THE
BEST
New England
STORIES

THE
BEST
New England
STORIES

INTRODUCTION BY
Robert Taylor
Former Book Editor of *The Boston Globe*

•

EDITED BY
Charles G. Waugh,
Martin H. Greenberg and
Robert Taylor

YANKEE BOOKS
CAMDEN • MAINE

COVER AND TEXT DESIGN BY LURELLE CHEVERIE
Typeset by Typeworks, Belfast, Maine
Printed and bound by Princeton University Press

Library of Congress Cataloguing-in-Publication Data

New England's best short stories / edited by Charles C. Waugh and Martin Harry Greenberg : Introduction by Robert Taylor.
    p.   cm.
   ISBN 0-912769-24-6 $12.95
   1. Short stories, American–New England. 2. New England–Fiction.
I. Waugh, Charles. II. Greenberg, Martin Harry.
PS541.N47 1990   90-12265
813'.0108974–dc20   CIP

To the memory of
CARL FREDERICK LEOPOLD RÖSSEL
January 7, 1909 to September 6, 1989
who liberated Naples during
World War II without even knowing it

CONTENTS

ROBERT TAYLOR

Introduction

Is there a distinctive New England voice? Memory summons from the airwaves the frail echo of a dry chuckle and the creak of a porch rocker–Titus Moody, the New England farmer on the old Fred Allen radio show. But Titus was a vaudeville rustic, far removed from the dedication to the written word of the demigods of the bygone New England literary establishment, foremost among them Ralph Waldo Emerson. A friend once confided to President Eliot of Harvard that he had heard most of the eminent American preachers and his general impression was that the sermon was always by Emerson–no matter who the preacher happened to be. Emerson's eloquence dominated the nineteenth-century American lyceum circuit. Still, as the captivating choice of short stories in this book discloses, his influence on fiction was oblique. The diversity of voices in New England writing is one of its refreshing characteristics.

We encounter too in these stories both Titus Moody and Emerson, the regional and the universal. The regional is not a matter of dialect; it is a matter of attitude. Stephen Vincent Benét's glorious fable, "The Devil and Daniel Webster," for example, does not resort to phonetics to reproduce the speech of the Prince of Darkness, but can anyone doubt that Benét must have listened carefully and at length to the inflections and cadences of New Hampshire hill-country speech? And as outstanding themes in Emerson concern the relationship of the individual to the timeless round of nature, a story of coastal Maine such as Lawrence Sargent Hall's "The Ledge" possesses the primal power of archaic legend. It could have happened in Homer or on a Norse voyage where existence is hammered bare as bone and flint, unfolding with tragic inevitability yet touched by filial devotion.

These stories provide a roughly equal representation of each New England state, and in most instances the flavor of the state is an atmospheric essential: the "hanging plants, unfinished wood paneling, butcherblock tables and captain's chairs" of Russell Banks's Concord, New Hampshire, cocktail lounge; the snowy isolation of Mark Helprin's Vermont attic amid a blizzard so thick "that the air was like tightly loomed cloth"; the silhouette of the menacing steeple on Federal Hill in the Gothic Providence, Rhode Island, of H.P. Lovecraft. Now and then the locale is incidental as it is in James Thurber's Waterbury, Connecticut, which serves as a backdrop to Walter Mitty's garish dreams. Nor is Edith Wharton as absorbed by the terrain of her tale, "Xingu," as she is in exposing with zestful malice the clubable intellectual pretensions of society ladies.

Which brings up the question, what exactly is a New England story? Like a New England "voice," the role of place is and is not fundamental. It is impossible to imagine Hawthorne's "Young Goodman Brown" apart from Puritan New England, or Ward Just's transplanted Chicago lawyer—even though he's an outsider—beyond the confines of Boston's Back Bay; on the other hand, Sidney Dow, the shambling but attractive hero of Sinclair Lewis's "Land," could have fallen in love with almost any bucolic eden, although Vermont is his particular passion, while Eunice, the addled morning drinker in Joyce Carol Oates's "Presque Isle," would probably have a shattered psyche in small-town Ohio or Beverly Hills. Indeed, authors Lawrence Hall and Thomas Bailey Aldrich, native New Englanders, share these pages with Oates, presently teaching at Princeton; Alice Adams, resident in San Francisco since her college graduation; and Ward Just of Waukegan, Illinois; Washington, D.C.; Andover, Massachusetts; and, at the moment, Paris, France.

So a New England story is not simply a matter of geography; all the same, the qualities of New England stamp it, however elusively. Van Wyck Brooks saw New England haunting the imagination of the country, "for, generally speaking, Americans had a stake in New England. They were deeply implicated in it, as the seat of their deepest, their stoutest, their greatest tradition. . . . It meant much to Americans that this old region should fare well, as their palladium of truth, justice, freedom and learning. They could not rest until they were reconciled to it, and until it was reconciled to them." American writers from other literary environs often react to New England as if registering the extremes, stormy or idyllic, of a skittish courtship. The dialogue between New England, the narrator, and the world at large may constitute the story's true subject. Fresh from Colorado, Jean Stafford examined the social nuances of "The Wedding: Beacon Hill." Her story in one sense represents a British eighteenth-century literary tradition in which a female secretary in the household of a rich woman serves as narrator; in another sense it is a mordant comedy of manners, shadowed by contemporary alienation in the suggestion that the wedding is only a sham attended by the bride's scapegrace lover. Reconciling oneself to the infinite contradictions of New England may well prove as difficult as that wedding.

The impressive range of the stories corresponds to the inexhaustible possibilities of a region layered by venerable history and the latest gossip. The earliest work is Hawthorne's (1835), the most recent is Russell Banks's "Sarah Cole: A Type of Love Story" (1984), but common elements of guilt and anguished self-discovery bridge the distance between them. Young Goodman Brown discovers the falsity of the social façades of Salem Village; the first-person narrator of "Sarah Cole," who elects to tell the story in an affectless, distanced manner as though he is witnessing himself, "slender, symmetrical and clean" Ron, in a performance, also discovers that class does not shield him against the lacerating truth about himself. Ron and Goodman Brown are victims of their own deceptions. Moreover, the moral as well as the physical darkness of Salem has its duplicate in the decaying neighborhoods of Concord, New Hampshire, with their cracked sidewalks, shadowy hallways, and spillage of uncollected garbage.

Hawthorne's grip on the New England imagination remains strong. For example, Benét's "The Devil and Daniel Webster" is a teeming WPA mural of a story; and a reader might consider it in terms of the American Scene painters of the 1930s, the Grant Woods and Thomas Hart Bentons turning away from Europe toward native subject matter, American myths, and histories commissioned for post offices and libraries. But the connection with Hawthorne should not be ignored. Have literary critics detected the parallels between the devil's comments to Young Goodman Brown—

"I have been as well acquainted with your family as with ever a one among the Puritans; and that's no trifle to say. I helped your grandfather, the constable, when he lashed the Quaker woman so smartly through the streets of Salem; and it was I that brought your father a pine-pitch knot, kindled at my own hearth, to set fire to an Indian village in King Philip's war. They were my good friends, both; and many a pleasant walk have we had along this path, and returned merrily after midnight."

—and the devil's comments to Dan'l Webster after the latter calls him a foreigner?

"When the first wrong was done to the first Indian I was there. When the first slaver put out for the Congo, I stood on her deck. Am I not in your books and stories and beliefs, from the first settlements on? Am I not spoken of, still, in every church in New England? 'Tis true the North claims me for a Southerner and the South for a Northerner, but I am neither. I am merely an honest American like yourself—and of the best descent—for, to tell the truth,

Mr. Webster, though I don't like to boast of it, my name is older in this country than yours."

With its economy of statement, the short-story form is peculiarly appropriate to New England. The extraordinary American renaissance of short fiction during the past decade is rooted in an older tradition, in the way Van Wyck Brooks suggested, a tradition represented by these stories. The Maine of Joyce Carol Oates and Alice Adams is a summer visitor's Maine, far removed from the regionalism of a late-nineteenth-century writer Mary Wilkins Freeman, but all three stories move us, and while different, they are in the same tradition. Surprisingly, it is Freeman who has written a feminist story, notwithstanding its picture of a farm where the women dutifully bake mince pies twice a week to satisfy the patriarchal tastes of the farmer. Perhaps the initial critical response to this gentle and good-humored tale of domestic rebellion (the critics usually chided Freeman for her "bleak" outlook, so different from the sentimental female authorship of her day) represented over-reaction to its implied message of independent behavior. "The Revolt of Mother," incidentally, comes from Freeman's second collection, *A New England Nun* (1891), when she was at the peak of her powers. The title of the book itself says a great deal about her audience's expectations.

Oates's portrait of a woman who dodges the reality of alcoholism, her desolate marriage, and her retinue of effete spongers is as penetrating as a characterization developed over the length of a novel. The relations between Eunice, the mother, and her partially alienated daughter, Jean-Marie, are developed with tenderness and poignant insight. "Alternatives," by Alice Adams, opens upon the sound of slapping wavelets at a lakeside house in Maine during the summer of 1935 and closes over thirty years later on the screened-in porch of that same house. The story is an astonishing technical feat. Because of the compressions of a short narrative, apprentice writers learn it is best to observe the classical unities of place and time, to concentrate on a few characters. Yet Adams presents an unforgettable family saga, a multiplicity of characters, each clearly delineated, and great movement through time and space – including a San Francisco detour – all within a dozen or so pages.

The unities, however, are integral to the emotional wallop of Lawrence Sargent Hall's "The Ledge": Christmas Day, a duck-hunting fisherman and his two boys, and an arthritic eleven-year-old black retriever. The details of the story have as much authenticity and power as the most persuasive passages of those other two hunters, Hemingway and Faulkner, and the intense climax with its final aching glimpse of the dog and the fisherman and the boys stays in the mind long after the story's conclusion. Close to Hall in spirit is another moving testament, "The Line Fence" of Curtis K. Stadtfeld, which deals with elementals and can even be read as a prose reflection of Robert Frost's poem, "Mending Wall."

To the reader who recalls James Gould Cozzens only for the polysyllabic sinuosities of his best-selling novel, *By Love Possessed,* the cool prose of the 1936 story "Total Stranger" will be a surprise. (The ironic detachment survives.) It is, I think, one of three instances in this anthology in which an author discloses a profile other than his public persona. The others are Sinclair Lewis, who in "Land" reveals an almost lyrical sympathy for a character, a clumsy dentist with the kind of limitations, cultural and intellectual, Lewis was otherwise inclined to mock; and Henry James in the little-known story "Osborne's Revenge." A Newport coquette confounds a New York lawyer, Philip Osborne, following the suicide of a friend, Robert Graham, presumably over his obsession with the young lady. She is described like a painting, her "dress of white grenadine, covered with ornaments and arabesques of crimson silk," and similar pictorial touches abound in the story's Winslow Homer-like depictions of Newport's private theatricals and island picnics.

Meeting James on his own territory, the story of manners, Ward Just in "About Boston" more than holds his own. His divorce lawyer is a traditional interloper into the inner circles of hereditary power. Unlike Jean Stafford's heroine, content to observe folly, he is bent on bulldozing his way to acceptance in a city he despises. Acceptance, however, doesn't mean social status, as in Stafford's "The Wedding: Beacon Hill": although status is involved, for the lawyer it means money. When an old flame consults him because of the breakdown of her marriage, he listens to her as avidly as a psychoanalyst, but the upshot of the interview ought to startle the reader as much as the lawyer. The energy of the style never flags; it is full of shrewd asides. The lawyer's metamorphosis from wills and trusts to the divorce courts, for instance, requires him to hear stories of another sort than those he once heard in his old-line firm. "The view from the bedroom was different from the view from the locker room. It was as if a light-bulb joke had been turned around and told from the point of view of the bulb."

Two of these stories are parables about the artist: Dorothy Canfield Fisher's "The Bedquilt" and Kurt Vonnegut, Jr.'s "Who Am I This Time?" They contrast markedly in tone, for Fisher's story belongs to the consciously regional school of Freeman in turn-of-the-century New England, while Vonnegut's is a genial romance on a favorite theme of identity—we become what we pretend to be—interpreted by the players of a little theater group rehearsing *A Streetcar Named Desire.* If Vonnegut's characters are interpretive artists, Fisher's Aunt Mehetabel realizes her latent creative gifts in a quilt that serves to liberate her from a lifetime of servitude.

Mark Helprin's "A Vermont Tale" is harder to classify since it features an allegorical story-within-a-story, but its pastoral images of snow and loons and lakes glide by with a lyric poise that never descends into the banal. Idiosyncratic, too, is H.P. Lovecraft's "The Haunter of the Dark," a spook sonata that succeeds because it emphasizes realism rather than fantasy. The Providence topography has so many recognizable everyday details, one has to accept, when it arrives, the story's demonology. "The Summer People," on the other hand, by Shirley Jackson, is a story that could frighten the wits out of the most stolid reader because it approaches realism via the mysterious and inexplicable; suggestion enhances its eerie mood.

The comic muse has been kind to the New England short story: Edith Wharton's "Xingu" and Christopher La Farge's "The Three Aspects" take obvious relish in the eccentricities of their characters, and James Thurber's "The Secret Life of Walter Mitty" has always been *sui generis,* even when Danny Kaye attempted the movie version. A first-time reader will experience one of the funniest stories produced by midcentury America while a Thurber fan will rediscover the nimble felicities of a unique stylist. Let us hope "Mitty" avoids the fate of that neglected nineteenth-century comic gem, Thomas Bailey Aldrich's epistolary "Marjorie Daw." Though almost forgotten today, Aldrich was a minor master whose story contains one of the exemplary surprise endings in the language. Who is Marjorie, that incredibly glamorous young woman, lying in her hammock, delicately swaying in the dappled shade? What is the book she holds in her hands? Is it *The Best New England Stories?* Finding out is part of the fun of this jubilant gathering.

NATHANIEL HAWTHORNE

1835

Young Goodman Brown

Young Goodman Brown came forth at sunset into the street at Salem village; but put his head back, after crossing the threshold, to exchange a parting kiss with his young wife. And Faith, as the wife was aptly named, thrust her own pretty head into the street, letting the wind play with the pink ribbons of her cap while she called to Goodman Brown.

"Dearest heart," whispered she, softly and rather sadly, when her lips were close to his ear, "prithee put off your journey until sunrise and sleep in your own bed to-night. A lone woman is troubled with such dreams and such thoughts that she's afeard of herself sometimes. Pray tarry with me this night, dear husband, of all nights in the year."

"My love and my Faith," replied young Goodman Brown, "of all nights in the year, this one night must I tarry away from thee. My journey, as thou callest it, forth and back again, must needs be done 'twixt now and sunrise. What, my sweet, pretty wife, dost thou doubt me already, and we but three months married?"

"Then God bless you!" said Faith, with the pink ribbons; "and may you find all well when you come back."

"Amen!" cried Goodman Brown. "Say thy prayers, dear Faith, and go to bed at dusk, and no harm will come to thee."

So they parted; and the young man pursued his way until, being about

1

to turn the corner by the meeting-house, he looked back and saw the head of Faith still peeping after him with a melancholy air, in spite of her pink ribbons.

"Poor little Faith!" thought he, for his heart smote him. "What a wretch am I to leave her on such an errand! She talks of dreams, too. Methought as she spoke there was trouble in her face, as if a dream had warned her what work is to be done to-night. But no, no; 't would kill her to think it. Well, she's a blessed angel on earth; and after this one night I'll cling to her skirts and follow her to heaven."

With this excellent resolve for the future, Goodman Brown felt himself justified in making more haste on his present evil purpose. He had taken a dreary road, darkened by all the gloomiest trees of the forest, which barely stood aside to let the narrow path creep through, and closed immediately behind. It was all as lonely as could be; and there is this peculiarity in such a solitude, that the traveller knows not who may be concealed by the innumerable trunks and the thick boughs overhead; so that with lonely footsteps he may yet be passing through an unseen multitude.

"There may be a devilish Indian behind every tree," said Goodman Brown to himself; and he glanced fearfully behind him as he added, "What if the devil himself should be at my very elbow!"

His head being turned back, he passed a crook of the road, and, looking forward again, beheld the figure of a man, in grave and decent attire, seated at the foot of an old tree. He arose at Goodman Brown's approach and walked onward side by side with him.

"You are late, Goodman Brown," said he. "The clock of the Old South was striking as I came through Boston, and that is full fifteen minutes agone."

"Faith kept me back a while," replied the young man, with a tremor in his voice, caused by the sudden appearance of his companion, though not wholly unexpected.

It was now deep dusk in the forest, and deepest in that part of it where these two were journeying. As nearly as could be discerned, the second traveller was about fifty years old, apparently in the same rank of life as Goodman Brown, and bearing a considerable resemblance to him, though perhaps more in expression than features. Still they might have been taken for father and son. And yet, though the elder person was as simply clad as the younger, and as simple in manner too, he had an indescribable air of one who knew the world, and who would not have felt abashed at the governor's dinner table or in King William's court, were it possible that his affairs should call him thither. But the only thing about him that could be fixed upon as remarkable was his staff, which bore the likeness of a great black snake, so curiously wrought that it might almost be seen to twist and wriggle itself like a living serpent. This, of course, must have been an ocular deception, assisted by the uncertain light.

"Come, Goodman Brown," cried his fellow-traveller, "this is a dull pace for the beginning of a journey. Take my staff, if you are so soon weary."

"Friend," said the other, exchanging his slow pace for a full stop, "having kept covenant by meeting thee here, it is my purpose now to return whence I came. I have scruples touching the matter thou wot'st of."

"Sayest thou so?" replied he of the serpent, smiling apart. "Let us walk on, nevertheless, reasoning as we go; and if I convince thee not thou shalt turn back. We are but a little way in the forest yet."

"Too far! too far!" exclaimed the goodman, unconsciously resuming his walk. "My father never went into the woods on such an errand, nor his father before him. We have been a race of honest men and good Christians since the days of the martyrs; and shall I be the first of the name of Brown that ever took this path and kept"–

"Such company, thou wouldst say," observed the elder person, interpreting his pause. "Well said, Goodman Brown! I have been as well acquainted with your family as with ever a one among the Puritans; and that's no trifle to say. I helped your grandfather, the constable, when he lashed the Quaker woman so smartly through the streets of Salem; and it was I that brought your father a pitch-pine knot, kindled at my own hearth, to set fire to an Indian village, in King Philip's war. They were my good friends, both; and many a pleasant walk have we had along this path, and returned merrily after midnight. I would fain be friends with you for their sake."

"If it be as thou sayest," replied Goodman Brown, "I marvel they never spoke of these matters; or, verily, I marvel not, seeing that the least rumor of the sort would have driven them from New England. We are a people of prayer, and good works to boot, and abide no such wickedness."

"Wickedness or not," said the traveller with the twisted staff, "I have a very general acquaintance here in New England. The deacons of many a church have drunk the communion wine with me; the selectman of divers towns make me their chairman; and a majority of the Great and General Court are firm supporters of my interest. The governor and I, too–But these are state secrets."

"Can this be so?" cried Goodman Brown, with a stare of amazement at his undisturbed companion. "Howbeit, I have nothing to do with the governor and council; they have their own ways, and are no rule for a simple husbandman like me. But, were I to go on with thee, how should I meet the eye of that good old man, our minister, at Salem village? Oh, his voice would make me tremble both Sabbath day and lecture day."

Thus far the elder traveller had listened with due gravity; but now burst into a fit of irrepressible mirth, shaking himself so violently that his snake-like staff actually seemed to wriggle in sympathy.

"Ha! ha! ha!" shouted he again and again; then composing himself, "Well go on, Goodman Brown, go on; but, prithee, don't kill me with laughing."

"Well, then, to end the matter at once," said Goodman Brown, considerably nettled, "there is my wife, Faith. It would break her dear little heart; and I'd rather break my own."

"Nay, if that be the case," answered the other, "e'en go thy ways, Goodman Brown. I would not for twenty old women like the one hobbling before us that Faith should come to any harm."

As he spoke he pointed his staff at a female figure on the path, in whom Goodman Brown recognized a very pious and exemplary dame, who had taught him his catechism in youth, and was still his moral and spiritual adviser, jointly with the minister and Deacon Gookin.

"A marvel, truly, that Goody Cloyse should be so far in the wilderness at nightfall," said he. "But with your leave, friend, I shall take a cut through the woods until we have left this Christian woman behind. Being a stranger to you, she might ask whom I was consorting with and whither I was going."

"Be it so," said his fellow-traveller. "Betake you to the woods, and let me keep the path."

Accordingly the young man turned aside, but took care to watch his companion, who advanced softly along the road until he had come within a staff's length of the old dame. She, meanwhile, was making the best of her way, with singular speed for so aged a woman, and mumbling some indistinct words—a prayer, doubtless—as she went. The traveller put forth his staff and touched her withered neck with what seemed the serpent's tail.

"The devil!" screamed the pious old lady.

"Then Goody Cloyse knows her old friend?" observed the traveller, confronting her and leaning on his writhing stick.

"Ah, forsooth, and is it your worship indeed?" cried the good dame. "Yea, truly is it, and in the very image of my old gossip, Goodman Brown, the grandfather of the silly fellow that now is. But—would your worship believe it?—my broomstick hath strangely disappeared, stolen, as I suspect, by that unhanged witch, Goody Cory, and that, too, when I was all anointed with the juice of smallage, and cinquefoil, and wolf's bane"—

"Mingled with fine wheat and the fat of a new-born babe," said the shape of old Goodman Brown.

"Ah, your worship knows the recipe," cried the old lady, cackling aloud. So, as I was saying, being all ready for the meeting, and no horse to ride on, I made up my mind to foot it; for they tell me there is a nice young man to be taken into communion tonight. But now your good worship will lend me your arm, and we shall be there in a twinkling."

"That can hardly be," answered her friend. "I may not spare you my arm, Goody Cloyse; but here is my staff, if you will."

So saying, he threw it down at her feet, where, perhaps, it assumed life, being one of the rods which its owner had formerly lent to the Egyptian magi. Of this fact, however, Goodman Brown could not take cognizance. He had cast up his eyes in astonishment, and, looking down again, beheld neither Goody Cloyse nor the serpentine staff, but his fellow-traveller alone, who waited for him as calmly as if nothing had happened.

"That old woman taught me my catechism," said the young man; and there was a world of meaning in this simple comment.

They continued to walk onward, while the elder traveller exhorted his companion to make good speed and persevere in the path, discoursing so aptly that his arguments seemed rather to spring up in the bosom of his auditor than to be suggested by himself. As they went, he plucked a branch of maple to serve for a walking stick, and began to strip it of the twigs and little boughs, which were wet with evening dew. The moment his fingers touched them they became strangely withered and dried up as with a week's sunshine. Thus the pair proceeded, at a good free pace, until suddenly, in a gloomy hollow of the road, Goodman Brown sat himself down on the stump of a tree and refused to go any farther.

"Friend," said he, stubbornly, "my mind is made up. Not another step will I budge on this errand. What if a wretched old woman do choose to go to the devil when I thought she was going to heaven: is that any reason why I should quit my dear Faith and go after her?"

"You will think better of this by and by," said his acquaintance, composedly. "Sit here and rest yourself a while; and when you feel like moving again, there is my staff to help you along."

Without more words, he threw his companion the maple stick, and was as speedily out of sight as if he had vanished into the deepening gloom. The young man sat a few moments by the roadside, applauding himself greatly, and thinking with how clear a conscience he should meet the minister in his morning walk, nor shrink from the eye of good old Deacon Gookin. And what calm sleep would be his that very night, which was to have been spent so wickedly, but so purely and sweetly now, in the arms of Faith! Amidst these pleasant and praiseworthy meditations, Goodman Brown heard the tramp of horses along the road, and deemed it advisable to conceal himself within the verge of the forest, conscious of the guilty purpose that had brought him thither, though now so happily turned from it.

On came the hoof tramps and the voices of the riders, two grave old voices, conversing soberly as they drew near. These mingled sounds appeared to pass along the road, within a few yards of the young man's hiding-place; but, owing doubtless to the depth of the gloom at that particular spot, neither the travellers nor their steeds were visible. Though their figures brushed the small boughs by the wayside, it could not be seen that they intercepted, even for a moment, the faint gleam from the strip of bright sky athwart which they must have passed. Goodman Brown alternately crouched and stood on tiptoe, pulling aside the branches and thrusting forth his head as far as he durst without discerning so much as a shadow. It vexed him the more, because he could have sworn, were such a thing possible, that he recognized the voices of the minister and Deacon Gookin, jogging along quietly, as they were wont to do, when bound to some ordination or ecclesiastical council. While yet within hearing, one of the riders stopped to pluck a switch.

"Of the two, reverend sir," said the voice like the deacon's, "I had rather miss an ordination dinner than tonight's meeting. They tell me that some of our community are to be here from Falmouth and beyond, and others from Connecticut and Rhode Island, besides several of the Indian powwows, who, after their fashion, know almost as much deviltry as the best of us. Moreover, there is a goodly young woman to be taken into communion."

"Mighty well, Deacon Gookin!" replied the solemn old tones of the minister. "Spur up, or we shall be late. Nothing can be done, you know, until I get on the ground."

The hoofs clattered again; and the voices, talking so strangely in the empty air, passed on through the forest, where no church had ever been gathered or solitary Christian prayed. Whither, then, could these holy men be journeying so deep into the heathen wilderness? Young Goodman Brown caught hold of a tree for support, being ready to sink down on the ground, faint and overburdened with the heavy sickness of his heart. He looked up to the sky, doubting whether there really was a heaven above him. Yet there was the blue arch, and the stars brightening in it.

"With heaven above and Faith below, I will yet stand firm against the devil!" cried Goodman Brown.

While he still gazed upward into the deep arch of the firmament and had lifted his hands to pray, a cloud, though no wind was stirring, hurried across the zenith and hid the brightening stars. The blue sky was still visible, except directly overhead, where this black mass of cloud was sweeping swiftly northward. Aloft in the air, as if from the depths of the cloud, came a confused and doubtful sound of voices. Once the listener fancied that he could distinguish the accents of towns-people of his own, men and women, both pious and ungodly, many of whom he had met at the communion table, and had seen others rioting at the tavern. The next moment, so indistinct were the sounds, he doubted whether he had heard aught but the murmur of the old forest, whispering without a wind. Then came a stronger swell of those familiar tones, heard daily in the sunshine at Salem village, but never until now from a cloud of night. There was one voice, of a young woman, uttering lamentations, yet with an uncertain sorrow, and entreating for some favor, which, perhaps, it would grieve her to obtain; and all the unseen multitude, both saints and sinners, seemed to encourage her onward.

"Faith!" shouted Goodman Brown, in a voice of agony and desperation; and the echoes of the forest mocked him, crying, "Faith! Faith!" as if bewildered wretches were seeking her all through the wilderness.

The cry of grief, rage, and terror was yet piercing the night, when the unhappy husband held his breath for a response. There was a scream, drowned immediately in a louder murmur of voices, fading into far-off laughter, as the dark cloud swept away, leaving the clear and silent sky above Goodman Brown. But something fluttered lightly down through the air and caught on the branch of a tree. The young man seized it, and beheld a pink ribbon.

"My Faith is gone!" cried he, after one stupefied moment. "There is no good on earth; and sin is but a name. Come, devil; for to thee is this world given."

And, maddened with despair, so that he laughed loud and long, did Goodman Brown grasp his staff and set forth again, at such a rate that he seemed to fly along the forest path rather than to walk or run. The road grew wilder and drearier and more faintly traced, and vanished at length, leaving him in the heart of the dark wilderness, still rushing onward with the instinct that guides mortal man to evil. The whole forest was peopled with frightful sounds—the creaking of the tress, the howling of wild beasts, and the yell of Indians; while sometimes the wind tolled like a distant church bell, and sometimes gave a broad roar around the traveller, as if all Nature were laughing him to scorn. But he was himself the chief horror of the scene, and shrank not from its other horrors.

"Ha! ha! ha!" roared Goodman Brown when the wind laughed at him. "Let us hear which will laugh loudest. Think not to frighten me with your deviltry. Come witch, come wizard, come Indian powwow, come devil himself, and here comes Goodman Brown. You may as well fear him as he fear you."

In truth, all through the haunted forest there could be nothing more frightful than the figure of Goodman Brown. On he flew among the black pines, brandishing his staff with frenzied gestures, now giving vent to an inspiration of horrid blasphemy, and now shouting forth such laughter as set all the echoes of the forest laughing like demons around him. The fiend in his own shape is less hideous than when he rages in the breast of man. Thus sped the demoniac on his course, until, quivering among the trees, he saw a red light before him, as when the felled trunks and branches of a clearing have been set on fire, and throw up their lurid blaze against the sky, at the hour of midnight. He paused, in a lull of the tempest that had driven him onward, and heard the swell of what seemed a hymn, rolling solemnly from a distance with the weight of many voices. He knew the tune; it was a familiar one in the choir of the village meeting-house. The verse died heavily away, and was lengthened by a chorus, not of human voices, but of all the sounds of the benighted wilderness pealing in awful harmony together. Goodman Brown cried out, and his cry was lost to his own ear by its unison with the cry of the desert.

In the interval of silence he stole forward until the light glared full upon his eyes. At one extremity of an open space, hemmed in by the dark wall of the forest, arose a rock, bearing some rude, natural resemblance either to an altar or a pulpit, and surrounded by four blazing pines, their tops aflame, their stems untouched, like candles at an evening meeting. The mass of foliage that had overgrown the summit of the rock was all on fire, blazing high into the night and fitfully illuminating the whole field. Each pendent twig and leafy festoon was in a blaze. As the red light arose and fell, a numerous congregation alternately shone forth, then disappeared in shadow, and again grew, as it were, out of the darkness, peopling the heart of the solitary woods at once.

"A grave and dark-clad company," quoth Goodman Brown.

In truth they were such. Among them, quivering to and fro between gloom and splendor, appeared faces that would be seen next day at the council board of the province, and others which, Sabbath after Sabbath, looked devoutly heavenward, and benignantly over the crowded pews, from the holiest pulpits in the land. Some affirm that the lady of the governor was there. At least there were high dames well known to her, and wives of honored husbands, and widows, a great multitude, and ancient maidens, all of excellent repute, and fair young girls, who trembled lest their mothers should espy them. Either the sudden gleams of light flashing over the obscure field bedazzled Goodman Brown, or he recognized a score of the church members of Salem village famous for their especial sanctity. Good old Deacon Gookin had arrived, and waited at the skirts of that venerable saint, his revered pastor. But, irreverently consorting with these grave, reputable, and pious people, these elders of the church, these chaste dames and dewy virgins, there were men of dissolute lives and women of spotted fame, wretches given over to all mean and filthy vice, and suspected even of horrid crimes. It was strange to see that the good shrank not from the wicked, nor were the sinners abashed by the saints. Scattered also among their pale-faced enemies were the Indian priests, or powwows, who had often scared their native forest with more hideous incantations than any known to English witchcraft.

"But where is Faith?" thought Goodman Brown; and, as hope came into his heart, he trembled.

Another verse of the hymn arose, a slow and mournful strain, such as the pious love, but joined to words which expressed all that our nature can conceive of sin, and darkly hinted at far more. Unfathomable to mere mortals is the lore of fiends. Verse after verse was sung; and still the chorus of the desert swelled between like the deepest tone of a mighty organ; and with the final peal of that dreadful anthem there came a sound, as if the roaring wind, the rushing streams, the howling beasts, and every other voice of the unconcerted wilderness were mingling and according with the voice of guilty man in homage to the prince of all. The four blazing pines threw up a loftier flame, and obscurely discovered shapes and visages of horror on the smoke wreaths above the impious assembly. At the same moment the fire on the rock shot redly forth and formed a glowing arch above its base, where now appeared a figure. With reverence be it spoken, the figure bore no slight similitude, both in garb and manner, to some grave divine of the New England churches.

"Bring forth the converts!" cried a voice that echoed through the field and rolled into the forest.

At the word, Goodman Brown stepped forth from the shadow of the trees and approached the congregation, with whom he felt a loathful brotherhood by the sympathy of all that was wicked in his heart. He could have well-nigh sworn that the shape of his own dead father beckoned him to advance, looking downward from a smoke wreath, while a woman, with dim features of despair, threw out her hand to warn him back. Was it his mother? But he had no power to retreat one step, nor to resist, even in thought, when the minister and good old Deacon Gookin seized his arms and led him to the blazing rock. Thither came also the slender form of a veiled female, led between Goody Cloyse, that pious teacher of the catechism, and Martha Carrier, who had received the devil's promise to be queen of hell. A rampant hag was she. And there stood the proselytes beneath the canopy of fire.

"Welcome, my children," said the dark figure, "to the communion of your race. Ye have found thus young your nature and your destiny. My children, look behind you!"

They turned; and flashing forth, as it were, in a sheet of flame, the fiend worshippers were seen; the smile of welcome gleamed darkly on every visage.

"There," resumed the sable form, "are all whom ye have reverenced from youth. Ye deemed them holier than yourselves, and shrank from your own sin, contrasting it with their lives of righteousness and prayerful aspirations heavenward. Yet here are they all in my worshipping assembly. This night it shall be granted you to know their secret deeds: how hoary-bearded elders of the church have whispered wanton words to the young maids of their households; how many a woman, eager for widows' weeds, has given her husband a drink at bedtime and let him sleep his last sleep in her bosom; how beardless youths have made haste to inherit their fathers' wealth; and how fair damsels—blush not, sweet ones—have dug little graves in the garden, and bidden me, the sole guest, to an infant's funeral. By the sympathy of your human hearts for sin ye shall scent out all the places—whether in church, bedchamber, street, field, or forest—where crime has been committed, and shall exult to behold the whole earth one stain of guilt, one mighty blood spot. Far more than this. It shall by yours to penetrate, in every bosom, the deep mystery of sin, the fountain of all wicked arts, and which inexhaustibly supplies more evil impulses than human power—than my power at its utmost—can make manifest in deeds. And now, my children, look upon each other."

They did so; and, by the blaze of the hell-kindled torches, the wretched man beheld his Faith, and the wife her husband, trembling before that unhallowed altar.

"Lo, there ye stand, my children," said the figure, in a deep and solemn tone, almost sad with its despairing awfulness, as if his once angelic nature could yet mourn for our miserable race. "Depending upon one another's hearts, ye had still hoped that virtue were not all a dream. Now are ye undeceived. Evil is the nature of mankind. Evil must be your only happiness. Welcome again, my children, to the communion of your race."

"Welcome," repeated the fiend worshippers, in one cry of despair and triumph.

And there they stood, the only pair, as it seemed, who were yet hesitating on the verge of wickedness in this dark world. A basin was hollowed, naturally, in the rock. Did it contain water, reddened by the lurid light? or was it blood? or, perchance, a liquid flame? Herein did the shape of evil dip his hand and prepare to lay the mark of baptism upon their foreheads, that they might be partakers of the mystery of sin, more conscious of the secret guilt of others, both indeed and thought, than they could now be of their own. The husband cast one look at his pale wife, and Faith at him. What polluted wretches would the next glance show them to each other, shuddering alike at what they disclosed and what they saw!

"Faith! Faith!" cried the husband, "look up to heaven, and resist the wicked one."

Whether Faith obeyed he knew not. Hardly had he spoken when he found himself amid calm night and solitude, listening to a roar of the wind which died heavily away through the forest. He staggered against the rock, and felt it chill and damp; while a hanging twig, that had been all on fire, besprinkled his cheek with the coldest dew.

The next morning young Goodman Brown came slowly into the street of Salem village, staring around him like a bewildered man. The good old minister was taking a walk along the graveyard to get an appetite for breakfast and meditate his sermon, and bestowed a blessing, as he passed, on Goodman Brown. He shrank from the venerable saint as if to avoid an anathema. Old Deacon Gookin was at domestic worship, and the holy words of his prayer were heard through the open window. "What God doth the wizard pray to?" quoth Goodman Brown. Goody Cloyse, that excellent old Christian, stood in the early sunshine at her own lattice, catechizing a little girl who had brought her a pint of morning's milk. Goodman Brown snatched away the child as from the grasp of the fiend himself. Turning the corner by the meeting-house, he spied the head of Faith, with the pink ribbons, gazing anxiously forth, and bursting into such joy at sight of him that she skipped along the street and almost kissed her husband before the whole village. But Goodman Brown looked sternly and sadly into her face, and passed on without a greeting.

Had Goodman Brown fallen asleep in the forest and only dreamed a wild dream of a witch-meeting?

Be it so if you will; but, alas! it was a dream of evil omen for young Goodman Brown. A stern, a sad, a darkly meditative, a distrustful, if not a desperate man did he become from the night of that fearful dream. On the Sabbath day, when the congregation were singing a holy psalm, he could not listen because an anthem of sin rushed loudly upon his ear and drowned all the blessed strain. When the minister spoke from the pulpit with power and fervid eloquence, and, with his hand on the open Bible, of the sacred truths of our religion, and of saint-like lives and triumphant deaths, and of future bliss or misery unutterable, then did Goodman Brown turn pale, dreading lest the roof should thunder down upon the gray blasphemer and his hearers. Often, awaking suddenly at midnight, he shrank from the bosom of Faith; and at morning or eventide, when the family knelt down at prayer, he scowled and muttered to himself, and gazed sternly at his wife, and turned away. And when he had lived long, and was borne to his grave a hoary corpse, followed by Faith, an aged woman, and children and grandchildren, a goodly procession, besides neighbors not a few, they carved no hopeful verse upon his tombstone, for his dying hour was gloom.

HENRY JAMES

1868

Osborne's Revenge

I

Philip Osborne and Robert Graham were intimate friends. The latter had been spending the summer at certain medicinal springs in New York, the use of which had been recommended by his physician. Osborne, on the other hand—a lawyer by profession, and with a rapidly increasing practice—had been confined to the city, and had suffered June and July to pass, not unheeded, heaven knows, but utterly unhonored. Toward the middle of July he began to feel uneasy at not hearing from his friend, habitually the best of correspondents. Graham had a charming literary talent, and plenty of leisure, being without a family, and without business. Osborne wrote to him, asking the reason of his silence, and demanding an immediate reply. He received in the course of a few days the following letter:

> DEAR PHILIP: I am as you conjectured, not well. These infernal waters have done me no good. On the contrary—they have poisoned me. They have poisoned my life, and I wish to God I had never come to them. Do you remember the *White Lady* in *The Monastery*, who used to appear to the hero at the spring? There is such a one here, at this spring—which you know tastes of sulphur. Judge of the quality of the young woman. She has charmed me, and I can't get away.

But I mean to try again. Don't think I'm cracked, but expect me next week. Yours always,

R.G.

The day after he received this letter, Osborne met, at the house of a female friend detained in town by the illness of one of her children, a lady who had just come from the region in which Graham had fixed himself. This lady, Mrs Dodd by name, and a widow, had seen a great deal of the young man, and she drew a very long face and threw great expression into her eyes as she spoke of him. Seeing that she was inclined to be confidential, Osborne made it possible that she should converse with him privately. She assured him, behind her fan, that his friend was dying of a broken heart. Something should be done. The story was briefly this. Graham had made the acquaintance, in the early part of the summer, of a young lady, a certain Miss Congreve, who was living in the neighborhood with a married sister. She was not pretty, but she was clever, graceful, and pleasing, and Graham had immediately fallen in love with her. She had encouraged his addresses, to the knowledge of all their friends, and at the end of a month – heart-histories are very rapid at the smaller watering places – their engagement, although not announced, was hourly expected. But at this moment a stranger had effected an entrance into the little society of which Miss Congreve was one of the most brilliant ornaments – a Mr Holland, out of the West – a man of Graham's age, but better favoured in person. Heedless of the circumstance that her affections were notoriously preoccupied, he had immediately begun to be attentive to the young girl. Equally reckless of the same circumstance, Henrietta Congreve had been all smiles – all seduction. In the course of a week, in fact, she had deliberately transferred her favors from the old love to the new. Graham had been turned out into the cold; she had ceased to look at him, to speak to him, to think of him. He nevertheless remained at the springs, as if he found a sort of fascination in the sense of his injury, and in seeing Miss Congreve and Holland together. Besides, he doubtless wished people to fancy that, for good reasons, he had withdrawn his suit, and it was therefore not for him to hide himself. He was proud, reserved, and silent, but his friends had no difficulty in seeing that his pain was intense, and that his wound was almost mortal. Mrs Dodd declared that unless he was diverted from his sorrow, and removed from contact with the various scenes and objects which reminded him of his unhappy passion – and above all, deprived of the daily chance of meeting Miss Congreve – she would not answer for his sanity.

Osborne made all possible allowances for exaggeration. A woman, he reflected, likes so to round off her story – especially if it is a dismal one. Nevertheless he felt very anxious, and he forthwith wrote his friend a long letter, asking him to what extent Mrs Dodd's little romance was true, and urging him to come immediately to town, where, if it is was substantially true, he might look for diversion. Graham answered by arriving in person. At first, Osborne was decidedly relieved. His friend looked better and stronger than he had looked for months. But on coming to talk with him, he found him morally, at least, a sad invalid. He was listless, abstracted, and utterly inactive in mind. Osborne observed with regret that he made no response to his attempts at interrogation and to his proffered sympathy. Osborne had by nature no great respect for sentimental woes. He was not a man to lighten his tread because his neighbor below stairs was laid up with a broken heart. But he saw that it would never do to poke fun at poor Graham, and that he was quite proof against the contagion of gayety. Graham begged him not to think him morbid or indifferent to his kindness, and to allow him not to speak of his trouble until it was over. He had resolved to forget it. When he had forgotten it—as one forgets such things—when he had contrived to push the further end of it at least into the past—then he would tell him all about it. For the present he must occupy his thoughts with something else. It was hard to decide what to do. It was hard to travel without an aim. Yet the intolerable heat made it impossible that he should stay in New York. He might go to Newport.

"A moment," said Osborne. "Has Miss Congreve gone to Newport?"

"Not that I know of."

"Does she intend to go?"

Graham was silent. "Good heavens!" he cried, at last, "forbid it then! All I want is to have it forbidden. *I* can't forbid it. Did you ever see a human being so degraded?" he added, with a ghastly smile. "Where *shall* I go?"

Philip went to his table and began to overhaul a mass of papers fastened with red tape. He selected several of these documents and placed them apart. Then, turning to his friend, "You're to go out to Minnesota," he said, looking him in the eyes. The proposal was a grave one, and gravely as it was meant, Osborne would have been glad to have Graham offer some resistance. But he sat looking at him with a solemn stare which (in the light of subsequent events) cast a lugubrious shade over the whole transaction. "The deuce!" thought Osborne. "Has it made him stupid?—What you need," he said aloud, "is to have something else to think about. An idle man can't expect to get over such troubles. I have some business to be done at St. Paul, and I know that if you'll give your attention to it, you're as well able to do it as any man. It's a simple matter, but it needs a trustworthy person. So I shall depend upon you."

Graham came and took up the papers and looked over them mechanically.

"Never mind them now," said Osborne; "it's past midnight; you must go to bed. To-morrow morning I'll put you *au fait*, and the day after, if you like, you can start."

The next morning Graham seemed to have recovered a considerable portion of his old cheerfulness. He talked about indifferent matters, laughed, and seemed for a couple of hours to have forgotten Miss Congreve. Osborne began to doubt that the journey was necessary, and he was glad to be able to think, afterwards, that he had expressed his doubts, and that his friend had strongly combatted them and insisted upon having the affair explained to him. He mastered it, to Osborne's satisfaction, and started across the continent.

During the ensuing week Philip was so pressed with business that he had very little time to think of the success of Graham's mission. Within the fortnight he received the following letter:

> DEAR PHILIP: Here I am, safe, but anything but sound. I don't know what to think of it, but I have completely forgotten the terms of my embassy. I can't for my life remember what I'm to do or say, and neither the papers nor your notes assist me a whit. 12th–I wrote so much yesterday and then went out to take a walk and collect my thoughts. I *have* collected them once for all. Do you understand, dearest Philip? Don't call me insane, or impious, or anything that merely expresses your own impatience and intolerance, without throwing a ray of light on the state of my own mind. He can only understand it who has felt it, and he who has felt it can do but as I do. Life has lost, I don't say its charm–that I could willingly dispense with–but its meaning. I shall live in your memory and your love, which is a vast deal better than living in my own self-contempt. Farewell.
>
> R.G.

Osborne learned the circumstances of his friend's death three days later, through his correspondent at St Paul–the person to whom Graham had been addressed. The unhappy young man had shot himself through the head in his room at the hotel. He had left money, and written directions for the disposal of his remains–directions which were, of course, observed. As Graham possessed no near relative, the effect of his death was confined to a narrow circle; to the circle, I may say, of Philip Osborne's capacious personality. The two young men had been united by an almost passionate friendship. Now that Graham had ceased to be, Osborne became sensible of the strength of this bond; he felt that he cared more for it than for any human tie. They had known each other ten years, and their intimacy had grown with their growth during the most active period of their lives. It had been strengthened within and without by the common enjoyment of so many pleasures, the experience of so many hazards, the exchange of so much advice, so much confidence, and so many pledges of mutual interest, that each had grown to regard it as the single absolute certainty in life, the one fixed fact in a shifting world. As constantly happens with intimate friends, the two were perfectly diverse in character, tastes and appearance. Graham was three years the elder, slight, undersized, feeble in health, sensitive, indolent, whimsical, generous, and in reality of a far finer clay than his friend, as the latter, moreover, perfectly well knew. Their intimacy was often a puzzle to observers. Disinterested parties were at a loss to discover how Osborne had come to set his heart upon an insignificant, lounging invalid, who, in general company, talked in monosyllables, in a weak voice, and gave himself the airs of one whom nature had endowed with the right to be fastidious, without ever having done a stroke of work. Graham's partisans, on the other hand, who were chiefly women (which, by the way, effectually relieves him from the accusation occasionally brought against him of being "effeminate") were quite unable to penetrate the motives of his interest in a commonplace, hard-working lawyer, who addressed a charming woman as if he were exhorting a jury of grocers and undertakers, and viewed the universe as one vast "case." This account of Osborne's mind and manners would have been too satirical to be wholly just, and yet it would have been excusable as an attempt to depict a figure in striking contrast with poor Graham. Osborne was in all respects a large fellow. He was six feet two in height, with a chest like a boxing-master, and a clear, brown, complexion, which successfully resisted the deleterious action of a sedentary life. He was, in fact, without a particle of vanity, a particularly handsome man. His character corresponded to his person, or, as one may say, continued and completed it, and his mind kept the promise of his character. He was all of one piece–all health and breadth, capacity and energy. Graham had once told his friend somewhat brutally–for in his little, weak voice Graham said things far more brutal than Osborne, just as he said things far more fine–he had told him that he worked like a horse and loved like a dog.

Theoretically, Osborne's remedy for mental trouble was work. He re-doubled his attention to his professional affairs, and strove to reconcile himself, once for all, to his loss. But he found his grief far stronger than his will, and felt that it obstinately refused to be pacified without some act of sacrifice or devotion. Osborne had an essentially kind heart and plenty of pity and charity for deserving objects; but at the bottom of his soul there lay a well of bitterness and resentment which, when his nature was strongly shaken by a sense of wrong, was sure to ferment and raise its level, and at last to swamp his conscience. These bitter waters had been stirred, and he felt that they were rising fast. His thoughts travelled back with stubborn iteration from Graham's death to the young girl who figured in the prologue to the tragedy. He felt in his breast a savage need of hating her. Osborne's friends observed in these days that he looked by no means pleasant; and if he had not been such an excellent fellow he might easily have passed for an intolerable brute. He was not softened and mellowed by suffering; he was exasperated. It seemed to him that justice cried aloud that Henrietta Congreve should be confronted with the results of her folly, and made to carry forever in her thoughts, in all the hideousness of suicide, the image of her miserable victim. Osborne was, perhaps, in error, but he was assuredly sincere; and it is strong evidence of the energy of genuine affection that this lusty intellect should have been brought, in the interest of another, to favor a scheme which it would have deemed wholly, ludicrously impotent to assuage the injured dignity of his own possessor. Osborne must have been very fond of his friend not to have pronounced him a drivelling fool. It is true that he had always pitied him as much as he loved him, although Graham's incontestable gifts and virtues had kept this feeling in the background. Now that he was gone, pity came uppermost, and bade fair to drive him to a merciless disallowance of all claims to extenuation on the part of the accused. It was unlikely that, for a long time at least, he would listen to anything but that Graham had been foully wronged, and that the light of his life had been wantonly quenched. He found it impossible to sit down in resignation. The best that he could do, indeed, would not call Graham back to life; but he might at least discharge his gall, and have the comfort of feeling that Miss Congreve was the worse for it. He was quite unable to work. He roamed about for three days in a disconsolate, angry fashion. On the third, he called upon Mrs Dodd, from whom he learned that Miss Congreve had gone to Newport, to stay with a second married sister. He went home and packed up a valise, and—without knowing why, feeling only that to do so was to do something, and to put himself in the way of doing more—drove down to the Newport boat.

II

His first inquiry on his arrival, after he had looked up several of his friends and encountered a number of acquaintances, was about Miss Congreve's whereabouts and habits. He found that she was very little known. She lived with her sister, Mrs Wilkes, and as yet had made but a single appearance in company. Mrs Wilkes, moreover, he learned, was an invalid and led a very quiet life. He ascertained the situation of her house and gave himself the satisfaction of walking past it. It was a pretty place, on a secluded by-road, marked by various tokens of wealth and comfort. He heard, as he passed, through the closed shutters of the drawing-room window, the sound of a high, melodious voice, warbling and trilling to the accompaniment of a piano. Osborne had no soul for music, but he stopped and listened, and as he did so, he remembered Graham's passion for the charming art and fancied that these were the very accents that had lured him to his sorrow. Poor Graham! here too, as in all things, he had showed his taste. The singer discharged a magnificent volley of roulades and flourishes and became silent. Osborn, fancying he heard a movement of the lattice of the shutters, slowly walked away. A couple of days later he found himself strolling, alone and disconsolate, upon the long avenue which runs parallel to the Newport cliffs, which, as all the world knows, may be reached by five minutes' walk from any part of it. He had been on the field, now, for nearly a week, and he was no nearer his revenge. His unsatisfied desire haunted his steps and hovered in a ghostly fashion about thoughts which perpetual contact with old friends and new, and the entertaining spectacle of a heterogeneous throng of pleasure seekers and pleasure vendors, might have made free and happy. Osborne was very fond of the world, and while he still clung to his resentment, he yet tacitly felt that it lurked as a skeleton at his banquet. He was fond of nature, too, and betwixt these two predelictions, he grew at moments ashamed of his rancor. At all events, he felt a grateful sense of relief when as he pursued his course along this sacred way of fashion, he caught a glimpse of the deep blue expanse of the ocean, shining at the end of a cross road. He forthwwith took his way down the cliffs. At the point where the road ceased, he found an open barouche whose occupants appeared to have wandered out of sight. Passing this carriage, he reached a spot where the surface of the cliff communicates with the beach, by means of an abrupt footpath. This path he descended and found himself on a level with the broad expanse of sand and the rapidly rising tide. The wind was blowing fresh from the sea and the little breakers tumbling in with their multitudinous liquid clamor. In a very few moments Osborne felt a sensible exhilaration of spirits. He had not advanced many steps under the influence of this joyous feeling, when, on turning a slight projection in the cliff, he descried a sight which caused him to hasten forward. On a broad flat rock, at about a dozen yards from the shore, stood a child of some five years—a handsome boy, fair-haired and well dressed—stamping his feet and wringing his hands in an apparent agony of terror. It was easy to understand the situation. The child had ventured out on the rock while the water was still low, and had become so much absorbed in paddling with his little wooden spade among the rich marine deposits on its surface, that he had failed to observe the advance of the waves, which had now completely covered the intermediate fragments of rock and were foaming and weltering betwixt him and the shore. The poor little fellow stood screaming to the winds and waters, and quite unable to answer Osborne's shouts of interrogation and comfort. Meanwhile, the latter prepared to fetch him ashore. He saw with some disgust that the channel was too wide to warrant a leap, and yet, as the child's companions might at any moment appear, in the shape of distracted importunate women, he judged it imprudent to divest himself of any part of his apparel. He accordingly plunged in without further ado, waded forward, seized the child and finally restored him to *terra firma*. He felt him trembling in his arms like a frightened bird. He set him on his feet, soothed him, and asked him what had become of his guardians.

The boy pointed toward a rock, lying at a certain distance, close under the cliff, and Osborne, following his gesture, distinguished what seemed to be the hat and feather of a lady sitting on the further side of it.

"That's Aunt Henrietta," said the child.

"Aunt Henrietta deserves a scolding," said Osborne. "Come, we'll go and give it to her." And he took the boy's hand and led him toward his culpable relative. They walked along the beach until they came abreast of the rock, and approached the lady in front. At the sound of their feet on the stones, she raised her head. She was a young woman, seated on a boulder, with an album in her lap, apparently absorbed in the act of sketching. Seeing at a glance that something was amiss, she rose to her feet and thrust the album into her pocket. Osborne's wet trousers and the bespattered garments and discomposed physiognomy of the child revealed the nature of the calamity. She held out her arms to her little nephew. He dropped Philip's hand, and ran and threw himself on his aunt's neck. She raised him up and kissed him, and looked interrogatively at Osborne.

"I couldn't help seeing him safely in your hands," said the latter, removing his hat. "He has had a terrific adventure."

"What is it, darling?" cried the young lady, again kissing the little fellow's bloodless face.

"He came into the water after me," cried the boy. "Why did you leave me there?"

"What has happened sir?" asked the young girl, in a somewhat preemptory tone.

"You had apparently left him on that rock, madame, with a channel betwixt him and the shore deep enough to drown him. I took the liberty of displacing him. But he's more frightened than hurt."

The young girl had a pale face and dark eyes. There was no beauty in her features; but Osborne had already perceived that they were extremely expressive and intelligent. Her face flushed a little, and her eyes flashed; the former, it seemed to Philip, with mortification at her own neglect, and the latter in irritation at the reproach conveyed in his accents. But he may have been wrong. She sat down on the rock, with the child on her knees, kissing him repeatedly and holding him with a sort of convulsive pressure. When she looked up, the flashes in her eyes had melted into a couple of tears. Seeing that Philip was a gentleman, she offered a few words of self-justification. She had kept the boy constantly within sight, and only within a few minutes had allowed her attention to be drawn away. Her apology was interrupted by the arrival of a second young woman—apparently a nursery-maid—who emerged from the concealment of the neighboring rocks, leading a little girl by the hand. Instinctively, her eyes fell upon the child's wet clothes.

"Ah, Miss Congreve," she cried, in true nursery-maid style, "what'll Mrs Wilkes say to that?"

"She will say that she is very thankful to this gentleman," said Miss Congreve, with decision.

Philip had been looking at the young girl as she spoke, forcibly struck by her face and manner. He detected in her appearance a peculiar union of modesty and frankness, of youthful freshness and elegant mannerism, which suggested vague possibilities of further acquaintance. He had already found it pleasant to observe her. He had been for ten days in search of a wicked girl, and it was a momentary relief to find himself suddenly face to face with a charming one. The nursery-maid's apostrophe was like an electric shock.

It is, nevertheless, to be supposed that he concealed his surprise, inasmuch as Miss Congreve gave no sign of having perceived that he was startled. She had come to a tardy sense of his personal discomfort. She besought him to make use of her carriage, which he would find on the cliff, and quickly return home. He thanked her and declined her offer, declaring that it was better policy to walk. He put out his hand to his little friend and bade him good-bye. Miss Congreve liberated the child and he came and put his hand in Philip's.

"One of these days," said Osborne, "you'll have long legs, too, and then you'll not mind the water." He spoke to the boy, but he looked hard at Miss Congreve, who, perhaps, thought he was asking for some formal expression of gratitude.

"His mother," she said, "will give herself the pleasure of thanking you."

"The trouble," said Osborne, "the very unnecessary trouble. Your best plan," he added, with a smile (for, wonderful to tell, he actually smiled) "is to say nothing about it."

"If I consulted my interests alone," said the young girl, with a gracious light in her dark eyes, "I should certainly hold my tongue. But I hope my little victim is not so ungrateful as to promise silence."

Osborne stiffened himself up; for this was more or less of a compliment. He made his bow in silence and started for home at a rapid pace. On the following day he received this note by post:

> Mrs Wilkes begs to thank Mr Osborne most warmly for the prompt and generous relief afforded to her little boy. She regrets that Mr Osborne's walk should have been interrupted, and hopes that his exertions have been attended with no bad effects.

Enclosed in the note was a pocket-handkerchief, bearing Philip's name, which he remembered to have made the child take, to wipe his tears. His answer was, of course, brief.

> Mr Osborne begs to assure Mrs Wilkes that she exaggerates the importance of the service rendered to her son, and that he has no cause to regret his very trifling efforts. He takes the liberty of

presenting his compliments to Master Wilkes, and of hoping that he
has recovered from his painful sensations.

The correspondence naturally went no further, and for some days no ad-
ditional light was thrown upon Miss Congreve. Now that Philip had met her,
face to face, and found her a commonplace young girl—a clever girl, doubtless, for she looked it, and an agreeable one—but still a mere young lady,
mindful of the proprieties, with a face innocent enough, and even a trifle sad,
and a couple of pretty children who called her "aunt," and whom, indeed, in
a moment of enthusiastic devotion to nature and art, she left to the mercy of
the waves, but whom she finally kissed and comforted and handled with all
due tenderness—now that he had met Miss Congreve under these circumstances, he felt his mission sitting more lightly on his conscience. Ideally
she had been repulsive; actually, she was a person whom, if he had not been
committed to detest her, he would find it very pleasant to like. She had been
humanized, to his view, by the mere accidents of her flesh and blood. Philip
was by no means prepared to give up his resentment. Poor Graham's ghost
sat grim and upright in his memory, and fed the flickering flame. But it was
something of a problem to reconcile the heroine of his vengeful longings,
with the heroine of the little scene on the beach, and to accommodate this
inoffensive figure, in turn, to the color of his retribution. A dozen matters
conspired to keep him from coming to the point, and to put him in a com-
paratively good humor. He was invited to the right and the left; he lounged
and bathed, and talked, and smoked, and rode, and dined out, and saw an
endless succession of new faces, and in short, reduced the vestments of his
outward mood to a suit of very cheerful half-mourning. And all this,
moreover, without any sense of being faithless to his friend. Oddly enough,
Graham had never seemed so living as now that he was dead. In the flesh,
he had possessed but a half-vitality. His spirit had been exquisitely willing,
but his flesh had been fatally weak. He was at best a baffled, disappointed
man. It was his spirit, his affections, his sympathies and perceptions, that
were warm and active, and Osborne knew that he had fallen sole heir to
these. He felt his bosom swell with a wholesome sense of the magnitude of
the heritage, and he was conscious with each successive day, of less desire to
invoke poor Graham in dark corners, and mourn him in lonely places. By a
single solemn, irrevocable aspiration, he had placed his own tough organism
and his energetic will at the service of his friend's virtues. So as he found his
excursion turning into a holiday, he stretched his long limbs and with the
least bit of a yawn whispered *Amen*.

Within a week after his encounter with Miss Congreve, he went with a
friend to witness some private theatricals, given in the house of a lady of
great social repute. The entertainment consisted of two plays, the first of
which was so flat and poor that when the curtain fell Philip prepared to

make his escape, thinking he might easily bring the day to some less impotent conclusion. As he passed along the narrow alley between the seats
and the wall of the drawing-room, he brushed a printed programme out of a
lady's hand. Stooping to pick it up, his eye fell upon the name of Miss Congreve among the performers in the second piece. He immediately retraced
his steps. The overture began, the curtain rose again, and several persons
appeared on the stage, arrayed in the powder and patches of the last century.
Finally, amid loud acclamations, walked on Miss Congreve, as the heroine,
powdered and patched in perfection. She represented a young countess – a
widow in the most interesting predicament – and for all good histrionic purposes, she was irresistibly beautiful. She was dressed, painted, and equipped
with great skill and in the very best taste. She looked as if she had stepped
out of the frame of one of those charming full-length pastel portraits of fine
ladies in Louis XV's time, which they show you in French palaces. But she
was not alone all grace and elegance and *finesse*; she had dignity; she was
serious at moments, and severe; she frowned and commanded; and, at the
proper time, she wept the most natural tears. It was plain that Miss Congreve was a true artist. Osborne had never seen better acting – never, indeed,
any so good; for here was an actress who was at once a perfect young lady
and a consummate mistress of dramatic effect. The audience was roused to
the highest pitch of enthusiasm, and Miss Congreve's fellow-players were
left quite in the lurch. The beautiful Miss Latimer, celebrated in polite society
for her face and figure, who had undertaken the second female part, was
compelled for the nonce to have neither figure nor face. The play had been
marked in the bills as adapted from the French "especially for this occasion";
and when the curtain fell for the last time, the audience, in great good
humor, clamoured for the adapter. Some time elapsed before any notice was
taken of their call, which they took as a provocation of their curiosity. Finally, a gentleman made his way before the curtain, and proclaimed that the
version of the piece which his associates had had the honor of performing
was from the accomplished pen of the young lady who had won their ap-
plause in the character of the heroine. At this announcement, a dozen en-
thusiasts lifted their voices and demanded that Miss Congreve should be
caused to re-appear; but the gentleman cut short their appeal by saying that
she had already left the house. This was not true, as Osborne subsequently
learned. Henrietta was sitting on a sofa behind the scenes, waiting for her
carriage, fingering an immense bouquet, and listening with a tired smile to
compliments – hard by Miss Latimer, who sat eating an ice beside her
mother, the latter lady looking in a very grim fashion at that very plain,
dreadfully thin Miss Congreve.

Osborne walked home thrilled and excited, but decidedly bewildered. He
felt that he had reckoned without his host, and that Graham's fickle mistress
was not a person to be snubbed and done for. He was utterly at a loss as to

what to think of her. She broke men's hearts and turned their heads; whatever she put her hand to she marked with her genius. She was a co-quette, a musician, an artist, an actress, and author—a prodigy. Of what stuff was she made? What had she done with her heart and her conscience? She painted her face, and frolicked among lamps and flowers to the clapping of a thousand hands, while poor Graham lay imprisoned in eternal silence. Osborne was put on his mettle. To draw a penitent tear from those deep and charming eyes was assuredly a task for a clever man.

The plays had been acted on a Wednesday. On the following Saturday Philip was invited to take part in a picnic, organized by Mrs Carpenter, the lady who had conducted the plays, and who had a mania for making up parties. The persons whom she had now enlisted were to proceed by water to a certain pastoral spot consecrated by nature to picnics, and there to have lunch upon the grass, to dance and play nursery-games. They were carried over in two large sailing boats, and during the transit Philip talked a while with Mrs Carpenter, whom he found a very amiable, loquacious person. At the further end of the boat in which, with his hostess, he had taken his place, he observed a young girl in a white dress, with a thick, blue veil drawn over her face. Through the veil, directed towards his person, he per-ceived the steady glance of two fine, dark eyes. For a moment he was at a loss to recognise their possessor; but his uncertainty was rapidly dispelled.

"I see you have Miss Congreve," he said to Mrs Carpenter—"the actress of the other evening."

"Yes," said Mrs Carpenter, "I persuaded her to come. She's all the fashion since Wednesday."

"Was she unwilling to come?" asked Philip.

"Yes, at first. You see, she's a good, quiet girl; she hates to have a noise made about her."

"She had enough noise the other night. She has wonderful talent."

"Wonderful, wonderful. And heaven knows where she gets it. Do you know her family? The most matter-of-fact, least dramatic, least imaginative people in the world—people who are shy of the theatre on moral grounds."

"I see. They won't go to the theatre; the theatre comes to them."

"Exactly. It serves them right. Mrs Wilkes, Henrietta's sister, was in a dreadful state about her attempting to act. But now, since Henrietta's suc-cess, she's talking about it to all the world."

When the boat came to shore, a plank was stretched from the prow to an adjacent rock for the accommodation of the ladies. Philip stood at the head of the plank, offering his hand for their assistance. Mrs Carpenter came last, with Miss Congreve, who declined Osborne's aid but gave him a little bow, through her veil. Half an hour later Philip again found himself at the side of his hostess, and again spoke of Miss Congreve. Mrs Carpenter warned him that she was standing close at hand, in a group of young girls.

"Have you heard," he asked, lowering his voice "of her being engaged to be married – or of her having been?"

"No," said Mrs Carpenter, "I've heard nothing. To whom? – stay. I've heard vaguely of something this summer at Sharon. She had a sort of flirtation with some man, whose name I forget."

"Was it Holland?"

"I think not. He left her for that very silly little Mrs Dodd – who hasn't been a widow six months. I think the name was Graham."

Osborne broke into a peal of laughter so loud and harsh that his companion turned upon him in surprise. "Excuse me," said he. "It's false."

"You ask questions, Mr Osborne," said Mrs Carpenter, "but you seem to know more about Miss Congreve than I do."

"Very likely. You see, I knew Robert Graham." Philip's words were uttered with such emphasis and resonance that two or three of the young girls in the adjoining group turned about and looked at him.

"She heard you," said Mrs Carpenter.

"She didn't turn round," said Philip.

"That proves what I say. I meant to introduce you, and now I can't."

"Thank you," said Philip. "I shall introduce myself." Osborne felt in his bosom all the heat of his old resentment. This perverse and heartless girl, then, his soul cried out, not content with driving poor Graham to impious self-destruction had caused it to be believed that he had killed himself from remorse at his own misconduct. He resolved to strike while the iron was hot. But although he was an avenger, he was still a gentleman, and he approached the young girl with a very civil face.

"If I am not mistaken," he said, removing his hat, "you have already done me the honor of recognising me."

Miss Congreve's bow, as she left the boat, had been so obviously a sign of recognition, that Philip was amazed at the vacant smile with which she received his greeting. Something had happened in the interval to make her change her mind. Philip could think of no other motive than her having overheard his mention of Graham's name.

"I have an impression," she said, "of having met you before; but I confess that I'm unable to place you."

Osborne looked at her a moment. "I can't deny myself," he said, "the pleasure of asking about little Mr Wilkes."

"I remember you now," said Miss Congreve, simply. "You carried my nephew out of the water."

"I hope he has got over his fright."

"He denies, I believe, that he was frightened. Of course, for my credit, I don't contradict him."

Miss Congreve's words were followed by a long pause, by which she seemed in no degree embarrassed. Philip was confounded by her apparent self-possession—to call it by no worse name. Considering that she had Graham's death on her conscience, and that, hearing his name on Osborne's lips, she must have perceived the latter to be identical with that dear friend of whom Graham must often have spoken, she was certainly showing a very brave face. But had she indeed heard of Graham's death? For a moment Osborne gave her the benefit of the doubt. He felt that he would take a grim satisfaction in being bearer of the tidings. In order to confer due honor on the disclosure, he saw that it was needful to detach the young girl from her companions. As, therefore, the latter at this moment began to disperse in clusters and couples along the shore, he proposed that they should stroll further a-field. Miss Congreve looked about at the other young girls as if to call one of them to her side, but none of them seemed available. So she slowly moved forward under Philip's guidance, with a half-suppressed look of reluctance. Philip began by paying her a very substantial compliment upon her acting. It was a most inconsequential speech, in the actual state of his feelings, but he couldn't help it. She was perhaps as wicked a girl as you shall easily meet, but her acting was perfect. Having paid this little tribute to equity, he broke ground for Graham.

"I don't feel, Miss Congreve," he said, "as if you were a new acquaintance. I have heard you a great deal talked about." This was not literally true, the reader will remember. All Philip's information had been acquired in his half hour with Mrs Dodd.

"By whom, pray?" asked Henrietta.

"By Robert Graham."

"Ah, yes. I was half prepared to hear you speak of him. I remember hearing him speak of a person of your name."

Philip was puzzled. Did she know, or not? "I believe you knew him quite well yourself," he said, somewhat preemptorily.

"As well as he would let me—I doubt if any one knew him well."

"So you've heard of his death," said Philip.

"Yes, from himself."

"How, from himself?"

"He wrote me a letter, in his last hours, leaving his approaching end to be inferred, rather than positively announcing it. I wrote an answer, with the request that if my letter was not immediately called for, it should be returned by the post office. It was returned within a week—And now, Mr Osborne," the young girl added, "let me make a request."

Philip bowed.

"I shall feel particularly obliged if you will say no more about Mr Graham."

This was a stroke for which Osborne was not prepared. It had at least the merit of directness. Osborne looked at his companion. There was a faint flush in her cheeks, and a serious light in her eyes. There was plainly no want of energy in her wish. He felt that he must suspend operations and make his approach from another quarter. But it was some moments before he could bring himself to accede to her request. She looked at him, expecting an answer, and he felt her dark eyes on his face.

"Just as you please," he said, at last, mechanically.

They walked along for some moments in silence. Then, suddenly coming upon a young married woman, whom Mrs Carpenter had pressed into her service as a lieutenant, Miss Congreve took leave of Philip, on a slight pretext, and entered into talk with this lady. Philip strolled away and walked about for an hour alone. He had met with a check, but he was resolved that, though he had fallen back, it would be only to leap the further. During the half-hour that Philip sauntered along by the water, the dark cloud suspended above poor Miss Congreve's head doubled in portentous volume. And, indeed, from Philip's point of view, could anything well be more shameless and more heartless than the young girl's request?

At last Osborne remembered that he was neglecting the duties laid upon him by Mrs Carpenter. He retraced his steps and made his way back to the spot devoted to the banquet. Mrs Carpenter called him to her, said that she had been looking for him for an hour, and, when she learned how he had been spending his time, slapped him with her parasol, called him a horrid creature, and declared that she would never again invite him to anything of hers. She then introduced him to her niece, a somewhat undeveloped young lady, with whom he went and sat down over the water. They found very little to talk about. Osborne was thinking of Miss Congreve, and Mrs Carpenter's niece, who was very timid and fluttering, having but one foot yet, as one may say, in society, was abashed and unnerved at finding herself alone with so very tall and mature and handsome a gentleman as Philip. He gave her a little confidence in the course of time, however, by making little stones skip over the surface of the water for her amusement. But he still kept thinking of Henrietta Congreve, and he at last bethought himself of asking his companion whether she knew her. Yes, she knew her slightly; but she threw no light on the subject. She was evidently not of an analytical turn of mind, and she was too innocent to gossip. She contended herself with saying that she believed Henrietta was wonderfully clever, and that she read Latin and Greek.

"Clever, clever," said Philip, "I hear nothing else. I shall begin to think she's a demon."

"No, Henrietta Congreve is very good," said his companion. "She's very religious. She visits the poor and reads sermons. You know the other night she acted for the poor. She's anything but a demon. I think she's so nice."

Before long the party was summoned to lunch. Straggling couples came wandering into sight, gentlemen assisting young girls out of rocky retreats into which no one would have supposed them capable of penetrating, and to which–more wonderful still–no one had observed them to direct their steps.

The table was laid in the shade, and on the grass, and the feasters sat about on rugs and shawls. As Osborne took his place along with Mrs Carpenter's niece, he noticed that Miss Congreve had not yet re-appeared. He called his companion's attention to the circumstance, and she mentioned it to her aunt, who said that the young girl had last been seen in company with Mr Stone–a person unknown to Osborne–and that she would, doubtless, soon turn up.

"I suppose she's quite safe," said Philip's neighbor–innocently or wittily, he hardly knew which; "she's with a clergyman."

In a few moments the missing couple appeared on the crest of an adjacent hill. Osborne watched them as they came down. Mr Stone was a comely-faced young man, in a clerical necktie and garments of an exaggerated sacerdotal cut–a divine, evidently of strong "ritualistic" tendencies. Miss Congreve drew near, pale, graceful, and grave, and Philip, with his eyes fixed on her in the interval, lost not a movement of her person, nor a glance of her eyes. She wore a white muslin dress, short, in the prevailing fashion, with trimmings of yellow ribbon inserted in the skirt; and round her shoulders a shawl of heavy black lace, crossed over her bosom and tied in a big knot behind. In her hand she carried a great bunch of wild flowers, with which, as Philip's neighbor whispered to him, she had "ruined" her gloves. Osborne wondered whether there was any meaning in her having taken up with a clergyman. Had she suddenly felt the tardy pangs of remorse, and been moved to seek spiritual advice? Neither on the countenance of her ecclesiastical gallant, nor on her own, were there any visible traces of pious discourse. On the contrary, poor Mr Stone looked sadly demoralized; their conversation had been wholly of profane things. His white cravat had lost its conservative rigidity, and his hat its unimpassioned equipoise. Worse than all, a little blue forget-me-not had found its way into his button-hole. As for Henrietta, her face wore that look of half-severe serenity which was its wonted expression, but there was no sign of her having seen her lover's ghost.

Osborne went mechanically through the movements of being attentive to the insipid little person at his side. But his thoughts were occupied with Miss Congreve and his eyes constantly turning to her face. From time to time, they met her own. A fierce disgust muttered in his bosom. What Henrietta Congreve needed, he said to himself, was to be used as she used others, as she was evidently now using this poor little parson. He was already over his ears in love–vainly feeling for bottom in midstream, while she sat dry-shod on the brink. She needed a lesson; but who should give it? She knew more than all her teachers. Men approached her only to be dazzled and charmed. If she could only find her equal or her master! one with as clear a head, as lively a fancy, as relentless a will as her own; one who would turn the tables, anticipate her, fascinate her, and then suddenly look at his watch and bid her good morning. Then, perhaps, Graham might settle to sleep in his grave. Then she would feel what it was to play with hearts, for then her own would have been as glass against bronze. Osborne looked about the table, but none of Mrs Carpenter's male guests bore the least resemblance to the hero of his vision—a man with a heart of bronze and a head of crystal. They were, indeed, very proper swains for the young ladies at their sides, but Henrietta Congreve was not one of these. She was not a mere twaddling ballroom flirt. There was in her coquetry something serious and exalted. It was an intellectual joy. She drained honest men's hearts to the last drop, and bloomed white upon the monstrous diet. As Philip glanced around the circle, his eye fell upon a young girl who seemed for a moment to have forgotten her neighbors, her sandwiches and her champagne, and was very innocently contemplating his own person. As soon as she perceived that he had observed her, she of course dropped her eyes on her plate. But Philip had read the meaning of her glance. It seemed to say—this lingering virginal eyebeam—in language easily translated, Thou art the man! It said, in other words, in less transcendental fashion, My dear Mr Osborne, you are a very good looking fellow. Philip felt his pulse quicken; he had received his baptism. Not that good looks were a sufficient outfit for breaking Miss Congreve's heart; but they were the outward signs of his mission.

The feasting at last came to an end. A fiddler, who had been brought along, began to tune his instrument, and Mrs Carpenter proceeded to organize a dance. The *débris* of the collation was cleared away, and the level space thus uncovered converted into a dancing floor. Osborne, not being a dancing man, sat at a distance, with two or three other spectators, among whom was the Rev. Mr Stone. Each of these gentlemen watched with close attention the movements of Henrietta Congreve. Osborne, however, occasionally glanced at his companion, who, on his side, was quite too absorbed in looking at Miss Congreve to think of anything else.

"They look very charming, those young ladies,"said Philip, addressing the young clergyman, to whom he had just been introduced. "Some of them dance particularly well."

"Oh, yes!" said Mr Stone, with fervor. And then, as if he feared that he had committed himself to an invidious distinction unbecoming of his cloth: "I think they all dance well."

But Philip, as a lawyer, naturally took a different view of the matter from Mr Stone, as a clergyman. "Some of them very much better than others, it seems to me. I had no idea that there could be such a difference. Look at Miss Congreve, for instance."

Mr Stone, whose eyes were fixed on Miss Congreve, obeyed his injunction by moving them away for a moment, and directing them to a very substantial and somewhat heavy-footed young lady, who was figuring beside her. "Oh, yes, she's very graceful," he said, with unction. "So light, so free, so quiet!"

Philip smiled. "You, too, most excellent simpleton," he said to himself– "you, too, shall be avenged." And then–"Miss Congreve is a very remarkable person," he added, aloud.

"Oh, very!"

"She has extraordinary versatility."

"Most extraordinary."

"Have you seen her act?"

"Yes–yes; I infringed upon my usage in regard to entertainments of that nature, and went the other evening. It was a most brilliant performance."

"And you know she wrote the play."

"Ah, not exactly," said Mr Stone, with a little protesting gesture; "she translated it."

"Yes; but she had to write it quite over. Do you know it in French?"–and Philip mentioned the original title.

Mr Stone signified that he was unacquainted with the work.

"It would never have done, you know," said Philip, "to play it as it stands. I saw it in Paris. Miss Congreve eliminated the little difficulties with uncommon skill."

Mr Stone was silent. The violin uttered a long-drawn note, and the adies curtsied low to their gentlemen. Miss Congreve's partner stood with his back to our two friends, and her own obeisance was, therefore, executed directly in front of them. If Mr Stone's enthusiasm had been damped by Philip's irreverent freedom, it was rekindled by this glance. "I suppose you've heard her sing," he said, after a pause.

"Yes, indeed," said Philip, without hesitation.

"She sings sacred music with the most beautiful fervor."

"Yes, so I'm told. And I'm told, moreover, that she's very learned–that she has a passion for books."

"I think it very likely. In fact, she's quite an accomplished theologian. We had this morning a very lively discussion."

"You differed, then?" said Philip.

"Oh," said Mr Stone, with charming *naïveté*, "*I* didn't differ. It was she!"

Isn't she a little–the least bit–" and Philip paused, to select his word.

"The least bit?" asked Mr Stone, in a benevolent tone. And then, as Philip still hesitated–"The least bit heterodox?"

"The least bit of a coquette?"

"Oh, Mr Osborne!" cried the young divine–"that's the last thing I should call Miss Congreve."

At this moment, Mrs Carpenter drew nigh. "What is the last thing you should call Miss Congreve?" she asked, overhearing the clergyman's words.

"A coquette."

"It seems to me," said the lady, "that it's the first thing I should call her. You have to come to it, I fancy. You always do, you know. I should get it off my mind at once, and then I should sing her charms."

"Oh, Mrs Carpenter!" said Mr Stone.

"Yes, my dear young man. She's quiet but she's deep–I see Mr Osborne knows," and Mrs Carpenter passed on.

"She's deep–that's what I say," said Mr Stone, with mild firmness–"What do you know, Mr Osborne?"

Philip fancied that the poor fellow had turned pale; he certainly looked grave.

"Oh, I know nothing," said Philip. "I affirmed nothing. I merely inquired."

"Well then, my dear sir"–and the young man's candid visage flushed a little with the intensity of his feelings–"I give you my word for it, that I believe Miss Congreve to be not only the most accomplished, but the most noble-minded, the most truthful, the most truly christian young lady–in this whole assembly."

"I'm sure, I'm much obliged to you for the assurance," said Philip. "I shall value and remember it."

It would not have been hard for Philip to set down Mr Stone as a mere soft-hearted, philandering parson–a type ready made to his hand. Mrs Carpenter, on the other hand, was a shrewd sagacious woman. But somehow he was impressed by the minister's words, and quite untouched by those of the lady. At last those of the dancers who were tired of the sport, left the circle and wandered back to the shore. The afternoon was drawing to a close, the western sky was beginning to blush crimson and the shadows to grow long on the grass. Only half an hour remained before the moment fixed for the return to Newport. Philip resolved to turn it to account. He followed Miss Congreve to a certain rocky platform, overlooking the water, whither, with a couple of elderly ladies, she had gone to watch the sunset. He found no difficulty in persuading her to wander aside from her companions. There was no distrust in her keen and delicate face. It was incredible that she should have meant defiance; but her very repose and placidity had a strangely irritating action upon Philip. They affected him as the climax of insolence. He drew from his breast-pocket a small portfolio, containing a dozen letters, among which was the last one he had received from Graham.

"I shall take the liberty, for once, Miss Congreve," he said, "of violating the injunction which you laid upon me this morning with regard to Robert Graham. I have here a letter which I should like you to see."

"From Mr Graham himself?"

"From Graham himself–written just before his death." He held it out, but Henrietta made no movement to take it.

"I have no desire to see it," she said. "I had rather not. You know he wrote also to me at that moment."

"I'm sure," said Philip, "I should not refuse to see your letter."

"I can't offer to show it to you. I immediately destroyed it."

"Well, you see I've kept mine—It's not long," Osborne pursued.

Miss Congreve, as if with a strong effort, put out her hand and took the document. She looked at the directions for some moments, in silence, and then raised her eyes toward Osborne. "Do you value it?" she asked. "Does it contain anything you wish to keep?"

"No; I give it to you, for that matter."

"Well then!" said Henrietta. And she tore the letter twice across, and threw the scraps into the sea.

"Ah!" cried Osborne, "what the devil have you done?"

"Don't be violent, Mr Osborne," said the young girl. "I hadn't the slightest intention of reading it. You are properly punished for having disobeyed me."

Philip swallowed his rage at a gulp, and followed her as she turned away.

III

In the middle of September, Mrs Dodd came to Newport, to stay with a friend—somewhat out of humor at having been invited at the fag end of the season, but on the whole very much the same Mrs Dodd as before; or rather not quite the same, for, in her way, she had taken Graham's death very much to heart. A couple of days after her arrival, she met Philip in the street, and stopped him, "I'm glad to find *some one* still here," she said; for she was with her friend, and having introduced Philip to this lady, she begged him to come and see her. On the next day but one, accordingly, Philip presented himself, and saw Mrs Dodd alone. She began to talk about Graham; she became very much affected, and with a little more encouragement from Osborne, she would certainly have shed tears. But, somehow, Philip was loth to countenance her grief; he made short responses. Mrs Dodd struck him as weak and silly and morbidly sentimental. He wondered whether there could have been any truth in the rumor that Graham had cared for her. Not certainly if there was any truth in the story of his passion for Henrietta Congreve. It was impossible that he should have cared for both. Philip made this reflection, but he stopped short of adding that Mrs Dodd failed signally to please him, because during the past three weeks he had constantly enjoyed Henrietta's society.

For Mrs Dodd, of course, the transition was easy from Graham to Miss Congreve. "I'm told Miss Congreve is still here," she said. "Have you made her acquaintance?"

"Perfectly," said Philip.

"You seem to take it very easily. I hope you have brought her to a sense of her iniquities. There's a task, Mr Osborne. You ought to convert her."

"I've not attempted to convert her. I've taken her as she is."

"Does she wear mourning for Mr. Graham? It's the least she can do."

"Wear mourning?" said Philip. "Why, she has been going to a party every other night."

"Of course I don't suppose she has put on a black dress. But does she mourn *here*?" And Mrs Dodd laid her hand on her heart.

"You mean in her heart? Well, you know, it's problematical that she has one."

"I suppose she disapproves of suicide," said Mrs Dodd, with a little acrid smile. "Bless my soul, so do I."

"So do I, Mrs Dodd," said Philip. And he remained for a moment thoughtful. "I wish to heaven," he cried, "that Graham were here! It seems to me at moments that he and Miss Congreve might have come to an understanding again."

Mrs Dodd threw out her hands in horror. "Why, has she given up her last lover?"

"Her last lover? Whom do you mean?"

"Why, the man I told you of—Mr Holland."

Philip appeared quite to have forgotten this point in Mrs Dodd's recital. He broke into a loud, nervous laugh. "I'll be hanged," he cried, "if I know! One thing is certain," he pursued, with emphasis, recovering himself; "Mr Holland—whoever he is—has for the past three weeks seen nothing of Miss Congreve."

Mrs Dodd sat silent, with her eyes lowered. At last, looking up, "You, on the other hand, I infer," she said, "have seen a great deal of her."

"Yes, I've seen her constantly."

Mrs Dodd raised her eyebrows and distended her lips in a smile which was emphatically not a smile. "Well, you'll think it an odd question, Mr Osborne," she said, "but how do you reconcile your intimacy with Miss Congreve with your devotion to Mr Graham?"

Philip frowned—quite too severely for good manners. Decidedly, Mrs Dodd was extremely silly. "Oh," he rejoined, "I reconcile the two things perfectly. Moreover, my dear Mrs. Dodd allow me to say that it's my own business. At all events," he added, more gently, "perhaps, one of these days, you'll read the enigma."

"Oh, if it's an enigma," cried the lady, "perhaps I can guess it."

Philip had risen to his feet to take his leave, and Mrs Dodd threw herself back on the sofa, clasped her hands in her lap, and looked up at him with a penetrating smile. She shook her finger at him reproachfully. Philip saw that she had an idea; perhaps it was the right one. At all events, he blushed. Upon this Mrs Dodd cried out.

"I've guessed it," she said. "Oh, Mr Osborne!"

"What have you guessed?" asked Philip, not knowing why in the world he should blush.

"If I've guessed right," said Mrs Dodd, "it's a charming idea. It does you credit. It's quite romantic. It would do in a novel."

"I doubt," said Philip, "whether I know what you're talking about."

"Oh, yes, you do. I wish you good luck. To another man I should say it was a dangerous game. But to you!"–and with an insinuating movement of her head, Mrs Dodd measured with a glance the length and breadth of Philip's fine person.

Osborne was inexpressibly disgusted, and without further delay he took his leave.

The reader will be at a loss to understand why Philip should have been disgusted with the mere foreshadowing on the part of another, of a scheme which, three weeks before, he had thought a very happy invention. For we may as well say outright, that although Mrs Dodd was silly, she was not so silly but that she had divined his original intentions with regard to Henrietta. The fact is that in three weeks Philip's humor had undergone a great change. The reader has gathered for himself that Henrietta Congreve was no ordinary girl, that she was on the contrary, a person of distinguished gifts and remarkable character. Until within a very few months she had seen very little of the world, and her mind and talents had been gradually formed in seclusion, study, and it is not too much to say, meditation. Thanks to her circumscribed life and her long contemplative leisures, she had reached a pitch of rare intellectual perfection. She was educated, one may say, in a sense in which the term may be used of very few young girls, however richly endowed by nature. When at a later period than most girls, owing to domestic circumstances which it is needless to unfold, she made her entrance into society and learned what it was to be in the world and of the world, to talk and listen, to please and be pleased, to be admired, flattered and interested, her admirable faculties and beautiful intellect, ripened in studious solitude, burst into luxuriant bloom and bore the fairest fruit. Miss Congreve was accordingly a person for whom a man of taste and of feeling could not help entertaining a serious regard. Philip Osborne was emphatically such a man; the manner in which he was affected by his friend's death proves, I think, that he had feeling; and it is ample evidence of his taste that he had chosen such a friend. He had no sooner begun to act in obedience to the impulse mystically bestowed, as it were, at the close of Mrs Carpenter's feast–he had no sooner obtained an introduction at Mrs Wilkes's, and, with excellent tact and discretion, made good his footing there, than he began to feel in his

inmost heart that in staking his life upon Miss Congreve's favor, poor Graham had indeed revealed the depths of his exquisite sensibility. For a week
at least–a week during which, with unprecedented good fortune, and a
degree of assurance worthy of a better cause, Philip contrived in one way
and other to talk with his fair victim no less than a dozen times–he was
under the empire of a feverish excitement which kept him from seeing the
young girl in all her beautiful integrity. He was pre-occupied with his own
intentions and the effect of his own manoeuvres. But gradually he quite
forgot himself while he was in her presence, and only remembered that he
had a sacred part to play, after he had left the house. Then it was that he
conceived the intensity of Graham's despair, and then it was that he began to
be sadly, wofully puzzled by the idea that a woman could unite so much love-
liness with so much treachery, so much light with so much darkness. He
was as certain of the bright surface of her nature as of its cold and dark
reverse, and he was utterly unable to discover a link of connection between
the two. At moments he wondered how in the world he had become saddled
with this metaphysical burden: *que diable venait-il faire dans cette galère?* But
nevertheless he was afloat; he must row his boat over the current to where
the restless spirit of his friend paced the opposite shore.

Henrietta Congreve, after a first movement of apparent aversion, was
very well pleased to accept Osborne as a friend and as an *habitué* of her
sister's house. Osborne fancied that he might believe without fatuity–for
whatever the reader may think, it is needless to say that Philip was very far
from supposing his whole course to be a piece of infatuated coxcombry–that
she preferred him to most of the young men of her circle. Philip had a just
estimate of his own endowments, and he knew that for the finer social purposes, if not for strictly sentimental ones, he contained the stuff of an important personage. He had no taste for trivialities, but trivialities played but a
small part in Mrs Wilkes's drawing-room. Mrs Wilkes was a simple woman,
but she was neither silly nor frivolous; and Miss Congreve was exempt from
these foibles for even better reasons. "Women really care only for men who
can tell them something," Osborne remembered once to have heard Graham
say, not without bitterness. "They are always famished for news." Philip now
reflected with satisfaction that he could give Miss Congreve more news than
most of her constituted gossips. He had an admirable memory and a very
lively observation. In these respects Henrietta was herself equally well endowed; but Philip's experience of the world had of course been tenfold more
extensive, and he was able continually to complete her partial inductions
and to rectify her false conjectures. Sometimes they seemed to him wonderfully shrewd, and sometimes delightfully innocent. He nevertheless frequently found himself in a position to make her acquainted with facts
possessing the charm of absolute novelty. He had travelled and seen a great
variety of men and women, and of course he had read a number of books

which a woman is not expected to read. Philip was keenly sensible of these advantages; but it nevertheless seemed to him that if the exhibition of his mental treasures furnished Miss Congreve with a great deal of entertainment, her attention, on the other hand, had a most refreshing effect upon his mind.

At the end of three weeks Philip might, perhaps not unreasonably, have supposed himself in a position to strike his blow. It is true that, for a woman of sense, there is a long step between thinking a man an excellent friend and a charming talker, and surrendering her heart to him. Philip had every reason to believe that Henrietta thought these good things of himself; but if he had hereupon turned about to make his exit, with the conviction that when he had closed the parlor-door behind him he should, by lending an attentive ear, hear her fall in a swoon on the carpet, he might have been sadly snubbed and disappointed. He longed for an opportunity to test the quality of his empire. If he could only pretend for a week to be charmed by another woman, Miss Congreve might perhaps commit herself. Philip flattered himself that he could read very small signs. But what other woman could decently serve as the object of a passion thus extemporized? The only woman Philip could think of was Mrs Dodd; and to think of Mrs Dodd was to give it up. For a man who was intimate with Miss Congreve to pretend to care for any other woman (except a very old friend) was to act in flagrant contempt of all verisimilitude. Philip had, therefore, to content himself with playing off his own assumed want of heart against Henrietta's cordial regard. But at this rate the game moved very slowly. Work was accumulating at a prodigious rate at his office, and he couldn't dangle about Miss Congreve forever. He bethought himself of a harmless artifice for drawing her out. It seemed to him that his move was not altogether unsuccessful, and that, at a pinch, Henrietta might become jealous of a rival in his affections. Nevertheless, he was strongly tempted to take up his hand and leave the game. It was too confoundedly exciting.

The incident of which I speak happened within a few days after Osborne's visit to Mrs Dodd. Finding it impossible to establish an imaginary passion for an actual, visible young lady, Philip resolved to invent not only the passion, but the young lady, too. One morning, as he was passing the showcase of one of the several photographers who came to Newport for the season, he was struck by the portrait of a very pretty young girl. She was fair in color, graceful, well-dressed, well placed, her face was charming, she was plainly a lady. Philip went in and asked who she was. The photographer had destroyed the negative and had kept no register of her name. He remembered her, however, distinctly. The portrait had not been taken during the summer; it had been taken during the preceding winter, in Boston, the photographer's headquarters. "I kept it," he said, "because I thought it so very perfect a picture. And such a charming sitter! We haven't many like that."

He added, however, that it was too good to please the masses, and that Philip was the first gentleman who had had the taste to observe it.

"So much the better," thought Philip, and forthwith proposed to the man to part with it. The latter, of course, had conscientious scruples; it was against his principles to dispose of the portraits of ladies who came to him in confidence. To do him justice, he adhered to his principles, and Philip was unable to persuade him to sell it. He consented, however, to give it to Mr Osborne, *gratis*. Mr Osborne deserved it, and he had another for himself. By this time Philip had grown absolutely fond of the picture; at this latter intelligence he looked grave, and suggested that if the artist would not sell one, perhaps he would sell two. The photographer declined, reiterated his offer, and Philip finally accepted. By way of compensation, however, he proceeded to sit for his own portrait. In the course of half an hour the photographer gave him a dozen reflections of his head and shoulders, distinguished by as many different attitudes and expressions.

"You sit first-rate, sir," said the artist. "You take beautifully. You're quite a match for my young lady."

Philip went off with his dozen prints, promising to examine them at his leisure, select and give a liberal order.

In the evening he went to Mrs Wilkes's. He found this lady on her verandah, drinking tea in the open air with a guest, whom in the darkness he failed to recognize. As Mrs Wilkes proceeded to introduce him, her companion graciously revealed herself as Mrs Dodd. "How on earth," thought Philip, "did she get here?" To find Mrs Dodd instead of Miss Congreve was, of course, a gross discomforture. Philip sat down, however, with a good grace, to all appearance, hoping that Henrietta would turn up. finally, moving his chair to a line with the drawing-room window, he saw the young girl within, reading by the lamp. She was alone and intent upon her book. She wore a dress of white grenadine, covered with ornaments and arabesques of crimson silk, which gave her a somewhat fantastical air. For the rest, her expression was grave enough, and her brows contracted, as if she were completely absorbed in her book. Her right elbow rested on the table, and with her hand she mechanically twisted the long curl depending from her *chignon*. Watching his opportunity, Osborne escaped from the ladies on the verandah and made his way into the drawing-room. Miss Congreve received him as an old friend, without rising from her chair.

Philip began by pretending to scold her for shirking the society of Mrs Dodd.

"Shirking!" said Henrietta. "You are very polite to Mrs Dodd."

"It seems to me," rejoined Osborne, "that I'm quite as polite as you."

"Well, perhaps you are. To tell the truth, I'm not very polite. At all events, she don't care to see me. She must have come to see my sister."

"I didn't know she knew Mrs Wilkes."

"It's an acquaintance of a couple hours' standing. I met her, you know, at Sharon in July. She was once very impertinent to me, and I fancied she had quite given me up. But this afternoon during our drive, as my sister and I got out of the carriage, on the rocks, who should I see but Mrs Dodd, wandering about alone, with a bunch of sea-weed as big as her head. She rushed up to me; I introduced her to Anna, and finding that she had walked quite a distance, Anna made her get into the carriage. It appears that she's staying with a friend, who has no carriage, and she's very miserable. We drove her about for an hour. Mrs Dodd was fascinating, she threw away her sea-weed, and Anna asked her to come home to tea. After tea, having endured her for two mortal hours, I took refuge here."

"If she was fascinating," said Philip, "why do you call it enduring her?"

"It's all the more reason, I assure you."

"I see, you have not forgiven her impertinence."

"No, I confess I have not. The woman was positively revolting."

"She appears, nevertheless, to have forgiven you."

"She has nothing to forgive."

In a few moments Philip took his photographs out of his pocket, handed them to Henrietta, and asked her advice as to which he should choose. Miss Congreve inspected them attentively, and selected but one. "This one is excellent," she said. "All the others are worthless in comparison."

"You advise me then to order that alone?"

"Why, you'll do as you please. I advise you to order that, at any rate. If you do, I shall ask you for one; but I shall care nothing for the rest."

Philip protested that he saw very little difference between this favoured picture and the others, and Miss Congreve declared that there was all the difference in the world. As Philip replaced the specimens in his pocket-book, he dropped on the carpet the portrait of the young lady of Boston.

"Ah," said Henrietta, "a young lady. I suppose I may see it."

"On one condition," said Philip, picking it up. "You'll please not to look at the back of the card."

I am very much ashamed to have to tell such things of poor Philip; for in point of fact, the back of the card was a most innocent blank. If Miss Congreve had ventured to disobey him, he would have made a very foolish figure. But there was so little that was boisterous in Henrietta's demeanor, that Osborne felt that he ran no risk.

"Who is she?" asked Henrietta, looking at the portrait. "She's charming."

"She's a Miss Thompson, of Philadelphia."

"Dear me, Not Dora Thompson, assuredly."

"No, indeed," said Philip, a little nervously. "Her name's not Dora—nor anything like it."

"You needn't resent the insinuation, sir. Dora's a very pretty name."

"Yes, but her own is prettier."

"I'm very curious to hear it."

Philip suddenly found himself in deep waters. He struck out blindly and answered at random, "Angelica."

Miss Congreve smiled—somewhat ironically, it seemed to Philip. "Well," she said, "I like her face better than her name."

"Dear me, if you come to that, so do I," cried Philip, with a laugh.

"Tell me about her, Mr. Osborne," pursued Henrietta. "She must be, with the face and figure, just the nicest girl in the world."

"Well, well, well," said Philip, leaning back in his chair, and looking at the ceiling—"perhaps she is—or at least, you'll excuse me if I say *I* think she is."

"I should think it inexcusable if you didn't say so," said Henrietta, giving him the card. "I'm sure I've seen her somewhere."

"Very likely. She comes to New York," said Philip. And he thought it prudent, on the whole, to divert the conversation to another topic. Miss Congreve remained silent and he fancied pensive. Was she jealous of Angelica Thompson? It seemed to Philip that, without fatuity, he might infer that she was, and that she was too proud to ask questions.

Mrs Wilkes had enabled Mrs Dodd to send tidings to her hostess of her whereabouts, and had promised to furnish her with an escort on her return. When Mrs Dodd prepared to take her leave, Philip, finding himself also ready to depart, offered to walk home with her.

"Well, sir," said the lady, when they had left the house, "your little game seems to be getting on."

Philip said nothing.

"Ah, Mr Osborne," said Mrs Dodd, with ill-concealed impatience, "I'm afraid you're too good for it."

"Well, I'm afraid I am."

"If you hadn't been in such a hurry to agree with me," said Mrs Dodd, "I should have said that I meant, in other words, that you're too stupid."

"Oh, I agree to that, too," said Philip.

The next day he received a letter from his partner in business, telling him of a great pressure of work, and urging him to return at his earliest convenience. "We are told," added this gentleman, "of a certain Miss—, I forget the name. If she's essential to your comfort, bring her along; but, at any rate, come yourself. In your absence the office is at a standstill—a fearful case of repletion without digestion."

This appeal came home to Philip's mind, to use a very old metaphor, like the sound of the brazen trumpet to an old cavalry charger. He felt himself overwhelmed with a sudden shame at the thought of the precious hours he had wasted and the long mornings he had consigned to perdition. He had been burning incense to a shadow, and the fumes had effaced it. In the afternoon he walked down toward the cliffs, feeling wofully perplexed, and exasperated in mind, and longing only to take a farewell look at the sea. He was not prepared to admit that he had played with fire and burned his fingers, but it was certain that he had gained nothing at the game; How the deuce had Henrietta Congreve come to thrust herself into his life–to steal away his time and his energies and to put him into a savage humor with himself? He would have given a great deal to be able to banish her from his thoughts; but she remained, and, while she remained, he hated her. After all, he had not been wholly cheated of his revenge. He had begun by hating her and he hated her still. On his way to the cliffs he met Mrs Wilkes, driving alone. Henrietta's place, vacant beside her, seemed to admonish him that she was at home, and almost, indeed, that she expected him. At all events, instead of going to bid farewell to the sea, he went to bid farewell to Miss Congreve. He felt that his farewell might easily be cold and formal, and indeed bitter.

He was admitted, he passed through the drawing-room to the verandah, and found Henrietta sitting on the grass, in the garden, holding her little nephew on her knee and reading him a fairy tale. She made room for him on the garden bench beside her, but kept the child. Philip felt himself seriously discomposed by this spectacle. In a few moments he took the boy upon his own knees. He then told Miss Congreve briefly that he intended that evening to leave Newport. "And you," he said, "when are you coming?"

"My sister," said Henrietta, "means to stay till Christmas. I hope to be able to remain as long."

Poor Philip bowed his head and heard his illusions tumbling most unmusically about his ears. His blow had smitten but the senseless air. He waited to see her color fade, or to hear her voice tremble. But he waited in vain. When he looked up and his eyes met Henrietta's, she was startled by the expression of his face.

"Tom," she said to the child, "go and ask Jane for my fan."

The child walked off, and Philip rose to his feet. Henrietta, hesitating a moment, also rose. "Must you go?" she asked.

Philip made no answer, but stood looking at her with blood-shot eyes, and with an intensity which puzzled and frightened the young girl.

"Miss Congreve," he said abruptly, "I'm a miserable man!"

"Oh, no!" said Henrietta, gently.

"I love a woman who doesn't care a straw for me."

"Are you sure?" said Henrietta, innocently.

"Sure! I adore her!"

"Are you sure she doesn't care for you?"

"Ah, Miss Congreve!" cried Philip. "If I could imagine, if I could hope–" and he put out his hand, as if to take her own.

Henrietta drew back, pale and frowning, carrying her hand to her heart. "Hope for nothing!" she said.

At this moment, little Tom Wilkes re-appeared issuing from the drawing-room window. "Aunt Henrietta," he cried, "here's a new gentleman!"

Miss Congreve and Philip turned about, and saw a young man step out upon the verandah from the drawing-room. Henrietta, with a little cry, hastened to meet him. Philip stood in his place. Miss Congreve exchanged a cordial greeting with the stranger, and led him down to the lawn. As she came toward him, Philip saw that Henrietta's pallor had made way for a rosy flush. She was beautiful.

"Mr Osborne," she said, "Mr Holland."

Mr Holland bowed graciously; but Philip bowed not at all. "Good-bye, then," he said, to the young girl.

She bowed, without speaking.

"Who's your friend, Henrietta?" asked her companion, when they were alone.

"He's a Mr Osborne, of New York," said Miss Congreve; "a friend of poor Mr Graham."

"By the way, I suppose you've heard of poor Graham's death."

"Oh, yes; Mr Osborne told me. And indeed—what do you think? Mr Graham wrote to me that he expected to die."

"Expected? Is that what he said?"

"I don't remember his words. I destroyed the letter."

"I must say, I think it would have been in better taste not to write."

"Taste! He had long since parted company with taste."

"I don't know. There was a method in his madness; and, as a rule, when a man kills himself, he shouldn't send out circulars."

"Kills himself? Good heavens, George! what do you mean?" Miss Congreve had turned pale, and stood looking at her companion with eyes dilated with horror.

"Why, my dear Henrietta," said the young man, "excuse my abruptness. Didn't you know it?"

"How strange—how fearful!" said Henrietta, slowly. "I wish I had kept his letter."

"I'm glad you didn't," said Holland. "It's a horrible business. Forget it."

"Horrible—horrible," murmured the young girl, in a tremulous tone. Her voice was shaken with irrepressible tears. Poor girl! in the space of five minutes she had been three times surprised. She gave way to her emotion and burst into sobs. George Holland drew her against him, and pressed his arms about her, and kissed her, and whispered comfort in her ear.

In the evening, Philip started for New York. On the steamer he found Mrs Dodd, who had come to an end of her visit. She was accompanied by a certain Major Dodd, of the Army, a brother of her deceased husband, and in addition, as it happened, her cousin. He was an unmarried man, a good-natured man, and a very kind friend to his sister-in-law, who had no family of her own, and who was in a position to be grateful for the services of a gentleman. In spite of a general impression to the contrary, I may affirm that the Major had no desire to make his little services a matter of course. "I'm related to Maria twice over already," he had been known to say, in a moment of expansion. "If I ever marry, I shall prefer to do it not quite so much in the family." He had come to Newport to conduct his sister home, who forthwith introduced him to Philip.

It was a clear, mild night, and, when the steamer had got under way, Mrs Dodd and the two gentlemen betook themselves to the upper deck, and sat down in the starlight. Philip, it may be readily imagined, was in no humour for conversation; but he felt that he could not wholly neglect Mrs Dodd. Under the influence of the beautiful evening, the darkly-shining sea, the glittering constellations, this lady became rabidly sentimental. She talked of friendship, and love, and death, and immortality. Philip saw what was coming. Before many moments, she had the bad taste (considering the Major's presence, as it seemed to Philip) to take poor Graham as a text for a rhapsody. Osborne lost patience, and interrupted her by asking if she would mind his lighting a cigar. She was scandalised, and immediately announced that she would go below. Philip had no wish to be uncivil. He attempted to restore himself to her favour by offering to see her down to the cabin. She accepted his escort, and he went with her to the door of her state-room, where she gave him her hand for good-night.

"Well," she said—"and Miss Congreve?"

Philip positively scowled. "Miss Congreve," he said, "is engaged to be married."

"To Mr—?"

"To Mr Holland."

"Ah!" cried Mrs Dodd, dropping his hand, "why didn't you break the engagement?"

"My dear Mrs Dodd," said Philip, "you don't know what you're talking about."

Mrs Dodd smiled a pitiful smile, shrugged her shoulders, and turned away. "Poor Graham!" she said.

Her words came to Philip like a blow in the face. "Graham!" he cried. "Graham was a fool!" He had struck back; he couldn't help it.

He made his way up stairs again, and came out on the deck, still trembling with the violence of his retort. He walked to the edge of the boat and leaned over the railing, looking down into the black gulfs of water which foamed and swirled in the wake of the vessel. He knocked off the end of his cigar, and watched the red particles fly downward and go out in the darkness. He was a disappointed, saddened man. There in the surging, furious darkness, yawned instant death. Did it tempt him, too? He drew back with a shudder, and returned to his place by Major Dodd.

The Major preserved for some moments a meditative silence. Then, at last, with a half apologetic laugh, "Mrs Dodd," he said, "labours under a singular illusion."

"Ah?" said Philip.

"But you knew Mr Graham yourself?" pursued the Major.

"Oh, yes; I knew him."

"It was a very melancholy case," said Major Dodd.

"A very melancholy case;" and Philip repeated his words.

"I don't know how it is that Mrs Dodd was beguiled into such fanaticism on the subject. I believe she went so far as once to blow out at the young lady."

"The young lady?" said Philip.

"Miss Congreve, you know, the object of his persecutions."

"Oh, yes," said Philip, painfully mystified.

"The fact is," said the Major, leaning over, and lowering his voice confidentially, "Mrs Dodd was in love with him—as far, that is, as a woman can be in love with a man in that state."

"Is it possible?" said Philip, disgusted and revolted at he knew not what; for his companion's allusions were an enigma.

"Oh, I was at Sharon for three weeks," the Major continued; "I went up for my sister-in-law; I saw it all. I wanted to bring poor Graham away, but he wouldn't listen to me—not that he wasn't very quiet. He made no talk, and opened himself only to Mrs Dodd and me—we lived in the same house, you know. Of course I very soon saw through it, and I felt very sorry for poor Miss Congreve. She bore it very well, but it must have been very annoying."

Philip started up from his chair. "For heaven's sake, Major Dodd," he cried, "what are you talking about?"

The Major started a moment, and then burst into a peal of laughter. "You agree, then, with Mrs Dodd?" he said, recovering himself.

"I understand Mrs Dodd no better than I do you."

"Why, my dear sir," said the Major, rising to his feet and extending his hand. "I beg a hundred pardons. But you must excuse me if I adhere to my opinion."

"First, please, be so good as to inform me of your opinion."

"Why, sir, the whole story is simply bosh."

"Good heavens," cried Philip, "that's no opinion!"

"Well, then, sir, if you will have it: the man was as mad as a March hare."

"Oh!" said Philip. His exclamation said a great many things, but the Major took it as a protest.

"He was a monomaniac."

Philip said nothing.

"The idea is not new to you?"

"Well," said Philip, "to tell the truth, it is."

"Well," said the Major, with a courteous flourish, "there you have it—for nothing."

Philip drew a long breath. "Ah, no!" he said gravely, "not for nothing." He stood silent for some time, with his eyes fixed on the deck. Major Dodd puffed his cigar and eyed him askance. At last Philip looked up. "And Henrietta Congreve?"

"Henrietta Congreve," said the Major, with military freedom and gallantry, "is the sweetest girl in the world. Don't talk to me! I know her."

"She never became engaged to Graham?"

"Engaged? She never looked at him."

"But he was in love with her."

"Ah, that was his own business. He worried her to death. She tried gentleness and kindness—it made him worse. Then, when she declined to see him, the poor fellow swore that she had jilted him. It was a fixed idea. He got Mrs Dodd to believe it."

Philip's silent reflections—the hushed eloquence of his amazed unburdened heart—we have no space to interpret. But as the Major lightened the load with one hand, he added to it with the other. Philip had never pitied his friend till now. "I knew him very well," he said, aloud. "He was the best of men. She might very well have cared for him."

"Good heavens! my dear sir, how could the woman love a madman?"

"You use strong language. When I parted with him in June, he was sane as you or I."

"Well, then, apparently, he lost his mind in the interval. He was in wretched health."

"But a man doesn't lose his mind without a cause."

"Let us admit, then," said the Major, "that Miss Congreve was the cause. I insist that she was the innocent cause. How should she have trifled with him? She was engaged to another man. The ways of the Lord are inscrutable. Fortunately," continued the Major, "she doesn't know the worst."

"How, the worst?"

"Well, you know he shot himself."

"Bless your soul, Miss Congreve knows it."

"I think you're mistaken. She didn't know it this morning."

Philip was sickened and bewildered by the tissue of horrors in which he found himself entangled. "Oh," he said, bitterly, "she has forgotten it then. She knew it a month ago."

"No, no, no," rejoined the Major, with decision. "I took the liberty, this morning, of calling upon her, and as we had had some conversation upon Mr Graham at Sharon, I touched upon his death. I saw she had heard of it, and I said nothing more—"

"Well, then?" said Philip.

"Well, then, my dear sir, she thinks he died in his bed. May she never think otherwise!"

In the course of that night—he sat out on the deck till two o'clock, alone—Philip, revolving many things, fervently echoed this last wish of Major Dodd.

Aux grands maux les grands remedes. Philip is now a married man; and curious to narrate, his wife bears a striking likeness to the young lady whose photograph he purchased for the price of six dozen of his own. And yet her name is not Angelica Thompson—nor even Dora.

THOMAS BAILEY ALDRICH

1873

Marjorie Daw

Dr. Dillon to Edward Delaney, Esq.,
at The Pines, Near Rye, N.H.

August 8, 187 –

MY DEAR SIR: I am happy to assure you that your anxiety is without reason. Flemming will be confined to the sofa for three or four weeks, and will have to be careful at first how he uses his leg. A fracture of this kind is always a tedious affair. Fortunately, the bone was very skillfully set by the surgeon who chanced to be in the drug-store where Flemming was brought after his fall, and I apprehend no permanent inconvenience from the accident. *Flemming is doing perfectly well physically*; but I must confess that the irritable and morbid state of mind into which he has fallen causes me a great deal of uneasiness. He is the last man in the world who ought to break his leg. You know how impetuous our friend is ordinarily, what a soul of restlessness and energy, never content unless he is rushing at some object, like a sportive bull at a red shawl, but amiable withal. He is no longer amiable. His temper has become something frightful. Miss Fanny Flemming came up from Newport, where the family are staying for the summer, to nurse him; but he packed her off the next morning in tears. He has a complete set of Balzac's works, twenty-seven volumes piled up near his sofa, to throw at Watkins whenever that exemplary serving-man appears with his meals. Yesterday I very innocently brought Flemming a small basket of lemons. You know it was a strip of lemon-peel on the curbstone that caused our friend's mischance. Well, he no sooner set his eyes upon

45

these lemons than he fell into such a rage as I cannot adequately describe. This is only one of his moods, and the least distressing. At other times he sits with bowed head regarding his splintered limb, silent, sullen, despairing. When this fit is on him – and it sometimes lasts all day – nothing can distract his melancholy. He refuses to eat, does not even read the newspapers; books, except as projectiles for Watkins, have no charms for him. His state is truly pitiable.

Now, if he were a poor man, with a family depending on his daily labor, this irritability and despondency would be natural enough. But in a young fellow of twenty-four, with plenty of money and seemingly not a care in the world, the thing is monstrous. If he continues to give way to his vagaries in this manner, he will end by bringing on an inflammation of the fibula. It was the fibula he broke. I am at my wits' end to know what to prescribe for him. I have anaesthetics and lotions, to make people sleep and to soothe pain; but I've no medicine that will make a man have a little common-sense. That is beyond my skill, but maybe it is not beyond yours. You are Flemming's intimate friend, his *fidus Achates*. Write to him, write to him frequently, distract his mind, cheer him up, and prevent him from becoming a confirmed case of melancholia. Perhaps he has some important plans disarranged by his present confinement. If he has you will know, and will know how to advise him judiciously. I trust your father finds the change beneficial? I am, my dear sir, with great respect, etc.

II

Edward Delaney to John Flemming,
West 38th Street, New York

August 9, –

MY DEAR JACK: I had a line from Dillon this morning, and was rejoiced to learn that your hurt is not so bad as reported. Like a certain personage, you are not so black and blue as you are painted. Dillon will put you on your pins again in two or three weeks, if you will only have patience and follow his counsels. Did you get my note of last Wednesday? I was greatly troubled when I heard of the accident.

I can imagine how tranquil and saintly you are with your leg in a trough! It is deuced awkward, to be sure, just as we had promised ourselves a glorious month together at the seaside; but we must make the best of it. It is unfortunate, too, that my father's health renders it impossible for me to leave him. I think he has much improved; the sea air is his native element; but he still needs my arm to lean upon in his walks, and requires some one more careful than a servant to look after him. I cannot come to you, dear Jack, but I have hours of unemployed time on hand, and I will write you a whole post-office full of letters if that will divert you. Heaven knows, I haven't anything to write about. It isn't as if we were living at one of the beach houses; then I could do you some character studies, and fill your imagination with groups of sea-goddesses, with their (or somebody else's) raven and blond manes hanging down their shoulders. You should have Aphrodite in morning wrapper, in evening costume, and in her prettiest bathing suit. But we are far from all that here. We have rooms in a farm-house, on a cross-road, two miles from the hotels, and lead the quietest of lives.

I wish I were a novelist. This old house, with its sanded floors and high wainscots, and its narrow windows looking out upon a cluster of pines that turn themselves into aeolian-harps every time the wind blows, would be the place in which to write a summer romance. It should be a story with the odors of the forest and the breath of the sea in it. It should be a novel like one of that Russian fellow's,—what's his name?—Tourguénieff, Turgenef, Turgenif, Toorguniff, Turgénjew,—nobody knows how to spell him. Yet I wonder if even a Liza or an Alexandra Paulovna could stir the heart of a man who has constant twinges in his leg. I wonder if one of our own Yankee girls of the best type, haughty and *spirituelle*, would be of any comfort to you in your present deplorable condition. If I thought so, I would hasten down to the Surf House and catch one for you; or, better still, I would find you one over the way.

Picture to yourself a large white house just across the road, nearly opposite our cottage. It is not a house, but a mansion, built, perhaps, in the colonial period, with rambling extensions, and gambrel roof, and a wide piazza on three sides—a self-possessed, high-bred piece of architecture, with its nose in the air. It stands back from the road, and has an obsequious retinue of fringed elms and oaks and weeping willows. Sometimes in the morning, and oftener in the afternoon, when the sun has withdrawn from that part of the mansion, a young woman appears on the piazza with some mysterious Penelope web of embroidery in her hand, or a book. There is a hammock over there,—of pineapple fibre, it looks from here. A hammock is very becoming when one is eighteen, and has golden hair, and dark eyes, and an emerald-colored illusion dress looped up after the fashion of a Dresden china shepherdess, and is *chaussée* like a belle of the time of Louis Quatorze. All this splendor goes into that hammock, and sways there like a pond-lily in the golden afternoon. The window of my bedroom looks down on that piazza,—and so do I.

But enough of this nonsense, which ill becomes a sedate young attorney taking his vacation with an invalid father. Drop me a line, dear Jack, and tell me how you really are. State your case. Write me a long, quiet letter. If you are violent or abusive, I'll take the law to you.

III

John Flemming to Edward Delaney

August 11, –

Your letter, dear Ned, was a godsend. Fancy what a fix I am in,–I, who never had a day's sickness since I was born. My left leg weighs three tons. It is embalmed in spices and smothered in layers of fine linen, like a mummy. I can't move. I haven't moved for five thousand years. I'm of the time of Pharaoh.

I lie from morning till night on a lounge, staring into the hot street. Everybody is out of town enjoying himself. The brown-stone-front houses across the street resemble a row of particularly ugly coffins set up on end. A green mould is settling on the names of the deceased, carved on the silver door-plates. Sardonic spiders have sewed up the key-holes. All is silence and dust and desolation. –I interrupt this a moment, to take a shy at Watkins with the second volume of César Birotteau. Missed him! I think I could bring him down with a copy of Sainte-Beuve or the Dictionnaire Universel, if I had it. These small Balzac books somehow don't quite fit my hand; but I shall fetch him yet. I've an idea Watkins is tapping the old gentleman's Château Yquem. Duplicate key of the wine-cellar. Hibernian swarries in the front basement. Young Cheops up stairs, snug in his cerements. Watkins glides into my chamber, with that colorless, hypocritical face of his drawn out long like an accordion; but I know he grins all the way down stairs, and is glad I have broken my leg. Was not my evil star in the very zenith when I ran up to town to attend that dinner at Delmonico's? I didn't come up altogether for that. It was partly to buy Frank Livingstone's roan mare Margot. And now I shall not be able to sit in the saddle these two months. I'll send the mare down to you at The Pines,–is that the name of the place?

Old Dillon fancies that I have something on my mind. He drives me wild with lemons. Lemons for a mind diseased! Nonsense. I am only as restless as the devil under this confinement,–a thing I'm not used to. Take a man who has never had so much as a headache or a toothache in his life, strap one of his legs in a section of water-spout, keep him in a room in the city for weeks, with the hot weather turned on, and then expect him to smile and purr and be happy! It is preposterous. I can't be cheerful or calm.

Your letter is the first consoling thing I have had since my disaster, ten days ago. It really cheered me up for half an hour. Send me a screed, Ned, as often as you can, if you love me. Anything will do. Write me more about that little girl in the hammock. That was very pretty, all that about the Dresden china shepherdess and the pond-lily; the imagery a little mixed, perhaps, but very pretty. I didn't suppose you had so much sentimental furniture in your upper story. It shows how one may be familiar for years with the reception-room of his neighbor, and never suspect what is directly under his mansard. I supposed your loft stuffed with dry legal parchments, mortgages and affidavits; you take down a package of manuscript, and lo! there are lyrics and sonnets and canzonettas. You really have a graphic descriptive touch, Edward Delaney, and I suspect you of anonymous love-tales in the magazines.

I shall be a bear until I hear from you again. Tell me all about your pretty *inconnue* across the road. What is her name? Who is she? Who's her father? Where's her mother? Who's her lover? You cannot imagine how this will occupy me. The more trifling the better. My imprisonment has weakened me intellectually to such a degree that I find your epistolary gifts quite considerable. I am passing into my second childhood. In a week or two I shall take to India-rubber rings and prongs of coral. A silver cup, with an appropriate inscription, would be a delicate attention on your part. In the meantime, write!

IV

Edward Delaney to John Flemming

August 12, –

The sick pasha shall be amused. *Bismillah!* he wills it so. If the storyteller becomes prolix and tedious,–the bow-string and the sack, and two Nubians to drop him into the Piscataqua! But truly, Jack, I have a hard task. There is literally nothing here,–except the little girl over the way. She is swinging in the hammock at this moment. It is to me compensation for many of the ills of life to see her now and then put out a small kid boot, which fits like a glove, and set herself going. Who is she, and what is her name? Her name is Daw. Only daughter of Mr. Richard W. Daw, ex-colonel and banker. Mother dead. One brother at Harvard, elder brother killed at the battle of Fair Oaks, nine years ago. Old, rich family, the Daws. This is the homestead, where father and daughter pass eight months of the twelve; the rest of the year in Baltimore and Washington. The New England winter too many for the old gentleman. The daughter is called Marjorie,–Marjorie Daw. Sounds odd at first, doesn't it? But after you say it over to yourself half a dozen times, you like it. There's a pleasing quaintness to it, something prim and violet-like. Must be a nice sort of girl to be called Marjorie Daw.

I had mine host of The Pines in the witness-box last night, and drew the foregoing testimony from him. He has charge of Mr. Daw's vegetable-garden, and has known the family these thirty years. Of course I shall make the acquaintance of my neighbors before many days. It will be next to impossible for me not to meet Mr. Daw or Miss Daw in some of my walks. The young lady has a favorite path to the sea-beach. I shall intercept her some morning, and touch my hat to her. Then the princess will bend her fair head to me with courteous surprise not unmixed with haughtiness. Will snub me, in fact. All this for thy sake, O Pasha of the Snapt Axle-tree! . . . How oddly things fall out! Ten minutes ago I was called down to the parlor,—you know the kind of parlors in farm-houses on the coast, a sort of amphibious parlor, with sea-shells on the mantel-piece and spruce branches in the chimney-place,—where I found my father and Mr. Daw doing the antique polite to each other. He had come to pay his respects to his new neighbors. Mr. Daw is a tall, slim gentleman of about fifty-five, with a florid face and snow-white mustache and side-whiskers. Looks like Mr. Dombey, or as Mr. Dombey would have looked if he had served a few years in the British Army. Mr. Daw was a colonel in the late war, commanding the regiment in which his son was a lieutenant. Plucky old boy, backbone of New Hampshire granite. Before taking his leave, the colonel delivered himself of an invitation as if he were issuing a general order. Miss Daw has a few friends coming, at 4 P.M., to play croquet on the lawn (parade-ground) and have tea (cold rations) on the piazza. Will we honor them with our company? (or be sent to the guard-house.) My father declines on the plea of ill-health. My father's son bows with as much suavity as he knows, and accepts.

In my next I shall have something to tell you. I shall have seen the little beauty face to face. I have a presentiment, Jack, that this Daw is a *rara avis*! Keep up your spirits, my boy, until I write you another letter,—and send me along word how's your leg.

V

Edward Delaney to John Flemming

August 13, –

The party, my dear Jack, was as dreary as possible. A lieutenant of the navy, the rector of the Episcopal church at Stillwater, and a society swell from Nahant. The lieutenant looked as if he had swallowed a couple of his buttons, and found the bullion rather indigestible; the rector was a pensive youth, of the daffydowndilly sort; and the swell from Nahant was a very weak tidal wave indeed. The women were much better, as they always are; the two Miss Kingsburys of Philadelphia, staying at the Seashell House, two bright and engaging girls. But Marjorie Daw!

The company broke up soon after tea, and I remained to smoke a cigar with the colonel on the piazza. It was like seeing a picture to see Miss Marjorie hovering around the old soldier, and doing a hundred gracious little things for him. She brought the cigars and lighted the tapers with her own delicate fingers, in the most enchanting fashion. As we sat there, she came and went in the summer twilight, and seemed, with her white dress and pale gold hair, like some lovely phantom that had sprung into existence out of the smoke-wreaths. If she had melted into air, like the statue of Galatea in the play, I should have been more sorry than surprised.

It was easy to perceive that the old colonel worshipped her, and she him. I think the relation between an elderly father and a daughter just blooming into womanhood the most beautiful possible. There is in it a subtile sentiment that cannot exist in the case of mother and daughter, or that of son and mother. But this is getting into deep water.

I sat with the Daws until half past ten, and saw the moon rise on the sea. The ocean, that had stretched motionless and black against the horizon, was changed by magic into a broken field of glittering ice, interspersed with marvellous silvery fjords. In the far distance the Isles of Shoals loomed up like a group of huge bergs drifting down on us. The Polar Regions in a June thaw! It was exceedingly fine. What did we talk about? We talked about the weather—and *you*! The weather has been disagreeable for several days past,—and so have you. I glided from one topic to the other very naturally. I told my friends of your accident; how it had frustrated all our summer plans, and what our plans were. I played quite a spirited solo on the fibula. Then I described you; or, rather, I didn't. I spoke of your amiability, of your patience under this severe affliction; of your touching gratitude when Dillon brings you little presents of fruit; of your tenderness to your sister Fanny, whom you would not allow to stay in town to nurse you, and how you heroically sent her back to Newport, preferring to remain alone with Mary, the cook, and your man Watkins, to whom, by the way, you were devotedly attached. If you had been there, Jack, you wouldn't have known yourself. I should have excelled as a criminal lawyer, if I had not turned my attention to a different branch of jurisprudence.

Miss Marjorie asked all manner of leading questions concerning you. It did not occur to me then, but it struck me forcibly afterwards, that she evinced a singular interest in the conversation. When I got back to my room, I recalled how eagerly she leaned forward, with her full, snowy throat in strong moonlight, listening to what I said. Positively, I think I made her like you!

Miss Daw is a girl whom you would like immensely, I can tell you that. A beauty without affectation, a high and tender nature,—if one can read the soul in the face. And the old colonel is a noble character, too.

I am glad the Daws are such pleasant people. The Pines is an isolated spot, and my resources are few. I fear I should have found life here somewhat monotonous before long, with no other society than that of my excellent sire. It is true, I might have made a target of the defenceless invalid; but I haven't a taste for artillery, *moi*.

VI

John Flemming to Edward Delaney

August 17, –

For a man who hasn't a taste for artillery, it occurs to me, my friend, you are keeping up a pretty lively fire on my inner works. But go on. Cynicism is a small brass field-piece that eventually bursts and kills the artilleryman.

You may abuse me as much as you like, and I'll not complain; for I don't know what I should do without your letters. They are curing me. I haven't hurled anything at Watkins since last Sunday, partly because I have grown more amiable under your teaching, and partly because Watkins captured my ammunition one night, and carried it off to the library. He is rapidly losing the habit he had acquired of dodging whenever I rub my ear, or make any slight motion with my right arm. He is still suggestive of the wine-cellar, however. You may break, you may shatter Watkins, if you will, but the scent of the Roederer will hang round him still.

Ned, that Miss Daw must be a charming person. I should certainly like her. I like her already. When you spoke in your first letter of seeing a young girl swinging in a hammock under your chamber window, I was somehow strangely drawn to her. I cannot account for it in the least. What you have subsequently written of Miss Daw has strengthened the impression. You seem to be describing a woman I have known in some previous state of existence, or dreamed of in this. Upon my word, if you were to send me her photograph, I believe I should recognize her at a glance. Her manner, that listening attitude, her traits of character, as you indicate them, the light hair and the dark eyes,–they are all familiar things to me. Asked a lot of questions, did she? Curious about me? That is strange.

You would laugh in your sleeve, you wretched old cynic, if you knew how I lie awake nights, with my gas turned down to a star, thinking of The Pines and the house across the road. How cool it must be down there! I long for the salt smell in the air. I picture the colonel smoking his cheroot on the piazza. I send you and Miss Daw off on afternoon rambles along the beach. Sometimes I let you stroll with her under the elms in the moonlight, for you are great friends by this time, I take it, and see each other every day. I know your ways and your manners! Then I fall into a truculent mood, and would like to destroy somebody. Have you noticed anything in the shape of a lover hanging around the colonial Lares and Penates? Does that lieutenant of the horse-marines or that young Stillwater parson visit the house much? Not that I am pining for news of them, but any gossip of the kind would be in order. I wonder, Ned, you don't fall in love with Miss Daw. I am ripe to do it myself. Speaking of photographs, couldn't you manage to slip one of her *cartes-de-visite* from her album,–she must have an album, you know,–and send it to me? I will return it before it could be missed. That's a good fellow!

Did the mare arrive safe and sound? It will be a capital animal this autumn for Central Park.

O—my leg? I forgot about my leg. It's better.

VII

Edward Delaney to John Flemming

August 20, —

You are correct in your surmises. I am on the most friendly terms with our neighbors. The colonel and my father smoke their afternoon cigar together in our sitting-room or on the piazza opposite, and I pass an hour or two of the day or the evening with the daughter. I am more and more struck by the beauty, modesty, and intelligence of Miss Daw.

You ask me why I do not fall in love with her. I will be frank, Jack: I have thought of that. She is young, rich, accomplished, uniting in herself more attractions, mental and personal, than I can recall in any girl of my acquaintance; but she lacks the something that would be necessary in inspire in me that kind of interest. Possessing this unknown quality, a woman neither beautiful nor wealthy nor very young could bring me to her feet. But not Miss Daw. If we were shipwrecked together on an uninhabited island,— let me suggest a tropical island, for it costs no more to be picturesque,—I would build her a bamboo hut, I would fetch her bread-fruit and cocoanuts, I would fry yams for her, I would lure the ingenuous turtle and make her nourishing soups, but I wouldn't make love to her,—not under eighteen months. I would like to have her for a sister, that I might shield her and counsel her, and spend half my income on thread-laces and camel's-hair shawls. (We are off the island now.) If such were not my feeling, there would still be an obstacle to my loving Miss Daw. A greater misfortune could scarcely befall me than to love her. Flemming, I am about to make a revelation that will astonish you. I may be all wrong in my premises and consequently in my conclusions; but you shall judge.

That night when I returned to my room after the croquet party at the Daws', and was thinking over the trivial events of the evening, I was suddenly impressed by the air of eager attention with which Miss Daw had followed my account of your accident. I think I mentioned this to you. Well, the next morning, as I went to mail my letter, I overtook Miss Daw on the road to Rye, where the post-office is, and accompanied her thither and back, an hour's walk. The conversation again turned on you, and again I remarked that inexplicable look of interest which had lighted up her face the previous evening. Since then, I have seen Miss Daw perhaps ten times, perhaps oftener, and on each occasion I found that when I was not speaking of you, or your sister, or some person or place associated with you, I was not holding her attention. She would be absent-minded, her eyes would wander away from me to the sea, or to some distant object in the landscape; her fingers would play with the leaves of a book in a way that convinced me she was not listening. At these moments if I abruptly changed the theme,—I did it several times as an experiment,—and dropped some remark about my friend Flemming, then the sombre blue eyes would come back to me instantly.

Now, is this not the oddest thing in the world? No, not the oddest. The effect which you tell me was produced on you by my casual mention of an unknown girl swinging in a hammock is certainly as strange. You can conjecture how that passage in your letter of Friday startled me. Is it possible, then, that two people who have never met, and who are hundreds of miles apart, can exert a magnetic influence on each other? I have read of such psychological phenomena, but never credited them. I leave the solution of the problem to you. As for myself, all other things being favorable, it would be impossible for me to fall in love with a woman who listens to me only when I am talking of my friend!

I am not aware that any one is paying marked attention to my fair neighbor. The lieutenant of the navy—he is stationed at Rivermouth—sometimes drops in of an evening, and sometimes the rector from Stillwater; the lieutenant the oftener. He was there last night. I would not be surprised if he had an eye to the heiress; but he is not formidable. Mistress Daw carries a neat little spear of irony, and the honest lieutenant seems to have a particular facility for impaling himself on the point of it. He is not dangerous, I should say; though I have known a woman to satirize a man for years, and marry him after all. Decidedly, the lowly rector is not dangerous; yet, again, who has not seen Cloth of Frieze victorious in the lists where Cloth of Gold went down?

As to the photograph. There is an exquisite ivorytype of Marjorie, in *passe-partout*, on the drawing-room mantel-piece. It would be missed at once, if taken. I would do anything reasonable for you, Jack, but I've no burning desire to be hauled up before the local justice of the peace, on a charge of petty larceny.

P. S.—Enclosed is a spray of mignonette, which I advise you to treat tenderly. Yes, we talked of you again last night, as usual. It is becoming a little dreary for me.

VIII

Edward Delaney to John Flemming

August 22, –

Your letter in reply to my last has occupied my thoughts all the morning. I do not know what to think. Do you mean to say that you are seriously half in love with a woman whom you have never seen,—with a shadow, a chimera? for what else can Miss Daw be to you? I do not understand it at all. I understand neither you nor her. You are a couple of ethereal beings moving in finer air that I can breathe with my commonplace lungs. Such delicacy of sentiment is something I admire without comprehending. I am bewildered. I am of the earth earthy, and I find myself in the incongruous position of having to do with mere souls, with natures so finely tempered that I run some risk of shattering them in my awkwardness. I am as Caliban among the spirits!

Reflecting on your letter, I am not sure it is wise in me to continue this correspondence. But no, Jack; I do wrong to doubt the good sense that forms the basis of your character. You are deeply interested in Miss Daw; you feel that she is a person whom you may perhaps greatly admire when you know her: at the same time you bear in mind that the chances are ten to five that, when you do come to know her, she will fall far short of your ideal, and you will not care for her in the least. Look at it in this sensible light, and I will hold back nothing from you.

Yesterday afternoon my father and myself rode over to Rivermouth with the Daws. A heavy rain in the morning had cooled the atmosphere and laid the dust. To Rivermouth is a drive of eight miles, along a winding road lined all the way with wild barberry-bushes. I never saw anything more brilliant than these bushes, the green of the foliage and the pink of the coral berries intensified by the rain. The colonel drove, with my father in front, Miss Daw and I on the back seat. I resolved that for the first five miles your name should not pass my lips. I was amused by the artful attempts she made, at the start, to break through my reticence. Then a silence fell upon her; and then she became suddenly gay. That keenness which I enjoyed so much when it was exercised on the lieutenant was not so satisfactory directed against myself. Miss Daw has great sweetness of disposition, but she can be disagreeable. She is like the young lady in the rhyme, with the curl on her forehead,

> "When she is good,
> She is very, very good,
> And when she is bad, she is horrid!"

I kept to my resolution, however; but on the return home I relented, and talked of your mare! Miss Daw is going to try a side-saddle on Margot some morning. The animal is a trifle too light for my weight. By the by, I nearly forgot to say Miss Daw sat for a picture yesterday to a Rivermouth artist. If the negative turns out well, I am to have a copy. So our ends will be accomplished without crime. I wish, though, I could send you the ivorytype in the drawing-room; it is cleverly colored, and would give you an idea of her hair and eyes, which of course the other will not.

No, Jack, the spray of mignonette did not come from me. A man of twenty-eight doesn't enclose flowers in his letters – to another man. But don't attach too much significance to the circumstance. She gives sprays of mignonette to the rector, sprays to the lieutenant. She has even given a rose from her bosom to your slave. It is her jocund nature to scatter flowers, like Spring.

If my letters sometimes read disjointedly, you must understand that I never finish one at a sitting, but write at intervals, when the mood is on me. The mood is not on me now.

IX

Edward Delaney to John Flemming

August 23, –

I have just returned from the strangest interview with Marjorie. She has all but confessed to me her interest in you. But with what modesty and dignity! Her words elude my pen as I attempt to put them on paper; and, indeed, it was not so much what she said as her manner; and that I cannot reproduce. Perhaps it was of a piece with the strangeness of this whole business, that she should tacitly acknowledge to a third party the love she feels for a man she has never beheld! But I have lost, through your aid, the faculty of being surprised. I accept things as people do in dreams. Now that I am again in my room, it all appears like an illusion,—the black masses of Rembrandtish shadow under the trees, the fireflies whirling in Pyrrhic dances among the shrubbery, the sea over there, Marjorie sitting on the hammock!

It is past midnight, and I am too sleepy to write more.

Thursday Morning.

My father has suddenly taken it into his head to spend a few days at the Shoals. In the meanwhile you will not hear from me. I see Marjorie walking in the garden with the colonel. I wish I could speak to her alone, but shall probably not have an opportunity before we leave.

X

Edward Delaney to John Flemming

August 28, –

You were passing into your second childhood, were you? Your intellect was so reduced that my epistolary gifts seemed quite considerable to you, did they? I rise superior to the sarcasm in your favor of the 11th instant, when I notice that five days' silence on my part is sufficient to throw you into the depths of despondency.

We returned only this morning from Appledore, that enchanted island, –at four dollars per day. I find on my desk three letters from you! Evidently there is no lingering doubt in *your* mind as to the pleasure I derive from your correspondence. These letters are undated, but in what I take to be the latest are two passages that require my consideration. You will pardon my candor, dear Flemming, but the conviction forces itself upon me that as your leg grows stronger your head becomes weaker. You ask my advice on a certain point. I will give it. In my opinion you could do nothing more unwise than to address a note to Miss Daw, thanking her for the flower. It would, I am sure, offend her delicacy beyond pardon. She knows you only through me; you are to her an abstraction, a figure in a dream,–a dream from which the faintest shock would awaken her. Of course, if you enclose a note to me and insist on its delivery, I shall deliver it; but I advise you not to do so.

You say you are able, with the aid of a cane, to walk about your chamber, and that you purpose to come to The Pines the instant Dillon thinks you strong enough to stand the journey. Again I advise you not to. Do you not see that every hour you remain away, Marjorie's glamour deepens, and your influence over her increases? You will ruin everything by precipitancy. Wait until you are entirely recovered; in any case, do not come without giving me warning. I fear the effect of your abrupt advent here–under the circumstances.

Miss Daw was evidently glad to see us back again, and gave me both hands in the frankest way. She stopped at the door a moment, this afternoon, in the carriage; she had been over to Rivermouth for her pictures. Unluckily the photographer had spilt some acid on the plate, and she was obliged to give him another sitting. I have an intuition that something is troubling Marjorie. She had an abstracted air not usual with her. However, it may be only my fancy . . . I end this, leaving several things unsaid, to accompany my father on one of those long rides which are now his chief medicine,–and mine!

XI

Edward Delaney to John Flemming

August 29, –

I write in great haste to tell you what has taken place here since my letter of last night. I am in the utmost perplexity. Only one thing is plain,–*you* must not dream of coming to The Pines. Marjorie has told her father everything! I saw her for a few minutes, an hour ago, in the garden; and, as near as I could gather from her confused statement, the facts are these: Lieutenant Bradly–that's the naval officer stationed at Rivermouth–has been paying court to Miss Daw for some time past, but not so much to her liking as to that of the colonel, who it seems is an old friend of the young gentleman's father. Yesterday (I knew she was in some trouble when she drove up to our gate) the colonel spoke to Marjorie of Bradly,–urged his suit, I infer. Marjorie expressed her dislike for the lieutenant with characteristic frankness, and finally confessed to her father–well, I really do not know what she confessed. It must have been the vaguest of confessions, and must have suffi-

ciently puzzled the colonel. At any rate, it exasperated him. I suppose I am
implicated in the matter, and that the colonel feels bitterly towards me. I do
not see why: I have carried no messages between you and Miss Daw; I have
behaved with the greatest discretion. I can find no flaw anywhere in my
proceeding. I do not see that anybody has done anything,—except the colonel
himself.

It is probable, nevertheless, that the friendly relations between the two
houses will be broken off. "A plague o' both your houses," say you. I will keep
you informed, as well as I can, of what occurs over the way. We shall remain
here until the second week in September. Stay where you are, or, at all
events, do not dream of joining me . . . Colonel Daw is sitting on the piazza
looking rather wicked. I have not seen Marjorie since I parted with her in
the garden.

XII

Edward Delaney to Thomas Dillon, M.D.,
Madison Square, New York

August 30, –

MY DEAR DOCTOR: If you have any influence over Flemming, I beg of you to
exert it to prevent his coming to this place at present. There are circumstances, which I will explain to you before long, that make it of the first
importance that he should not come into this neighborhood. His appearance
here, I speak advisedly, would be disastrous to him. In urging him to remain
in New York, or to go to some inland resort, you will be doing him and me a
real service. Of course you will not mention my name in this connection. You
know me well enough, my dear doctor, to be assured that, in begging your
secret co-operation, I have reasons that will meet your entire approval when
they are made plain to you. We shall return to town on the 15th of next
month, and my first duty will be to present myself at your hospitable door
and satisfy your curiosity, if I have excited it. My father, I am glad to state,
has so greatly improved that he can no longer be regarded as an invalid.
With great esteem, I am, etc., etc.

XIII

Edward Delaney to John Flemming

August 31, –

Your letter, announcing your mad determination to come here, has just
reached me. I beseech you to reflect a moment. The step would be fatal to your
interests and hers. You would furnish just cause for irritation to R. W. D.;
and, though he loves Marjorie tenderly, he is capable of going to any lengths

if opposed. You would not like, I am convinced, to be the means of causing him to treat *her* with severity. That would be the result of your presence at The Pines at this juncture. I am annoyed to be obliged to point out these things to you. We are on very delicate ground, Jack; the situation is critical, and the slightest mistake in a move would cost us the game. If you consider it worth the winning, be patient. Trust a little to my sagacity. Wait and see what happens. Moreover, I understand from Dillon that you are in no condition to take so long a journey. He thinks the air of the coast would be the worst thing possible for you; that you ought to go inland, if anywhere. Be advised by me. Be advised by Dillon.

XIV

Telegrams

September 1, –

1. – To EDWARD DELANEY
Letter received. Dillon be hanged. I think
I ought to be on the ground.
J.F.

2. – To JOHN FLEMMING
Stay where you are. You would only complicate
matters. Do not move until you hear from me.
E.D.

3. – To EDWARD DELANEY
My being at The Pines could be kept secret.
I must see her.
J.F.

4. – To JOHN FLEMMING
Do not think of it. It would be useless.
R. W. D. has locked M. in her room. You would
not be able to effect an interview.
E.D.

5. – To EDWARD DELANEY
Locked her in her room. Good God.
That settles the question. I shall leave by
the twelve-fifteen express.
J.F.

XV

The Arrival

On the second of September, 187–, as the down express due at 3:40 left the station at Hampton, a young man, leaning on the shoulder of a servant, whom he addressed as Watkins, stepped from the platform into a hack, and requested to be driven to "The Pines." On arriving at the gate of a modest farm-house, a few miles from the station, the young man descended with difficulty from the carriage, and, casting a hasty glance across the road, seemed much impressed by some peculiarity in the landscape. Again leaning on the shoulder of the person Watkins, he walked to the door of the farm-house and inquired for Mr. Edward Delaney. He was informed by the aged man who answered his knock, that Mr. Edward Delaney had gone to Boston the day before, but that Mr. Jonas Delaney was within. This information did not appear satisfactory to the stranger, who inquired if Mr. Edward Delaney had left any message for Mr. John Flemming. There *was* a letter for Mr. Flemming, if he were that person. After a brief absence the aged man reappeared with a letter.

XVI

Edward Delaney to John Flemming

September 1, –

I am horror-stricken at what I have done! When I began this correspondence I had no other purpose than to relieve the tedium of your sick-chamber. Dillon told me to cheer you up. I tried to. I thought you entered into the spirit of the thing. I had no idea, until within a few days, that you were taking matters *au sérieux*.

What can I say? I am in sackcloth and ashes. I am a pariah, a dog of an outcast. I tried to make a little romance to interest you, something soothing and idyllic, and, by Jove! I have done it only too well! My father doesn't know a word of this, so don't jar the old gentleman any more than you can help. I fly from the wrath to come—when you arrive! For O, dear Jack, there isn't any colonial mansion on the other side of the road, there isn't any piazza, there isn't any hammock,–there isn't any Marjorie Daw!!

MARY WILKINS FREEMAN

1891

The Revolt of Mother

 "Father!"

"What is it?"

"What are them men diggin' over in the field for?"

There was a sudden dropping and enlarging of the lower part of the old man's face, as if some heavy weight had settled therein; he shut his mouth tight, and went on harnessing the great bay mare. He hustled the collar on to her neck with a jerk.

"Father!"

The old man slapped the saddle on the mare's back.

"Look here, Father, I want to know what them men are diggin' over in the field for, an' I'm goin' to know."

"I wish you'd go into the house, Mother, an' 'tend to your own affairs," the old man said then. He ran his words together, and his speech was almost as inarticulate as a growl.

But the woman understood; it was her most native tongue. "I ain't goin' into the house till you tell me what them men are doin' over there in the field," said she.

Then she stood waiting. She was a small woman, short and straight-waisted like a child in her brown cotton gown. Her forehead was mild and benevolent between the smooth curves of gray hair; there were meek down-ward lines about her nose and mouth; but her eyes, fixed upon the old man,

61

looked as if the meekness had been the result of her own will, never of the will of another.

They were in the barn, standing before the wide-open doors. The spring air, full of the smell of growing grass and unseen blossoms, came in their faces. The deep yard in front was littered with farm wagons and piles of wood; on the edges, close to the fence and the house, the grass was a vivid green, and there were some dandelions.

The old man glanced doggedly at his wife as he tightened the last buckles on the harness. She looked as immovable to him as one of the rocks in his pasture land, bound to the earth with generations of blackberry vines. He slapped the reins over the horse, and started forth from the barn.

"Father!" said she.

The old man pulled up. "What is it?"

"I want to know what them men are diggin' over there in that field for."

"They're diggin' a cellar, I s'pose, if you've got to know."

"A cellar for what?"

"A barn."

"A barn? You ain't goin' to build a barn over there where we was goin' to have a house, Father?"

The old man said not another word. He hurried the horse into the farm wagon and clattered out of the yard, jouncing as sturdily on his seat as a boy.

The woman stood a moment looking after him, then she went out of the barn across a corner of the yard to the house. The house, standing at right angles with the great barn and a long reach of sheds and out-buildings, was infinitesimal compared with them. It was scarcely as commodious for people as the little boxes under the barn eaves were for doves.

A pretty girl's face, pink and delicate as a flower, was looking out of one of the house windows. She was watching three men who were digging over in the field which bounded the yard near the road line. She turned quickly when the woman entered.

"What are they diggin' for, Mother?" said she. "Did he tell you?"

"They're diggin' for—a cellar for a new barn."

"Oh, Mother, he ain't going to build another barn?"

"That's what he says."

A boy stood before the kitchen glass combing his hair. He combed slowly and painstakingly, arranging his brown hair in a smooth hillock over his forehead. He did not seem to pay any attention to the conversation.

"Sammy, did you know Father was going to build a new barn?" asked the girl.

He turned, and showed a face like his father's under his smooth crest of hair. "Yes, I s'pose I did," he said, reluctantly.

"How long have you known it?" asked his mother.

" 'Bout three months, I guess."

"Why didn't you tell of it?"

"Didn't think 'twould do no good."

"I don't see what Father wants another barn for," said the girl, in her sweet, slow voice. She turned again to the window and stared out at the digging men in the field. Her tender, sweet face was full of a gentle distress. Her forehead was as bald and innocent as a baby's, with the light hair strained from it in a row of curl papers. She was quite large, but her soft curves did not look as if they covered muscles.

Her mother looked sternly at the boy. "Is he goin' to buy more cows?" said she.

The boy did not reply; he was tying his shoes.

"Sammy, I want you to tell me if he's going' to buy more cows."

"I s'pose he is."

"How many?"

"Four, I guess."

His mother said nothing more. She went into the pantry, and there was a clatter of dishes. The boy got his cap from a nail behind the door, took an old arithmetic from the shelf, and started for school. He was lightly built, but clumsy. He went out of the yard with a curious spring in his hips that made his loose homemade jacket tilt up in the rear.

The girl went to the sink and began to wash the dishes that were piled up there. Her mother came promptly out of the pantry and shoved her aside. "You wipe 'em," said she. "I'll wash. There's a good many this mornin'."

The mother plunged her hands vigorously into the water, the girl wiped the plates slowly and dreamily. "Mother," said she, "don't you think it's too bad Father's going to build that new barn, much as we need a decent house to live in?"

Her mother scrubbed a dish fiercely. "You ain't found out yet, we're womenfolks, Nanny Penn," said she. "You ain't seen enough of menfolks yet to. One of these days you'll find it out, and then you'll know that we know only what menfolks think we do, so far as any use of it goes, an' how we'd ought to reckon menfolks in with Providence, an' not complain of what they do any more than we do of the weather."

"I don't care; I don't believe George is anything like that, anyhow," said Nanny. Her delicate face flushed pink; her lips pouted softly, as if she were going to cry.

"You wait an' see. I guess George Eastman ain't no better than other men. You hadn't ought to judge Father, though. He can't help it, 'cause he don't look at things jest the way we do. An' we've been pretty comfortable here, after all. The roof don't leak–ain't never but once–that's one thing. Father's kept it shingled right up."

"I do wish we had a parlor."

"I guess it won't hurt George Eastman any to come to see you in a nice clean kitchen. I guess a good many girls don't have as good a place as this. Nobody's ever heard me complain."

"I ain't complained either, Mother."

"Well, I don't think you'd better, a good father an' a good home as you've got. S'pose your father made you go out an' work for your livin'? Lots of girls have to that ain't no better able to than you be."

Sarah Penn washed the frying pan with a conclusive air. She scrubbed the outside of it as faithfully as the inside. She was a masterly keeper of her box of a house. Her one living room never seemed to have in it any of the dust which the friction of life with inanimate matter produces. She swept, and there seemed to be no dirt to go before the broom; she cleaned, and one could see no difference. She was like an artist so perfect that he has apparently no art. Today she got out a mixing bowl and a board, and rolled some pies, and there was no more flour upon her than upon her daughter who was doing finer work. Nanny was to be married in the fall, and she was sewing on some white cambric and embroidery. She sewed industriously while her mother cooked; her soft milk-white hands and wrists showed whiter than her delicate work.

"We must have the stove moved out in the shed before long," said Mrs. Penn. "Talk about not havin' things, it's been a real blessin' to be able to put a stove up in that shed in hot weather. Father did one good thing when he fixed that stove pipe out there."

Sarah Penn's face as she rolled her pies had that expression of meek vigor which might have characterized one of the New Testament saints. She was making mince pies. Her husband, Adoniram Penn, liked them better than any other kind. She baked twice a week. Adoniram often liked a piece of pie between meals. She hurried this morning. It had been later than usual when she began, and she wanted to have a pie baked for dinner. However deep a resentment she might be forced to hold against her husband, she would never fail in sedulous attention to his wants.

Nobility of character manifests itself at loopholes when it is not provided with large doors. Sarah Penn's showed itself today in flaky dishes of pastry. She made the pies faithfully, while across the table she could see, when she glanced up from work, the sight that rankled in her patient and steadfast soul—the digging of the cellar of the new barn in the place where Adoniram forty years ago had promised her their new house should stand.

The pies were done for dinner. Adoniram and Sammy were home a few minutes after twelve o'clock. The dinner was eaten with serious haste. There was never much conversation at the table in the Penn family. Adoniram asked a blessing, and they ate promptly, then rose up and went about their work.

Sammy went back to school, taking soft sly lopes out of the yard like a rabbit. He wanted a game of marbles before school, and feared his father would give him chores to do. Adoniram hastened to the door and called after him, but he was out of sight.

"I don't see what you let him go for, Mother," said he. "I wanted him to help me unload that wood."

Adoniram went to work out in the yard unloading wood from the wagon. Sarah put away the dinner dishes, while Nanny took down her curl papers and changed her dress. She was going down to the store to buy some more embroidery and thread.

When Nanny was gone, Mrs. Penn went to the door. "Father!" she called.

"Well, what is it!"

"I want to see you jest a minute, Father."

"I can't leave this wood nohow. I've got to git it unloaded and go for a load of gravel afore two o'clock. Sammy had ought to help me. You hadn't ought to let him go to school so early."

"I want to see you jest a minute."

"I tell ye I can't, nohow, Mother."

"Father, you come here." Sarah Penn stood in the door like a queen; she held her head as if it bore a crown; there was that patience which makes authority in her voice. Adoniram went.

Mrs. Penn led the way into the kitchen, and pointed to a chair. "Sit down, Father," said she; "I've got somethin' I want to say to you."

He sat down heavily; his face was quite stolid, but he looked at her with restive eyes. "Well, what is it, Mother?"

"I want to know what you're buildin' that new barn for, Father?"

"I ain't got nothin' to say about it."

"It cain't be you think you need another barn?"

"I tell ye I ain't got nothin' to say about it, Mother; an' I ain't goin' to say nothin'."

"Be you goin' to buy more cows?"

Adoniram did not reply; he shut his mouth tight.

"I know you be, as well as I want to. Now, Father, look here"–Sarah Penn had not sat down; she stood before her husband in the humble fashion of a Scripture woman–"I'm goin' to talk real plain to you; I never have sence I married you, but I'm goin' to now. I ain't never complained, an' I ain't goin' to complain now, but I'm goin' to talk plain. You see this room here, Father; you look at it well. You see there ain't no carpet on the floor, an' you see the paper is all dirty and droppin' off the walls. We ain't had no new paper on it for ten year, an' then I put it on myself, an' it didn't cost but nine cents a roll. You see this room, Father; it's all the one I've had to work in an' eat in an' sit in sence we was married. There ain't another woman in the whole town whose husband ain't got half the means you have but what's got better. It's all the room Nanny's got to have her company in; an' there ain't one of her mates but what's got better, an' their fathers not so able as hers is. It's all the room she'll have to be married in. What would you have thought, Father, if we had had our weddin' in a room no better than this? I was married in my mother's parlor, with a carpet on the floor, an' stuffed furniture, an' a mahogany card table. An' this is all the room my daughter will have to be married in. Look here, Father!"

Sarah Penn went across the room as though it were a tragic stage. She flung open a door and disclosed a tiny bedroom only large enough for a bed and bureau, with a path between. "There, Father," said she, "there's all the room I've had to sleep in in forty year. All my children were born there–the two that died an' the two that's livin'. I was sick with a fever, there."

She stepped to another door and opened it. It led into the small ill-lighted pantry. "Here," said she, "is all the buttery I've got–every place I've got for my dishes, to set away my victuals in, an' to keep my milk pans in. Father, I've been takin' care of the milk of six cows in this place, an' now you're goin' to build a new barn, an' keep more cows, an' give me more to do in it."

She threw open another door. A narrow, crooked flight of stairs wound upward from it. "There, Father," said she, "I want you to look at the stairs that go up to them two unfinished chambers that are all the places our son and daughter have had to sleep in all their lives. There ain't a prettier girl in town nor a more ladylike one than Nanny, an' that's the place she has to sleep in. It ain't so good as your horse's stall; it ain't so warm an' tight."

Sarah Penn went back and stood before her husband. "Now, Father," said she," I want to know if you think you're doin' right and accordin' to what you profess. Here, where we was married forty year ago, you promised me faithful that we should have a new house built in that lot over in the field before the year was out. You said you had money enough, an' you wouldn't ask me to live in no such place as this. It is forty year now, an' you've been makin' more money an' I've been savin' of it for you ever sence, an' you ain't built no house yet. You've built sheds an' cow houses an' one new barn, an' now you're goin' to build another. Father, I want to know if you think it's right. You're lodgin' your dumb beasts better than you are your own flesh and blood. I want to know if you think it's right."

"I ain't got nothin' to say."

"You can't say nothin' without ownin' it ain't right, Father. An' there's another thing–I ain't complained; I've got along forty year an' I s'pose I should forty more, if it wa'n't for that–if we don't have another house, Nanny, she can't live with us after she's married. She'll have to go somewhere else to live away from us, an' it don't seem as if I could have it so, noways, Father. She wa'n't ever strong. She's got considerable color, but there wa'n't never any backbone to her. I've always took the heft of everything off her, an' she ain't fit to keep house an' do everything herself. Think of her doin' all the washin' and ironin' and bakin' with them soft white hands and arms, an' sweepin'. I can't have it so, noways, Father."

Mrs. Penn's face was burning; her mild eyes gleamed. She had pleaded her little cause like a Webster; she had ranged from severity to pathos; but her opponent employed that obstinate silence which makes eloquence futile with mocking echoes. Adoniram arose clumsily.

"Father, ain't you got nothin' to say?" said Mrs. Penn.

"I've got to go off after that load of gravel. I can't stan' talkin' all day."

"Father, won't you think it over an' have a house built there instead of a barn?"

"I ain't got nothin' to say."

Adoniram shuffled out. Mrs. Penn went into her bedroom. When she came out, her eyes were red. She had a roll of unbleached cotton. She spread it out on the kitchen table, and began cutting out some shirts for her husband. The men over in the field had a team to help them this afternoon; she could hear their halloos. She had a scanty pattern for the shirts; she had to plan and piece the sleeves.

Nanny came home with her embroidery and sat down with her needlework. She had taken down her curl papers, and there was a soft roll of fair hair like an aureole over her forehead; her face was as delicately fine and clear as porcelain. Suddenly she looked up and the tender red flamed over her face and neck. "Mother," said she.

"What say?"

"I've been thinking—I don't see how we're goin' to have any wedding in this room. I'd be ashamed to have his folks come if we didn't have anybody else."

"Mebbe we can have some new paper before then; I can put it on. I guess you won't have no call to be ashamed of your belongin's."

"We might have the wedding in the new barn," said Nanny, with gentle pettishness. "Why, Mother, what makes you look so?"

Mrs. Penn had started and was staring at her with a curious expression. She turned again to her work, and spread out a pattern carefully on the cloth. "Nothin'," said she.

Presently Adoniram clattered out of the yard in his two-wheeled dump cart, standing as proudly upright as a Roman charioteer. Mrs. Penn opened the door and stood there a minute looking out; the halloos of the men sounded louder.

It seemed to her all through the spring months that she heard nothing but the halloos and the noises of saws and hammers. The new barn grew fast. It was a fine edifice for this little village. Men came on pleasant Sundays, in their meeting suits and clean shirt bosoms, and stood around it admiringly. Mrs. Penn did not speak of it and Adoniram did not mention it to her, although sometimes upon a return from inspecting it, he bore himself with injured dignity.

"It's a strange thing how your mother feels about the new barn," he said, confidentially, to Sammy one day.

Sammy only grunted after an odd fashion for a boy; he had learned it from his father.

The barn was all completed ready for us by the third week in July. Adoniram had planned to move his stock in on Wednesday; on Tuesday he received a letter which changed his plans. He came in with it early in the morning. "Sammy's been to the post office," said he, "an' I've got a letter from Hiram." Hiram was Mrs. Penn's brother who lived in Vermont.

"Well," said Mrs. Penn, "what does he say about the folks?"

"I guess they're all right. He says he thinks if I come up country right off ther's a chance to buy jest the kind of a horse I want." He stared reflectively out of the window at the new barn.

Mrs. Penn was making pies. She went on clapping the rolling pin into the crust, although she was very pale, and her heart beat loudly.

"I dun' know but what I'd better go," said Adoniram. "I hate to go off jest now, right in the midst of hayin', but the ten-acre lot's cut, an' I guess Rufus an' the others can git along without me three or four days. I can't get a horse round here to suit me, nohow, an' I've got to have another for all that wood haulin' in the fall. I told Hiram to watch out an' if he got wind of a good horse to let me know. I guess I'd better go."

"I'll get out your clean shirt an' collar," said Mrs. Penn calmly.

She laid out Adoniram's Sunday suit and his clean clothes on the bed in the little bedroom. She got his shaving water and razor ready. At last she buttoned on his collar and fastened his black cravat.

Adoniram never wore his collar and cravat except on extra occasions. He held his head high, with a rasped dignity. When he was all ready, with coat and hat brushed, and a lunch of pie and cheese in a paper bag, he hesitated on the threshold of the door. He looked at his wife and his manner was defiantly apologetic. "*If* them cows come today Sammy can drive them into the new barn," said he, "an' when they bring the hay up they can pitch it in there."

"Well," replied Mrs. Penn.

Adoniram set his shaven face ahead and started. When he had cleared the doorstep, he turned and looked back with a kind of nervous solemnity. "I shall be back by Saturday if nothin' happens," said he.

"Do be careful, Father," returned his wife.

She stood in the door with Nanny at her elbow and watched him out of sight. Her eyes had a strange, doubtful expression in them; her peaceful forehead was contracted. Nanny sat sewing. Her wedding day was drawing nearer and she was getting pale and thin with her steady sewing. Her mother kept glancing at her.

"Have you got that pain in your side this mornin'?" she asked.

"A little."

Mrs. Penn's face as she worked, changed; her perplexed forehead smoothed; her eyes were steady, her lips firmly set. She formed a maxim for herself, although incoherently with her unlettered thoughts. "Unsolicited opportunities are the guideposts of the Lord to the new roads of Life," she repeated in effect, and she made up her mind to her course of action.

"S'posin' I *had* wrote to Hiram," she muttered once, when she was in the pantry. "S'posin' I had wrote and asked him if he knew of any horse? But I didn't, an' Father's goin' wa'n't any of my doin'. It looks like a providence." Her mother's voice rang out quite loud at the last.

"What you talkin' about, Mother?" called Nanny.

"Nothin'."

Mrs. Penn hurried her baking; at eleven o'clock it was all done. The load of hay from the west field came slowly down the cart track and drew up at the new barn. Mrs. Penn ran out. "Stop!" she screamed. "Stop!"

The men stopped and looked; Sammy upreared from the top of the load and stared at his mother.

"Stop!" she cried out again. "Don't you put the hay in that barn; put it in the old one."

"Why, he said to put it in here," returned one of the haymakers, wonderingly. He was a young man, a neighbor's son, whom Adoniram hired by the year to work on the farm.

"Don't you put the hay in the new barn; there's room enough in the old one, ain't there?" said Mrs. Penn.

"Room enough," returned the hired man, in his thick, rustic tones. "Didn't need the new barn, nohow, as far as room's concerned. Well, I s'pose he changed his mind." He took hold of the horses' bridles.

Mrs. Penn went back to the house. Soon the kitchen windows were darkened and a fragrance like warm honey came into the room.

Nanny laid down her work. "I thought Father wanted them to put the hay into the new barn?" she said, wonderingly.

"It's all right," replied her mother.

Sammy slid down from the load of hay and came in to see if dinner was ready.

"I ain't goin' to get a regular dinner today, as long as Father's gone," said his mother. "I've let the fire go out. You can have some bread an' milk an' pie. I thought we could get along." She set out some bowls of milk, some bread and a pie on the kitchen table. "You'd better eat your dinner now," said she. "You might jest as well get through with it. I want you to help me afterward."

Nanny and Sammy stared at each other. There was something strange in their mother's manner. Mrs. Penn did not eat anything herself. She went into the pantry and they heard her moving dishes while they ate. Presently she came out with a pile of plates. She got the clothes basket out of the shed and packed them in it. Nanny and Sammy watched. She brought out cups and saucers and put them in with the plates.

"What you goin' to do, Mother?" inquired Nanny, in a timid voice. A sense of something unusual made her tremble, as if it were a ghost. Sammy rolled his eyes over his pie.

"You'll see what I'm goin' to do," replied Mrs. Penn. "If you're through, Nanny, I want you to go upstairs and pack your things; an' I want you, Sammy, to help me take down the bed in the bedroom."

"Oh, Mother, what for?" gasped Nanny.

"You'll see."

During the next few hours a feat was performed by this simple pious New England mother which was equal in its way to Wolfe's storming of the Heights of Abraham. It took no more genius and audacity of bravery for Wolfe to cheer his wondering soldiers up those steep precipices, under the sleeping eyes of the enemy, than for Sarah Penn, at the head of her children, to move all their little house-hold goods into the new barn while her husband was away.

Nanny and Sammy followed their mother's instructions without a murmur; indeed, they were overawed. There is a certain uncanny and superhuman quality about all such purely original undertakings as their mother's was to them. Nanny went back and forth with her light loads and Sammy tugged with sober energy.

At five o'clock in the afternoon the little house in which the Penns had lived for forty years had emptied itself into the new barn.

Every builder builds somewhat for unknown purposes, and is in a measure a prophet. The architect of Adoniram Penn's barn, while he designed it for the comfort of four-footed animals, had planned better than he knew for the comfort of humans. Sarah Penn saw at a glance its possibilities. Those great box stalls, with quilts hung before them, would make better bedrooms than the one she had occupied for forty years, and there was a tight carriage room. The harness room, with its chimney and shelves, would make a kitchen of her dreams. The great middle space would make a parlor, by-and-by, fit for a palace. Upstairs there was as much room as down. With partitions and windows, what a house there would be! Sarah looked at the row of stanchions before the allotted space for cows, and reflected she would have a front entry there.

At six o'clock the stove was up in the harness room, the kettle was boiling, and the table set for tea. It looked almost as homelike as the abandoned house across the yard had ever done. The young hired man milked, and Sarah directed him calmly to bring the milk to the new barn. He came gasping, dropping little blots of foam from the brimming pails on the grass. Before the next morning he had spread the story of Adoniram Penn's wife moving into the new barn all over the little village. Men assembled in the store and talked it over; women with shawls over their heads scuttled into each other's houses before their work was done. Any deviation from the ordinary course of life in this quiet town was enough to stop all progress in it. Everybody paused to look at the staid, independent figure on the side track. There was a difference of opinion with regard to her. Some held her to be insane; some, of a lawless and rebellious spirit.

Friday the minister went to see her. It was in the forenoon, and she was at the barn door shelling peas for dinner. She looked up and returned his salutation with dignity; then she went on with her work. She did not invite him in. The sanity expression of her face remained fixed, but there was an angry flush over it.

The minister stood awkwardly before her, and talked. She handled the peas as if they were bullets. At last she looked up and her eyes showed a spirit that her meek front had covered for a lifetime.

"There ain't no use talkin', Mr. Hersey," said she. "I've thought it all over and over, an' I believe I'm doin' what's right. I've made it the subject of prayer, and it's betwixt me an' the Lord an' Adoniram. There ain't no call for nobody else to worry about it."

"Well, of course, if you have brought it to the Lord in prayer, and feel satisfied that you are doing right, Mrs. Penn," said the minister helplessly. His thin, gray-bearded face was pathetic. He was a sickly man; his youthful confidence had cooled; he had to scourge himself up to some of his pastoral duties, and then he was prostrated by the smart.

"I think it's right jest as much as I think it was right for our forefathers to come over from the old country 'cause they didn't have what belonged to 'em," said Mrs. Penn. She arose. The barn threshold might have been Plymouth Rock from her bearing. "I don't doubt you mean well, Mr. Hersey," said she, "but there are things people hadn't ought to interfere with. I've been a member of the church for over forty year. I've got my mind an' my own feet, an' I'm goin' to think my own thoughts an' go my own ways, an' nobody but the Lord is goin' to dictate to me unless I've a mind to have him. Won't you come in an' set down? How is Mis' Hersey?"

"She is well, I thank you," replied the minister. He added some more perplexed, apologetic remarks; then he retreated.

He could expound the intricacies of every character study in the Scriptures; he was competent to grasp the Pilgrim Fathers and all historical innovators; but Sarah Penn was beyond him. He could deal with primal cases, but parallel ones worsted him. But, after all, although it was aside from his province, he wondered more how Adoniram Penn would deal with his wife than how the Lord would. Everybody shared the wonder. When Adoniram's four new cows arrived, Sarah ordered three put in the old barn, the other in the house shed where the cooking stove had stood. That added to the excitement. It was whispered that all four cows were domiciled in the house.

Toward sunset on Saturday, when Adoniram was expected home, there was a knot of men in the road near the new barn. The hired man milked, but he still hung around the premises. There were brown bread and baked beans and a custard pie; it was the supper that Adoniram loved on a Saturday night. She had on a clean calico and she bore herself imperturbably. Nanny and Sammy kept close at her heels. Their eyes were large, and Nanny was full of nervous tremors. Still there was to them more pleasant excitement than anything else. An inborn confidence in their mother over their father asserted itself.

Sammy looked out of the harness-room window. "There he is," he announced, in an awed whisper. He and Nanny peeped around the casing. Mrs. Penn kept on about her work. The children watched Adoniram leave the new horse standing in the drive while he went to the house door. It was fastened. Then he went around to the shed. That door was seldom locked, even when the family was away. The thought how her father would be confronted by the cow flashed upon Nanny. There was a hysterical sob in her throat. Adoniram emerged from the shed and stood looking about in a dazed fashion. His lips moved; he was saying something, but they could not hear what it was. The hired man was peeping around a corner of the old barn but nobody saw him.

Adoniram took the new horse by the bridle and led him across the yard to the new barn. Nanny and Sammy slunk close to their mother. The barn doors rolled back and there stood Adoniram, with the long mild face of the great Canadian farm horse looking over his shoulder.

Nanny kept behind her mother, but Sammy stepped suddenly forward and stood in front of her.

Adoniram stared at the group. "What on airth you all down here for?" said he. "What's the matter over to the house?"

"We've come here to live, Father," said Sammy. His shrill voice quavered out bravely.

"What—" Adoniram sniffed—"what is it smells like cookin'?" said he. He stepped forward and looked in at the open door of the harness room. Then he turned to his wife. His old bristling face was pale and frightened. "What on airth does this mean, Mother?"

"You come in here, Father," said Sarah. She led the way into the harness room and shut the door. "Now, Father," said she, "you needn't be scared. I ain't crazy. There ain't nothin' to be upset over. But we've come here to live an' we're goin' to live here. We've got jest as good a right here as new horses and cows. The house wa'n't fit for us to live in any longer, an' I made up my mind I wa'n't goin' to stay there. I've done my duty by you forty year an' I'm goin' to do it now, but I'm goin' to live here. You've got to put in some windows an' partitions, an' you'll have to buy some furniture."

"Why, Mother!" the old man gasped.

"You'd better take your coat off an' get washed–there's the wash basin–an' then we'll have supper."

"Why, Mother!"

Sammy went past the window, leading the new horse to the old barn. The old man saw him and shook his head speechlessly. He tried to take off his coat, but his arms seemed to lack the power. His wife helped him. She poured some water into the tin basin and put in a piece of soap. She got the comb and brush and smoothed his thin gray hair after he had washed. Then she put the beans, hot bread and tea on the table. Sammy came in and the family drew up. Adoniram sat looking dazedly at his plate and they waited.

"Ain't you goin' to ask a blessin', Father?" said Sarah.

And the old man bent his head and mumbled.

All through the meal he stopped eating at intervals and stared furtively at his wife, but he ate well. The home food tasted good to him and his old frame was too sturdily healthy to be affected by his mind. But after supper he went out and sat down on the step of the smaller door at the right of the barn, through which he had meant his Jerseys to pass in stately file, but which Sarah designed for her front house-door, and he leaned his head on his hands.

After the supper dishes were cleared away and the milkpans washed, Sarah went out to him. The twilight was deepening. There was a clear green glow in the sky. Before them stretched the smooth level of field; in the distance was a cluster of haystacks like the huts of a village; the air was very calm and sweet. The landscape might have been an ideal one of peace.

Sarah bent over and touched her husband on one of his thin, sinewy shoulders. "Father!"

The old man's shoulders heaved; he was weeping.

"Why, don't do so, Father," said Sarah.

"I'll–put up the–partitions, an'–everything you–want, Mother."

Sarah put her apron up to her face; she was overcome by her own triumph.

Adoniram was life a fortress whose walls had no active resistance, and went down the instant the right besieging tools were used. "Why, Mother," he said hoarsely, "I hadn't no idee you was so set on't it as all this comes to."

DOROTHY CANFIELD FISHER

1908

The Bedquilt

Of all the Elwell family Aunt Mehetabel was certainly the most unimportant member. It was in the New England days, when an unmarried woman was an old maid at twenty, at forty was everyone's servant, and at sixty had gone through so much discipline that she could need no more in the next world. Aunt Mehetabel was sixty-eight.

She had never for a moment known the pleasure of being important to anyone. Not that she was useless in her brother's family; she was expected, as a matter of course, to take upon herself the most tedious and uninteresting part of the household labors. On Mondays she accepted as her share the washing of the men's shirts, heavy with sweat and stiff with dirt from the fields and from their own hard-working bodies. Tuesdays she never dreamed of being allowed to iron anything pretty or even interesting, like the baby's white dresses or the fancy aprons of her young lady nieces. She stood all day pressing out a tiresome monotonous succession of dish-cloths and towels and sheets.

In preserving-time she was allowed to have none of the pleasant responsibility of deciding when the fruit had cooked long enough, nor did she share in the little excitement of pouring the sweet-smelling stuff into the stone jars. She sat in a corner with the children and stoned cherries incessantly, or hulled strawberries until her fingers were dyed red to the bone.

The Elwells were not consciously unkind to their aunt, they were even in a vague way fond of her; but she was so utterly insignificant a figure in their lives that they bestowed no thought whatever on her. Aunt Mehetabel did not resent this treatment; she took it quite as unconsciously as they gave

74

it. It was to be expected when one was an old-maid dependent in a busy family. She gathered what crumbs of comfort she could from their occasional careless kindnesses and tried to hide the hurt which even yet pierced her at her brother's rough joking. In the winter when they all sat before the big hearth, roasted apples, drank mulled cider, and teased the girls about their beaux and the boys about their sweethearts, she shrank into a dusky corner with her knitting, happy if the evening passed without her brother saying, with a crude sarcasm, "Ask your Aunt Mehetabel about the beaux that used to come a-sparkin' her!" or, "Mehetabel, how was't when you was in love with Abel Cummings." As a matter of fact, she had been the same at twenty as at sixty, a quiet, mouse-like little creature, too timid and shy for anyone to notice, or to raise her eyes for a moment and wish for a life of her own.

Her sister-in-law, a big hearty housewife, who ruled indoors with as autocratic a sway as did her husband on the farm, was rather kind in an absent, offhand way to the shrunken little old woman, and it was through her that Mehetabel was able to enjoy the one pleasure of her life. Even as a girl she had been clever with her needle in the way of patching bedquilts. More than that she could never learn to do. The garments which she made for herself were the most lamentable affairs, and she was humbly grateful for any help in the bewildering business of putting them together. But in patch-work she enjoyed a tepid importance. She could really do that as well as anyone else. During years of devotion to this one art she had accumulated a considerable store of quilting patterns. Sometimes the neighbors would send over and ask "Miss Mehetabel" for such and such a design. It was with an agreeable flutter at being able to help someone that she went to the dresser, in her bare little room under the eaves, and extracted from her crowded portfolio the pattern desired.

She never knew how her great idea came to her. Sometimes she thought she must have dreamed it, sometimes she even wondered reverently, in the phraseology of the weekly prayer-meeting, if it had not been "sent" to her. She never admitted to herself that she could have thought of it without other help; it was too great, too ambitious, too lofty a project for her humble mind to have conceived. Even when she finished drawing the design with her own fingers, she gazed at it incredulously, not daring to believe that it could indeed be her handiwork. At first it seemed to her only like a lovely but quite unreal dream. She did not think of putting it into execution—so elaborate, so complicated, so beautifully difficult a pattern could be only for the angels in heaven to quilt. But so curiously does familiarity accustom us even to very wonderful things, that as she lived with this astonishing creation of her mind, the longing grew stronger and stronger to give it material life with her nimble old fingers.

She gasped at her daring when this idea first swept over her and put it away as one does a sinfully selfish notion, but she kept coming back to it again and again. Finally she said compromisingly to herself that she would make one "square," just one part of her design, to see how it would look. Accustomed to the most complete dependence on her brother and his wife, she dared not do even this without asking Sophia's permission. With a heart full of hope and fear thumping furiously against her old ribs, she approached the mistress of the house on churning-day, knowing with the innocent guile of a child that the country woman was apt to be in a good temper while working over the fragrant butter in the cool cellar.

Sophia listened absently to her sister-in-law's halting, hesitating petition. "Why, yes, Mehetabel," she said, leaning far down into the huge churn for the last golden morsels—"why, yes, start another quilt if you want to. I've got a lot of pieces from the spring sewing that will work in real good." Mehetabel tried honestly to make her see that this would be no common quilt, but her limited vocabulary and her emotion stood between her and expression. At last Sophia said, with a kindly impatience: "Oh, there! Don't bother me. I never could keep track of your quiltin' patterns, anyhow. I don't care what pattern you go by."

With this overwhelmingly, although unconsciously, generous permission Mehetabel rushed back up the steep attic stairs to her room, and in a joyful agitation began preparations for the work of her life. It was even better than she hoped. By some heaven-sent inspiration she had invented a pattern beyond which no patchwork quilt could go.

She had but little time from her incessant round of household drudgery for this new and absorbing occupation, and she did not dare sit up late at night lest she burn too much candle. It was weeks before the little square began to take on a finished look, to show the pattern. Then Mehetabel was in a fever of impatience to bring it to completion. She was too conscientious to shirk even the smallest part of her share of the work of the house, but she rushed through it with a speed which left her panting as she climbed to the little room. This seemed like a radiant spot to her as she bent over the innumerable scraps of cloth which already in her imagination ranged themselves in the infinitely diverse pattern of her masterpiece. Finally she could wait no longer, and one evening ventured to bring her work down beside the fire where the family sat, hoping that some good fortune would give her a place near the tallow candles on the mantelpiece. She was on the last corner of the square, and her needle flew in and out with inconceivable rapidity. No one noticed her, a fact which filled her with relief, and by bedtime she had but a few more stitches to add.

As she stood up with the others, the square fluttered out of her trembling old hands and fell on the table. Sophia glanced at it carelessly. "Is that the new quilt you're beginning on?" she asked with a yawn. "It looks like a real pretty pattern. Let's see it." Up to that moment Mehetabel had labored in the purest spirit of disinterested devotion to an ideal, but as Sophia held her work toward the candle to examine it, and exclaimed in amazement and admiration, she felt an astonished joy to know that her creation would stand the test of publicity.

"Land sakes!" ejaculated her sister-in-law, looking at the many-colored square. "Why, Mehetabel Elwell, where'd you git that pattern?"

"I made it up," said Mehetabel quietly, but with unutterable pride.

"No!" exclaimed Sophia incredulously. "*Did* you! Why, I never see such a pattern in my life. Girls, come here and see what your Aunt Mehetabel is doing."

The three tall daughters turned back reluctantly from the stairs. "I don't seem to take much interest in patchwork," said one listlessly.

"No, nor I neither!" answered Sophia; "but a stone image would take an interest in this pattern. Honest, Mehetabel, did you think of it yourself? And how under the sun and stars did you ever git your courage up to start in a-making it? Land! Look at all those tiny squinchy little seams! Why the wrong side ain't a thing *but* seams!"

The girls echoed their mother's exclamations, and Mr. Elwell himself came over to see what they were discussing. "Well, I declare!" he said, looking at his sister with eyes more approving than she could ever remember. "That beats old Mis' Wightman's quilt that got the blue ribbon so many times at the county fair."

Mehetabel's heart swelled within her, and tears of joy moistened her old eyes as she lay that night in her narrow, hard bed, too proud and excited to sleep. The next day her sister-in-law amazed her by taking the huge pan of potatoes out of her lap and setting one of the younger children to peeling them. "Don't you want to go on with that quiltin' pattern?" she said; "I'd kind o' like to see how you're goin' to make the grape-vine design come out on the corner."

By the end of the summer the family interest had risen so high that Mehetabel was given a little stand in the sitting-room where she could keep her pieces, and work in odd minutes. She almost wept over such kindness, and resolved firmly not to take advantage of it by neglecting her work, which she performed with a fierce thoroughness. But the whole atmosphere of her world was changed. Things had a meaning now. Through the longest task of washing milk-pans there rose the rainbow of promise of her variegated work. She took her place by the little table and put the thimble on her knotted, hard finger with the solemnity of a priestess performing a sacred rite.

She was even able to bear with some degree of dignity the extreme honor of having the minister and the minister's wife comment admiringly on her great project. The family felt quite proud of Aunt Mehetabel as Minister Bowman had said it was work as fine as any he had ever seen, "and he didn't know but finer!" The remark was repeated verbatim to the neighbors in the following weeks when they dropped in and examined in a perverse silence some astonishingly difficult *tour de force* which Mehetabel had just finished.

The family especially plumed themselves on the slow progress of the quilt. "Mehetabel has been to work on that corner for six weeks, come Tuesday, and she ain't half done yet," they explained to visitors. They fell out of the way of always expecting her to be the one to run on errands, even for the children. "Don't bother your Aunt Mehetabel," Sophia would call. "Can't you see she's got to a ticklish place on the quilt?"

The old woman sat up straighter and looked the world in the face. She was a part of it at last. She joined in the conversation and her remarks were listened to. The children were even told to mind her when she asked them to do some service for her, although this she did but seldom, the habit of self-effacement being too strong.

One day some strangers from the next town drove up and asked if they could inspect the wonderful quilt which they had heard of, even down in their end of the valley. After that such visitations were not uncommon, making the Elwell's house a notable object. Mehetabel's quilt came to be one of the town sights, and no one was allowed to leave the town without having paid tribute to its worth. The Elwells saw to it that their aunt was better dressed than she had ever been before, and one of the girls made her a pretty little cap to wear on her thin white hair.

A year went by and a quarter of the quilt was finished; a second year passed and half was done. The third year Mehetabel had pneumonia and lay ill for weeks and weeks, overcome with terror lest she die before her work was completed. A fourth year and one could really see the grandeur of the whole design; and in September of the fifth year, the entire family watching her with eager and admiring eyes, Mehetabel quilted the last stitches in her creation. The girls held it up by the four corners, and they all looked at it in a solemn silence. Then Mr. Elwell smote one horny hand within the other and exclaimed: "By ginger! That's goin' to the county fair!" Mehetabel blushed a deep red at this. It was a thought which had occurred to her in a bold moment, but she had not dared to entertain it. The family acclaimed the idea, and one of the boys was forthwith dispatched to the house of the neighbor who was chairman of the committee for their village. He returned with radiant face. "Of course he'll take it. Like's not it may git a prize, so he says; but he's got to have it right off, because all the things are goin' to-morrow morning."

Even in her swelling pride Mehetabel felt a pang of separation as the bulky package was carried out of the house. As the days went on she felt absolutely lost without her work. For years it had been her one preoccupation, and she could not bear even to look at the little stand, now quite bare of the litter of scraps which had lain on it so long. One of the neighbors, who took the long journey to the fair, reported that the quilt was hung in a place of honor in a glass case in "Agricultural Hall." But that meant little to Mehetabel's utter ignorance of all that lay outside of her brother's home. The family noticed the old woman's depression, and one day Sophia said kindly, "You feel sort o' lost without the quilt, don't you, Mehetabel?"

"They took it away so quick!" she said wistfully; "I hadn't hardly had one real good look at it myself."

Mr. Elwell made no comment, but a day or two later he asked his sister how early she could get up in the morning.

"I dun'no'. Why?" she asked.

"Well, Thomas Ralston has got to drive clear to West Oldton to see a lawyer there, and that is four miles beyond the fair. He says if you can git up so's to leave here at four in the morning he'll drive you over to the fair, leave you there for the day, and bring you back again at night."

Mehetabel looked at him with incredulity. It was as though someone had offered her a ride in a golden chariot up to the gates of heaven. "Why, you can't *mean* it!" she cried, paling with the intensity of her emotion. Her brother laughed a little uneasily. Even to his careless indifference this joy was a revelation of the narrowness of her life in his home. "Oh, 'tain't so much to go to the fair. Yes, I mean it. Go git your things ready, for he wants to start to-morrow morning."

All that night a trembling, excited old woman lay and stared at the rafters. She, who had never been more than six miles from home in her life, was going to drive thirty miles away—it was like going to another world. She who had never seen anything more exciting than a church supper was to see the county fair. To Mehetabel it was like making the tour of the world. She had never dreamed of doing it. She could not at all imagine what it would be like.

Nor did the exhortations of the family, as they bade good-by to her, throw any light on her confusion. They had all been at least once to the scene of gayety she was to visit, and as she tried to eat her breakfast they called out conflicting advice to her till her head whirled. Sophia told her to be sure and see the display of preserves. Her brother said not to miss inspecting the stock, her nieces said the fancywork was the only thing worth looking at, and her nephews said she must bring them home an account of the races. The buggy drove up to the door, she was helped in, and her wraps tucked about her. They all stood together and waved good-by to her as she drove out of the yard. She waved back, but she scarcely saw them. On her return home that evening she was very pale, and so tired and stiff that her brother had to lift her out bodily, but her lips were set in a blissful smile. They crowded around her with thronging questions, until Sophia pushed them all aside, telling them Aunt Mehetabel was too tired to speak until she had had her supper. This was eaten in an enforced silence on the part of the children, and then the old woman was helped into an easy-chair before the fire. They gathered about her, eager for news of the great world, and Sophia said, "Now, come, Mehetabel, tell us all about it!"

Mehetabel drew a long breath. "It was just perfect!" she said; "finer even than I thought. They've got it hanging up in the very middle of a sort o' closet made of glass, and one of the lower corners is ripped and turned back so's to show the seams on the wrong side."

"What?" asked Sophia, a little blankly.

"Why, the quilt!" said Mehetabel in surprise. "There are a whole lot of other ones in that room, but not one that can hold a candle to it, if I do say it who shouldn't. I heard lots of people say the same thing. You ought to have heard what the women said about that corner, Sophia. They said—well, I'd be ashamed to *tell* you what they said. I declare if I wouldn't!"

Mr. Elwell asked, "What did you think of that big ox we've heard so much about?"

"I didn't look at the stock," returned his sister indifferently. "That set of pieces you gave me, Maria, from your red waist, come out just lovely!" she assured one of her nieces. "I heard one woman say you could 'most smell the red silk roses."

"Did any of the horses in our town race?" asked young Thomas.

"I didn't see the races."

"How about the preserves?" asked Sophia.

"I didn't see the preserves," said Mehetabel calmly. "You see, I went right to the room where the quilt was, and then I didn't want to leave it. It had been so long since I'd seen it. I had to look at it first real good myself, and then I looked at the others to see if there was any that could come up to it. And then the people begun comin' in and I got so interested in hearin' what they had to say I couldn't think of goin' anywheres else. I ate my lunch right there too, and I'm as glad as can be I did, too; for what do you think?"—she gazed about her with kindling eyes—"while I stood there with a sandwich in one hand didn't the head of the hull concern come in and open the glass door and pin 'First Prize' right in the middle of the quilt!"

There was a stir of congratulation and proud exclamation. Then Sophia returned again to the attack. "Didn't you go to see anything else?" she queried.

"Why, no," said Mehetabel. "Only the quilt. Why should I?"

She fell into a reverie where she saw again the glorious creation of her hand and brain hanging before all the world with the mark of highest approval on it. She longed to make her listeners see the splendid vision with her. She struggled for words; she reached blindly after unknown superlatives. "I tell you it looked like—" she said, and paused, hesitating. Vague recollections of hymn-book phraseology came into her mind, the only form of literary expression she knew; but they were dismissed as being sacrilegious, and also not sufficiently forcible. Finally, "I tell you it looked real *well!*" she assured them, and sat staring into the fire, on her tired old face the supreme content of an artist who has realized his ideal.

EDITH WHARTON

1911

Xingu

Mrs. Ballinger is one of the ladies who pursue Culture in bands, as though it were dangerous to meet alone. To this end she had founded the Lunch Club, an association composed of herself and several other indomitable huntresses of erudition. The Lunch Club, after three or four winters of lunching and debate, had acquired such local distinction that the entertainment of distinguished strangers became one of its accepted functions; in recognition of which it duly extended to the celebrated Osric Dane, on the day of her arrival in Hillbridge, an invitation to be present at the next meeting.

The club was to meet at Mrs. Ballinger's. The other members, behind her back, were of one voice in deploring her unwillingness to cede her rights in favor of Mrs. Plinth, whose house made a more impressive setting for the entertainment of celebrities; while, as Mrs. Leveret observed, there was always the picture gallery to fall back on.

Mrs. Plinth made no secret of sharing this view. She had always regarded it as one of her obligations to entertain the Lunch Club's distinguished guests. Mrs. Plinth was almost as proud of her obligations as she was of her picture gallery; she was in fact fond of implying that the one possession implied the other, and that only a woman of her wealth could afford to live up to a standard as high as that which she had set herself. An all-round sense of duty, roughly adaptable to various ends, was, in her opinion, all that Providence exacted of the more humbly stationed; but the power which had predestined Mrs. Plinth to keep a footman clearly intended her to maintain an equally specialized staff of responsibilities. It was the more to be regretted that Mrs. Ballinger, whose obligations to society were bounded by the narrow scope of two parlormaids, should have been so tenacious of the right to entertain Osric Dane.

The question of that lady's reception had for a month past profoundly moved the members of the Lunch Club. It was not that they felt themselves unequal to the task, but that their sense of the opportunity plunged them into the agreeable uncertainty of the lady who weighs the alternatives of a well-stocked wardrobe. If such subsidiary members as Mrs. Leveret were fluttered by the thought of exchanging ideas with the author of *The Wings of Death*, no forebodings disturbed the conscious adequacy of Mrs. Plinth, Mrs. Ballinger and Miss Van Vluyck. *The Wings of Death* had, in fact, at Miss Van Vluyck's suggestion, been chosen as the subject of discussion at the last club meeting, and each member had thus been enabled to express her own opinion or to appropriate whatever sounded well in the comments of the others.

Mrs. Roby alone had abstained from profiting by the opportunity but it was now openly recognized that, as a member of the Lunch Club, Mrs. Roby was a failure. "It all comes," as Mrs. Van Vluyck put it, "of accepting a woman on a man's estimation." Mrs. Roby, returning to Hillbridge from a prolonged sojourn in exotic lands – the other ladies no longer took the trouble to remember where – had been heralded by the distinguished biologist, Professor Foreland, as the most agreeable woman he had ever met; and the members of the Lunch Club, impressed by an encomium that carried the weight of a diploma, and rashly assuming that the Professor's social sympathies would follow the line of his professional bent, had seized the chance of annexing a biological member. Their disillusionment was complete. At Miss Van Vluyck's first offhand mention of the pterodactyl Mrs. Roby had confusedly murmured: "I know so little about meters –" and after that painful betrayal of incompetence she had prudently withdrawn from further participation in the mental gymnastics of the club.

"I suppose she flattered him," Miss Van Vluyck summed up – "or else it's the way she does her hair."

The dimensions of Miss Van Vluyck's dining room having restricted the membership of the club to six, the nonconductiveness of one member was a serious obstacle to the exchange of ideas, and some wonder had already been expressed that Mrs. Roby should care to live, as it were, on the intellectual bounty of the others. This feeling was increased by the discovery that she had not yet read *The Wings of Death*. She owned to having heard the name of Osric Dane; but that – incredible as it appeared – was the extent of her acquaintance with the celebrated novelist. The ladies could not conceal their surprise; but Mrs. Ballinger, whose pride in the club made her wish to put even Mrs. Roby in the best possible light, gently insinuated that, though she had not had time to acquaint herself with *The Wings of Death*, she must at least be familiar with its equally remarkable predecessor, *The Supreme Instant*.

Mrs. Roby wrinkled her sunny brows in a conscientious effort of memory, as a result of which she recalled that, oh, yes, she *had* seen the book at her brother's, when she was staying with him in Brazil, and had even carried it off to read one day on a boating party; but they had all got to shying things at each other in the boat, and the book had gone overboard, so she had never had the chance—

The picture evoked by this anecdote did not increase Mrs. Roby's credit with the club, and there was a painful pause, which was broken by Mrs. Plinth's remarking: "I can understand that, with all your other pursuits, you should not find much time for reading; but I should have thought you might at least have *got up The Wings of Death* before Osric Dane's arrival."

Mrs. Roby took this rebuke good-humoredly. She had meant, she owned, to glance through the book; but she had been so absorbed in a novel of Trollope's that—

"No one reads Trollope now," Mrs. Ballinger interrupted.

Mrs. Roby looked pained. "I'm only just beginning," she confessed.

"And does he interest you?" Mrs. Plinth inquired.

"He amuses me."

"Amusement," said Mrs. Plinth, "is hardly what I look for in my choice of books."

"Oh, certainly, *The Wings of Death* is not amusing," ventured Mrs. Leveret, whose manner of putting forth an opinion was like that of an obliging salesman with a variety of other styles to submit if his first selection does not suit.

"Was it *meant* to be?" inquired Mrs. Plinth, who was fond of asking questions that she permitted no one but herself to answer. "Assuredly not."

"Assuredly not—that is what I was going to say," assented Mrs. Leveret, hastily rolling up her opinion and reaching for another. "It was meant to—to elevate."

Miss Van Vluyck adjusted her spectacles as though they were the black cap of condemnation. "I hardly see," she interposed, "how a book steeped in the bitterest pessimism can be said to elevate, however much it may instruct."

"I meant, of course, to instruct," said Mrs. Leveret, flurried by the unexpected distinction between two terms which she had supposed to be synonymous. Mrs. Leveret's enjoyment of the Lunch Club was frequently marred by such surprises; and not knowing her own value to the other ladies as a mirror for their mental complacency she was sometimes troubled by a doubt of her worthiness to join in their debates. It was only the fact of having a dull sister who thought her clever that saved her from a sense of hopeless inferiority.

"Do they get married in the end?" Mrs. Roby interposed.

"They—who?" the Lunch Club collectively exclaimed.

"Why, the girl and man. It's a novel, isn't it? I always think that's the one thing that matters. If they're parted, it spoils my dinner."

Mrs. Plinth and Mrs. Ballinger exchanged scandalized glances, and the latter said: "I should hardly advise you to read *The Wings of Death* in that spirit. For my part, when there are so many books one *has* to read, I wonder how any one can find time for those that are merely amusing."

"The beautiful part of it," Laura Glyde murmured, "is surely just this—that no one can tell *how The Wings of Death* ends. Osric Dane, overcome by the awful significance of her own meaning, has mercifully veiled it—perhaps even from herself—as Apelles, in representing the sacrifice of Iphigenia, veiled the face of Agamemnon."

"What's that? Is it poetry?" whispered Mrs. Leveret to Mrs. Plinth; who, disdaining a definite reply, said coldly: "You should look it up. I always make it a point to look things up." Her tone added—"Though I might easily have it done for me by the footman."

"I was about to say," Mrs. Van Vluyck resumed, "that it must always be a question whether a book *can* instruct unless it elevates."

"Oh—" murmured Mrs. Leveret, now feeling herself hopelessly astray.

"I don't know," said Mrs. Ballinger, scenting in Miss Van Vluyck's tone a tendency to depreciate the coveted distinction of entertaining Osric Dane; "I don't know that such a question can seriously be raised as to a book which has attracted more attention among thoughtful people than any novel since *Robert Elsmere.*"

"Oh, but don't you see," exclaimed Laura Glyde, "that it's just the dark hopelessness of it all—the wonderful tone scheme of black on black—that makes it such an artistic achievement? It reminded me when I read it of Prince Rupert's *manière noire* . . . the book is etched, not painted, yet one feels the color values so intensely. . . ."

"Who is *he?*" Mrs. Leveret whispered to her neighbor. "Someone she's met abroad?"

"The wonderful part of the book," Mrs. Ballinger conceded, "is that it may be looked at from so many points of view. I hear that as a study of determinism Professor Lupton ranks it with *The Data of Ethics.*"

"I'm told that Osric Dane spent ten years in preparatory studies before beginning to write it," said Mrs. Plinth. "She looks up everything—verifies everything. It had always been my principle, as you know. Nothing would induce me, now, to put aside a book before I'd finished it, just because I can buy as many more as I want."

"And what do *you* think of *The Wings of Death?*" Mrs. Roby abruptly asked her.

It was the kind of question that might be termed out of order, and the ladies glanced at each other as though disclaiming any share in such a breach of discipline. They all knew there was nothing Mrs. Plinth so disliked as being asked her opinion of a book. Books were written to read; if one read them what more could be expected? To be questioned in detail regarding the contents of a volume seemed to her as great an outrage as being searched for smuggled laces at the Custom House. The club had always respected this idiosyncrasy of Mrs. Plinth's. Such opinions as she had were imposing and substantial: her mind, like her house, was furnished with monumental "pieces" that were not meant to be disarranged; and it was one of the unwritten rules of the Lunch Club that, within her own province, each member's habits of thought should be respected. The meeting therefore closed with an increased sense, on the part of the other ladies, of Mrs. Roby's hopeless unfitness to be one of them.

II

Mrs. Leveret, on the eventful day, arrived early at Mrs. Ballinger's, her volume of *Appropriate Allusions* in her pocket.

It always flustered Mrs. Leveret to be late at the Lunch Club: she liked to collect her thoughts and gather a hint, as the others assembled, of the turn the conversation was likely to take. Today, however, she felt herself completely at a loss; and even the familiar contact of *Appropriate Allusions*, which stuck into her as she sat down, failed to give her any reassurance. it was an admirable little volume, compiled to meet all the social emergencies; so that, whether on the occasion of Anniversaries, joyful or melancholy (as the classification ran), of Banquets, social or municipal, or of Baptisms, Church of England or sectarian, its student need never be at a loss for a pertinent reference. Mrs. Leveret, though she had for years devoutly conned its pages, valued it, however, rather for its moral support than for its practical services; for though in the privacy of her own room she commanded an army of quotations, these invariably deserted her at the critical moment, and the only phrase she retained—*canst thou draw out leviathan with a hook?*—was one she had never yet found occasion to apply.

Today she felt that even the complete mastery of the volume would hardly have insured her self-possession; for she thought it probable that, even if she *did*, in some miraculous way, remember an Allusion, it would be only to find that Osric Dane used a different volume (Mrs. Leveret was convinced that literary people always carried them), and would consequently not recognize her quotations.

Mrs. Leveret's sense of being adrift was intensified by the appearance of Mrs. Ballinger's drawing room. To a careless eye its aspect was unchanged; but those acquainted with Mrs. Ballinger's way of arranging her books would instantly have detected the marks of recent perturbation. Mrs. Ballinger's province, as a member of the Lunch Club, was the Book of the Day. On that, whatever it was, from a novel to a treatise on experimental psychol-

ogy, she was confidently, authoritatively "up." What became of last year's
books, or last week's even; what she did with the "subjects" she had previously professed with equal authority; no one had ever yet discovered. Her
mind was an hotel where facts came and went like transient lodgers,
without leaving their address behind, and frequently without paying for
their board. It was Mrs. Ballinger's boast that she was "abreast with the
Thoughts of the Day," and her pride that this advanced position should be
expressed by the books on her table. These volumes, frequently renewed,
and almost always damp from the press, bore names generally unfamiliar to
Mrs. Leveret, and giving her, as she furtively scanned them, a disheartening
glimpse of new fields of knowledge to be breathlessly traversed in Mrs. Ballinger's wake. But today a number of maturer-looking volumes were adroitly
mingled with the *primeurs* of the press—Karl Marx jostled Professor Berg-
son, and the *Confessions of St. Augustine* lay beside the last work on "Men-
delism"; so that even to Mrs. Leveret's fluttered perceptions it was clear that
Mrs. Ballinger didn't in the least know what Osric Dane was likely to talk
about, and had taken measures to be prepared for anything. Mrs. Leveret felt
like a passenger on an ocean steamer who is told that there is no immediate
danger, but that she had better put on her lifebelt.

It was a relief to be roused from these forebodings by Miss Van Vluyck's
arrival.

"Well, my dear," the newcomer briskly asked her hostess, "what subjects
are we to discuss today?"

Mrs. Ballinger was furtively replacing a volume of Wordsworth by a
copy of Verlaine. "I hardly know," she said, somewhat nervously. "Perhaps
we had better leave that to circumstances."

"Circumstances?" said Miss Van Vluyck drily. "that means, I suppose,
that Laura Glyde will take the floor as usual, and we shall be deluged with
literature."

Philanthropy and statistics were Miss Van Vluyck's province, and she
resented any tendency to divert their guest's attention from these topics.

Mrs. Plinth at this moment appeared.

"Literature?" she protested in a tone of remonstrance. "But this is perfectly unexpected. I understood we were to talk of Osric Dane's novel."

Mrs. Ballinger winced at the discrimination, but let it pass. "We can
hardly make that our chief subject—at least not *too* intentionally," she suggested. "Of course we can let our talk *drift* in that direction; but we ought to
have some other topic as an introduction, and that is what I wanted to con-
sult you about. The fact is, we know so little of Osric Dane's tastes and interests that it is difficult to make any special preparation."

"It may be difficult," said Mrs. Plinth with decision, "but it is necessary.
I know what that happy-go-lucky principle leads to. As I told one of my
nieces the other day, there are certain emergencies for which a lady should

always be prepared. It's in shocking taste to wear colors when one pays a visit of condolence, or a last year's dress when there are reports that one's husband is on the wrong side of the market; and so it is with conversation. All I ask is that I should know beforehand what is to be talked about; then I feel sure of being able to say the proper thing."

"I quite agree with you," Mrs. Ballinger assented; "but—"

And at that instant, heralded by the fluttered parlormaid, Osric Dane appeared upon the threshold.

Mrs. Leveret told her sister afterward that she had known at a glance what was coming. She saw that Osric Dane was not going to meet them halfway. That distinguished personage had indeed entered with an air of compulsion not calculated to promote the easy exercise of hospitality. She looked as though she were about to be photographed for a new edition of her books.

The desire to propitiate a divinity is general in inverse ratio to its responsiveness, and the sense of discouragement produced by Osric Dane's entrance visibly increased the Lunch Club's eagerness to please her. Any lingering idea that she might consider herself under an obligation to her entertainers was at once dispelled by her manner: as Mrs. Leveret said afterward to her sister, she had a way of looking at you that made you feel as if there was something wrong with your hat. This evidence of greatness produced such an immediate impression on the ladies that a shudder of awe ran through them when Mrs. Roby, as their hostess led the great personage into the dining room, turned back to whisper to the others: "What a brute she is!"

The hour about the table did not tend to revise this verdict. It was passed by Osric Dane in the silent deglutition of Mrs. Ballinger's menu, and by the members of the club in the emission of tentative platitudes which their guest seemed to swallow as perfunctorily as the successive courses of the luncheon.

Mrs. Ballinger's reluctance to fix a topic had thrown the club into a mental disarray which increased with the return to the drawing room, where the actual business of discussion was to open. Each lady waited for the other to speak; and there was a general shock of disappointment when their hostess opened the conversation by the painfully commonplace inquiry: "Is this your first visit to Hillbridge?"

Even Mrs. Leveret was conscious that this was a bad beginning; and a vague impulse of deprecation made Miss Glyde interject: "It is a very small place indeed."

Mrs. Plinth bristled. "We have a great many representative people," she said, in the tone of one who speaks for her order.

Osric Dane turned to her. "What do they represent?" she asked.

Mrs. Plinth's constitutional dislike to being questioned was intensified by her sense of unpreparedness; and her reproachful glance passed the question on to Mrs. Ballinger.

"Why," said that lady, glancing in turn to the other members, "as a community I hope it is not too much to say that we stand for culture."

"For art—" Miss Glyde interjected.

"For art and literature," Mrs. Ballinger amended.

"And for sociology, I trust," snapped Miss Van Vluyck.

"We have a standard," said Mrs. Plinth, feeling herself suddenly secure on the vast expanse of a generalization; and Mrs. Leveret, thinking there must be room for more than one on so broad a statement, took courage to murmur: "Oh, certainly; we have a standard."

"The object of our little club," Mrs. Ballinger continued, "is to concentrate the highest tendencies of Hillbridge—to centralize and focus its intellectual effort."

This was felt to be so happy that the ladies drew an almost audible breath of relief.

"We aspire," the President went on, "to be in touch with whatever is highest in art, literature and ethics."

Osric Dane again turned to her. "What ethics?" she asked.

A tremor of apprehension encircled the room. None of the ladies required any preparation to pronounce on a question of morals; but when they were called ethics it was different. The club, when fresh from the *Encyclopedia Britannica*, the *Reader's Handbook* or Smith's *Classical Dictionary*, could deal confidently with any subject; but when taken unawares it had been known to define agnosticism as a heresy of the Early Church and Professor Froude as a distinguished histologist; and such minor members as Mrs. Leveret still secretly regarded ethics as something vaguely pagan.

Even to Mrs. Ballinger, Osric Dane's question was unsettling, and there was a general sense of gratitude when Laura Glyde leaned forward to say, with her most sympathetic accent: "You must excuse us, Mrs. Dane, for not being able, just at present, to talk of anything but *The Wings of Death*."

"Yes," said Miss Van Vluyck, with a sudden resolve to carry the war into the enemy's camp. "We are so anxious to know the exact purpose you had in mind in writing your wonderful book."

"You will find," Mrs. Plinth interposed, "that we are not superficial readers."

"We are eager to hear from you," Miss Van Vluyck continued, "if the pessimistic tendency of the book is an expression of your own convictions or—"

"Or merely," Miss Glyde thrust in, "a somber background brushed in to throw your figures into more vivid relief. *Are* you not primarily plastic?"

"*I* have always maintained," Mrs. Ballinger interposed, "that you represent the purely objective method—"

Osric Dane helped herself critically to coffee. "How do you define objective?" she then inquired.

There was a flurried pause before Laura Glyde intensely murmured: "In reading *you* we don't define, we feel."

Osric Dane smiled. "The cerebellum," she remarked, "is not infrequently the seat of the literary emotions." And she took a second lump of sugar.

The sting that this remark was vaguely felt to conceal was almost neutralized by the satisfaction of being addressed in such technical language.

"Ah, the cerebellum," said Miss Van Vluyck complacently. "The club took a course in psychology last winter."

"Which psychology?" asked Osric Dane.

There was an agonizing pause, during which each member of the club secretly deplored the distressing inefficiency of the others. Only Mrs. Roby went on placidly sipping her chartreuse. At last Mrs. Ballinger said, with an attempt at a high tone: "Well, really, you know, it was last year that we took psychology, and this winter we have been so absorbed in—"

She broke off, nervously trying to recall some of the club's discussions; but her faculties seemed to be paralyzed by the petrifying stare of Osric Dane. What *had* the club been absorbed in? Mrs. Ballinger, with a vague purpose of gaining time, repeated slowly: "We've been so intensely absorbed in—"

Mrs. Roby put down her liqueur glass and drew near the group with a smile.

"In Xingu?" she gently prompted.

A thrill ran through the other members. They exchanged confused glances, and then, with one accord, turned a gaze of mingled relief and interrogation on their rescuer. The expression of each denoted a different phase of the same emotion. Mrs. Plinth was the first to compose her features to an air of reassurance: after a moment's hasty adjustment her look almost implied that it was she who had given the word to Mrs. Ballinger.

"Xingu, of course!" exclaimed the latter with her accustomed promptness, while Miss Van Vluyck and Laura Glyde seemed to be plumbing the depths of memory, and Mrs. Leveret, feeling apprehensively for *Appropriate Allusions*, was somehow reassured by the uncomfortable pressure of its bulk against her person.

Osric Dane's change of countenance was no less striking than that of her entertainers. She too put down her coffee cup, but with a look of distinct annoyance; she too wore, for a brief moment, what Mrs. Roby afterward described as the look of feeling for something in the back of her head; and before she could dissemble these momentary signs of weakness, Mrs. Roby, turning to her with a deferential smile, had said: "And we've been so hoping that today you would tell us just what you think of it."

Osric Dane received the homage of the smile as a matter of course; but the accompanying question obviously embarrassed her, and it became clear to her observers that she was not quick at shifting her facial scenery. It was as though her countenance had so long been set in an expression of un-challenged superiority that the muscles had stiffened, and refused to obey her orders.

"Xingu–" she said, as if seeking in her turn to gain time.

Mrs. Roby continued to press her. "Knowing how engrossing the subject is, you will understand how it happens that the club has let everything else go to the wall for the moment. Since we took up Xingu I might say–were it not for your books–that nothing else seems to us worth remembering."

Osric Dane's stern features were darkened rather than lit up by an un-easy smile. "I am glad to hear that you make on exception," she gave out between narrowed lips.

"Oh, of course," Mrs. Roby said prettily; "but as you have shown us that–so very naturally!–you don't care to talk of your own things, we really can't let you off from telling us exactly what you think about Xingu; especial-ly," she added, with a still more persuasive smile, "as some people say that one of your last books was saturated with it."

It was an *it* then–the assurance sped like fire through the parched minds of the other members. In their eagerness to gain the least little clue to Xingu they almost forgot the joy of assisting at the discomfiture of Mrs. Dane.

The latter reddened nervously under her antagonist's challenge. "May I ask," she faltered out, "to which of my books you refer?"

Mrs. Roby did not falter. "That's just what I want you to tell us; because, though I was present, I didn't actually take part."

"Present at what?" Mrs. Dane took her up; and for an instant the trem-bling members of the Lunch Club thought that the champion Providence had raised up for them had lost a point. But Mrs. Roby explained herself gaily: "At the discussion, of course. And so we're dreadfully anxious to know just how it was that you went into the Xingu."

There was a portentous pause, a silence so big with incalculable dangers that the members with one accord checked the words on their lips, like sol-diers dropping their arms to watch a single combat between their leaders. Then Mrs. Dane gave expression to their inmost dread by saying sharply: "Ah–you say *the* Xingu, do you?"

Mrs. Roby smiled undauntedly. "It *is* a shade pedantic, isn't it? Personal-ly, I always drop the article: but I don't know how the other members feel about it."

The other members looked as though they would willingly have dis-pensed with this appeal to their opinion, and Mrs. Roby, after a bright glance about the group, went on: "They probably think, as I do, that nothing really matters except the thing itself–except Xingu."

No immediate reply seemed to occur to Mrs. Dane, and Mrs. Ballinger gathered courage to say: "Surely everyone must feel that about Xingu."

Mrs. Plinth came to her support with a heavy murmur of assent, and Laura Glyde sighed out emotionally: "I have known cases where it has changed a whole life."

"It has done me worlds of good," Mrs. Leveret interjected, seeming to herself to remember that she had either taken it or read it the winter before.

"Of course," Mrs. Roby admitted, "the difficulty is that one must give up so much time to it. It's very long."

"I can't imagine," said Mrs. Van Vluyck, "grudging the time given to such a subject."

"And deep in places," Mrs. Roby pursued; (so then it was a book!) "And it isn't easy to skip."

"I never skip," said Mrs. Plinth dogmatically.

"Ah, it's dangerous to, in Xingu. Even at the start there are places where one can't. One must just wade through."

"I should hardly call it *wading*," said Mrs. Ballinger sarcastically.

Mrs. Roby sent her a look of interest. "Ah—you always found it went swimmingly?"

Mrs. Ballinger hesitated. "Of course there are difficult passages," she conceded.

"Yes; some are not at all clear—even," Mrs. Roby added, "if one is familiar with the original."

"As I suppose you are?" Osric Dane interposed, suddenly fixing her with a look of challenge.

Mrs. Roby met it by a deprecating gesture. "Oh, it's really not difficult up to a certain point; though some of the branches are very little known, and it's almost impossible to get at the source."

"Have you ever tried?" Mrs. Plinth inquired, still distrustful of Mrs. Roby's thoroughness.

Mrs. Roby was silent for a moment; then she replied with lowered lids: "No—but a friend of mine did; a very brilliant man; and he told me it was best for women—not to. . . . "

A shudder ran around the room. Mrs. Leveret coughed so that the parlormaid, who was handing the cigarettes, should not hear; Miss Van Vluyck's face took on a nauseated expression, and Mrs. Plinth looked as if she were passing someone she did not care to bow to. But the most remarkable result of Mrs. Roby's words was the effect they produced on the Lunch Club's distinguished guest. Osric Dane's impassive features suddenly softened to an expression of the warmest human sympathy, and edging her chair toward Mrs. Roby's she asked: "Did he really? And—did you find he was right?"

Mrs. Ballinger, in whom annoyance at Mrs. Roby's unwonted assumption of prominence was beginning to displace gratitude for the aid she had rendered, could not consent to her being allowed, by such dubious means, to monopolize the attention of their guest. If Osric Dane had not enough self-respect to resent Mrs. Roby's flippancy, at least the Lunch Club would do so in the person of its President.

Mrs. Ballinger had laid her hand on Mrs. Roby's arm. "We must not forget," she said with a frigid amiability, "that absorbing as Xingu is to *us*, it may be less interesting to–"

"Oh, no, on the contrary, I assure you," Osric Dane intervened.

"–to others," Mrs. Ballinger finished firmly; "and we must not allow our little meeting to end without persuading Mrs. Dane to say a few words to us on a subject which, today, is much more present in all our thoughts. I refer, of course, to *The Wings of Death*."

The other members, animated by various degrees of the same sentiment, and encouraged by the humanized mien of their redoubtable guest, repeated after Mrs. Ballinger: "Oh, yes, you really *must* talk to us a little about your book."

Osric Dane's expression became as bored, though not as haughty, as when her work had been previously mentioned. But before she could respond to Mrs. Ballinger's request, Mrs. Roby had risen from her seat, and was pulling down her veil over her frivolous nose.

"I'm so sorry," she said, advancing toward her hostess with outstretched hand, "but before Mrs. Dane begins I think I'd better run away. Unluckily, as you know, I haven't read her books, so I should be at a terrible disadvantage among you all, and besides, I've an engagement to play bridge."

If Mrs. Roby had simply pleaded her ignorance of Osric Dane's works as a reason for withdrawing, the Lunch Club, in view of her recent prowess, might have approved such evidence of discretion; but to couple this excuse with the brazen announcement that she was foregoing the privilege for the purpose of joining a bridge party was only one more instance of her deplorable lack of discrimination.

The ladies were disposed, however, to feel that her departure–now that she had performed the sole service she was ever likely to render them–would probably make for greater order and dignity in the impending discussion, besides relieving them of the sense of self-distrust which her presence always mysteriously produced. Mrs. Ballinger therefore restricted herself to a formal murmur of regret, and the other members were just grouping themselves comfortably about Osric Dane when the latter, to their dismay, started up from the sofa on which she had been seated.

"Oh wait–do wait, and I'll go with you!" she called out to Mrs. Roby; and, seizing the hands of the disconcerted members, she administered a series of farewell pressures with the mechanical haste of a railway conductor punching tickets.

"I'm so sorry–I'd quite forgotten–" she flung back at them from the threshold; and as she joined Mrs. Roby, who had turned in surprise at her appeal, the other ladies had the mortification of hearing her say, in a voice which she did not take the pains to lower: "If you'll let me walk a little way with you, I should so like to ask you a few more questions about Xingu. . . . "

III

The incident had been so rapid that the door closed on the departing pair before the other members had time to understand what was happening. Then a sense of the indignity put upon them by Osric Dane's unceremonious desertion began to contend with the confused feeling that they had been cheated out of their due without exactly knowing how or why.

There was a silence, during which Mrs. Ballinger, with a perfunctory hand, rearranged the skillfully grouped literature at which her distinguished guest had not so much as glanced; then Miss Van Vluyck tartly pronounced: "Well, I can't say that I consider Osric Dane's departure a great loss."

This confession crystallized the resentment of the other members, and Mrs. Leveret exclaimed: "I do believe she came on purpose to be nasty!"

It was Mrs. Plinth's private opinion that Osric Dane's attitude toward the Lunch Club might have been very different had it welcomed her in the majestic setting of the Plinth drawing rooms; but not liking to reflect on the inadequacy of Mrs. Ballinger's establishment she sought a roundabout satisfaction in deprecating her lack of foresight.

"I said from the first that we ought to have had a subject ready. It's what always happens when you're unprepared. Now if we'd only got up Xingu—"

The slowness of Mrs. Plinth's mental processes was always allowed for by the club; but this instance of it was too much for Mrs. Ballinger's equanimity.

"Xingu!" she scoffed. "Why, it was the fact of our knowing so much more about it than she did—unprepared though we were—that made Osric Dane so furious. I should have thought that was plain enough to everybody!"

This retort impressed even Mrs. Plinth, and Laura Glyde, moved by an impulse of generosity, said: "Yes, we really ought to be grateful to Mrs. Roby for introducing the topic. It may have made Osric Dane furious, but at least it made her civil."

"I am glad we were able to show her," added Miss Van Vluyck, "that a broad and up-to-date culture is not confined to the great intellectual centers."

This increased the satisfaction of the other members, and they began to forget their wrath against Osric Dane in the pleasure of having contributed to her discomfiture.

Miss Van Vluyck thoughtfully rubbed her spectacles. "What surprised me most," she continued, "was that Fanny Roby should be so up on Xingu."

This remark threw a slight chill on the company, but Mrs. Ballinger said with an air of indulgent irony: "Mrs. Roby always has the knack of making a little go a long way; still, we certainly owe her a debt for happening to remember that she'd heard of Xingu." And this was felt by the other members to be a graceful way of canceling once and for all the club's obligation to Mrs. Roby.

Even Mrs. Leveret took courage to speed a timid shaft of irony. "I fancy Osric Dane hardly expected to take a lesson in Xingu at Hillbridge!"

Mrs. Ballinger smiled. "When she asked me what we represented–do you remember?–I wish I'd simply said we represented Xingu!"

All the ladies laughed appreciatively at this sally, except Mrs. Plinth, who said, after a moment's deliberation: "I'm not sure it would have been wise to do so."

Mrs. Ballinger, who was already beginning to feel as if she had launched at Osric Dane the retort which had just occurred to her, turned ironically on Mrs. Plinth. "May I ask why?" she inquired.

Mrs. Plinth looked grave. "Surely," she said, "I understood from Mrs. Roby herself that the subject was one it was well not to go into too deeply?"

Miss Van Vluyck rejoined with precision: "I think that applied only to an investigation of the origin of the–of the–"; and suddenly she found that her usually accurate memory had failed her. "It's part of the subject I never studied myself," she concluded.

"Nor I," said Mrs. Ballinger.

Laura Glyde bent toward them with widened eyes. "And yet it seems– doesn't it–the part that is fullest of an esoteric fascination?

"I don't know on what you base that," said Miss Van Vluyck argumentatively.

"Well, didn't you notice how intensely interested Osric Dane became as soon as she heard what the brilliant foreigner–he *was* a foreigner, wasn't he–had told Mrs. Roby about the origin–the origin of the rite–or whatever you called it?"

Mrs. Plinth looked disapproving, and Mrs. Ballinger visibly wavered. Then she said: "It may not be desirable to touch on the–on that part of the subject in general conversation; but, from the importance it evidently has to a woman of Osric Dane's distinction, I feel as if we ought not to be afraid to discuss it among ourselves–without gloves–though with closed doors, if necessary."

"I'm quite of your opinion," Miss Van Vluyck came briskly to her support; "on condition, that is, that all grossness of language is avoided."

"Oh, I'm sure we shall understand without that," Mrs. Leveret tittered; and Laura Glyde added significantly: "I fancy we can read between the lines," while Mrs. Ballinger rose to assure herself that doors were really closed.

Mrs. Plinth had not yet given her adhesion. "I hardly see," she began, "what benefit is to be derived from investigating such peculiar customs–"

But Mrs. Ballinger's patience had reached the extreme limit of tension.

"This at least," she returned; "that we shall not be placed again in the humiliating position of finding ourselves less up on our own subjects than Fanny Roby!"

Even to Mrs. Plinth this argument was conclusive. She peered furtively about the room and lowered her commanding tones to ask: "Have you got a copy?"

"A–a copy?" stammered Mrs. Ballinger. She was aware that the other members were looking at her expectantly, and that this answer was inadequate, so she supported it by asking another question. "A copy of what?"

Her companions bent their expectant gaze on Mrs. Plinth, who, in turn, appeared less sure of herself than usual. "Why, of–of–the book," she explained.

"What book?" snapped Miss Van Vluyck, almost as sharply as Osric Dane.

Mrs. Ballinger looked at Laura Glyde, whose eyes were interrogatively fixed on Mrs. Leveret. The fact of being deferred to was so new to the latter that it filled her with an insane temerity. "Why, Xingu, of course!" she exclaimed.

A profound silence followed this challenge to the resources of Mrs. Ballinger's library, and the latter, after glancing nervously toward the Books of the Day, returned with dignity: "It's not a thing one cares to leave about."

"I should think *not*!" exclaimed Mrs. Plinth.

"It *is* a book, then?" said Miss Van Vluyck.

This again threw the company into disarray, and Mrs. Ballinger, with an impatient sigh, rejoined: "Why–there *is* a book–naturally. . . . "

"Then why did Miss Glyde call it a religion?"

Laura Glyde started up."A religion? I never–"

"Yes, you did," Miss Van Vluyck insisted; "You spoke of rites; and Mrs. Plinth said it was a custom."

Miss Glyde was evidently making a desperate effort to recall her statement; but accuracy of detail was not her strongest point. At length she began in a deep murmur: "Surely they used to do something of the kind at the Eleusinian mysteries–"

"Oh–" said Miss Van Vluyck, on the verge of disapproval; and Mrs. Plinth protested: "I understood there was to be no indelicacy!"

Mrs. Ballinger could not control her irritation. "Really, it is too bad that we should not be able to talk the matter over quietly among ourselves. Personally, I think that if one goes into Xingu at all–"

"Oh, so do I!" cried Miss Glyde.

"And I don't see how one can avoid doing so, if one wishes to keep up with the Thought of the Day–"

Mrs. Leveret uttered an exclamation of relief. "There–that's it!" she interposed.

"What's it?" the President took her up.

"Why—it's a—a Thought: I mean a philosophy."

This seemed to bring a certain relief to Mrs. Ballinger and Laura Glyde, but Miss Van Vluyck said: "Excuse me if I tell you that you're all mistaken. Xingu happens to be a language."

"A language!" the Lunch Club cried.

"Certainly. Don't you remember Fanny Roby's saying that there were several branches, and that some were hard to trace? What could that apply to but dialects?"

Mrs. Ballinger could not longer restrain a contemptuous laugh. "Really, if the Lunch Club has reached such a pass that it has to go to Fanny Roby for instruction on a subject like Xingu, it had almost better cease to exist!"

"It's really her fault for not being clearer," Laura Glyde put in.

"Oh, clearness and Fanny Roby!" Mrs. Ballinger shrugged. "I dare say we shall find she was mistaken on almost every point."

"Why not look it up?" said Mrs. Plinth.

As a rule this recurrent suggestion of Mrs. Plinth's was ignored in the heat of discussion, and only resorted to afterward in the privacy of each member's home. But on the present occasion the desire to ascribe their own confusion of thought to the vague and contradictory nature of Mrs. Roby's statements caused the members of the Lunch Club to utter a collective demand for a book of reference.

At this point the production of her treasured volume gave Mrs. Leveret, for a moment, the unusual experience of occupying the center front; but she was not able to hold it long, for *Appropriate Allusions* contained no mention of Xingu.

"Oh, that's not the kind of thing we want!" exclaimed Miss Van Vluyck. She cast a disparaging glance over Mrs. Ballinger's assortment of literature, and added impatiently: "Haven't you any useful books?"

"Of course I have," replied Mrs. Ballinger indignantly; "I keep them in my husband's dressing room."

From this region, after some difficulty and delay, the parlormaid produced the W-Z volume of an *Encyclopedia* and, in deference to the fact that the demand for it had come from Miss Van Vluyck, laid the ponderous tome before her.

There was a moment of painful suspense while Miss Van Vluyck rubbed her spectacles, adjusted them, and turned to Z; and a murmur of surprise when she said: "It isn't here."

"I suppose," said Mrs. Plinth, "it's not fit to be put in a book of reference."

"Oh, nonsense!" exclaimed Mrs. Ballinger. "Try X."

Miss Van Vluyck turned back through the volume, peering shortsightedly up and down the pages, till she came to a stop and remained motionless, like a dog on a point.

"Well, have you found it?" Mrs. Ballinger inquired after a considerable delay.

"Yes. I've found it," said Mrs. Van Vluyck in a queer voice.

Mrs. Plinth hastily interposed: "I beg you won't read it aloud if there's anything offensive."

Miss Van Vluyck, without answering, continued her silent scrutiny.

"Well, what *is* it?" exclaimed Laura Glyde excitedly.

"*Do* tell us!" urged Mrs. Leveret, feeling that she would have something awful to tell her sister.

Miss Van Vluyck pushed the volume aside and turned slowly toward the expectant group.

"It's a river."

"A *river*?"

"Yes: in Brazil. Isn't that where she's been living?"

"Who? Fanny Roby? Oh, but you must be mistaken. You've been reading the wrong thing," Mrs. Ballinger exclaimed, leaning over her to seize the volume.

"It's the only Xingu in the *Encyclopedia*; and she *has* been living in Brazil," Miss Van Vluyck persisted.

"Yes: her brother has a consulship there," Mrs. Leveret interposed.

"But it's too ridiculous! I—we—why we *all* remember studying Xingu last year—or the year before last," Mrs. Ballinger stammered.

"I thought I did when *you* said so," Laura Glyde avowed.

"*I* said so?" cried Mrs. Ballinger.

"Yes. You said it had crowded everything else out of your mind."

"Well *you* said it had changed your whole life!"

"For that matter Miss Van Vluyck said she had never grudged the time she'd given it."

Mrs. Plinth interposed: "I made it clear that I knew nothing whatever of the original."

Mrs. Ballinger broke off the dispute with a grown. "Oh, what does it all matter if she's been making fools of us? I believe Miss Van Vluyck's right—she was talking of the river all the while!"

"How could she? It's too preposterous," Mrs. Glyde exclaimed.

"Listen." Mrs. Van Vluyck had repossessed herself of the Encyclopedia, and restored her spectacles to a nose reddened by excitement. " 'The Xingu, one of the principal rivers of Brazil, rises on the plateau of Mato Grosso, and flows in a northerly direction for a length of no less than one-thousand one hundred and eighteen miles, entering the Amazon near the mouth of the latter river. The upper course of the Xingu is auriferous and fed by numerous branches. Its source was first discovered in 1884 by the German explorer von den Steinen, after a difficult and dangerous expedition through a region inhabited by tribes still in the Stone Age of culture.' "

The ladies received this communication in a state of stupefied silence from which Mrs. Leveret was the first to rally. "She certainly *did* speak of its having branches."

The word seemed to snap the last thread of their incredulity. "And of its great length," gasped Mrs. Ballinger.

"She said it was awfully deep, and you couldn't skip—you just had to wade through," Mrs. Glyde added.

The idea worked its way more slowly through Mrs. Plinth's compact resistances. "How could there be anything improper about a river?" she inquired.

"Improper?"

"Why, what she said about the source—that it was corrupt?"

"Not corrupt, but hard to get at," Laura Glyde corrected. "Someone who'd been there had told her so. I dare say it was the explorer himself—doesn't it say the expedition was dangerous?"

"'Difficult and dangerous,'" read Miss Van Vluyck.

Mrs. Ballinger pressed her hands to her throbbing temples. "There's nothing she said that wouldn't apply to a river—to this river!" She swung about excitedly to the other members. "Why, do you remember her telling us that she hadn't read *The Supreme Instant* because she'd taken it on a boating party while she was staying with her brother, and someone had 'shied' it overboard—'shied' of course was her own expression."

The ladies breathlessly signified that the expression had not escaped them.

"Well—and then didn't she tell Osric Dane that one of her books was simply saturated with Xingu? Of course it was, if one of Mrs. Roby's rowdy friends had thrown it into the river!"

This surprising reconstruction of the scene in which they had just participated left the members of the Lunch Club inarticulate. At length, Mrs. Plinth, after visibly laboring with the problem, said in a heavy tone: "Osric Dane was taken in too."

Mrs. Leveret took courage at this. "Perhaps that's what Mrs. Roby did it for. She said Osric Dane was a brute, and she may have wanted to give her a lesson."

Miss Van Vluyck frowned. "It was hardly worth-while to do it at our expense."

"At least," said Miss Glyde with a touch of bitterness, "she succeeded in interesting her, which was more than we did."

"What chance had we?" rejoined Mrs. Ballinger. "Mrs. Roby monopolized her from the first. And *that,* I've no doubt, was her purpose—to give Osric Dane a false impression of her own standing in the club. She would hesitate at nothing to attract attention: we all know how she took in poor Professor Foreland."

"She actually makes him give bridge teas every Thursday," Mrs. Leveret piped up.

Laura Glyde struck her hands together. "Why this is Thursday, and it's *there* she's gone, of course; and taken Osric with her!"

"And they're shrieking over us at this moment," said Mrs. Ballinger between her teeth.

This possibility seemed too preposterous to be admitted. "She would hardly dare," said Miss Van Vluyck, "confess the imposture to Osric Dane."

"I'm not so sure: I thought I saw her make a sign as she left. If she hadn't made a sign, why should Osric Dane have rushed out after her?"

"Well, you know, we'd all been telling her how wonderful Xingu was, and she said she wanted to find out more about it," Mrs. Leveret said, with a tardy impulse of justice to the absent.

This reminder, far from mitigating the wrath of the other members, gave it a stronger impetus.

"Yes—and that's exactly what they're both laughing over now," said Laura Glyde ironically.

Mrs. Plinth stood up and gathered her expensive furs about her monumental form. "I have no wish to criticize," she said; "but unless the Lunch Club can protect its members against the recurrence of such—such unbecoming scenes, I for one—"

"Oh, so do I!" agreed Miss Glyde, rising also.

Miss Van Vluyck closed the Encyclopedia and proceeded to button herself into her jacket. "My time is really too valuable—" she began.

"I fancy we are all of one mind," said Mrs. Ballinger, looking searchingly at Mrs. Leveret, who looked at the others.

"I always deprecate anything like a scandal—" Mrs. Plinth continued.

"She has been the cause of one today!" exclaimed Miss Glyde.

Mrs. Leveret moaned: "I don't see how she *could*!" and Miss Van Vluyck said, picking up her notebook: "Some women stop at nothing."

"—But if," Mrs. Plinth took up her argument impressively, "anything of the kind had happened in *my* house" (it never would have, her tone implied), "I should have felt that I owed it to myself either to ask for Mrs. Roby's resignation—or to offer mine."

"Oh, Mrs. Plinth—" gasped the Lunch Club.

"Fortunately for me," Mrs. Plinth continued with an awful magnanimity, "the matter was taken out of my hands by our President's decision that the right to entertain distinguished guests was a privilege vested in her office; and I think the other members will agree that, as she was alone in this opinion, she ought to be alone in deciding on the best way of effacing its—its really deplorable consequences."

A deep silence followed this outbreak of Mrs. Plinth's long-stored resentment.

"I don't see why *I* should be expected to ask her to resign—" Mrs. Ballinger at length began; but Laura Glyde turned back to remind her: "You know she made you say that you'd got on swimmingly in Xingu."

An ill-timed giggle escaped from Mrs. Leveret, and Mrs. Ballinger energetically continued "—But you needn't think for a moment that I'm afraid to!"

The door of the drawing room closed on the retreating backs of the Lunch Club, and the President of that distinguished association, seating herself at her writing table, and pushing away a copy of *The Wings of Death* to make room for her elbow, drew forth a sheet of the club's notepaper, on which she began to write: "My dear Mrs. Roby—"

SINCLAIR LEWIS

1931

Land

He was named Sidney, for the sake of elegance, just as his parents had for elegance in their Brooklyn parlor a golden-oak
combination bookcase, desk, and shield-shaped mirror. But Sidney Dow was
descended from generations of Georges and Johns, of Lorens and Lukes and
Nathans.

He was little esteemed in the slick bustle of his city school. He seemed
a loutish boy, tall and heavy and slow-spoken, and he was a worry to his
father. For William Dow was an ambitious parent. Born on a Vermont farm,
William felt joyously that he had done well in the great city of Brooklyn. He
had, in 1885, when Sidney was born, a real bathroom with a fine tin tub, gas
lights, and a handsome phaeton with red wheels, instead of the washtub in
the kitchen for Saturday-night baths, the kerosene lamps, and the heavy old
buggy which his father still used in Vermont. Instead of being up at 5:30, he
could loll abed till a quarter of seven, and he almost never, he chuckled in
gratification at his progress, was in his office before a quarter to eight.

But the luxury of a red-wheeled carriage and late lying did not indicate
that William's Yankee shrewdness had been cozened by urban vice, or that he
was any less solid and respectable than old George, his own father. He was a
deacon in the Universalist church, he still said grace before meals, and he
went to the theater only when Ben-Hur was appearing.

For his son, Sidney, William Dow had even larger ambitions. William
himself had never gone to high school, and his business was only a cautious
real-estate and insurance agency, his home a squatting two-story brick
house in a red, monotonous row. But Sidney—he should go to college, he

should be a doctor or a preacher or a lawyer, he should travel in Europe, he should live in a three-story graystone house in the Forties in Manhattan, he should have a dress suit and wear it to respectable but expensive hops!

William had once worn dress clothes at an Odd Fellows' ball, but they had been rented.

To enable Sidney to attain all these graces, William toiled and sacrificed and prayed. American fathers have always been as extraordinary as Scotch fathers in their heroic ambitions for their sons—and sometimes as unscrupulous and as unwise. It bruised William and often it made him naggingly unkind to see that Sidney, the big slug, did not "appreciate how his parents were trying to do for him and give him every opportunity." When they had a celebrated Columbia Heights physician as guest for dinner, Sidney merely gawked at him and did not at all try to make an impression.

"Suffering cats! You might have been one of your uncles still puttering around with dirty pitchforks back on the farm! What are you going to do with yourself, anyway?" raged William.

"I guess maybe I'd like to be a truck driver," mumbled Sidney.

Yet, even so, William should not have whipped him. It only made him sulkier.

To Sidney Dow, at sixteen, his eagerest memories were of occasional weeks he had spent with his grandfather and uncles on the Vermont farm, and the last of these was seven years back now. He remembered Vermont as an enchanted place, with curious and amusing animals—cows, horses, turkeys. He wanted to return, but his father seemed to hate the place. Of Brooklyn, Sidney liked nothing save livery stables and occasional agreeable gang fights, with stones inside iced snowballs. He hated school, where he had to cramp his big knees under trifling desks, where irritable lady teachers tried to make him see the importance of A's going more rapidly than B to the town of X, a town in which he was even less interested than in Brooklyn—school where hour on hour he looked over the top of his geography and stolidly hated the whiskers of Longfellow, Lowell, and Whittier. He hated the stiff, clean collar and the itchy, clean winter underwear connected with Sunday school. He hated hot evenings smelling of tarry pavements, and cold evenings when the pavements were slippery.

But he didn't know that he hated any of these things. He knew only that his father must be right in saying that he was a bad, disobedient, ungrateful young whelp, and in his heart he was as humble as in his speech he was sullen.

Then, at sixteen, he came to life suddenly, on an early June morning, on his grandfather's farm. His father had sent him up to Vermont for the summer, had indeed exiled him, saying grimly, "I guess after you live in that tumble-down big old shack and work in the fields and have to get up early, instead of lying abed till your majesty is good and ready to have the girl wait on you—I guess that next fall you'll appreciate your nice home and school and church here, young man!" So sure of himself was his father that Sidney was convinced he was going to encounter hardship on the farm, and all the way up, in the smarting air of the smoker on the slow train, he wanted to howl. The train arrived at ten in the evening, and he was met by his uncle Rob, a man rugged as a pine trunk and about as articulate.

"Well! Come for the summer!" said Uncle Rob; and after they had driven three miles: "Got new calf—yeh, new calf"; and after a mile more: "Your pa all right?" And that was all the conversation of Uncle Rob.

Seven years it was since Sidney had been in any country wilder than Far Rockaway, and the silent hills of night intimidated him. It was a roaring silence, a silence full of stifled threats. The hills that cut the stars so high up on either side the road seemed walls that would topple and crush him, as a man would crush a mosquito between his two palms. And once he cried out when, in the milky light from the lantern swung beneath the wagon, he saw a porcupine lurch into the road before them. It was dark, chill, unfriendly, and, to the boy, reared to the lights and cheery voices of the city, even though he hated them, it was appallingly lonely.

His grandfather's house was dark when they arrived. Uncle Rob drove into the barn, jerked his thumb at a ladder up to the haymow and muttered, "Y'sleep up there. Not allowed t' smoke. Take this lantern when we've unharnessed. Sure to put it out. No smoking in the barn. Too tired to help?"

Too tired? Sidney would have been glad to work till daylight if Uncle Rob would but stay with him. He was in a panic at the thought of being left in the ghostly barn where, behind the pawing of horses and the nibble of awakened cows, there were the sounds of anonymous wild animals—scratchings, squeaks, patterings overhead. He made the task as slow as possible, though actually he was handy with horses, for the livery stables of Brooklyn had been his favorite refuge and he had often been permitted to help the hostlers, quite free.

"Gee, Uncle Rob, I guess I'm kind of all thumbs about unharnessing and like that. Seven years since I been here on the farm."

"That so? G'night. Careful of that lantern now. And no smoking!"

The barn was blank as a blind face. The lantern was flickering, and in that witching light the stalls and the heap of sleighs, plows, old harness, at the back wall of the barn were immense and terrifying. The barn was larger than his whole house in Brooklyn, and ten times as large it seemed in the dimness. He could not see clear to the back wall, and he imagined abominable monsters lurking there. He dashed at the ladder up to the haymow, the lantern handle in his teeth and his imitation-leather satchel in one hand.

And the haymow, rising to the darkness of its hand-hewn rafters, seemed vaster and more intimidating than the space below. It one corner a space had been cleared of hay for a cot, with a blanket and a pea-green comforter, and for a chair and a hinged box. Sidney dashed at the cot and crawled into it, waiting only to take off his shoes and jacket. Till the lantern flame died down to a red rim of charred wick, he kept it alight. Then utter darkness leaped upon him.

A rooster crowed, and he startled. Past him things scampered and chittered. The darkness seemed to swing in swift eddies under the rafters, the smell of dry hay choked him—and he awoke to light slipping in silver darts through cracks in the roof, and to jubilant barn swallows diving and twittering.

"Gee, I must have fell asleep!" he thought. He went down the ladder, and now, first, he saw the barn.

Like many people slow of thought and doubtful of speech, Sidney Dow had moments of revelation as complete as those of a prophet, when he beheld a scene or a person or a problem in its entirety, with none of the confusing thoughts of glibber and more clever people with their minds forever running off on many tracks. He saw the barn—really saw it, instead of merely glancing at it, like a normal city boy. He saw that the beams, hand-hewn, gray with sixty years, were beautiful; that the sides of the stalls, polished with rubbing by the shoulders of cattle dead these fifty years, were beautiful; that the harrow, with its trim spikes kept sharp and rustless, was beautiful; that most beautiful of all were the animals—cows and horses, chickens that walked with bobbing heads through the straw, and a calf tethered to the wall. The calf capered with alarm as he approached it; then stood considering him with great eyes, letting him stroke its head and at last licking his hand. He slouched to the door of the barn and looked down the valley. More radiant in that early morning light than even the mountain tops covered with maples and hemlock were the upland clearings with white houses and red barns.

"Gosh, it looks nice! It's—it's sort of—it looks nice! I didn't hardly get it when I was here before. But gee"—with all the scorn of sixteen—"I was just a kid then!"

With Uncle Rob he drove the cows to pasture; with Uncle Ben he plowed; with his grandfather, sourly philanthropic behind his beard, he split wood. He found an even greater menagerie than in the barn—turkeys, geese, ducks, pigs and, in the woods and mowings, an exciting remnant of woodchucks, chipmunks, rabbits, and infrequent deer. With all of them—uncles and grandfather, beasts, wild or tame—he felt at home. They did not expect him to chatter and show off, as had his gang in Brooklyn; they accepted him.

That, perhaps, more than any ancestral stoutness, more than the beauty of the land, made a farmer of him. He was a natural hermit, and here he could be a hermit without seeming queer.

And a good farmer he was – slow but tireless, patient, unannoyed by the endless work, happy to go to bed early and be up at dawn. For a few days his back felt as though he were burning at the stake, but after that he could lift all day in the hayfield or swing the scythe or drive the frisky young team. He was a good farmer, and he slept at night. The noises which on his first night had fretted his city-tortured nerves were soporific now, and when he heard the sound of a distant train, the barking of a dog on the next farm, he inarticulately told himself that they were lovely.

"You're pretty fair at working," said Uncle Rob, and that was praise almost hysterical.

Indeed, in one aspect of labor, Sidney was better than any of them, even the pine-carved Uncle Rob. He could endure wet dawns, wild winds, all-day drenching. It seems to be true that farmers are more upset by bad weather than most outdoor workers – sailors, postmen, carpenters, brakemen, teamsters. Perhaps it is because they are less subject to higher authority; except for chores and getting in the hay, they can more nearly do things in their own time, and they build up a habit of taking shelter on nasty days. Whether or no, it was true that just the city crises that had vexed Sidney, from icy pavements to sudden fire alarms, had given him the ability to stand discomforts and the unexpected, like a little Cockney surprisingly stolid in the trenches.

He learned the silent humor of the authentic Yankee. Evenings he sat with neighbors on the bench before the general store. To a passing stranger they seemed to be saying nothing, but when the stranger had passed, Uncle Rob would drawl, "Well, if I had fly nets on my hosses, guess I'd look stuck-up too!" and the others would chuckle with contempt at the alien.

This, thought Sidney, was good talk – not like the smart gabble of the city. It was all beautiful, and he knew it, though in his vocabulary there was no such word as "beautiful," and when he saw the most flamboyant sunset he said only, "Guess going to be clear tomorrow."

And so he went back to Brooklyn, not as to his home but as to prison, and as a prison corridor he saw the narrow street with little houses like little cells.

Five minutes after he had entered the house, his father laughed. "Well, did you get enough of farming? I guess you'll appreciate your school now! I won't rub it in, but I swear, how Rob and Ben can stand it –"

"I kind of liked it, Dad. I think I'll be a farmer. I – kind of liked it."

His father had black side whiskers, and between them he had thin cheeks that seemed, after Uncle Rob and Uncle Ben, pallid as the under side of a toadstool. They flushed now, and William shouted:

"You're an idiot! What have I done to have a son who is an idiot? The way I've striven and worked and economized to give you a chance to get ahead, to do something worth while, and then you want to slip right back and be ordinary, like your uncles! So you think you'd like it! You're a fool! Sure you like it in summer, but if you knew it like I do—rousted out to do the chores five o'clock of a January morning, twenty below zero, and maybe have to dig through two feet of snow to get to the barn! Have to tramp down to the store, snowstorm so thick you can't see five feet in front of you!"

"I don't guess I'd mind it much."

"Oh, you don't! Don't be a fool! And no nice company like here—go to bed with the chickens, a winter night, and no nice lodge meeting or church supper or lectures like there is here!"

"Don't care so much for those things. Everybody talking all the while. I like it quiet, like in the country."

"Well, you will care so much for those things, or I'll care you, my fine young man! I'm not going to let you slump back into being a rube like Ben, and don't you forget it! I'll make you work at your books! I'll make you learn to appreciate good society and dressing proper and getting ahead in the world and amounting to something! Yes, sir, amounting to something! Do you think for one moment that after the struggle I've gone through to give you a chance—the way I studied in a country school and earned my way through business college and went to work at five dollars a week in real-estate office and studied and economized and worked late, so I could give you this nice house and advantages and opportunity— No, sir! You're going to be a lawyer or a doctor or somebody that amounts to something, and not a rube!"

It would have been too much to expect of Sidney's imagination that he should have seen anything fine and pathetic in William's fierce ambition. That did not move him, but rather fear. He could have broken his father in two, but the passion in this blenched filing-case of a man was such that it hypnotized him.

For days, miserably returned to high school, he longed for the farm. But his mother took him aside and begged: "You musn't oppose your father so, dearie. He knows what's best for you, and it would just break his heart if he thought you were going to be a common person and not have something to show for all his efforts."

So Sidney came to feel that it was some wickedness in him that made him prefer trees and winds and meadows and the kind cattle to trolley cars and offices and people who made little, flat, worried jokes all day long.

He barely got through high school. His summer vacations he spent in warehouses, hoisting boxes. He failed to enter medical school, botched his examinations shockingly—feelingly wicked at betraying his father's ambitions—and his father pushed him into a second-rate dental school with sketchy requirements, a school now blessedly out of existence.

"Maybe you'd be better as a dentist anyway. Requires a lot of manipulation, and I will say you're good with your hands," his father said, in relief that now Sidney was on the highway to fortune and respectability.

But Sidney's hands, deft with hammer and nails, with reins or hoe or spade, were too big, too awkward for the delicate operations of dentistry. And in school he hated the long-winded books with their queer names and shocking colored plates of man's inwards. The workings of a liver did not interest him. He had never seen a liver, save that of a slain chicken. He would turn from these mysteries to a catalogue of harvesting machinery or vegetable seed. So with difficulty he graduated from this doubtful school, and he was uneasy at the pit of his stomach, even when his father, much rejoicing now, bought for him a complete dental outfit, and rented an office, on the new frontier of the Bronx, in the back part of a three-story red-brick apartment house.

His father and mother invited their friends over from Brooklyn to admire the office, and served them coffee and cake. Not many of them came, which was well, for the office was not large. It was really a single room, divided by a curtain to make a reception hall. The operating room had pink-calcimined walls and, for adornment, Sidney's diploma and a calendar from a dental supply house which showed, with no apparent appropriateness, a view of Pike's Peak.

When they had all gone, mouthing congratulations, Sidney looked wistfully out on the old pasture land which, fifteen years later, was to be filled solidly with tall, cheap apartment houses and huge avenues with delicatessen shops and movie palaces. Already these pastures were doomed and abandoned. Cows no longer grazed there. Gaunt billboards lined the roads and behind their barricades were unkempt waste lands of ashes and sodden newspapers. But they were open grass, and they brought back the valleys and uplands of Vermont. His great arms were hungry for the strain of plowing, and he sighed and turned back to his shining new kit of tools.

The drill he picked up was absurd against his wide red palm. All at once he was certain that he knew no dentistry, and that he never would; that he would botch every case; that dreadful things would happen – suits for malpractice –

Actually, as a few and poorly paying neighborhood patients began to come in, the dreadful things didn't happen. Sidney was slow, but he was careful; if he did no ingenious dental jeweling, he did nothing wrong. He learned early what certain dentists and doctors never learn – that nature has not yet been entirely supplanted by the professions. It was not his patients who suffered; it was he.

All day long to have to remain indoors, to stand in one place, bent over gaping mouths, to fiddle with tiny instruments, to produce unctuous sounds of sympathy for cranks who complained of trivial aches, to try to give brisk and confident advice which was really selling talk—all this tortured him.

Then, within one single year, his mother died, his grandfather died on the Vermont farm, Uncle Rob and Uncle Ben moved West, and Sidney met the most wonderful girl in the world. The name of this particular most wonderful girl in the world, who unquestionably had more softness and enchantment and funny little ways of saying things than Helen of Troy, was Mabelle Ellen Pflugmann, and she was cultured; she loved the theater, but rarely attended it; loved also the piano, but hadn't time, she explained, to keep up her practice, because, her father's laundry being in a state of debility, for several years she had temporarily been cashier at the Kwiturwurry Lunch.

They furnished a four-room apartment and went to Vermont for their honeymoon. His grandfather's farm—Sidney wasn't quite sure just who had bought it—was rented out to what the neighborhood considered foreigners— that is, Vermonters from way over beyond the Ridge, fifteen miles away. They took in Sidney and Mabelle. She enjoyed it. She told how sick she had become of the smell and dish clatter of the ole lunch and the horrid customers who were always trying to make love to her. She squealed equally over mountains and ducklings, sunsets and wild strawberries, and as for certain inconveniences—washing with a pitcher and bowl, sleeping in a low room smelling of the chicken run, and having supper in the kitchen with the menfolks in shirt sleeves—she said it was just too darling for words—it was, in fact, sweet. But after ten days of the fortnight on which they had planned, she thought perhaps they had better get back to New York and make sure all the furniture had arrived.

They were happy in marriage. Mabelle saw him, and made him see himself, as a man strong and gallant but shy and blundering. He needed mothering, she said, and he got it and was convinced that he liked it. He was less gruff with his patients, and he had many more of them, for Mabelle caused him to be known socially. Till marriage he had lived in a furnished room, and all evening he had prowled alone, or read dentistry journals and seed catalogues. Now Mabelle arranged jolly little parties—beer and Welsh rabbit and a game of five hundred. If at the Kwiturwurry Lunch she had met many light fellows, West Farms Lotharios, she had also met estimable but bohemian families of the neighborhood—big traveling men whose territory took them as far west as Denver, assistant buyers from the downtown department stores, and the office manager of a large insurance agency.

Mabelle, a chatelaine now, wanted to shine among them, and wanted Sidney to shine. And he, feeling a little cramped in a new double-breasted blue serge coat, solemnly served the beer, and sometimes a guest perceived that here was an honest and solid dentist upon whom to depend. And once they gave a theater party—six seats at a vaudeville house.

Yet Sidney was never, when he awoke mornings, excited about the adventure of standing with bent, aching shoulders over patients all this glorious coming day.

They had two children in three years and began to worry a little about the rent bill and the grocery bill, and Sidney was considerably less independent with grumbling patients that he had been. His broad shoulders had a small stoop, and he said quite humbly, "Well, I'll try my best to fix 'em to your satisfaction, Mrs. Smallberg," and sometimes his thick fingers tapped nervously on his chin as he talked. And he envied now, where once he had despised them, certain dental-school classmates who knew little of dentistry, but who were slick dressers and given to verbal chucklings under the chin, who had made money and opened three-room offices with chintz chairs in the waiting room. Sidney still had his old office, with no assistant, and the jerry-built tenement looked a little shabby now beside the six-story apartment houses of yellow brick trimmed with marble which had sprung up all about it.

Then their children, Rob and Willabette, were eight and six years old, and Mabelle began to nag Sidney over the children's lack of clothes as pretty as those of their lovely little friends at school.

And his dental engine—only a treadle affair at that—was worn out. And his elbows were always shiny. And in early autumn his father died.

His father died, muttering, "You've been a good boy, Sid, and done what I told you to. You can understand and appreciate now why I kept you from being just a farmer and gave you a chance to be a professional man. I don't think Mabelle comes from an awful good family, but she's a spunky little thing, and real bright, and she'll keep you up to snuff. Maybe some day your boy will be a great, rich banker or surgeon. Keep him away from his Vermont relations—no ambition, those folks. My chest feels so tight! Bless you, Sid!"

He was his father's sole heir. When the will was read in the shabby lawyer's office in Brooklyn, he was astonished to find that his father still owned—that he himself now owned—the ancestral Vermont home. His slow-burning imagination lighted. He was touched by the belief that his father, for all his pretended hatred of the place, had cherished it and had wanted his son to own it. Not till afterward did he learn from Uncle Rob that William, when his own father had died, had, as eldest son, been given the choice of the farm or half the money in the estate, and had taken the farm to keep Sidney away from it. He had been afraid that if his brothers had it they would welcome Sidney as a partner before he became habituated as a dentist. But in his last days, apparently, William felt that Sidney was safely civilized now and caught. With the farm Sidney inherited some three thousand dollars—not more, for the Brooklyn home was mortgaged.

Instantly and ecstatically, while the lawyer droned senseless advice, Sidney decided to go home. The tenant on his farm—his!—had only two months more on his lease. He'd take it over. The three thousand dollars would buy eight cows—well, say ten—with a cream separator, a tractor, a light truck, and serve to put the old buildings into condition adequate for a few years. He'd do the repairing himself! He arched his hands with longing for the feel of a hammer or a crowbar.

In the hall outside the lawyer's office, Mabelle crowed: "Isn't it—oh, Sid, you do know how sorry I am your father's passed on, but won't it be just lovely! The farm must be worth four thousand dollars. We'll be just as sensible as can be—not blow it all in, like lots of people would. We'll invest the seven thousand, and that ought to give us three hundred and fifty dollars a year—think of it, an extra dollar every day! You can get a dress suit now, and at last I'll have some decent dresses for the evening, and we'll get a new suit for Rob right away—how soon can you get the money? did he say?—and I saw some lovely little dresses for Willabette and the cutest slippers, and now we can get a decent bridge table instead of that rickety old thing, and—"

As she babbled, which she did, at length, on the stairs down from the office, Sidney realized wretchedly that it was going to take an eloquence far beyond him to convert her to farming and the joys of the land. He was afraid of her, as he had been of his father.

"There's a drug store over across. Let's go over and have an ice-cream soda," he said mildly. "Gosh, it's hot for September! Up on the farm now it would be cool, and the leaves are just beginning to turn. They're awful pretty—all red and yellow."

"Oh, you and your old farm!" But in her joy she was amiable.

They sat at the bright-colored little table in the drug store, with cheery colored drinks between them. But the scene should have been an ancient castle at midnight, terrible with wind and lightning, for suddenly they were not bright nor cheery, but black with tragedy.

There was no manner of use in trying to cajole her. She could never understand how he hated the confinement of his dental office; she would say, "Why, you get the chance of meeting all sorts of nice, interesting people, while I have to stay home," and not perceive that he did not want to meet nice, interesting people. He wanted silence and the smell of earth! And he was under her spell as he had been under his father's. Only violently could he break it. He spoke softly enough, looking at the giddy marble of the soda counter, but he spoke sternly:

"Look here, May. This is our chance. You bet your sweet life we're going to be sensible and not blow in our stake! And we're not going to blow it in on a lot of clothes and a lot of fool bridge parties for a lot of fool folks that don't care one red hoot about us except what they get out of us! For that matter, if we were going to stay on in New York—"

"Which we most certainly are, young man!"

"Will you listen to me? I inherited this dough, not you! Gee, I don't want to be mean, May, but you got to listen to reason, and as I'm saying, if we were going to stay in the city, the first thing I'd spend money for would be a new dental engine – an electric one.

"Need it like the mischief – lose patients when they see me pumping that old one and think I ain't up-to-date – which I ain't, but that's no skin off their nose!"

Even the volatile Mabelle was silent at the unprecedented length and vigor of his oration.

"But we're not going to stay. No, sir! We're going back to the old farm, and the kids will be brought up in the fresh air instead of a lot of alleys. Go back and farm it—"

She exploded then, and as she spoke and looked at him with eyes hot with hatred, the first hatred he had ever known in her:

"Are you crazy? Go back to that hole? Have my kids messing around a lot of manure and dirty animals and out working in the hayfield like a lot of cattle? And attend a little one-room school with a boob for a teacher? And play with a lot of nitwit brats? Not on your life they won't! I've got some ambition for 'em, even if you haven't!"

"Why, May, I thought you liked Vermont and the farm! You were crazy about it on our honeymoon, and you said—"

"I did not! I hated it even then, I just said I liked it to make you happy. That stifling little bedroom, and kerosene lamps, and bugs, and no bathroom, and those fools of farmers in their shirt sleeves—Oh, it was fierce! If you go, you go without the kids and me! I guess I can still earn a living! And I guess there's still plenty of other men would like to marry me when I divorce you! And I mean it!"

She did, and Sidney knew she did. He collapsed as helplessly as he had with his father.

"Well, of course, if you can't stand it—" he muttered.

"Well, I'm glad you're beginning to come to your senses! Honest, I think you were just crazy with the heat! But listen, here's what I'll do: I won't kick about your getting the electric dental doodingus if it don't cost too much. Now how do you go about selling the farm?"

There began for this silent man a secret life of plotting and of lies. Somehow – he could not see how – he must persuade her to go to the farm. Perhaps she would die—But he was shocked at this thought, for he loved her and believed her to be the best woman living, as conceivably she may have been. But he did not obey her and sell the farm. He lied. He told her that a Vermont real-estate dealer had written that just this autumn there was no market for farms, but next year would be excellent. And the next year he repeated the lie, and rented the farm to Uncle Rob, who had done well enough on Iowa cornland but was homesick for the hills and sugar groves and placid maples of Vermont. Himself, Sidney did not go to the farm. It was not permitted.

Mabelle was furious that he had not sold, that they had only the three thousand—which was never invested—for clothes and bridge prizes and payments on the car and, after a good deal of irritated talk, his electric dental engine.

If he had always been sullenly restless in his little office, now he was raging. He felt robbed. The little back room, the view—not even of waste land now, but of the center of a cheap block and the back of new tenements —the anguish of patients, which crucified his heavy, unspoken sympathy for them, and that horrible, unending series of wide-stretched mouths and bad molars and tongues—it was intolerable. He thought of meadows scattered with daisies and devil's-paintbrush, of dark, healing thundershowers pouring up the long valley. He must go home to the land!

From the landlord who owned his office he got, in the spring a year and a half after his father's death, the right to garden a tiny patch amid the litter and cement areaways in the center of the block. Mabelle laughed at him, but he stayed late every evening to cultivate each inch of his pocket paradise— a large man, with huge feet, setting them carefully down in a plot ten feet square.

The earth understood him, as it does such men, and before the Long Island market gardeners had anything to display, Sidney had a row of beautiful radish plants. A dozen radishes, wrapped in a tabloid newspaper, he took home one night, and he said vaingloriously to Mabelle, "You'll never get any radishes like these in the market! right out of our own garden!"

She ate one absently. He braced himself to hear a jeering "You and your old garden!" What he did hear was, in its uncaring, still worse: "Yes, they're all right, I guess."

He'd show her! He'd make her see him as a great farmer! And with that ambition he lost every scruple. He plotted. And this was the way of that plotting:

Early in July he said, and casually, "Well, now we got the darn car all paid for, we ought to use it. Maybe we might take the kids this summer and make a little tour for a couple weeks or so."

"Where?"

She sounded suspicious, and in his newborn guile he droned, "Oh, wherever you'd like. I hear it's nice up around Niagara Falls and the Great Lakes. Maybe come back by way of Pennsylvania, and see Valley Forge and all them famous historical sites."

Well, yes, perhaps. The Golheims made a tour last summer and—they make me sick!—they never stop talking about it."

They went. And Mabelle enjoyed it. She was by no means always a nagger and an improver; she was so only when her interests or what she deemed the interests of her children were threatened. She made jokes about the towns through which they passed—any community of less than fifty thousand was to her New Yorkism a "hick hole"—and she even sang jazz and admired his driving, which was bad.

They had headed north, up the Hudson. At Glens Falls he took the highway to the right, instead of left toward the Great Lakes, and she, the city girl, the urban rustic, to whom the only directions that meant anything were East Side and West Side as applied to New York, did not notice, and she was still unsuspicious when he grumbled. "Looks to me like I'd taken the wrong road." Stopping at a filling station, he demanded, "How far is it to Lake George? We ought to be there now."

"Well, stranger, way you're headed, it'll be about twenty-five thousand miles. You're going plumb in the wrong direction."

"I'll be darned! Where are we? Didn't notice the name of the last town we went through."

"You're about a mile from Fair Haven."

"Vermont?"

"Yep."

"Well, I'll be darned! Just think of that! Can't even be trusted to stay in one state and not skid across the border line!"

Mabelle was looking suspicious, and he said with desperate gayety, "Say, do you know what, May? We're only forty miles from our farm! Let's go have a look at it." Mabelle made a sound of protest, but he turned to the children, in the back seat amid a mess of suitcases and tools and a jack and spare inner tubes, and gloated, "Wouldn't you kids like to see the farm where I worked as a kid—where your grandfather and great-grandfather were born? And see your Granduncle Rob? And see all the little chicks, and so on?"

"Oh, yes!" they shrilled together.

With that enthusiasm from her beloved young, with the smart and uniformed young filling-station attendant listening, Mabelle's talent for being righteous and indignant was gagged. Appearances! She said lightly to the filling-station man, "The doctor just doesn't seem to be able to keep the road at all, does he? Well, Doctor, shall we get started?"

Even when they had gone on and were alone and ready for a little sound domestic quarreling, she merely croaked, "Just the same, it seems mighty queer to me!" And after another mile of brooding, while Sidney drove silently and prayed: "Awfully queer!"

But he scarcely heard her. He was speculating, without in the least putting it into words, "I wonder if in the early summer evenings the fireflies still dart above the meadows? I wonder if the full moon, before it rises behind the hemlocks and sugar maples along the Ridge, still casts up a prophetic glory? I wonder if sleepy dogs still bark across the valley? I wonder if the night breeze slips through the mowing? I, who have for fortress and self-respect only a stuffy office room—I wonder if there are still valleys and stars and the quiet night? Or was that all only the dream of youth?"

They slept at Rutland, Sidney all impatient of the citified hotel bedroom. It was at ten in the morning—he drove in twenty minutes the distance which thirty years ago had taken Uncle Rob an hour and a half—that he drove up to the white house where, since 1800, the Dows had been born.

He could see Uncle Rob with the hayrake in the south mowing, sedately driving the old team and ignoring the visitors.

"I guess he prob'ly thinks we're bootleggers," chuckled Sidney. "Come on, you kids! Here's where your old daddy worked all one summer! Let's go! . . . Thirsty? Say, I'll give you a drink of real spring water—not none of this chlorinated city stuff! And we'll see the menagerie."

Before he had finished, Rob and Willabette had slipped over the rear doors of the car and were looking down into the valley with little sounds of excitement. Sidney whisked out almost as quickly as they, while Mabelle climbed down with the dignity suitable to a dweller in the Bronx. He ignored her. He clucked his children round the house to the spring-fed well and pumped a bucket of water.

"Oh, it's so cold, Daddy. It's swell!" said Rob.

"You bet your life it's cold and swell. Say! Don't use words like 'swell'! They're common. But hell with that! Come on, you brats! I'll show you something!"

There were kittens, and two old, grave, courteous cats. There was a calf—heaven knows by how many generations it was descended from the calf that on a June morning, when Sidney was sixteen, had licked his fingers. There were ducklings, and young turkeys with feathers grotesquely scattered over their skins like palm trees in a desert, and unexpected more kittens, and an old, brown-and-white, tail-wagging dog, and a pen of excited little pigs.

The children squealed over all of them until Mabelle caught up, puffing a little.

"Well," she said, "the kits are cute, ain't they?" Then, darkly: "Now that you've got me here, Sid, with your plans and all!"

Uncle Rob crept up, snarling, "What you folks want? . . . By Gracious, if it ain't Sid! This your wife and children? Well, sir!"

It was, Sidney felt, the climax of his plot, and he cried to his son, "Rob! This is your granduncle, that you were named for. How'd you like to stay here on the farm instead of in New York?"

"Hot dog! I'd love it! Them kittens and the li'l' ducks! Oh, they're the berries! You bet I'd like to stay!"

"Oh, I'd love it!" gurgled his sister.

"You would not!" snapped Mabelle. "With no bathroom?"

"We could put one in," growled Sidney.

"On what? On all the money you'd make growing orchids and bananas here, I guess! You kids—how'd you like to walk two miles to school, through the snow, in winter?"

"Oh, that would be slick! Maybe we could kill a deer," said young Rob.

"Yes, and maybe a field mouse could kill you, you dumb-bell! Sure! Lovely! All evening with not a dog-gone thing to do after supper!"

"Why, we'd go to the movies! Do you go to the movies often, Granduncle Rob?"

"Well, afraid in winter you wouldn't get to go to the movies at all. Pretty far into town," hesitated Uncle Rob.

"Not—go—to—the—movies?" screamed the city children, incredulous. It was the most terrible thing they had ever heard of.

Rob, Jr., mourned, "Oh, gee, that wouldn't be so good! Say, how do the hicks learn anything if they don't go to the movies? But still, we could go in the summer, Ma, and in the winter it would be elegant, with sliding and hunting and everything. I'd love it!"

Mabelle cooked supper, banging the pans a good deal and emitting opinions of a house that had no porcelain sink, no water taps, no refrigerator, no gas or electricity. She was silent through supper, silent as Sidney, silent as Uncle Rob. But Sidney was exultant. With the children for allies, he would win. And the children themselves, they were hysterical. Until Mabelle screamed for annoyance; they leaped up from the table, to come back with the most unspeakable and un-Bronxian objects—a cat affectionately carried by his hind leg, but squealing with misunderstanding of the affection, a dead mole, an unwiped oil can, a muck-covered spade.

"But, Mother," they protested, "in the city you never find anything, except maybe a dead lemon."

She shooed them off to bed at eight; herself, sniffily, she disappeared at nine, muttering to Sidney, "I hope you and your boy friend, Uncle Rob, chew the rag all night and get it out of your systems!"

He was startled, for indeed the next step of his plot did concern Uncle Rob and secret parleys.

For half an hour he walked the road, almost frightened by the intensity of stillness. He could fancy catamounts in the birch clumps. But between spasms of skittish city nerves he stretched out his arms, arched back his hands, breathed consciously. This was not just air, necessary meat for the lungs; it was a spirit that filled him.

He knew that he must not tarry after 9:30 for his intrigue with Uncle Rob. Uncle Rob was seventy-five, and in seventy-five times three hundred and sixty-five evenings he had doubtless stayed up later than 9:30 o'clock several times—dancing with the little French Canuck girls at Potsdam Forge as a young man, sitting up with a sick cow since then, or stuck in the mud on his way back from Sunday-evening meeting. But those few times were epochal. Uncle Rob did not hold with roistering and staying up till all hours just for the vanities of the flesh.

Sidney crept up the stairs to Uncle Rob's room.

Mabelle and Sidney had the best bedroom, on the ground floor; young Rob and Bette had Grampa's room, on the second; Uncle Rob lived in the attic.

City folks might have wondered why Uncle Rob, tenant and controller of the place, should have hidden in the attic, with three good bedrooms below him. It was simple. Uncle Rob had always lived there since he was a boy.

Up the narrow stairs, steep as a rock face, Sidney crept, and knocked.

"Who's there!" A sharp voice, a bit uneasy. How many years was it since Uncle Rob had heard anyone knock at his bedroom door?

"It's me, Rob—Sid."

"Oh, well—well, guess you can come in. Wait'll I unlock the door."

Sidney entered his uncle's room for the first time in his life. The hill people, anywhere in the world, do not intrude or encourage intrusion.

Perhaps to fastidious and alien persons Uncle Rob's room would have seemed unlovely. It was lighted by a kerosene lamp, smoking a little, with the wick burned down on one side. There was, for furniture, only a camp cot, with a kitchen chair, a washstand and a bureau. But to make up for this paucity, the room was rather littered. On the washstand, beside a pitcher dry from long disuse, there were a mail-order catalogue, a few packets of seed, a lone overshoe, a ball of twine, a bottle of applejack, and a Spanish War veteran's medal. The walls and ceiling were of plaster so old that they showed in black lines the edges of every lath.

And Sidney liked it—liked the simplicity, liked the freedom from neatness and order and display, liked and envied the old-bach quality of it all.

Uncle Rob, lying on the bed, had prepared for slumber by removing his shoes and outer clothing. He blinked at Sidney's amazing intrusion, but he said amiably enough, "Well, boy?"

"Uncle Rob, can't tell you how glad I am to be back at the old place!"

"H'm."

"Look, I—Golly, I feel skittish as a young colt! Hardly know the old doc, my patients wouldn't! Rob, you got to help me. Mabelle don't want to stay here and farm it—maybe me and you partners, eh? But the kids and I are crazy to. How I hate that ole city! So do the kids."

"Yeh?"

"Sure they do. Didn't you hear how they said they wouldn't mind tramping to school and not having any movies?"

"Sid, maybe you'll understand kids when you get to be a granddad. Kids will always agree with anything that sounds exciting. Rob thinks it would be dandy to hoof it two miles through the snow to school. He won't! Not once he's done it!" Uncle Rob thrust his hands behind his skinny, bark-brown old neck on the maculate pillow. He was making perhaps the longest oration of his life. The light flickered, and a spider moved indignantly in its web in a corner. "No," said Uncle Rob, "he won't like it. I never did. And the school-master used to lick me. I hated it, crawling through that snow and then get licked because you're late. And jiminy–haven't thought of it for thirty years, I guess, maybe forty, but I remember how some big fellow would dare you to put your tongue to your lunch pail, and it was maybe thirty below, and your tongue stuck to it and it took the hide right off! No, I never liked any of it, especially chores."

"Rob, listen! I'm serious! The kids will maybe kind of find it hard at first, but they'll get to like it, and they'll grow up real folks and not city saps. It'll be all right with them. I'll see to that. It's Mabelle. Listen, Rob, I've got a swell idea about her, and I want you to help me. You get hold of the ladies of the township–the Grange members and the Methodist ladies and like that. You tell 'em Mabelle is a swell city girl, and it would be dandy for the neigh-borhood if they could get her to stay here. She's grand, but she does kind of fall for flattery, and in the Bronx she ain't so important, and if these ladies came and told her they thought she was the cat's pajamas, maybe she'd fall for it, and then I guess maybe she might stay, if the ladies came—"

"They wouldn't!"

Uncle Rob had been rubbing his long and prickly chin and curling his toes in his gray socks.

"What do you mean?"

"Well, first place, the ladies round here would be onto your Mabelle. They ain't so backwoods as they was in your time. Take Mrs. Craig. Last three winters, her and her husband, Frank, have packed up the flivver and gone to Florida. But that ain't it. Fact is, Sid, I kind of sympathize with Mabelle."

"What do you mean?"

"Well, I never was strong for farming. Hard life, Sid. Always thought I'd like to keep store or something in the city. You forget how hard the work is here. You with your easy job, just filling a few teeth! No, I can't help you, Sid."

"I see. All right. Sorry for disturbing you."

As he crept downstairs in bewilderment, Sidney prayed–he who so rarely prayed–"O Lord, doesn't anybody but me love the land any more? What is going to happen to us? Why, all our life comes from the land!"

He knew that in the morning he would beg Mabelle to stay for a fortnight–and that she would not stay. It was his last night here. So all night long, slow and silent, he walked the country roads, looking at hemlock branches against the sky, solemnly shaking his head and wondering why he could never rid himself of this sinfulness of longing for the land; why he could never be grown-up and ambitious and worthy, like his father and Mabelle and Uncle Rob.

JAMES GOULD COZZENS

1936

Total Stranger

Clad in a long gray duster, wearing a soft gray cap, my father, who was short and strong, sat bolt upright. Stiffly, he held his gauntleted hands straight out on the wheel. The car jiggled scurrying along the narrow New England country road. Sometimes, indignant, my father drove faster. Then, to emphasize what he was saying, and for no other reason, he drove much slower. Though he was very fond of driving, he drove as badly as most people who had grown up before there were cars to drive.

"Well," I said, "I can't help it."

"Of course you can help it!" my father snorted, adding speed. His severe, dark mustache seemed to bristle a little. He had on tinted sunglasses, and he turned them on me.

"For heaven's sake, look what you're doing!" I cried. He looked just in time, but neither his dignity nor his train of thought was shaken. He continued: "Other boys help it, don't they?"

"If you'd just let me finish," I began elaborately. "If you'd just give me a chance to—"

"Go on, go on," he said. "Only don't tell me you can't help it! I'm very tired of hearing—"

"Well, it's mostly Mr Clifford," I said. "He has it in for me. And if you want to know why, it's because I'm not one of his gang of bootlickers, who hang around his study to bum some tea, every afternoon practically." As I spoke, I could really feel that I would spurn an invitation so dangerous to my independence. The fact that Mr Clifford rarely spoke to me except to give me another hour's detention became a point in my favor. "So, to get back at me, he tells the Old Man—"

"Do you mean Doctor Holt?"

"Everyone calls him that. Why shouldn't I?"

"If you were a little more respectful, perhaps you wouldn't be in trouble all the time."

"I'm not in trouble all the time. I'm perfectly respectful. This year I won't be in the dormitory any more, so Snifty can't make up a lot of lies about me."

My father drove dashing past a farmhouse in a billow of dust and flurry of panic-struck chickens. "Nonsense!" he said. "Sheer nonsense! Doctor Holt wrote that after a long discussion in faculty meeting he was satisfied that your attitude—"

"Oh, my attitude!" I groaned. "For heaven's sake, a fellow's attitude! Of course, I don't let Snifty walk all over me. What do you think I am? That's what that means. It means that I'm not one of Snifty's little pets, hanging around to bum some tea."

"You explained about the tea before," my father said. "I don't feel that it quite covers the case. How about the other masters? Do they also expect you to come around and take tea with them? When they tell the headmaster that you make no effort to do your work, does that mean that they are getting back at you?"

I drew a deep breath in an effort to feel less uncomfortable. Though I was experienced in defending myself, and with my mother, could do it very successfully, there was a certain remote solemnity about my father which made me falter. From my standpoint, talking to my father was a risky business, since he was only interested in proved facts. From his standpoint, I had reason to know, my remarks would form nothing but a puerile exhibition of sorry nonsense. The result was that he avoided, as long as he could, these serious discussions, and I avoided, as long as I could, any discussions at all.

I said laboriously, "Well, I don't think they told him that. Not all of them. And I can prove it, because didn't I get promoted with my form? What did I really flunk, except maybe algebra? I suppose Mr Blackburn was the one who said it." I nodded several times, as though it confirmed my darkest suspicions.

My father said frigidly, "In view of the fact that your grade for the year was forty-four, I wouldn't expect him to be exactly delighted with you."

"Well, I can tell you something about that," I said, ill at ease, but sufficiently portentous. "You can ask anyone. He's such a bum teacher that you don't learn anything in his courses. He can't even explain the simplest thing. Why, once he was working out a problem on the board, and I had to laugh, he couldn't get it himself. Until finally one of the fellows who is pretty good in math had to show him where he made a mistake even a first former wouldn't make. And that's how good he is."

My father said, "Now, I don't want any more argument. I simply want you to understand that this fall term will be your last chance. Doctor Holt is disgusted with you. I want you to think how your mother would feel if you disgrace her by being dropped at Christmas. I want you to stop breaking rules and wasting time."

He let the car slow down for emphasis. He gave me a look, at once penetrating and baffled. He could see no sense in breaking the simple, necessary rules of any organized society; and wasting time was worse than wrong, it was mad and dissolute. Time lost, he very well knew, can never be recovered. Left to himself, my father's sensible impulse would probably have been to give me a thrashing I'd remember. But this was out of the question, for my mother had long ago persuaded him that he, too, believed in reasoning with a child.

Looking at me, he must have found the results of reasoning as unimpressive as ever. He said, with restrained grimness, "And if you're sent home, don't imagine that you can go back to the academy. You'll go straight into the public school and stay there. So just remember that."

"Oh, I'll remember all right," I nodded significantly. I had not spent the last two years without, on a number of occasions, having to think seriously about what I'd do if I were expelled. I planned to approach a relative of mine connected with a steamship company and get a job on a boat.

"See that you do!" said my father. We looked at each other with mild antagonism. Though I was still full of arguments, I knew that none of them would get me anywhere, and I was, as always, a little alarmed and depressed by my father's demonstrable rightness about everything. In my position, I supposed that he would always do his lessons, never break any rules, and probably end up a prefect, with his rowing colors and a football letter—in fact, with everything that I would like, if only the first steps toward them did not seem so dull and difficult. Since they did, I was confirmed in my impression that it was impossible to please him. Since it was impossible, I had long been resolved not to care whether I pleased him or not. Practice had made not caring fairly easy.

As for my father, surely he viewed me with much the same resentful astonishment. My mother was accustomed to tell him that he did not understand me. He must have been prepared to believe it; indeed, he must have wondered if he understood anything when he tried to reconcile such facts as my marks with such contentions as my mother's that I had a brilliant mind. At the moment he could doubtless think of nothing else to say, so he drove faster, as if he wanted to get away from the whole irksome matter; but suddenly the movement of the car was altered by a series of heavy, jolting bumps.

"Got a flat," I said with satisfaction and relief. "Didn't I tell you? Everybody knows those tires pick up nails. You can ask anybody."

My father edged the limping car to the side of the road. In those day you had to expect punctures if you drove any distance, so my father was not particularly put out. He may have been glad to get his mind off a discussion which was not proving very profitable. When we had changed the tire—we had demountable rims, which made it wonderfully easy, as though you were putting something over on a puncture—we were both in better spirits and could resume our normal, polite and distant attitudes. That is, what I said was noncommittal, but not impertinent; and what he said was perfunctory, but not hostile. We got into Sansbury at five o'clock, having covered one hundred and three miles, which passed at the time for a long, hard drive.

When my father drove me up to school, we always stopped at Sansbury. The hotel was not a good or comfortable one, but it was the only convenient place to break the journey. Sansbury was a fair-sized manufacturing town, and the hotel got enough business from traveling salesmen—who, of course, traveled by train—to operate in a shabby way something like a metropolitan hotel. It had a gloomy little lobby with rows of huge armchairs and three or four imitation-marble pillars. There were two surly bellboys, one about twelve, the other about fifty. The elevator, already an antique, was made to rise by pulling on a cable. In the dark dining room a few sad, patient, middle-aged waitresses distributed badly cooked food, much of it, for some reason, served in separate little dishes of the heaviest possible china. It was all awful.

But this is in retrospect. At the time I thought the hotel more pleasant than not. My father had the habit, half stoical, half insensitive, of making the best of anything there was. Though he acted with promptness and decision when it was in his power to change circumstances, he did not grumble when it wasn't. If the food was bad, favored by an excellent digestion, he ate it anyway. If his surroundings were gloomy and the company either boring to him or nonexistent, he did not fidget.

When he could find one of the novels at the moment seriously regarded, he would read it critically. When he couldn't, he would make notes on business affairs in a shorthand of his own invention which nobody else could read. When he had no notes to make, he would retire, without fuss or regret, into whatever his thoughts were.

I had other ideas of entertainment. At home I was never allowed to go to the moving pictures, for my mother considered films themselves silly and cheap, and the theaters likely to be infested with germs. Away from home, I could sometimes pester my father into taking me. As we moved down the main street of Sansbury—my father serenely terrorizing all the rest of the traffic—I was watching to see what was at the motion-picture theater. To my chagrin, it proved to be Annette Kellerman in *A Daughter of the Gods*, and I could be sure I wouldn't be taken to that.

The hotel garage was an old stable facing the kitchen wing across a yard of bare dirt forlornly stained with oil. My father halted in the middle of it and honked his horn until finally the fifty-year-old bellboy appeared, scowling. While my father had an argument with him over whether luggage left in the car would be safe, I got out. Not far away there stood another car. The hood was up, and a chauffeur in his shirt sleeves had extracted and spread out on a sheet of old canvas an amazing array of parts. The car itself was a big impressive landaulet with carriage lamps at the doorposts. I moved toward it and waited until the chauffeur noticed me.

"What's the trouble?" I inquired professionally.

Busy with a wrench, he grunted, "Cam shaft."

"Oh! How much'll she do?"

"Hundred miles an hour."

"Ah, go on!"

"Beat it," he said. "I got no time."

My father called me, and, aggrieved, I turned away, for I felt sure that I had been treated with so little respect because I had been compelled to save my clothes by wearing for the trip an old knickerbocker suit and a gray cloth hat with the scarlet monogram of a summer camp I used to go to on it. Following the aged bellboy through the passage toward the lobby, I said to my father, "Well, I guess I'll go up and change."

My father said, "There's no necessity for that. Just see that you wash properly, and you can take a bath before you go to bed."

"I don't see how I can eat in a hotel, looking like this," I said. "I should think you'd want me to look halfway respectable. I—"

"Nonsense!" said my father. "If you wash your face and hands, you'll look perfectly all right."

The aged bellboy dumped the bags indignantly, and my father went up to the imitation-marble desk to register. The clerk turned the big book around and gave him a pen. I wanted to sign for myself, so I was standing close to him, watching him write in his quick, scratchy script, when suddenly the pen paused. He held his hand, frowning a little.

"Come on," I said, "I want to—"

"Now, you can just wait until I finish," he answered. When he had finished, he let me have the pen. To the clerk he said, "Curious coincidence! I used to know someone by that name." He stopped short, gave the clerk a cold, severe look, as though he meant to indicate that the fellow would be well advised to attend to his own business, and turned away.

The elevator was upstairs. While we stood listening to its creeping, creaky descent, my father said, "Hm!" and shook his head several times. The lighted cage came into view. My father gazed at it a moment. Then he said "Hm!" again. It came shaking to a halt in front of us. The door opened, and a woman walked out. Her eyes went over us in a brief, impersonal glance.

She took two steps, pulled up short, and looked at us again. Then, with a sort of gasp, she said, "Why, Will!"

My father seemed to have changed color a little, but he spoke with his ordinary equability: "How are you, May? I had an idea it might be you."

She came right up to him. She put her hand on his arm. "Will!" she repeated. "Well, now, honestly!" She gave his arm a quick squeeze, tapped it and dropped her hand. "Will, I can't believe it! Isn't it funny! You know, I never planned to stop here. If that wretched car hadn't broken down—"

I was looking at her with blank curiosity, and I saw at once that she was pretty–though not in the sense in which you applied pretty to a girl, exactly. In a confused way, she seemed to me to look more like a picture–the sort of woman who might appear on a completed jigsaw puzzle, or on the back of a pack of cards. Her skin had a creamy, powdered tone. Her eyes had a soft, gay shine which I knew from unconscious observation was not usual in a mature face. Her hair was just so. Very faint, yet very distinct, too, the smell of violets reached me. Although she was certainly not wearing anything resembling evening dress, and, in fact, had a hat on, something about her made me think of my mother when she was ready to go to one of the dances they called assemblies, or of the mothers of my friends who came to dinner looking not at all as they usually looked. I was so absorbed in this feeling of strangeness–I neither liked it nor disliked it; it simply bewildered me–that I didn't hear anything until my father said rather sharply, "John! Say how do you do to Mrs Prentice!"

"I can't get over it!" she was saying. She broke into a kind of bubbling laughter. "Why he's grown up, Will! Oh, dear, doesn't it make you feel queer?"

Ordinarily, I much resented that adult trick of talking about you as if you weren't there, but the grown-up was all right, and she looked at me without a trace of the customary patronage; as though, of course, I saw the joke too. She laughed again. I would not have had the faintest idea why, yet I was obliged to laugh in response.

She asked brightly, "Where's Hilda?"

My father answered, with slight constraint, that my mother was not with us, that he was just driving me up to school.

Mrs Prentice said, "Oh, that's too bad. I'd so like to see her." She smiled at me again and said, "Will, I can't face that dreadful dining room. I was going to have something sent up. They've given me what must be the bridal suite." She laughed. "You should see it! Why don't we all have supper up there?"

"Capital!" my father said.

The word astonished me. I was more or less familiar with most of my father's expressions, and that certainly was not one of them. I thought it sounded funny, but Mrs Prentice said, "Will, you haven't changed a bit! But then, you wouldn't. It comes from having such a wonderful disposition."

The aged bellboy had put our luggage in the elevator and shuffled his feet beside it, glowering at us. "Leave the supper to me," my father said. "I'll see if something fit to eat can be ordered. We'll be down in about half an hour."

In our room, my father gave the aged bellboy a quarter. It was more than a bellboy in a small-town hotel would ever expect to get, and so, more than my father would normally give, for he was very exact in money matters and considered lavishness not only wasteful but rather common, and especially bad for the recipient, since it made him dissatisfied when he was given what he really deserved. He said to me, "You can go in the bathroom first, and see that you wash your neck and ears. If you can get your blue suit out without unpacking everything else, change to that."

While I was splashing around I could hear him using the telephone. It did not work very well, but he must eventually have prevailed over it, for when I came out he had unpacked his shaving kit. With a strop hung on a clothes hook, he was whacking a razor up and down. Preoccupied, he sang, or rather grumbled, to himself, for he was completely tone-deaf: "I am the monarch of the sea, the ruler of the Queen's—"

The room where we found Mrs Prentice was quite a big one, with a large dark-green carpet on the floor, and much carved furniture, upholstered where possible in green velvet of the color of the carpet. Long full glass curtains and green velvet drapes shrouded the windows, so the lights—in brass wall brackets and a wonderfully coiled and twisted chandelier—were on. There was also an oil painting in a great gold frame showing a group of red-trousered French soldiers defending a farmhouse against the Prussians—the type of art I liked most. It all seemed to me tasteful and impressive, but Mrs Prentice said, "Try not to look at it!" She and my father both laughed.

"I don't know what we'll get," my father said. "I did what I could."

"Anything will do," she said. "Will, you're a godsend! I was expiring for a cocktail, but I hated to order one by myself."

I was startled. My father was not a drinking man. At home I could tell when certain people were coming to dinner, for a tray with glasses and a decanter of sherry would appear in the living room about the time I was going upstairs, and a bottle of sauterne would be put in the icebox.

My mother usually had a rehearsal after the table was set, to make sure that the maid remembered how wine was poured.

Sometimes, when I was at the tennis club, my father would bring me into the big room with the bar and we would both have lemonades. I had never actually seen him drink anything else, so I had an impression that drinking was unusual and unnecessary. I even felt that it was reprehensible, since I knew that the man who take care of the garden sometimes had to be spoken to about it.

To my astonishment, my father said, as though it were the most natural thing in the world, "Well, we can't let you expire, May. What'll it be?"

She said, "I'd love a Clover Club, Will. Do you suppose they could make one?"

My father said, "We'll soon find out! But I think I'd better go down and superintend it myself. That bar looks the reverse of promising."

Left alone with Mrs Prentice, my amazement kept me vaguely uncomfortable. I studied the exciting details of the fight for the farmhouse, but I was self-conscious, for I realized that she was looking at me. When I looked at her, she was lighting a gold-tipped cigarette which she had taken from a white cardboard box on the table. She seemed to understand something of my confusion. She said, "Many years ago your father and I were great friends, John. After I was married, I went to England to live – to London. I was there until my husband died, so we didn't see each other. That's why we were both so surprised."

I could not think of anything to say. Mrs Prentice tried again. "You two must have wonderful times together," she said. "He's a lot of fun, isn't he?"

Embarrassed, I inadvertently nodded; and thinking that she had found the right subject, she went on warmly, "He was always the most wonderful swimmer and tennis player, and a fine cyclist. I don't know how many cups he took for winning the century run."

Of course, I had often seen my father play tennis. He played it earnestly, about as well as a strong but short-legged amateur who didn't have much time for it could. He was a powerful swimmer, but he did not impress me particularly, even when he swam, as he was fond of doing, several miles; for he never employed anything but a measured, monotonous breast stroke which moved him through the water with unbending dignity. It was very boring to be in the boat accompanying him across some Maine lake. I had no idea what a century run was, but I guessed it meant bicycling, so my confusion and amazement were all the greater. The fad for bicycling wasn't within my memory. I could as easily imagine my father playing tag or trading cigarette pictures as riding a bicycle.

Mrs Prentice must have wondered what was wrong with me. She could see that I ought to be past the stage when overpowering shyness would be natural. She must have known, too, that she had a more than ordinary gift for attracting people and putting them at ease. No doubt, her failure with me mildly vexed and amused her.

She arose, saying, "Oh, I forgot! I have something." She swept into the room beyond. In a moment she came back with a box in her hands. I had stood up awkwardly when she stood up. She brought the box to me. It was very elaborate. A marvelous arrangement of candied fruits and chocolates filled it. I said, "Thank you very much," I took the smallest and plainest piece of chocolate I could see.

"You mustn't spoil your appetite, must you?" she said, her eyes twinkling, "You take what you want. We won't tell your father."

Her air of cordial conspiracy really warmed me. I tried to smile, but I didn't find myself any more articulate. I said again, "Thank you. This is really all I want."

"All right, John," she said. "We'll leave it on the desk there, in case you change your mind."

The door, which had stood ajar, swung open. In came my father, carrying a battered cocktail shaker wrapped in a napkin. He headed a procession made up of the young bellboy, with a folding table; the old bellboy, with a bunch of roses in a vase; and a worried-looking waitress, with a tray of silver and glasses and folded linen.

"Why, Will," Mrs Prentice cried, "it's just like magic!"

My father said, "What it will be just like, I'm afraid, is the old Ocean House."

"Oh, oh!" Mrs Prentice laughed. "The sailing parties! You know, I haven't thought of those – and those awful buffet suppers!"

"Very good," my father said, looking at the completed efforts of his procession. "Please try to see that the steak is rare and gets here hot. That's all." He filled two glasses with pink liquid from the cocktail shaker. He brought one of them to Mrs Prentice, and, lifting the other, said, "Well, May. Moonlight Bay!"

She looked at him, quick and intent. She began quizzically to smile. It seemed to me she blushed a little. "All right, Will," she said and drank.

They were both silent for an instant. Then, with a kind of energetic abruptness, she said, "Lottie Frazer! Oh, Will, do you know, I saw Lottie a month or two ago."

I sat quiet, recognizing adult conversation and knowing that it would be dull. I fixed my eyes on the battle picture. I tried to imagine myself behind the mottled stone wall with the French infantrymen, but constantly I heard Mrs Prentice laugh. My father kept responding, but with an odd, light, good-humored inflection, as though he knew that she would laugh again as soon as he finished speaking. I could not make my mind stay on the usually engrossing business of thinking myself into a picture.

". . . you were simply furious," I heard Mrs Prentice saying. "I didn't blame you."

My father said, "I guess I was."

"You said you'd break his neck."

They had my full attention, but I had missed whatever it was, for my father only responded, "Poor old Fred!" and looked thoughtfully at his glass. "So you're going back?"

Mrs Prentice nodded. "This isn't really home to me. Becky and I are – well, I can hardly believe we're sisters. She disapproves of me so."

"I don't remember Becky ever approving of anything," my father said, "There's frankness for you."

"Oh, but she approved of you!" Mrs. Prentice looked at him a moment.

"I never knew it," said my father. "She had a strange way of showing it. I had the impression that she thought I was rather wild, and hanging would be too good—"

"Oh, Will, the things you never knew!" Mrs. Prentice shook her head. "And of course, the person Becky really couldn't abide was Joe. They never spoke to each other. Not even at the wedding." Mrs. Prentice gazed at me, but abstractedly, without expression. She started to look back to my father, stopped herself, gave me a quick little smile, and then looked back. My father was examining his glass.

"Ah, well," he said, " 'there is a divinity that shapes our ends, rough-hew them—' "

Mrs. Prentice smiled. "Do you still write poetry?" she asked.

My father looked at her as though taken aback. "No," he said. He chuckled, but not with composure. "And what's more, I never did."

"Oh, but I think I could say some of it to you."

"Don't," said my father. "I'm afraid I was a very pretentious young man." At that moment, dinner arrived on two trays under a number of big metal covers.

I thought the dinner was good, and ate all that was offered me; yet eating seemed to form no more than a pleasant, hardly noticed undercurrent to my thoughts. From time to time I looked at the empty cocktail glasses or the great box of candied fruits and chocolates. I stole glances at Mrs. Prentice's pretty, lively face. Those fragments of conversation repeated themselves to me.

Intently, vainly, I considered "century run," "Ocean House," "Moonlight Bay." I wondered about Fred, whose neck, it seemed, my father thought of breaking; about this Becky and what she approved of; and about the writing of poetry. My mother had done a good deal to acquaint me with poetry. She read things like "Adonais," the "Ode to a Nightingale," "The Hound of Heaven" to me; and though I did not care much for them, I knew enough about poets to know that my father had little in common with pictures of Shelley and Keats. I had never seen a picture of Francis Thompson, but I could well imagine.

Thus I had already all I could handle; and though talk went on during the meal, I hardly heard what they were saying. My attention wasn't taken until Mrs. Prentice, pouring coffee from a little pot, said something about the car.

My father accepted the small cup and answered, "I don't know that it's wise."

"But I've just got to," she said. "I can't make the boat unless—"

"Well, if you've got to, you've got to," my father said. "Are you sure he knows the roads? There are one or two places where you can easily make the wrong turn. I think I'd better get a map I have and mark it for you. It will only take a moment."

"Oh, Will," she said, "that would be such a help."

My father set his cup down and arose with decision. When we were alone, Mrs. Prentice got up too. As I had been taught to, I jumped nervously to my feet. She went and took the box from the desk and brought it to me again.

"Thank you very much," I stammered. I found another small plain piece of chocolate. "I'm going to put the cover on," she said, "and you take it with you."

I made a feeble protesting sound. I was aware that I ought not to accept such a considerable present from a person I did not know, but I realized that, with it, I was bound to be very popular on my arrival – at least, until the evening school meeting, when anything left would have to be turned in.

She could see my painful indecision. She set the box down. She gave a clear warm laugh, extended a hand and touched me on the chin. "John, you're a funny boy!" she said. My mother had sometimes addressed those very words to me, but with an air of great regret; meaning that the way I had just spoken or acted, while not quite deserving punishment, saddened her. Mrs. Prentice's tone was delighted, as though the last thing she meant to do was reprove me. "You don't like strangers to bother you, do you?"

The touch of her hand so astonished me that I hadn't moved a muscle. "I didn't think you were, at first," she said, "but you are! You don't look very much like him, but you can't imagine how exactly—" She broke into that delighted little laugh again. Without warning, she bent forward and kissed my cheek.

I was frightfully embarrassed. My instant reaction was a sense of deep outrage, for I thought that I had been made to look like a child and a fool. Collecting my wits took me a minute, however; and I found then that I was not angry at all. My first fear – that she might mean to imply that I was just a baby or a little boy – was too clearly unfounded. I was not sure just what she did mean, but part of it, I realized was that I had pleased her somehow, that she had suddenly felt a liking for me, and that people she liked, she kissed.

I stood rigid, my face scarlet. She went on at once: "Will you do something for me, John? Run down and see if you can find my chauffeur. His name is Alex. Tell him to bring the car around as soon as he can. Would you do that?"

"Yes, Mrs. Prentice," I said.

I left the room quickly. It was only the second floor, so I found the stairs instead of waiting for the elevator. I went down slowly, gravely, and bewildered, thinking of my father and how extraordinary it all was; how different he seemed and yet I could see, too, that he really hadn't changed. What he said and did was new to me, but not new to him. Somehow it all fitted together. I could feel that.

I came into the lobby and went down the back passage and out to the yard. It was now lighted by an electric bulb in a tin shade over the stable door. A flow of thin light threw shadows upon the bare earth. The hood of the big landaulet was down in place, and the man was putting some things away. "Alex!" I said authoritatively.

He turned sharp, and I said, "Mrs Prentice wants you to bring the car around at once." He continued to look at me a moment. Then he smiled broadly. He touched his cap and said, "Very good, sir."

When I got back upstairs, my father had returned. The old bellboy was taking out a couple of bags. After a moment Mrs Prentice came from the other room with a coat on and a full veil pinned over her face and hat. "Thank you, John," she said to me. "Don't forget this." She nodded at the big box on the table. I blushed and took it.

"Aren't you going to thank Mrs Prentice?" my father asked.

She said, "Oh, Will, he's thanked me already. Don't bother him."

"Bother him!" said my father. "He's not bothered. Why I can remember my father saying to me, 'Step up here, sir, and I'll mend your manners!' And for less than not saying thank you. I'm slack, but I knew my parental duties."

They both laughed, and I found myself laughing too. We all went out to the elevator.

In front of the hotel, at the bottom of the steps, the car stood. "Just see he follows the map," my father said. "You can't miss it." He looked at the sky. "Fine moonlight night! I wouldn't mind driving myself."

"Will," said Mrs Prentice, "Will!" She took his hand in both of hers and squeezed it. "Oh, I hate to say good-by like this! Why, I've hardly seen you at all!"

"There," said my father. "It's wonderful to have seen you, May."

She turned her veiled face toward me. "Well, John! Have a grand time at school!"

I said, "Good-by, Mrs Prentice. Thank you very much for the—"

The chauffeur held the door open, and my father helped her in. There was a thick click of the latch closing. The chauffeur went around to his seat. We stood on the pavement, waiting while he started the engine. The window was down a little, and I could hear Mrs. Prentice saying, "Good-by, good-by."

My father waved a hand, and the car drew away with a quiet, powerful drone. It passed, the sound fading, lights glinting on it, down the almost empty street.

"Well, that's that!" said my father. He looked at me at last and said, "I think you might send a post card to your mother to tell her we got here all right."

I was feeling strangely cheerful and obedient. I thought fleetingly of making a fuss about the movies, but I decided not to. At the newsstand inside, my father bought me a post card showing a covered bridge near the town. I took it to one of the small writing tables by the wall.

"Dear Mother," I wrote with the bad pen, "arrived here safely." I paused. My father had bought a paper and, putting on his glasses, had settled in one of the big chairs. He read with close, critical attention, light shining on his largely bald head, his mustache drawn down sternly. I had seen him reading like that a hundred times, but tonight he did not look quite the same to me. I thought of Mrs Prentice a moment, but when I came to phrase it, I could not think of anything to say. Instead, I wrote: "We drove over this bridge." I paused again for some time, watching my father read, while I pondered. I wrote: "Father and I had a serious talk. Mean to do better at school—"

Unfortunately, I never did do much better at school. But that year and the years following, I would occasionally try to, for I thought it would please my father.

STEPHEN VINCENT BENÉT

1936

The Devil and Daniel Webster

It's a story they tell in the border country, where Massachusetts joins Vermont and New Hampshire.

Yes, Dan'l Webster's dead—or, at least, they buried him. But every time there's a thunderstorm around Marshfield, they say you can hear his rolling voice in the hollows of the sky. And they say that if you go to his grave and speak loud and clear, "Dan'l Webster—Dan'l Webster!" the ground'll begin to shiver and the trees begin to shake. And after a while you'll hear a voice saying, "Neighbor, how stands the Union?" Then you better answer the Union stands as she stood, rock-bottomed and copper-sheathed, one and indivisible, or he's liable to rear right out of the ground. At least, that's what I was told when I was a youngster.

You see, for a while, he was the biggest man in the country. He never got to be President, but he was the biggest man. There were thousands that trusted in him right next to God Almighty, and they told stories about him that were like the stories of patriarchs and such. They said, when he stood up to speak, stars and stripes came right out in the sky, and once he spoke against a river and made it sink into the ground. They said, when he walked the woods with his fishing rod, Killall, the trout would jump out of the streams right into his pockets, for they knew it was no use putting up a fight against him; and, when he argued a case, he could turn on the harps of the blessed and the shaking of the earth underground. That was the kind of man he was, and his big farm up at Marshfield was suitable to him. The chickens he raised were all white meat down through the drumsticks, the cows were tended like children, and the big ram he called Goliath had horns with a curl like a morning-glory vine and could butt through an iron door. But Dan'l wasn't one of your gentlemen farmers; he knew all the ways of the land, and he'd be up by candlelight to see that the chores got done. A man with a mouth like a mastiff, a brow like a mountain and eyes like burning anthracite—that was Dan'l Webster in his prime. And the biggest case he argued never got written down in the books, for he argued it against the devil, nip and tuck and no holds barred. And this is the way I used to hear it told.

There was a man named Jabez Stone, lived at Cross Corners, New Hampshire. He wasn't a bad man to start with, but he was an unlucky man. If he planted corn, he got borers; if he planted potatoes, he got blight. He had good-enough land, but it didn't prosper him; he had a decent wife and children, but the more children he had, the less there was to feed them. If stones cropped up in his neighbor's field, boulders boiled up in his; if he had a horse with the spavins, he'd trade it for one with the staggers and give something extra. There's some folks bound to be like that, apparently. But one day Jabez Stone got sick of the whole business.

He'd been plowing that morning and he'd just broke the plowshare on a rock that he could have sworn hadn't been there yesterday. And, as he stood looking at the plowshare, the off horse began to cough—that ropy kind of cough that means sickness and horse doctors. There were two children down with the measles, his wife was ailing, and he had a whitlow on his thumb. It was about the last straw for Jabez Stone. "I vow," he said, and he looked around him kind of desperate—"I vow it's enough to make a man want to sell his soul to the devil! And I would, too, for two cents!"

Then he felt a kind of queerness come over him at having said what he'd said; though, naturally, being a New Hampshireman, he wouldn't take it back. But, all the same, when it got to be evening and, as far as he could see, no notice had been taken, he felt relieved in his mind, for he was a religious man. But notice is always taken, sooner or later, just like the Good Book says. And, sure enough, next day, about suppertime, a soft-spoken, dark-dressed stranger drove up in a handsome buggy and asked for Jabez Stone.

Well, Jabez told his family it was a lawyer, come to see him about a legacy. But he knew who it was. He didn't like the looks of the stranger, nor the way he smiled with his teeth. They were white teeth, and plentiful—some say they were filed to a point, but I wouldn't vouch for that. And he didn't like it when the dog took one look at the stranger and ran away howling, with his tail between his legs. But having passed his word, more or less, he stuck to it, and they went out behind the barn and made their bargain. Jabez Stone had to prick his finger to sign, and the stranger lent him a silver pin. The wound healed clean, but it left a little white scar.

After that, all of a sudden, things began to pick up and prosper for Jabez Stone. His cows got fat and his horses sleek, his crops were the envy of the neighborhood, and lightning might strike all over the valley, but it wouldn't strike his barn. Pretty soon, he was one of the prosperous people of the country; they asked him to stand for selectman, and he stood for it; there began to be talk of running him for state senate. All in all, you might say the Stone family was as happy and contented as cats in a dairy. And so they were, except for Jabez Stone.

He'd been contented enough, for the first few years. It's a great thing when bad luck turns; it drives most other things out of your head. True, every now and then, especially in rainy weather, the little white scar on his finger would give him a twinge. And once a year, punctual as clockwork, the stranger with the handsome buggy would come driving by. But the sixth year, the stranger lighted, and, after that, his peace was over for Jabez Stone.

The stranger came up through the lower field, switching his boots with a cane—they were handsome black boots, but Jabez Stone never liked the look of them, particularly the toes. And, after he'd passed the time of day, he said, "Well, Mr. Stone, you're a hummer! It's a very pretty property you've got here, Mr. Stone."

"Well, some might favor it and others might not," said Jabez Stone, for he was a New Hampshireman.

"Oh, no need to decry your industry!" said the stranger, very easy, showing his teeth in a smile. "After all, we know what's been done, and it's been according to contract and specifications. So when—ahem—the mortgage falls due next year, you shouldn't have any regrets."

"Speaking of that mortgage, mister," said Jabez Stone, and he looked around for help to the earth and the sky, "I'm beginning to have one or two doubts about it."

"Doubts?" said the stranger, not quite so pleasantly.

"Why, yes," said Jabez Stone. "This being the U.S.A. and me always having been a religious man." He cleared his throat and got bolder. "Yes, sir," he said, "I'm beginning to have considerable doubts as to that mortgage holding in court."

"There's courts and courts," said the stranger, clicking his teeth. "Still, we might as well have a look at the original document." And he hauled out a big black pocketbook, full of papers. "Sherwin, Slater, Stevens, Stone," he muttered. "I Jabez Stone, for a term of seven years—Oh, it's quite in order, I think."

But Jabez Stone wasn't listening, for he saw something else flutter out of the black pocketbook. It was something that looked like a moth, but it wasn't a moth. And as Jabez Stone stared at it, it seemed to speak to him in a small sort of piping voice, terrible small and thin, but terrible human.

"Neighbor Stone!" it squeaked. "Neighbor Stone! Help me! For God's sake, help me!"

But before Jabez Stone could stir hand or foot, the stranger whipped out a big bandanna handkerchief, caught the creature in it, just like a butterfly, and started tying up the ends of the bandanna.

"Sorry for the interruption," he said. "As I was saying—"

But Jabez Stone was shaking all over like a scared horse.

"That's Miser Stevens' voice!" he said, in a croak. "And you've got him in your handkerchief!"

The stranger looked a little embarrassed.

"Yes, I really should have transferred him to the collecting box," he said with a simper, "But there were some rather unusual specimens there and I didn't want them crowded. Well, well, these little contretemps will occur."

"I don't know what you mean by contertan," said Jabez Stone, "but that was Miser Stevens' voice! And he ain't dead! You can't tell me he is! He was just as spry and mean as a woodchuck, Tuesday!"

"In the midst of life—" said the stranger, kind of pious. "Listen!" then a bell began to toll in the valley and Jabez Stone listened, with the sweat running down his face. For he knew it was tolled for Miser Stevens and that he was dead.

"These long-standing accounts," said the stranger with a sigh; "one really hates to close them. But business is business."

He still had the bandanna in his hand, and Jabez Stone felt sick as he saw the cloth struggle and flutter.

"Are they all as small as that?" he asked hoarsely.

"Small?" said the stranger. "Oh, I see what you mean. Why, they vary." He measured Jabez Stone with his eyes, and his teeth showed. "Don't worry, Mr. Stone," he said. "You'll go with a very good grade. I wouldn't trust you outside the collecting box. Now, a man like Dan'l Webster, of course—well, we'd have to build a special box for him, and even at that, I imagine the wingspread would astonish you. But, in your case, as I was saying—"

"Put that handkerchief away!" said Jabez Stone, and he began to beg and to pray. But the best he could get at the end was a three years' extension, with conditions.

But till you make a bargain like that, you've got no idea of how fast four years can run. By the last months of those years, Jabez Stone's known all over the state and there's talk of running him for governor—and it's dust and ashes in his mouth. For every day, when he gets up, he thinks. "There's one more night gone," and every night when he lies down, he thinks of the black pocketbook and the soul of Miser Stevens, and it makes him sick at heart. Till, finally, he can't bear it any longer, and, in the last days of the last year, he hitches up his horse and drives off to seek Dan'l Webster. For Dan'l was born in New Hampshire, only a few miles from Cross Corners, and it's well known that he has a particular soft spot for old neighbors.

It was early in the morning when he got to Marshfield, but Dan'l was up already, talking Latin to the farm hands and wrestling with the ram, Goliath, and trying out a new trotter and working up speeches to make against John C. Calhoun. But when he heard a New Hampshireman had come to see him, he dropped everything else he was doing, for that was Dan'l's way. He gave Jabez Stone a breakfast that five men couldn't eat, went into the living history of every man and woman in Cross Corners, and finally asked him how he could serve him.

Jabez Stone allowed that it was a kind of mortgage case.

"Well, I haven't pleaded a mortgage in a long time, and I don't generally plead now, except before the Supreme Court," said Dan'l, "but, if I can, I'll help you."

"Then I've got hope for the first time in ten years," said Jabez Stone, and told him the details.

Dan'l walked up and down as he listened, hands behind his back, now and then asking a question, now and then plunging his eyes at the floor, as if they'd bore through it like gimlets. When Jabez Stone had finished, Dan'l puffed out his cheeks and blew. Then he turned to Jabez Stone and a smile broke over his face like the sunrise over Monadnock.

"You've certainly given yourself the devil's own row to hoe, Neighbor Stone," he said, "but I'll take your case."

"You'll take it?" said Jabez Stone, hardly daring to believe.

"Yes," said Dan'l Webster. "I've got about seventy-five other things to do and the Missouri Compromise to straighten out, but I'll take your case. For if two New Hampshiremen aren't a match for the devil, we might as well give the country back to the Indians."

Then he shook Jabez Stone by the hand and said, "Did you come down here in a hurry?"

"Well, I admit I made time," said Jabez Stone.

"You'll go back faster," said Dan'l Webster, and he told 'em to hitch up Constitution and Constellation to the carriage. They were matched grays with one white forefoot, and they stepped like greased lightning.

Well, I won't describe how excited and pleased the whole Stone family was to have the great Dan'l Webster for a guest, when they finally got there. Jabez Stone had lost his hat on the way, blown off when they overtook a wind, but he didn't take much account of that. But after supper he sent the family off to bed, for he had most particular business with Mr. Webster. Mrs. Stone wanted them to sit in the front parlor, but Dan'l Webster knew front parlors and said he preferred the kitchen. So it was there they sat, waiting for the stranger, with a jug on the table between them and a bright fire on the hearth–the stranger being scheduled to show up on the stroke of midnight, according to specifications.

Well, most men wouldn't have asked for better company than Dan'l Webster and a jug. But with every tick of the clock Jabez Stone got sadder and sadder. His eyes roved round, and though he sampled the jug you could see he couldn't taste it. Finally, on the stroke of 11:30 he reached over and grabbed Dan'l Webster by the arm.

"Mr. Webster, Mr. Webster!" he said, and his voice was shaking with fear and a desperate courage. "For God's sake, Mr. Webster, harness your horses and get away from this place while you can!"

"You've brought me a long way, neighbor, to tell me you don't like my company," said Dan'l Webster, quite peaceable, pulling at the jug.

"Miserable wretch that I am!" groaned Jabez Stone. "I've brought you a devilish way, and now I see my folly. Let him take me if he wills. I don't hanker after it, I must say, but I can stand it. But you're the Union's stay and New Hampshire's pride! He mustn't get you, Mr. Webster! He mustn't get you!"

Dan'l Webster looked at the distracted man, all gray and shaking in the firelight, and laid a hand on his shoulder.

"I'm obliged to you, Neighbor Stone," he said gently. "It's kindly thought of. But there's a jug on the table and a case in hand. And I never left a jug or a case half finished in my life."

And just at that moment there was a sharp rap on the door.

"Ah," said Dan'l Webster, very coolly, "I thought your clock was a trifle slow, Neighbor Stone." He stepped to the door and opened it. "Come in!" he said.

The stranger came in–very dark and tall he looked in the firelight. He was carrying a box under his arm–a black, japanned box with little air holes in the lid. At the sight of the box, Jabez Stone gave a low cry and shrank into a corner of the room.

"Mr. Webster, I presume," said the stranger, very polite, but with his eyes glowing like a fox's deep in the woods.

"Attorney of record for Jabez Stone," said Dan'l Webster, but his eyes were glowing too. "Might I ask your name?"

"I've gone by a good many," said the stranger carelessly. "Perhaps Scratch will do for the evening. I'm often called that in these regions."

Then he sat down at the table and poured himself a drink from the jug. The liquor was cold in the jug, but it came steaming into the glass.

"And now," said the stranger, smiling and showing his teeth, "I shall call upon you, as a law-abiding citizen, to assist me in taking possession of my property."

Well, with that the argument began–and it went hot and heavy. At first, Jabez Stone had a flicker of hope, but when he saw Dan'l Webster being forced back at point after point, he just scrunched in his corner, with his eyes on that japanned box. For there wasn't any doubt as to the deed or the signature—that was the worst of it. Dan'l Webster twisted and turned and thumped his fist on the table, but he couldn't get away from that. He offered to compromise the case; the stranger wouldn't hear of it. He pointed out the property had increased in value, and state senators ought to be worth more; the stranger stuck to the letter of the law. He was a great lawyer, Dan'l Webster, but we know who's the King of Lawyers, as the Good Book tells us, and it seemed as if, for the first time, Dan'l Webster had met his match.

Finally, the stranger yawned a little. "Your spirited efforts on behalf of your client do you credit, Mr. Webster," he said, "but if you have no more arguments to adduce, I'm rather pressed for time"—and Jabez Stone shuddered.

Dan'l Webster's brow looked dark as a thundercloud.

"Pressed or not, you shall not have this man!" he thundered. "Mr. Stone is an American citizen, and no American citizen may be forced into the service of a foreign prince. We fought England for that in '12 and we'll fight all hell for it again!"

"Foreign?" said the stranger. "And who calls me a foreigner?"

"Well, I never yet heard of the dev—of your claiming American citizenship," said Dan'l Webster with surprise.

"And who with better right?" said the stranger, with one of his terrible smiles. "When the first wrong was done to the first Indian, I was there. When the first slaver put out for the Congo, I stood on her deck. Am I not in your books and stories and beliefs, from the first settlements on? Am I not spoken of, still, in every church of New England? 'Tis true the North claims me for a Southerner and the South for a Northerner, but I am neither. I am merely an honest American like yourself—and of the best descent—for, to tell the truth, Mr. Webster, though I don't like to boast of it, my name is older in this country than yours."

"Aha!" said Dan'l Webster, with the veins standing out in his forehead. "Then I stand on the Constitution! I demand a trial for my client!"

"The case is hardly one for an ordinary court," said the stranger, his eyes flickering. "And, indeed, the lateness of the hour—"

"Let it be any court you choose, so it is an American judge and an American jury!" said Dan'l Webster in his pride. "Let it be the quick or the dead; I'll abide the issue!"

"You have said it," said the stranger, and pointed his finger at the door. And with that, and all of a sudden, there was a rushing of wind outside and a noise of footsteps. They came, clear and distinct, through the night. And yet, they were not like the footsteps of living men.

"In God's name, who comes by so late?" cried Jabez Stone, in an ague of fear.

"The jury Mr. Webster demands," said the stranger, sipping at his boiling glass. "You must pardon the rough appearance of one or two; they will have come a long way."

And with that the fire burned blue and the door blew open and twelve men entered, one by one.

If Jabez Stone had been sick with terror before, he was blind with terror now. For there was Walter Butler, the loyalist, who spread fire and horror through the Mohawk Valley in the times of the Revolution; and there was Simon Girty, the renegade, who saw white men burned at the stake and whooped with the Indians to see them burn. His eyes were green, like a catamount's, and the stains on his hunting shirt did not come from the blood of the deer. King Philip was there, wild and proud as he had been in life, with the great gash in his head that gave him his death wound, and cruel Governor Dale, who broke men on the wheel. There was Morton of Merry Mount, who so vexed the Plymouth Colony, with his flushed, loose, handsome face and his hate of the godly. There was Teach, the bloody pirate, with his black beard curling on his breast. The Reverend John Smeet, with his strangler's hands and his Geneva gown, walked as daintily as he had to the gallows. The red print of the rope was still around his neck, but he carried a perfumed handkerchief in one hand. One and all, they came into the room with the fires of hell still upon them, and the stranger named their names and their deeds as they came, till the tale of twelve was told. Yet the stranger had told the truth—they had all played a part in America.

"Are you satisfied with the jury, Mr. Webster?" said the stranger mockingly, when they had taken their places.

The sweat stood upon Dan'l Webster's brow, but his voice was clear.

"Quite satisfied," he said. "Though I miss General Arnold from the company."

"Benedict Arnold is engaged upon other business," said the stranger, with a glower. "Ah, you asked for a justice, I believe."

He pointed his finger once more, and a tall man, soberly clad in Puritan garb, with the burning gaze of the fanatic, stalked into the room and took his judge's place.

"Justice Hathorne is a jurist of experience," said the stranger. "He presided at certain witch trials once held in Salem. There were others who repented of the business later, but not he."

"Repent of such notable wonders and undertakings?" said the stern old justice. "Nay, hang them—hang them all!" And he muttered to himself in a way that struck ice into the soul of Jabez Stone.

Then the trial began, and, as you might expect, it didn't look anyways good for the defense. And Jabez Stone didn't make much of a witness in his own behalf. He took one look at Simon Girty and screeched, and they had to put him back in his corner in a kind of swoon.

It didn't halt the trial, though; the trial went on, as trials do. Dan'l Webster had faced some hard juries and hanging judges in his time, but this was the hardest he'd ever faced, and he knew it. They sat there with a kind of glitter in their eyes, and the stranger's smooth voice went on and on. Every time he'd raise an objection, it'd be "Objection sustained," but whenever Dan'l objected, it'd be "Objection denied." Well, you couldn't expect fair play from a fellow like this Mr. Scratch.

It got to Dan'l in the end, and he began to heat, like iron in the forge. When he got up to speak he was going to flay that stranger with every trick known to the law, and the judge and jury too. He didn't care if it was contempt of court or what would happen to him for it. He didn't care any more what happened to Jabez Stone. He just got madder and madder, thinking of what he'd say. And yet, curiously enough, the more he thought about it, the less he was able to arrange his speech in his mind.

Till, finally, it was time for him to get up on his feet, and he did so, all ready to bust out with lightnings and denunciations. But before he started he looked over the judge and jury for a moment, such being his custom. And he noticed the glitter in their eyes was twice as strong as before, and they all leaned forward. Like hounds just before they get the fox, they looked, and the blue mist of evil in the room thickened as he watched them. Then he saw what he'd been about to do, and he wiped his forehead, as a man might who's just escaped falling into a pit in the dark.

For it was him they'd come for, not only Jabez Stone. He read it in the glitter of their eyes and in the way the stranger hid his mouth with one hand. And if he fought them with their own weapons, he'd fall into their power; he knew that, though he couldn't have told you how. It was his own anger and horror that burned in their eyes; and he'd have to wipe that out or the case was lost. He stood there for a moment, his black eyes burning like anthracite. And then he began to speak.

He started off in a low voice, though you could hear every word. They say he could call on the harps of the blessed when he chose. And this was just as simple and easy as a man could talk. But he didn't start out by condemning or reviling. He was talking about the things that make a country a country, and a man a man.

And he began with the simple things that everybody's known and felt—the freshness of a fine morning when you're young, and the taste of food when you're hungry, and the new day that's every day when you're a child. He took them up and he turned them in his hands. They were good things for any man. But without freedom, they sickened. And when he talked of those enslaved, and the sorrows of slavery, his voice got like a big bell. He talked of the early days of America and the men who had made those days. It wasn't spread-eagle speech, but he made you see it. He admitted all the wrong that had ever been done. But he showed how, out of the wrong and the right, the suffering and starvations, something new had come. And everybody had played a part in it, even the traitors.

Then he turned to Jabez Stone and showed him as he was—an ordinary man who'd had hard luck and wanted change it. And, because he'd wanted to change it, now he was going to be punished for all eternity. And yet there was good in Jabez Stone, and he showed that good. He was hard and mean, in some ways, but he was a man. There was sadness in being a man, but it was a proud thing too. And he showed what the pride of it was till you couldn't help feeling it. Yes, even in hell, if a man was a man, you'd know it. And he wasn't pleading for any one person any more, though his voice rang like an organ. He was telling the story and the failures and the endless journey of mankind. They got tricked and trapped and bamboozled, but it was a great journey. And no demon that was ever foaled could know the inwardness of it—it took a man to do that.

The fire began to die on the hearth and the wind before morning to blow. The light was getting gray in the room when Dan'l Webster finished. And his words came back at the end to New Hampshire ground, and the one spot of land that each man loves and clings to. He painted a picture of that, and to each one of that jury he spoke of things long forgotten. For his voice could search the heart, and that was his gift and his strength. And to one, his voice was like the forest and its secrecy, and to another like the sea and the storms of the sea; and one heard the cry of his lost nation in it, and another saw a little harmless scene he hadn't remembered for years. But each saw something. And when Dan'l Webster finished he didn't know whether or not he'd saved Jabez Stone. But he knew he'd done a miracle. For the glitter was gone from the eyes of judge and jury, and, for the moment, they were men again, and knew they were men.

"The defense rests," said Dan'l Webster, and stood there like a mountain. His ears were still ringing with his speech, and he didn't hear anything else till he heard Judge Hathorne say, "The jury will retire to consider its verdict."

Walter Butler rose in his place and his face had a dark, gay pride on it.

"The jury has considered its verdict," he said, and looked the stranger full in the eye. "We find for the defendant, Jabez Stone."

With that, the smile left the stranger's face, but Walter Butler did not flinch.

"Perhaps 'tis not strictly in accordance with the evidence," he said, "but even the damned may salute the eloquence of Mr. Webster."

With that, the long crow of a rooster split the gray morning sky, and judge and jury were gone from the room like a puff of smoke and as if they had never been there. The stranger turned to Dan'l Webster, smiling wryly.

"Major Butler was always a bold man," he said. "I had not thought him quite so bold. Nevertheless, my congratulations, as between two gentlemen."

"I'll have that paper first, if you please," said Dan'l Webster, and he took it and tore it into four pieces. It was queerly warm to the touch. "And now," he said, "I'll have you!" and his hand came down like a bear trap on the stranger's arm. For he knew that once you bested anybody like Mr. Scratch in fair fight, his power on you was gone. And he could see that Mr. Scratch knew it too.

The stranger twisted and wriggled, but he couldn't get out of that grip. "Come, come, Mr. Webster," he said, smiling palely. "This sort of thing is ridic—ouch!—is ridiculous. If you're worried about the costs of the case, naturally, I'd be glad to pay—"

"And so you shall!" said Dan'l Webster, shaking him till his teeth rattled. "For you'll sit right down at that table and draw up a document, promising never to bother Jabez Stone nor his heirs or assigns nor any other New Hampshireman till doomsday! For any hades we want to raise in this state, we can raise ourselves, without assistance from strangers."

"Ouch!" said the stranger. "Ouch! Well, they never did run very big to the barrel, but—ouch!—I agree!"

So he sat down and drew up the document. But Dan'l Webster kept his hand on his coat collar all the time.

"And, now, may I go?" said the stranger, quite humble, when Dan'l'd seen the document was in proper and legal form.

"Go?" said Dan'l, giving him another shake. "I'm still trying to figure out what I'll do with you. For you've settled the costs of the case, but you haven't settled with me. I think I'll take you back to Marshfield," he said, kind of reflective. "I've got a ram there name Goliath that can butt through an iron door. I'd kind of like to turn you loose in his field and see what he'd do."

Well, with that the stranger began to beg and to plead. And he begged and he pled so humble that finally Dan'l, who was naturally kindhearted, agreed to let him go. The stranger seemed terrible grateful for that and said, just to show they were friends, he'd tell Dan'l's fortune before leaving. So Dan'l agreed to that, though he didn't take much stock in fortune-tellers ordinarily. But, naturally, the stranger was a little different.

Well, he pried and he peered at the lines in Dan'l's hands. And he told him one thing and another that was quite remarkable. But they were all in the past.

"Yes, all that's true, and it happened," said Dan'l Webster. "But what's to come in the future?"

The stranger grinned, kind of happily, and shook his head.

"The future's not as you think it," he said. "It's dark. You have a great ambition, Mr. Webster."

"I have," said Dan'l firmly, for everybody knew he wanted to be President.

"It seems almost within your grasp," said the stranger," but you will not attain it. Lesser men will be made President and you will be passed over."

"And, if I am, I'll still be Daniel Webster," said Dan'l. "Say on."

"You have two strong sons," said the stranger, shaking his head. "You look to found a line. But each will die in war and neither reach greatness."

"Live or die, they are still my sons," said Dan'l Webster. "Say on."

"You have made great speeches," said the stranger. "You will make more."

"Ah," said Dan'l Webster.

H.P. LOVECRAFT

1936

The Haunter of the Dark

I have seen the dark universe yawning
Where the black planets roll without aim—
Where they roll in their horror unheeded,
Without knowledge or luster or name.
                                        —NEMESIS

Cautious investigators will hesitate to challenge the common belief that Robert Blake was killed by lightning or by some profound nervous shock derived from an electrical discharge. It is true that the window he faced was unbroken, but nature has shown herself capable of many freakish performances. The expression on his face may easily have arisen from some obscure muscular source unrelated to anything he saw, while the entries in his diary are clearly the result of a fantastic imagination aroused by certain local superstitions and by certain old matters he had uncovered. As for the anomalous conditions at the deserted church of Federal Hill—the shrewd analyst is not slow in attributing them to some charlatanry, conscious or unconscious, with at least some of which Blake was secretly connected.

For after all, the victim was a writer and painter and wholly devoted to the field of myth, dream, terror, and superstition, and avid in his quest for scenes and effects of a bizarre, spectral sort. His earlier stay in the city—a visit to a strange old man as deeply given to occult and forbidden lore as he–had ended amidst death and flame, and it must have been some morbid instinct which drew him back from his home in Milwaukee. He may have known of the old stories despite his statements to the contrary in the diary, and his death may have nipped in the bud some stupendous hoax destined to have a literary reflection.

Among those, however, who have examined and correlated all this evidence, there remain several who cling to less rational and commonplace theories. They are inclined to take much of Blake's diary at its face value, and point significantly to certain facts such as the undoubted genuineness of the old church record, the verified existence of the disliked and unorthodox Starry Wisdom sect prior to 1877, the recorded disappearance of an inquisitive reporter named Edwin M. Lillibridge in 1893, and–above all–the look of monstrous, transfiguring fear on the face of the young writer when he died. It was one of these believers who, moved to fanatical extremes, threw into the bay the curiously angled stone and its strangely adorned metal box found in the old church steeple–the black windowless steeple, and not the tower where Blake's diary and those things originally were. Though widely censured both officially and unofficially, this man–a reputable physician with a taste for odd folklore–averred that he had rid the earth of something too dangerous to rest upon it.

Between these two schools of opinion the reader must judge for himself. The papers have given the tangible details from a skeptical angle, leaving for others the drawing of the picture as Robert Blake saw it–or thought he saw it–or pretended to see it. Now, studying the diary closely, dispassionately, and at leisure, let us summarize the dark chain of events from the expressed point of view of their chief actor.

Young Blake returned to Providence in the winter of 1934–5, taking the upper floor of a venerable dwelling in a grassy court off College Street–on the crest of the great eastward hill near the Brown University campus and behind the marble John Hay Library. It was a cozy and fascinating place, in a little garden oasis of village-like antiquity where huge, friendly cats sunned themselves atop a convenient shed. The square Georgian house had a monitor roof, classic doorway with fan carving, small-paned windows, and all the other earmarks of early nineteenth-century workmanship. Inside were six-panelled doors, wide floor-boards, a curving colonial staircase, white Adam-period mantels, and a rear set of rooms three steps below the general level.

Blake's study, a large southwest chamber, overlooked the front garden on one side, while its west windows–before one of which he had his desk– faced off from the brow of the hill and commanded a splendid view of the lower town's outspread roofs and of the mystical sunsets that flamed behind them. On the far horizon were the open countryside's purple slopes. Against these, some two miles away, rose the spectral hump of Federal Hill, bristling with huddled roofs and steeples whose remote outlines wavered mysteriously, taking fantastic forms as the smoke of the city swirled up and enmeshed them. Blake had a curious sense that he was looking upon some unknown, ethereal world which might or might not vanish in dream if ever he tried to seek it out and enter it in person.

Having sent home for most of his books. Blake brought some antique furniture suitable to his quarters and settled down to write and paint–living alone, and attending to the simple housework himself. His studio was in a north attic room, where the panes of the monitor roof furnished admirable lightning. During that first winter he produced five of his best-known short stories–*The Burrower Beneath, The Stairs in the Crypt, Shaggai, In the Vale of Pnath,* and *The Feaster from the Stars*–and painted seven canvases; studies of nameless, unhuman monsters, and profoundly alien, non-terrestrial landscapes.

At sunset he would often sit at his desk and gaze dreamily off at the outspread west–the dark towers of Memorial Hall just below, the Georgian courthouse belfry, the lofty pinnacles of the downtown section, and that shimmering, spire-crowned mound in the distance whose unknown streets and labyrinthine gables so potently provoked his fancy. From his few local acquaintances he learned that the far-off slope was a vast Italian quarter, though most of the houses were remnants of older Yankee and Irish days. Now and then he would train his field-glasses on that spectral, unreachable world beyond the curling smoke; picking out individual roofs and chimneys and steeples, and speculating upon the bizarre and curious mysteries they might house. Even with optical aid Federal Hill seemed somehow alien, half fabulous, and linked to the unreal, intangible marvels of Blake's own tales and pictures. The feeling would persist long after the hill had faded into the violet, lamp-starred twilight, and the court-house floodlights and the red Industrial Trust beacon had blazed up to make the night grotesque.

Of all the distant objects on Federal Hill, a certain huge, dark church most fascinated Blake. It stood out with especial distinctness at certain hours of the day, and at sunset the great tower and tapering steeple loomed blackly against the flaming sky. It seemed to rest on especially high ground; for the grimy façade, and the obliquely seen north side with sloping roof and tops of great pointed windows, rose boldly above the tangle of surrounding ridgepoles and chimney-pots. Peculiarly grim and austere, it appeared to be built of stone, stained and weathered with the smoke and storms of a century and more. The style, so far as the glass could show, was that earliest experimental form of Gothic revival which preceded the stately Upjohn period and held over some of the outlines and proportions of the Georgian age. Perhaps it was reared around 1810 or 1815.

As months passed, Blake watched the far-off, forbidding structure with an oddly mounting interest. Since the vast windows were never lighted, he knew that it must be vacant. The longer he watched, the more his imagination worked, till at length he began to fancy curious things. He believed that a vague, singular aura of desolation hovered over the place, so that even the pigeons and swallows shunned its smoky eaves. Around other towers and belfries his glass would reveal great flocks of birds, but here they never rested. At least, that is what he thought and set down in his diary. He pointed the place out to several friends, but none of them had even been on Federal Hill or possessed the faintest notion of what the church was or had been.

In that spring a deep restlessness gripped Blake. he had begun his long-planned novel – based on a supposed survival of the witchcult in Maine – but was strangely unable to make progress with it. More and more he would sit at his westward window and gaze at the distant hill and the black, frowning steeple shunned by the birds. When the delicate leaves came out on the garden boughs the world was filled with a new beauty, but Blake's restlessness was merely increased. It was then that he first thought of crossing the city and climbing bodily up that fabulous slope into the smoke-wreathed world of dream.

Late in April, just before the eon-shadowed Walpurgis time, Blake made his first trip into the unknown. Plodding through the endless downtown streets and the bleak, decayed squares beyond, he came finally upon the ascending avenue of century-worn steps, sagging Doric porches, and blear-paned cupolas which he felt must lead up to the long-known, unreachable world beyond the mists. There were dingy blue-and-white street signs which meant nothing to him, and presently he noted the strange, dark faces of the drifting crowds, and the foreign signs over curious shops in brown, decade-weathered buildings. Nowhere could he find any of the objects he had seen from afar; so that once more he half fancied that the Federal Hill of that distant view was a dream-world never to be trod by living human feet.

Now and then a battered church façade or crumbling spire came in sight, but never the blackened pile that he sought. When he asked a shopkeeper about a great stone church the man smiled and shook his head, though he spoke English freely. As Blake climbed higher, the region seemed stranger and stranger, with bewildering mazes of brooding brown alleys leading eternally off to the south. He crossed two or three broad avenues, and once thought he glimpsed a familiar tower. Again he asked a merchant about the massive church of stone, and this time he could have sworn that the plea of ignorance was feigned. The dark man's face had a look of fear which he tried to hide, and Blake saw him make a curious sign with his right hand.

Then suddenly a black spire stood out against the cloudy sky on his left, above the tiers of brown roofs lining the tangled southerly alleys. Blake

knew at once what it was, and plunged toward it through the squalid, un-
paved lanes that climbed from the avenue. Twice he lost his way, but he
somehow dared not ask any of the patriarchs or housewives who sat on their
doorsteps, or any of the children who shouted and played in the mud of the
shadowy lanes.

At last he saw the tower plain against the southwest, and a huge stone
bulk rose darkly at the end of an alley. Presently he stood in a wind-swept
open square, quaintly cobblestoned, with a high bank wall on the farther
side. This was the end of his quest; for upon the wide, iron-railed, weed-
grown plateau which the wall supported—a separate, lesser world raised
fully six feet above the surrounding streets—there stood a grim, titan bulk
whose identity, despite Blake's new perspective, was beyond dispute.

The vacant church was in a state of great decrepitude. Some of the high
stone buttresses had fallen, and several delicate finials lay half lost among
the brown, neglected weeds and grasses. The sooty Gothic windows were
largely unbroken, though many of the stone mullions were missing. Blake
wondered how the obscurely painted panes could have survived so well, in
view of the known habits of small boys the world over. The massive doors
were intact and tightly closed. Around the top of the bank wall, fully enclos-
ing the grounds, was a rusty iron fence whose gate—at the head of a flight of
steps from the square—was visibly padlocked. The path from the gate to the
building was completely overgrown. Desolation and decay hung like a pall
above the place, and in the birdless eaves and black, ivyless walls Blake felt
a touch of the dimly sinister beyond his power to define.

There were very few people in the square, but Blake saw a policeman at
the northerly end and approached him with questions about the church. He
was a great wholesome Irishman, and it seemed odd that he would do little
more than make the sign of the cross and mutter that people never spoke of
that building. When Blake pressed him he said very hurriedly that the
Italian priests warned everybody against it, vowing that a monstrous evil
had once dwelt there and left its mark. He himself had heard dark whispers
of it from his father, who recalled certain sounds and rumors from his
boyhood.

There had been a bad sect there in the old days—an outlaw sect that
called up awful things from some unknown gulf of night. It had taken a good
priest to exercise what had come, though there did be those who said that
merely the light could do it. If Father O'Malley were alive there would be
many the thing he could tell. But now there was nothing to do but let it
alone. It hurt nobody now, and those that owned it were dead or far away.
They had run away like rats after the threatening talk in '77, when people
began to mind the way folks vanished now and then in the neighbourhood.
Some day the city would step in and take the property for lack of heirs, but
little good would come of anybody's touching it. Better it be left alone for the

years to topple, lest things be stirred that ought to rest for ever in their black abyss.

After the policeman had gone Blake stood staring at the sullen steepled pile. It excited him to find that the structure seemed as sinister to others as to him, and he wondered what grain of truth might lie behind the old tales the bluecoat had repeated. Probably they were mere legends evoked by the evil look of the place, but even so, they were like a strange coming to life of one of his own stories.

The afternoon sun came out from behind dispersing clouds, but seemed unable to light up the stained, sooty walls of the old temple that towered on its high plateau. It was odd that the green of spring had not touched the brown, withered growths in the raised, iron-fenced yard. Blake found himself edging nearer the raised area and examining the bank wall and rusted fence for possible avenues of ingress. There was a terrible lure about the blackened fane which was not to be resisted. The fence had no opening near the steps, but around on the north side were some missing bars. He could go up the steps and walk around on the narrow coping outside the fence till he came to the gap. If the people feared the place so wildly, he would encounter no interference.

He was on the embankment and almost inside the fence before anyone noticed him. Then, looking down, he saw the few people in the square edging away and making the same sign with their right hands that the shopkeeper in the avenue had made. Several windows were slammed down, and a fat woman darted into the street and pulled some small children inside a rickety, unpainted house. The gap in the fence was very easy to pass through, and before long Blake found himself wading amidst the rotting, tangled growths of the deserted yard. Here and there the worn stump of a headstone told him that there had once been burials in this field; but that, he saw, must have been very long ago. The sheer bulk of the church was oppressive now that he was close to it, but he conquered his mood and approached to try the three great doors in the façade. All were securely locked, so he began a circuit of the Cyclopean building in quest of some minor and more penetrable opening. Even then he could not be sure that he wished to enter that haunt of desertion and shadow, yet the pull of its strangeness dragged him on automatically.

A yawning and unprotected cellar window in the rear furnished the needed aperture. Peering in, Blake saw a subterrene gulf of cobwebs and dust faintly litten by the western sun's filtered rays. Debris, old barrels, and ruined boxes and furniture of numerous sorts met his eye, though over everything lay a shroud of dust which softened all sharp outlines. The rusted remains of a hot-air furnace showed that the building had been used and kept in shape as late as Mid-Victorian times.

Acting almost without conscious initiative, Blake crawled through the window and let himself down to the dust-carpeted and debris-strewn concrete floor. The vaulted cellar was a vast one, without partitions; and in a corner far to the right, amid dense shadows, he saw a black archway evidently leading upstairs. He felt a peculiar sense of oppression at being actually within the great spectral building, but kept it in check as he cautiously scouted about—finding a still-intact barrel amid the dust, and rolling it over to the open window to provide for his exit. Then, bracing himself, he crossed the wide, cobweb-festooned space toward the arch. Half choked with the omnipresent dust, and covered with ghostly gossamer fibers, he reached and began to climb the worn stone steps which rose into the darkness. He had no light, but groped carefully with his hands. After a sharp turn he felt a closed door ahead, and a little fumbling revealed its ancient latch. It opened inward, and beyond it he saw a dimly illumined corridor lined with worm-eaten paneling.

Once on the ground floor, Blake began exploring in rapid fashion. All the inner doors were unlocked, so that he freely passed from room to room. The colossal nave was an almost eldritch place with its drifts and mountains of dust over box pews, altar, hour-glass pulpit, and sounding-board, and its titanic ropes of cob-web stretching among the pointed arches of the gallery and entwining the clustered Gothic columns. Over all this hushed desolation played a hideous leaden light as the declining afternoon sun sent its rays through the strange, half-blackened panes of the great apsidal windows.

The paintings on those windows were so obscured by soot that Blake could scarcely decipher what they had represented, but from the little he could make out he did not like them. The designs were largely conventional, and his knowledge of obscure symbolism told him much concerning some of the ancient patterns. The few saints depicted bore expressions distinctly open to criticism, while one of the windows seemed to show merely a dark space with spirals of curious luminosity scattered about in it. Turning away from the windows, Blake noticed that the cobwebbed cross above the altar was not of the ordinary kind, but resembled the primordial ankh of crux ansata of shadowy Egypt.

In a rear vestry room beside the apse Blake found a rotting desk and ceiling-high shelves of mildewed, disintegrating books. Here for the first time he received a positive shock of objective horror, for the titles of those books told him much. They were the black, forbidden things which most sane people have never even heard of, or have heard of only in furtive, timorous whispers; the banned and dreaded repositories of equivocal secrets and immemorial formulae which have trickled down the stream of time from the days of man's youth, and the dim, fabulous days before man was. He had himself read many of them—a Latin version of the abhorred *Necronomicon*, the sinister *Liber Ivonis*, the infamous *Cultes des Goules* of Comte d'Erlette, the *Unaussprechlichen Kulten* of von Junzt, and old Ludvig Prinn's hellish

De Vermis Mysteriis. But there were others he had known merely by reputation or not at all–the *Pnakotic Manuscripts*, the *Book of Dzyan*, and a crumbling volume in wholly unidentifiable characters yet with certain symbols and diagrams shudderingly recognizable to the occult student. Clearly, the lingering local rumors had not lied. This place had once been the seat of an evil older than mankind and wider than the known universe.

In the ruined desk was a small leatherbound recordbook filled with entries in some odd cryptographic medium. The manuscript writing consisted of the common traditional symbols used today in astronomy and anciently in alchemy, astrology, and other dubious acts–the devices of the sun, moon, planets, aspects, and zodiacal signs–here massed in solid pages of text, with divisions and paragraphings suggesting that each symbol answered to some alphabetical letter.

In the hope of later solving the cryptogram, Blake bore off this volume in his coat pocket. Many of the great tomes on the shelves fascinated him unutterably, and he felt tempted to borrow them at some later time. He wondered how they could have remained undisturbed so long. Was he the first to conquer the clutching, pervasive fear which had for nearly sixty years protected this deserted place from visitors?

Having now thoroughly explored the ground floor, Blake plowed again through the dust of the spectral nave to the front vestibule, where he had seen a door and staircase presumably leading up to the blackened tower and steeple–objects so long familiar to him at a distance. The ascent was a choking experience, for dust lay thick, while the spiders had done their worst in this constricted place. The staircase was a spiral with high, narrow wooden treads, and now and then Blake passed a clouded window looking dizzily out over the city. Though he had seen no ropes below, he expected to find a bell or peal of bells in the tower whose narrow, louver-boarded lancet windows his field-glass had studied so often. Here he was doomed to disappointment; for when he attained the top of the stairs he found the tower chamber vacant of chimes, and clearly devoted to vastly different purposes.

The room, about fifteen feet square, was faintly lighted by four lancet windows, one on each side, which were glazed within their screening of decayed louver-boards. These had been further fitted with tight, opaque screens, but the latter were now largely rotted away. In the center of the dust-laden floor rose a curiously angled stone pillar some four feet in height and two in average diameter, covered on each side with bizarre, crudely incised and wholly unrecognizable hieroglyphs. On this pillar rested a metal box of peculiarly asymmetrical form, its hinged lid thrown back, and its interior holding what looked beneath the decade-deep dust to be an egg shaped or irregularly spherical object some four inches through. Around the pillar in a rough circle were seven high-backed Gothic chairs still largely intact, while behind them, ranging along the dark-paneled walls, were seven colossal images of crumbling, black-painted plaster, resembling more than any-thing else the cryptic carven megaliths of mysterious Easter Island. In one corner of the cobwebbed chamber a ladder was build into the wall, leading up to the closed trap door of the windowless steeple above.

As Blake grew accustomed to the feeble light he noticed odd bas-reliefs on the strange open box of yellowish metal. Approaching, he tried to clear the dust away with his hands and handkerchief, and saw that the figurings were of a monstrous and utterly alien kind; depicting entities which, though seemingly alive, resembled no known life-form ever evolved on this planet. This four-inch seeming sphere turned out to be a nearly black, red-striated polyhedron with many irregular flat surfaces; either a very remarkable crys-tal of some sort, or an artificial object of carved and highly polished mineral matter. It did not touch the bottom of the box, but was held suspended by means of a metal band around its center, with seven queerly-designed sup-ports extending horizontally to angles of the box's inner wall near the top. This stone, once exposed, exerted upon Blake an almost alarming fascina-tion. He could scarcely tear his eyes from it, and as he looked at its glisten-ing surfaces he almost fancied it was transparent, with half-formed worlds of wonder within. Into his mind floated pictures of alien orbs with great stone towers, and other orbs with titan mountains and no mark of life, and still remoter spaces where only a stirring in vague blacknesses told of the presence of consciousness and will.

When he did look away, it was to notice a somewhat singular mound of dust in the far corner near the ladder to the steeple. Just why, it took his attention he could not tell, but something in its contours carried a message to his unconscious mind. Plowing toward it, and brushing aside the hanging cobwebs as he went, he began to discern something grim about it. Hand and handkerchief soon revealed the truth, and Blake gasped with a baffling mix-ture of emotions. It was a human skeleton, and it must have been there for a very long time. The clothing was in shreds, but some buttons and frag-ments of cloth bespoke a man's gray suit. There were other bits of evidence –shoes, metal clasps, huge buttons for round cuffs, a stickpin of bygone pat-tern, a reporter's badge with the name of the old *Providence Telegram*, and a crumbling leather pocket-book. Blake examined the latter with care, finding within it several bills of antiquated issue, a celluloid advertising calendar for 1893, some cards with the name "Edwin M. Lillibridge," and a paper covered with penciled memoranda.

This paper held much of a puzzling nature, and Blake read it carefully at the dim westward window. Its disjointed text included such phrases as the following:

> "Prof. Enoch Bowen home from Egypt May 1844–buys old
> Free-Will Church in July–his archaeological work and studies in
> occult well known."

"Dr. Drowne of 4th Baptist warns against Starry Wisdom in sermon Dec. 29, 1844."

"Congregation 97 by end of '45."

"1846–3 disappearances–first mention of Shining Trapezohedron."

"7 disappearances 1848–stories of blood sacrifice begin."

"Investigation 1853 comes to nothing–stories of sounds."

"Fr. O'Malley tells of devil-worship with box found in great Egyptian ruins–says they call up something that can't exist in light. Flees a little light, and banished by strong light. Then has to be summoned again. Probably got this from death-bed confession of Francis X. Feeney, who had joined Starry Wisdom in '49. These people say the Shining Trapezohedron shows them heaven & other worlds, & that the Haunter of the Dark tells them secrets in some way."

"Story of Orrin B. Eddy 1857. They call it up by gazing at the crystal, & have a secret language of their own."

"200 or more in cong. 1863, exclusive of men at front."

"Irish boys mob church in 1869 after Patrick Regan's disappearance."

"Veiled article in J. March 14, '72, but people don't talk about it."

"6 disappearances 1876–secret committee calls on Mayor Doyle."

"Action promised Feb. 1877–church closes in April."

"Gang–Federal Hill Boys–threaten Dr. — and vestrymen in May."

"181 persons leave city before end of '77–mention no names."

"Ghost stories begin around 1880–try to ascertain truth of report that no human being has entered church since 1877."

"Ask Lanigan for photograph of place taken 1851. . . . "

Restoring the paper to the pocket-book and placing the latter in his coat, Blake turned to look down at the skeleton in the dust. The implications of the notes were clear, and there could be no doubt that this man had come to the deserted edifice forty-two years before in quest of a newspaper sensation which no one else had been bold enough to attempt. Perhaps no one else had known of his plan–who could tell? But he had never returned to his paper. Had some bravely-suppressed fear risen to overcome him and bring on sudden heart-failure? Blake stooped over the gleaming bones and noted their peculiar state. Some of them were badly scattered, and a few seemed oddly *dissolved* at the ends. Others were strangely yellowed, with vague suggestions of charring. This charring extended to some of the fragments of clothing. The skull was in a very peculiar state–stained yellow, and with a charred aperture in the top as if some powerful acid had eaten through the solid bone. What had happened to the skeleton during its four decades of silent entombment here Blake could not imagine.

Before he realized it, he was looking at the stone again, and letting its curious influence call up a nebulous pageantry in his mind. He saw processions of robed, hooded figures whose outlines were not human, and looked on endless leagues of desert lined with carved, sky-reaching monoliths. He saw towers and walls in nighted depths under the sea, and vortices of space where wisps of black mist floated before thin shimmerings of cold purple haze. And beyond all else he glimpsed an infinite gulf of darkness, where solid and semi-solid forms were known only by their windy stirrings, and cloudly patterns of force seemed to superimpose order to chaos and hold forth a key to all the paradoxes and arcana of the worlds we know.

Then all at once the spell was broken by an access of gnawing, indeterminate panic fear. Blake choked and turned away from the stone, conscious of some formless alien presence close to him and watching him with horrible intentness. He felt entangled with something–something which was not in the stone, but which had looked through it at him–something which would ceaselessly follow him with a cognition that was not physical sight. Plainly, the place was getting on his nerves–as well it might in view of his gruesome find. The light was waning, too, and since he had no illuminant with him he knew he would have to be leaving soon.

It was then, in the gathering twilight, that he thought he saw a faint trace of luminosity in the crazily angled stone. He had tried to look away from it, but some obscure compulsion drew his eyes back. Was there a subtle phosphorescence of radio-activity about the thing? What was it that the dead man's notes had said concerning a *Shining Trapezohedron*? What, anyway, was his abandoned lair of cosmic evil? What had been done here, and what might still be lurking in the bird-shunned shadows? It seemed now as if an elusive touch of fetor had arisen somewhere close by, though its source was not apparent. Blake seized the cover of the long-open box and snapped it down. It moved easily on its alien hinges, and closed completely over the unmistakably glowing stone.

At the sharp click of that closing a soft stirring sound seemed to come from the steeple's eternal blackness overhead, beyond the trap-door. Rats, without question–the only living things to reveal their presence in this accursed pile since he had entered it. And yet that stirring in the steeple frightened him horribly, so that he plunged almost wildly down the spiral stairs, across the ghoulish nave, into the vaulted basement, out amidst the gathering dusk of the deserted square, and down through the teeming, fear-haunted alleys and avenues of Federal Hill toward the sane central streets and the home-like brick sidewalks of the college district.

During the days which followed, Blake told no one of his expedition. Instead, he read much in certain books, examined long years of newspaper files downtown, and worked feverishly at the cryptogram in that leather volume from the cobwebbed vestry room. The cipher, he soon saw, was no simple one; and after a long period of endeavor he felt sure that its language could not be English, Latin, Greek, French, Spanish, Italian, or German. Evidently he would have to draw upon the deepest wells of his strange erudition.

Every evening the old impulse to gaze westward returned, and he saw the black steeple as of yore amongst the bristling roofs of a distant and half-fabulous world. But now it held a fresh note of terror for him. He knew the heritage of evil lore it masked, and with the knowledge his vision ran riot in queer new ways. The birds of spring were returning, and as he watched their sunset flights he fancied they avoided the gaunt, lone spire as never before. When a flock of them approached it, he thought, they would wheel and scatter in panic confusion—and he could guess at the wild twitterings which failed to reach him across the intervening miles.

It was in June that Blake's diary told of his victory over the cryptogram. The text was, he found, in the dark Aklo language used by certain cults of evil antiquity, and known to him in a halting way through previous researches. The diary is strangely reticent about what Blake deciphered, but he was patently awed and disconcerted by his results. There are references to a Haunter of the Dark awaked by gazing into the Shining Trapezohedron, and insane conjectures about the black gulfs of chaos from which it was called. The being is spoken of as holding all knowledge, and demanding monstrous sacrifices. Some of Blake's entries show fear lest the thing, which he seemed to regard as summoned, stalk abroad; though he adds that the streetlights form a bulwark which cannot be crossed.

Of the Shining Trapezohedron he speaks often, calling it a window of all time and space, and tracing its history from the days it was fashioned on dark Yoggoth, before ever the Old Ones brought it to earth. It was treasured and placed in its curious box by the crinoid things of Antarctica, salvaged from their ruins by the serpent-men of Valusia, and peered at eons later in Lemuria by the first human beings. It crossed strange lands and stranger seas, and sank with Atlantis before a Minoan fisher meshed it in his net and sold it to swarthy merchants from nighted Khem. The Pharoah Nephren-Ka built around it a temple with a windowless crypt, and did that which caused his name to be stricken from all monuments and records. Then it slept in the ruins of that evil fane which the priests and the new Pharoah destroyed, till the delver's spade once more brought it forth to curse mankind.

Early in July the newspapers oddly supplement Blake's entries, though in so brief and casual a way that only the diary has called general attention to their contribution. It appears that a new fear had been growing on Federal Hill since a stranger had entered the dreaded church. The Italians whispered of unaccustomed stirrings and bumpings and scrapings in the dark windowless steeple, and called on their priests to banish an entity which haunted their dreams. Something, they said, was constantly watching at a door to see if it were dark enough to venture forth. Press items mentioned the longstanding local superstitions, but failed to shed much light on the earlier background of the horror. It was obvious that the young reporters of today are no antiquarians. In writing of these things in his diary, Blake expresses a curious kind of remorse, and talks of the duty of burying the Shining Trapezohedron and of banishing what he had evoked by letting daylight into the hideous jutting spire. At the same time, however, he displays the dangerous extent of his fascination, and admits a morbid longing—pervading even his dreams–to visit the accursed tower and gaze again into the cosmic secrets of the glowing stone.

Then something in the *Journal* on the morning of July 17 threw the diarist into a veritable fever of horror. It was only a variant of the other half-humorous items about the Federal Hill restlessness, but to Blake it was somehow very terrible indeed. In the night a thunderstorm had put the city's lighting-system out of commission for a full hour, and in that black interval the Italians had nearly gone mad with fright. Those living near the dreaded church had sworn that the thing in the steeple had taken advantage of the street lamps' absence and gone down into the body of the church, flopping and bumping around in a viscous, altogether dreadful way. Toward the last it had bumped up to the tower, where there were sounds of the shattering of glass. It could go wherever the darkness reached, but light would always send it fleeing.

When the current blazed on again there had been a shocking commotion in the tower, for even the feeble light trickling through the grime-blackened, louver-boarded windows was too much for the thing. It had bumped and slithered up into its tenebrous steeple just in time–for a long dose of light would have sent it back into the abyss whence the crazy stranger had called it. During the dark hour praying crowds had clustered round the church in the rain with lighted candles and lamps somehow shielded with folded paper and umbrellas–a guard of light to save the city from the nightmare that stalks in darkness. Once, those nearest the church declared, the outer door had rattled hideously.

But even this was not the worst. That evening in the *Bulletin* Blake read of what the reporters had found. Aroused at last to the whimsical news value of the scare, a pair of them had defied the frantic crowds of Italians and crawled into the church through the cellar window after trying the doors in vain. They found the dust of the vestibule and of the special nave plowed up in a singular way, with pits of rotted cushions and satin pew-linings scattered curiously around. There was a bad odor everywhere, and here and there were bits of yellow stains and patches of what looked like charring. Opening the door to the tower, and pausing a moment at the suspicion of a scraping sound above, they found the narrow spiral stairs wiped roughly clean.

In the tower itself a similarly half-swept condition existed. They spoke of the heptagonal stone pillar, the overturned Gothic chairs, and the bizarre plaster images; though strangely enough the metal box and the old mutilated skeleton were not mentioned. What disturbed Blake the most–except for the hints of stains and charring and bad odors–was the final detail that explained the crashing glass. Every one of the tower's lancet windows was broken, and two of them had been darkened in a crude and hurried way by the stuffing of satin pew-linings and cushion-horsehair into the spaces between the slanting exterior louver-boards. More satin fragments and bunches of horsehair lay scattered around the newly swept floor, as if someone had been interrupted in the act of restoring the tower to the absolute blackness of its tightly curtained days.

Yellowish stains and charred patches were found on the ladder to the windowless spire, but when a reporter climbed up, opened the horizontally-sliding trapdoor and shot a feeble flashlight beam into the black and strangely fetid space, he saw nothing but darkness, and an heterogeneous litter of shapeless fragments near the aperture. The verdict, of course was charlatanry. Somebody had played a joke on the superstitious hill-dwellers, or else some fanatic had striven to bolster up their fears, for their own supposed good. Or perhaps some of the younger and more sophisticated dwellers had staged an elaborate hoax on the outside world. There was an amusing aftermath when the police sent an officer to verify the reports. Three men in succession found ways of evading the assignment, and the fourth went very reluctantly and returned very soon without adding to the account given by the reporters.

From this point onward Blake's diary shows a mounting tide of insidious horror and nervous apprehension. He upbraids himself for not doing something, and speculates wildly on the consequences of another electrical breakdown. It had been verified that on three occasions–during thunderstorms–he telephoned the electric light company in a frantic vein and asked that desperate precautions against a lapse of power be taken. Now and then his entries show concern over the failure of the reporters to find the metal box and stone, and the strangely marred old skeleton, when they explored the shadowy tower room. He assumed that these things had been removed–whither, and by whom or what, he could only guess. But his worst fears concerned himself, and the kind of unholy rapport he felt to exist between his mind and that lurking horror in the distant steeple–that monstrous thing of night which his rashness had called out of the ultimate black spaces. He seemed to feel a constant tugging at his will, and callers of that period remember how he would sit abstractedly at his desk and stare out of the west window at that far-off spirebristling mound beyond the swirling smoke of the city. His entries dwell monotonously on certain terrible dreams, and of a strengthening of the unholy rapport in his sleep. There is mention of a night when he awakened to find himself fully dressed, outdoors, and headed automatically down College Hill toward the west. Again and again he dwells on the fact that the thing in the steeple knows where to find him.

The week following July 30 is recalled as the time of Blake's partial breakdown. He did not dress, and ordered all his food by telephone. Visitors remarked the cords he kept near his bed, and he said that the sleep-walking had forced him to bind his ankles every night with knots which would probably hold or else waken him with the labor of untying.

In his diary he told of the hideous experience which had brought the collapse. After retiring on the night of the 30th he had suddenly found himself groping about in an almost black space. All he could see were short, faint, horizontal streaks of bluish light, but he could smell an overpowering foetor and hear a curious jumble of soft, furtive sounds above him. Whenever he moved he stumbled over something, and at each noise there would come a sort of answering sound from above – a vague stirring, mixed with the cautious sliding of wood on wood.

Once his groping hands encountered a pillar of stone with a vacant top, whilst later he found himself clutching the rungs of a ladder built into the wall, and fumbling his uncertain way upward toward some region of intenser stench where a hot, searing blast beat down against him. Before his eyes a kaleidoscopic range of fantasmal images played, all of them dissolving at intervals into the picture of a vast, unplumbed abyss of night wherein whirled suns and worlds of an even profounder blackness. He thought of the ancient legends of Ultimate Chaos, at whose center sprawls the blind idiot god Azathoth, Lord of All Things, encircled by his flopping horde of mindless and amorphous dancers, and lulled by the thin monotonous piping of a demoniac flute held in nameless paws.

Then a sharp report from the outer world broke through his stupor and roused him to the unutterable horror of his position. What it was, he never knew – perhaps it was some belated peal from the fireworks heard all summer on Federal Hill as the dwellers hail their various patron saints, or the saints of their native villages in Italy. In any event he shrieked aloud, dropped frantically from the ladder, and stumbled blindly across the obstructed floor of the almost lightless chamber that encompassed him.

He knew instantly where he was, and plunged recklessly down the narrow spiral staircase, tripping and bruising himself at every turn. There was a nightmare flight through a vast cobwebbed nave whose ghostly arches reached up to realms of leering shadow, a sightless scramble through the littered basement, a climb to regions of air and street lights outside, and a mad racing down a spectral hill of gibbering gables, across a grim, silent city of tall black towers, and up the steep eastward precipice to his own ancient door.

On regaining consciousness in the morning he found himself lying on his study floor fully dressed. Dirt and cobwebs covered him, and every inch of his body seemed sore and bruised. When he faced the mirror he saw that his hair was badly scorched, while a trace of strange, evil odor seemed to cling to his upper outer clothing. It was then that his nerves broke down. Thereafter, lounging exhaustedly about in a dressing gown, he did little but stare from his west window, shiver at the threat of thunder, and make wild entries in his diary.

The great storm broke just before midnight on August 8. Lightning struck repeatedly in all parts of the city and two remarkable fireballs were reported. The rain was torrential, while a constant fusillade of thunder brought sleeplessness to thousands. Blake was utterly frantic in his fear for the lighting system, and tried to telephone the company around one A.M., though by that time service had been temporarily cut off in the interest of safety. He recorded everything in his diary–the large, nervous, and often undecipherable hieroglyphs telling their own story of growing frenzy and despair, and of entries scrawled blindly in the dark.

He had to keep the house dark in order to see out the window, and it appears that most of his time was spent at his desk, peering anxiously through the rain across the glistening miles of downtown roofs at the constellation of distant lights marking Federal Hill. Now and then he would fumblingly make an entry in his diary, so that detached phrases such as "The lights must not go"; "It knows where I am"; "I must destroy it"; and "It is calling to me, but perhaps it means no injury this time"; are found scattered down two of the pages.

Then the lights went out all over the city. It happened at 2:12 A.M. according to power-house records, but Blake's diary gives no indication of the time. The entry is merely, "Lights out–God help me." On Federal Hill there were watchers as anxious as he, and rain-soaked knots of men paraded the square and alleys around the evil church with umbrella-shaded candles, electric flashlights, oil lanterns, crucifixes, and obscure charms of the many sorts common to southern Italy. They blessed each flash of lightning, and made cryptic signs of fear with their right hands when a turn in the storm caused the flashes to lessen and finally to cease altogether. A rising wind blew out most of the candles, so that the scene grew threatening dark. Someone roused Father Merluzzo of Spirto Santo Church, and he hastened to the dismal square to pronounce whatever helpful syllables he could. Of the restless and curious sounds in the blackened tower, there could be no doubt whatever.

For what happened at 2:35 we have the testimony of the priest, a young, intelligent, and well-educated person; of Patrolman William J. Monohan of the Central Station, an officer of the highest reliability who had paused at that part of his beat to inspect the crowd; and of most of the seventy-eight men who had gathered around the church's high bank wall– especially those in the square where the eastward façade was visible. Of course there was nothing which can be proved as being outside the order of nature. The possible causes of such an event are many. No one can speak with certainty of the obscure chemical processes arising in a vast, ancient, ill-aired, and long-deserted building of heterogeneous contents. Mephitic vapors – spontaneous combustion – pressure of gases born of long decay – any one of numberless phenomena might be responsible. And then, of course, the factor of conscious charlatanry can by no means be excluded. The thing was really quite simple in itself, and covered less than three minutes of actual time. Father Merluzzo, always a precise man, looked at his watch repeatedly.

It started with a definite swelling of the dull fumbling sounds inside the black tower. There had for some time been a vague exhalation of strange, evil odors from the church, and this had now become emphatic and offensive. Then at last there was a sound of splintering wood, and a large, heavy object crashed down in the yard beneath the frowning easterly façade. The tower was invisible now that the candles would not burn, but as the object neared the ground the people knew it was the smoke-grimed louver-boarding of that tower's east window.

Immediately afterward an utterly unbearable foetor welled forth from the unseen heights, choking and sickening the trembling watchers, and almost prostrating those in the square. At the same time the air trembled with a vibration as of flapping wings, and a sudden east-blowing wind more violent than any previous blast snatched off the hats and wrenched the drip-ping umbrellas of the crowd. Nothing definite could be seen in the candleless night, though some upward-looking spectators thought they glimpsed a great spreading blur of denser blackness against the inky sky – something like a formless cloud of smoke that shot with meteor-like speed toward the east.

That was all. The watchers were half numbed with fright, awe, and dis-comfort, and scarcely knew what to do, or whether to do anything at all. Not knowing what had happened, they did not relax their vigil; and a moment later they sent up a prayer as a sharp flash of belated lightning, followed by an earsplitting crash of sound, rent the flooded heavens. Half an hour later the rain stopped, and in fifteen minutes more the street lights sprang on again, sending the weary, bedraggled watchers relievedly back to their homes.

The next day's papers gave these matters minor mention in connection with the general storm reports. It seems that the great lightning flash and deafening explosion which followed he Federal Hill occurrence were even more tremendous farther east, where a burst of the singular foetor was like-wise noticed. The phenomenon was most marked over College Hill, where the crash awakened all the sleeping inhabitants and led to a bewildered round of speculations. Of those who were already awake only a few saw the anomalous blaze of light near the top of the hill, or noticed the inexplicable upward rush of air which almost stripped the leaves from the trees and blasted the plants in the gardens. It was agreed that the lone, sudden lightning-bolt must have struck somewhere in this neighborhood, though no trace of its striking could afterward be found. A youth in the Tau Omega fraternity house thought he saw a grotesque and hideous mass of smoke in the air just as the preliminary flash burst, but his observation has not been verified. All of the few observers, however, agree as to the violent gust from the west and the flood of intolerable stench which preceded the belated smoke; whilst evidence concerning the momentary burned odor after the stroke is equally general.

These points were discussed very carefully because of their probable connection with the death of Robert Blake. Students in the Psi Delta house, whose upper rear windows looked into Blake's study, noticed the blurred white face at the westward window on the morning of the ninth, and wondered what was wrong with the expression. When they saw the same face in the same position that evening, they felt worried, and watched for the lights to come up in his apartment. Later they rang the bell of the darkened flat, and finally had a policeman force the door.

The rigid body sat bolt upright at the desk by the window, and when the intruders saw the glossy, bulging eyes, and the marks of stark, convulsive fright on the twisted features, they turned away in sickened dismay. Shortly afterward the corner's physician made an examination, and despite the unbroken window reported electrical shock, or nervous tension induced by electrical discharge, as the cause of death. The hideous expression he ignored altogether, deeming it a not improbable result of the profound shock a experienced by a person of such abnormal imagination and unbalanced emotions. He deduced these latter qualities from the books, paintings, and manuscripts found in the apartment, and from the blindly scrawled entries in the diary on the desk. Blake had prolonged his frenzied jottings to the last, and the broken-pointed pencil was found clutched in his spasmodically contracted right hand.

The entries after the failure of the lights were highly disjointed, and legible only in part. From them certain investigators have drawn conclusions differing greatly from the materialistic official verdict, but such speculations have little chance for belief among the conservative. The case of these imaginative theorists has not been helped by the action of superstitious Dr. Dexter, who threw the curious box and angled stone—an object certainly self-luminous as seen in the black windowless steeple where it was found—into the deepest channel of Narragansett Bay. Excessive imagination and neurotic unbalance on Blake's part, aggravated by knowledge of the evil bygone cult whose startling taces he had uncovered, form the dominant interpretation given those final, frenzied jottings. These are the entries—or all that can be made of them.

"Lights still out—must be five minutes now. Everything depends on lightning. Yaddith grant it will keep up! . . . Some influence seems beating through it. . . . Rain and thunder and wind deafen. . . . The thing is taking hold of my mind. . . .

"Trouble with memory. I see things I never knew before. Other worlds and other galaxies. . . . Dark. . . . The lightning seems dark and the darkness seems light. . . .

"It cannot be the real hill and church that I see in the pitch-darkness. Must be retinal impression left by flashes. Heaven grant the Italians are out with their candles if the lightning stops!

"What am I afraid of? Is it not an avatar of Nyarlathotep, who in antique and shadowy Khem even took the form of man? I remember Yuggoth, and more distant Shaggai, and the ultimate void of the black planets. . . .

"The long, winging flight through the void . . . cannot cross the universe of light . . . re-created by the thoughts caught in the Shining Trapezohedron . . . send it through the horrible abysses of radiance. . . .

"My name is Blake—Robert Harrison Blake at 620 East Knapp Street, Milwaukee, Wisconsin. . . . I am on this planet. . . .

"Azathoth have mercy!—the lightning no longer flashes—horrible—I can see everything with a monstrous sense that is not sight—light is dark and dark is light . . . those people on the hill . . . guard . . . candle and charms . . . their priests . . .

"Sense of distance gone—far is near and near is far. No light—no glass—see that steeple—that tower—window—can hear—Roderick Usher—am mad or going mad—the thing is stirring and fumbling in the tower—I am it and it is I—I want to get out . . . must get out and unify the forces. . . . It knows where I am. . . .

"I am Robert Blake, but I see the tower in the dark. There is a monstrous odor . . . senses transfigured . . . boarding at that tower cracking and giving way. . . . Iä . . . ngai . . . ygg . . .

"I see it—coming here—hell-wind—titan blur—black wings—Yog-Sothoth save me—the three-lobed burning eye. . . ."

JAMES THURBER

1942

The Secret Life of
Walter Mitty

We're going through!" The Commander's voice was like thin ice breaking. He wore his full-dress uniform, with the heavily braided white cap pulled down rakishly over one cold gray eye. "We can't make it, sir. It's spoiling for a hurricane, if you ask me." "I'm not asking you, Lieutenant Berg," said the Commander. "Throw on the power light! Rev her up to 8, 500! We're going through!" The pounding of the cylinders increased: ta-pocketa-pocketa-pocketa-*pocketa-pocketa*. The Commander stared at the ice forming on the pilot window. He walked over and twisted a row of complicated dials. "Switch on No. 8 auxiliary!" he shouted. "Switch on No. 8 auxiliary!" repeated Lieutenant Berg. "Full strength in No. 3 turret!" shouted the Commander. "Full strength in No. 3 turret!" The crew, bending to their various tasks in the huge, hurtling eight-engined Navy hydroplane, looked at each other and grinned. "The Old Man'll get us through," they said to one another. "The Old Man ain't afraid of Hell!" . . .

"Not so fast! You're driving too fast!" said Mrs. Mitty. "What are you driving so fast for?"

"Hmm?" said Walter Mitty. He looked at his wife, in the seat beside him, with shocked astonishment. She seemed grossly unfamiliar, like a strange woman who had yelled at him in a crowd.

"You were up to fifty-five," she said. "You know I don't like to go more than forty. You were up to fifty-five." Walter Mitty drove on toward Waterbury in silence, the roaring of the SN202 through the worst storm in twenty years of Navy flying fading in the remote, intimate airways of his mind. "You're tensed up again," said Mrs. Mitty. "It's one of your days. I wish you'd let Dr. Renshaw look you over."

Walter Mitty stopped the car in front of the building where his wife went to have her hair done. "Remember to get those overshoes while I'm having my hair done," she said. "I don't need overshoes," said Mitty. She put her mirror back into her bag. "We've been all through that," she said, getting out of the car. "You're not a young man any longer." He raced the engine a little. "Why don't you wear your gloves? Have you lost your gloves?" Walter Mitty reached in a pocket and brought out the gloves. He put them on, but after she had turned and gone into the building and he had driven on to a red light, he took them off again. "Pick it up, brother!" snapped a cop as the light changed, and Mitty hastily pulled on his gloves and lurched ahead. He drove around the streets aimlessly for a time, and then he drove past the hospital on his way to the parking lot.

. . . "It's the millionaire banker, Wellington McMillan," said the pretty nurse. "Yes?" said Walter Mitty, removing his gloves slowly. "Who has the case?" "Dr. Renshaw and Dr. Benbow, but there are two specialists here, Dr. Remington from New York and Mr. Pritchard-Mitford from London. He flew over." A door opened down a long, cool corridor and Dr. Renshaw came out. He looked distraught and haggard. "Hello, Mitty," he said. "We're having the devil's own time with McMillan, the millionaire banker and close personal friend of Roosevelt. Obstreosis of the ductal tract. Tertiary. Wish you'd take a look at him." "Glad to," said Mitty.

In the operating room there were whispered introductions: "Dr. Remington, Dr. Mitty. Mr. Pritchard-Mitford, Dr. Mitty." "I've read your book on streptothricosis," said Pritchard-Mitford, shaking hands. "A brilliant performance, sir." "Thank you," said Walter Mitty. "Didn't know you were in the States, Mitty," grumbled Remington. "Coals to Newcastle, bringing Mitford and me up here for a tertiary." "You are very kind," said Mitty. A huge, complicated machine, connected to the operating table, with many tubes and wires, began at this moment to go pocketa-pocketa-pocketa. "The new anesthetizer is giving way!" shouted an interne. "There is no one in the East who knows how to fix it!" "Quiet, man!" said Mitty, in a low, cool voice. He sprang to the machine, which was now going pocketa-pocketa-queep-pocketa-queep. He began fingering delicately a row of glistening dials. "Give me a fountain pen!" he snapped. Someone handed him a fountain pen. He pulled a faulty piston out of the machine and inserted the pen in its place. "That will hold for ten minutes," he said. "Get on with the operation." A nurse hurried over and whispered to Renshaw, and Mitty saw the man turn pale. "Coreopsis has set in," said Renshaw nervously. "If you would take over, Mitty?" Mitty looked at him and at the craven figure of Benbow, who drank, and at the grave, uncertain faces of the two great specialists. "If you wish," he said. They slipped a white gown on him; he adjusted a mask and drew on thin gloves; nurses handed him shining . . .

"Back it up, Mac!" Look out for that Buick!" Walter Mitty jammed on the brakes. "Wrong lane, Mac," said the parking-lot attendant, looking at Mitty closely. "Gee. Yeh," muttered Mitty. He began cautiously to back out of the lane marked "Exit Only." "Leave her sit there," said the attendant. "I'll put her away." Mitty got out of the car. "Hey, better leave the key." "Oh," said Mitty, handing the man the ignition key. The attendant vaulted into the car, backed it up with insolent skill, and put it where it belonged.

They're so damn cocky, thought Walter Mitty, walking along Main Street: they think they know everything. Once he had tried to take his chains off, outside New Milford, and he had got them wound around the axles. A man had had to come out in a wrecking car and unwind them, a young, grinning garageman. Since then Mrs. Mitty always made him drive to a garage to have the chains taken off. The next time, he thought, I'll wear my right arm in a sling; they won't grin at me then. I'll have my right arm in a sling and they'll see I couldn't possibly take the chains off myself. He kicked at the slush on the sidewalk. "Overshoes," he said to himself, and he began looking for a shoe store.

When he came out into the street again, with the overshoes in a box under his arm, Walter Mitty began to wonder what the other thing was his wife had told him to get. She had told him twice, before they set out from their house for Waterbury. In a way he hated these weekly trips to town – he was always getting something wrong. Kleenex, he thought, Squibb's, razor blades? No. Toothpaste, toothbrush, bicarbonate, carborundum, initiative and referendum? He gave it up. But she would remember it. "Where's the what's-its-name?" she would ask. "Don't tell me you forgot the what's-its-name." A newsboy went by shouting something about the Waterbury trial.

. . . "Perhaps this will refresh your memory." The District Attorney suddenly thrust a heavy automatic at the quiet figure on the witness stand. "Have you ever seen this before?" Walter Mitty took the gun and examined it expertly. "This is my Webley-Vickers 50.80," he said calmly. An excited buzz ran around the courtroom. The judge rapped for order. "You are a crack shot with any sort of firearms, I believe?" said the District Attorney, insinuatingly. "Objection!" shouted Mitty's attorney. "We have shown that the defendant could not have fired the shot. We have shown that the defendant wore his right arm in a sling on the night of the fourteenth of July." Walter Mitty raised his hand briefly and the bickering attorneys were stilled. "With any known make of gun," he said evenly, "I could have killed Gregory Fitzhurst at three hundred feet *with my left hand.*" Pandemonium broke loose in the courtroom. A woman's scream rose above the bedlam and suddenly a lovely, dark-haired girl was in Walter Mitty's arms. The District Attorney struck at her savagely. Without rising from his chair, Mitty let the man have it on the point of the chin. "You miserable cur!" . . .

"Puppy biscuit," said Walter Mitty. He stopped walking and the buildings of Waterbury rose up out of the misty courtroom and surrounded him again. A woman who was passing laughed. "He said 'Puppy biscuit,' " she said to her companion. "That man said 'Puppy biscuit' to himself." Walter Mitty hurried on. He went into an A & P, not the first one he came to but a smaller one farther up the street. "I want some biscuit for small, young dogs," he said to the clerk. "Any special brand, sir?" The greatest pistol shot in the world thought a moment. "It says 'Puppies Bark for It' on the box," said Walter Mitty.

His wife would be through at the hairdresser's in fifteen minutes, Mitty saw in looking at his watch, unless they had trouble drying it; sometimes they had trouble drying it. She didn't like to get to the hotel first; she would want him to be there waiting for her as usual. He found a big leather chair in the lobby, facing a window, and he put the overshoes and the puppy biscuit on the floor beside it. He picked up an old copy of *Liberty* and sank down into the chair. "Can Germany Conquer the World Through the Air?" Walter Mitty looked at the pictures of bombing planes and of ruined streets.

. . . "The cannonading has got the wind up in young Raleigh, sir," said the sergeant. Captain Mitty looked up at him through tousled hair. "Get him to bed," he said wearily. "With the others. I'll fly alone." "But you can't sir," said the sergeant anxiously. "It takes two men to handle that bomber and the Archies are pounding hell out of the air. Von Richtman's circus is between here and Saulier. "Somebody's got to get that ammunition dump," said Mitty. "I'm going over. Spot of brandy?" He poured a drink for the sergeant and one for himself. War thundered and whined around the dugout and battered at the door. There was a rending of wood and splinters flew through the room. "A bit of a near thing," said Captain Mitty carelessly. "The box barrage is closing in," said the sergeant. "We only live once, Sergeant," said Mitty, with his faint, fleeting smile. "Or do we?" he poured another brandy and tossed it off. "I never see a man could hold his brandy like you, sir," said the sergeant. "Begging your pardon, sir," Captain Mitty stood up and strapped on his huge Webley-Vickers automatic. "It's forty kilometers through hell, sir," said the sergeant. Mitty finished one last brandy. "After all," he said softly, "what isn't?" The pounding of the cannon increased; there was the rat-tat-tatting of machine guns, and from somewhere came the menacing pocketa-pocketa-pocketa of the new flame-throwers. Walter Mitty walked to the door of the dugout humming "Auprès de Ma Blonde." He turned and waved to the sergeant. "Cheerio!" he said. . . .

Something struck his shoulder. "I've been looking all over this hotel for you," said Mrs. Mitty. "Why do you have to hide in this old chair? How did you expect me to find you?" "Things close in," said Walter Mitty vaguely.

"What?" Mrs. Mitty said. "Did you get the what's-its-name? The puppy biscuit? What's in that box?" "Overshoes," said Mitty. "Couldn't you have put them on in the store?" "I was thinking," said Walter Mitty. "Does it ever occur to you that I am sometimes thinking?" She looked at him. "I'm going to take your temperature when I get you home," she said.

They went out through the revolving doors that made a faintly derisive whistling sound when you pushed them. It was two blocks to the parking lot. At the drugstore on the corner she said, "Wait here for me. I forgot something. I won't be a minute." She was more than a minute. Walter Mitty lighted a cigarette. It began to rain, rain with sleet in it. He stood up against the wall of the drugstore, smoking. . . . He put his shoulders back and his heels together. "To hell with the handkerchief," said Walter Mitty scornfully. He took one last drag on his cigarette and snapped it away. Then, with that faint, fleeting smile playing about his lips, he faced the firing squad; erect and motionless, proud and disdainful, Walter Mitty the Undefeated, inscrutable to the last.

JEAN STAFFORD

1944

The Wedding: Beacon Hill

The dressmaker who had been imported from New York to make Hopestill's trousseau was known by her trade name, Mamselle Therese, which she herself always substituted for the nominative case of the first person as though she were her own interpreter. "Mamselle Therese does not touch the potatoes," she said on her first evening in Louisburg Square, as she and I dined alone. She said to me, "Mamselle Therese goes to a nightclub twice a week in New York," by which I understood she wanted me, as Miss Pride's deputy, to supply her with the Boston equivalent of this diversion, but I did not respond as she had hoped and thereafter she made no more such overtures but amused herself (and presumably me) in designing costumes which she said would "bring out" my personality. She spoke of Chanel, Lilly Daché, Mainbocher, as though they were Brahms, Bach, Mozart, or Plato, Descartes, and Hegel. "Daché composed a superb number for an archduchess last month, a really revolutionary turban. People were simply swept off their feet."

Like the bald barber recommending a hair restorer, like the dentist whose teeth are false, Mamselle Therese dressed most frumpishly. She wore a strange assemblage of seedy garments, too large for her spare, nimble frame, out-of-date, soiled, frayed. And it was not only that the little modiste had clothed herself out of a rag bag, but that she had very bad taste, burdening herself like a fancy woman with gimcracks from the five-and-ten-cent stores; wooden brooches in the unreasonable shape of a Scotty or of an ice skate or of a Dutch shoe or a football; enameled beetles or dragon flies or cobras made of tin, with blinding rhinestone eyes, earrings in the shape of oak leaves or candlesticks; and, with any costume, upon her right arm she wore nine thin silver bracelets which she clanked interminably. Her shabbiness could not be explained by poverty, for she had a flourishing business, and the expensive dresses of her two assistants, who had been lodged in a house on Joy Street, suggested that she could afford to be generous in their salaries. She was charging Miss Pride a shocking price for her niece's trousseau, as I knew from her estimate she had handed in on the day she arrived. She spoke quite openly of this as a "good thing."

"Now for you, angel," she said, "Mamselle Therese would sew for next to nothing, but for them, the price is in the hundreds, sometimes in the thousands. It is an art, *n'est-ce pas?* Wouldn't they pay ten thousand for a picture by Rousseau? Then why shouldn't they pay ten thousand for a dress by Chanel? Mainbocher? Mamselle Therese don't kid herself. She knows she isn't in that class yet, but she works slow and sure like a mole. Five years from now Mamselle Therese will be in the movies like Adrian."

Her ruling passion was business, and she could see nothing except in terms of its commercial value. Thus, when she learned that I had gone to a secretarial school, she said, "You must keep your eyes open and when the time comes, rush in and nab yourself a plum. Mamselle Therese's advice to a young girl like you that has a good head on her shoulders is: be a secretary to a big-time lawyer. There's the money! There's the prestige! I'm telling you. What good are you doing yourself fooling around up here with that *vieille furie* when you could be on Fifth Avenue, New York? Mamselle Therese has a girl-friend working at Number One Wall Street on the thirty-fourth floor and she makes fifty dollars a week. I'm telling you."

But she was not, as she seemed, out of touch with human affairs. She was not especially interested in them, but nothing escaped her shrewd French eye. Knowing me to be Miss Pride's secretary, she spoke unguardedly of the household. "*Mon dieu*, that bridegroom! Angel, he is a fool, I'm telling you. Mamselle Therese don't need to make his acquaintance to know that like she knows the palm of her own hand. She only has to contact the fiancée, *n'est-ce pas?* That rich *renarde.*"

"Why do you say he is *renarde?*" I asked.

"You can tell by the eyes. They are subzero. You know? It is on her part a *mariage de convenance.*"

"And how do you know that?"

"Because they haven't slept together. And how does Mamselle Therese know that?" She tapped her forehead. "*Par intuition.*"

"But perhaps it is a *mariage de convenance* on his part too?" I suggested.

"Maybe. Yes, maybe. It is a cold place, this Boston. He marries her because she is rich, beautiful, whatnot. Because a doctor should have a wife. She marries him because she is *enceinte, n'est-ce pas?*"

I should have laughed and denied the charge, but I was so astounded at the woman's wizardry that I could not gather my wits together, for a moment, and when I did, knowing that her conviction was not only right but that I could in no way shake her from it, I said, "You may be right, but I beg you to say nothing to anyone. It would kill Miss Pride."

Mamselle Therese was offended. "Why should Mamselle Therese gossip? She is here for the money. She don't care a damn about the *mariage*. Angel, it is a dirty business and not for me. This little up-and-coming *couturière* stays single. I'm telling you. Plenty of boy-friends and not a husband. Don't mix business with pleasure, angel. So why should she interfere with someone else's *mariage*? Mamselle Therese won't talk to the interested parties. She is interested only in the money from the interested parties."

We were sitting in my room at the time of this conversation and it was rather late, perhaps eleven o'clock. Both Miss Pride and Hopestill had gone out for the evening. Presently we heard light footsteps coming up the last flight of stairs and Hopestill's door was opened. Evidently she had come back to get something, for in ten minutes she went out again and back down the stairs. Mamselle Therese, not so much through the fear of being overheard as through boredom with the subject, dropped it instantly on hearing the footsteps and began telling me about a new costume she had designed for nuns which would be at once more sanitary and more beautiful than their present ones.

But her soliloquy did not prevent me from hearing through the wall which separated our rooms, the soft collapse of the girl's body on the chaise lounge and a sob, stifled at once as though she had pressed her face into a pillow. The sound would probably have escaped me if I had not heard it before and had not come to expect it as the expression, in a sense, of the reason for her visits to her room during the evening. Almost every night when there were dinner guests she came up two or three times, and usually I heard that secret, frustrated outburst like a checked curse. On such evenings she might stay as long as a quarter of an hour, and hearing her footsteps back and forth across the carpet, muted so that I could not be sure if I really heard them or only felt the vibrations of the floor, I sat at my typewriter unable to strike a key, embarrassed because she must have heard the clatter of the machine which stopped as her doorknob turned.

I could not immunize myself to her misery and pitied her for whatever punishment her conscience was meting out to her. I was impelled to go in to her in the way one may start, hearing a human cry in the night, and thinking it is someone lost or hurt and in need of help. Beside a warm fire in a light room, an impression of the night's cold and darkness superimposes itself upon the altruistic impulse, and one rationalizes, says the cry comes from the throat of a drunk or of a cat that can sound like a woman or even that it is the lure of a thief. I would wait until I heard her going down the stairs again and then I would shrug my shoulders with a resolute indifference and say aloud, "It's her affair, not mine."

Still, I could not help feeling that I was somehow better equipped to endure than Hopestill. She, the frail sheep lost from the herd, could not find her way back nor could she make her way alone. She knew already, as these flights to the privacy of her room showed, that she could not carry it off, for even if the discovery of her deception were long postponed or never made at all or made only by a few people who would not blame her or, if they did, would keep silent, she had nevertheless ruined herself in the only milieu for which she was trained. She had ruined herself even though there might never be suspicions or rumors, for she would never be *sure* that she was not suspected: she would hear the most innocent remark as a *double entendre*, the most amiable question as put with an ulterior design. It was possible, too, I thought, that after the secret gratitude to Philip for unknowingly saving her from disgrace had expired, she would commence to hate him.

By day our house was the scene of what Miss Pride crossly called "a needless hullabaloo" for which, as a matter of fact, she was largely responsible, for while Hopestill and Philip had wanted a small wedding, she had insisted that a step of this kind be taken with public pomp. It was typical of her to speak of it as "a step of this kind" as though it were some sort of sensible negotiation which had been undertaken after several other "kinds" had been discarded. It was she who had wired Mamselle Therese, and she who had sent out invitations to three hundred guests for the wedding breakfast, and she who had persuaded a notable clergyman who had left Boston several years before to perform the ceremony. There had been some argument about this last detail. Both Miss Pride and Dr. McAllister's father were Unitarians and did their best to dissuade Hopestill from being married in the Episcopal church in which, adopting her father's rather than her mother's sect, she had been confirmed. She was adamant and requested, moreover, that the minister from whom she had received the Eucharist at her first communion be brought back for the occasion. In only one other particular had she insisted on having her own way. She refused to be given away by her Uncle Arthur Hornblower or any other relative, and before even consulting her aunt conferred the honor upon her aunt's old admirer, Admiral Nephews.

I thought that she wanted to be married in the Episcopal church out of a nostalgic attachment to her childhood as having been a better and happier time. I could find no other reason, for she was altogether without religious conviction and never went to any services. I divined, too, that in denying any member of her family the right to participate actively in the ritual, she was relieving them, symbolically, of any accessory responsibility.

In the week before the wedding, my duties were many and complex. I acted as the intermediary between Miss Pride and the representatives of florists, liquor dealers, caterers, and took great pleasure in ordering such things as twelve cases of champagne and thirty pounds of filet of sole. Miss Pride would have preferred to attend to these matters herself because all tradespeople were scoundrels and I was both gullible and extravagant, but she was occupied with other things, among them with ridding the house of kinsfolk who came in droves beginning at nine o'clock in the morning, expecting to be asked to luncheon and then tea and even dinner.

They infuriated her by telling her that she looked "worn out" and that they were going to make her go to bed while they themselves took over, lock, stock and barrel. To such a suggestion, Miss Pride would say, turning her eyes like pistols on the offender, "If I want crutches, I'll *buy* them, Sally Hornblower." They were full of plans for what she would wear to the wedding (I knew what she would wear: a new black broadcloth suit and a green beaver hat) and for the most decorative way of arranging the display of gifts. She would nod her head and say, "I daresay that would be nice. But I shall just muddle on in my old way. You can't teach an old dog new tricks." Once, after this cliché, she gave a mirthless, "Ha, ha!" and sounded, indeed, like the dog that could not be taught but had learned in his youth the trick of biting trespassers.

The continual stir of the house was intoxicating. On my way out of the house to run some important errand, I would glance into the upstairs sitting room where the presents gradually were accumulating. Hopestill might, as I passed, be unwrapping something that had just come. She would hold up for me to see a blue plum-blossom jar or a silver pitcher. We could hear the bee-like flurry of the sewing machine and the animated conversation of Mamselle Therese and her two assistants. The doorbell and the telephone reiterated their clamorous demands until the servants were beside themselves. Leaving Hopestill surrounded by her treasure, I would go downstairs to receive a final instruction from Miss Pride.

Nearly always, on one of the tables in the hall, there was a silver bowl half-filled with water on whose surface floated the disintegrating but still fragrant flowers that Hopestill had worn the night before. I was curiously moved at the sight of them, and imagined her coming in late, the dangers of another day behind her, Philip's car already pulling away from the curb. I wondered if she would not ponder her face in the mirror above the table as she unpinned the orchid or the gardenias.

The churchly odor of old wood and stone was sweetened with the perfume and boutonnieres of the wedding guests assembled twenty minutes early. A beam of sunshine came through the open door and extended the length of the central aisle until, at the sanctuary, it joined in a pool of opaline light with another laden shaft sifted through the stained-glass windows, of which the three segments were so detailed that I could read in them no narrative but saw only brilliant colors throwing off the glitter of jewels.

From where I sat at the back of the chapel, I could see Miss Pride in the front row sitting between the Reverend McAllister and his wife. She was wearing a new suit, but as it was made in the same pattern as all her others and cut from the same wool, perhaps I alone knew that it was new, for I had seen the tailor's bill. She had made one concession to her relatives, and in place of her green beaver wore a small hat planted with red posies which caused her so much consternation, because she thought it would fall off, that during the ceremony, as she told everyone later, she could think of nothing but the moment when she might take it off.

Philip's mother, although she would have preferred to wear black as a sign of mourning for her son, had finally decided that it would be too much of a good thing if all four of the chief relatives were attired as for a funeral, and was dressed in pale blue, becoming to her rosy cheeks and her white hair and her blue eyes, which had not been reddened but made only prettily clouded by the incessant stream of tears they had released ever since the engagement was announced. She had lost her appetite, had been unable to sleep a night through, and had not appeared at any of the prenuptial parties. It was said by her husband that her heart was temporarily "out of kilter." She had several times written Hopestill begging her to come to Concord: "We have so much to talk about," she wrote. "I feel there are many things you must know about Philip which only I can tell you. The hastiness of your wedding has prevented us from getting really well acquainted, but perhaps we can make up for lost time if only you will agree to spend two or three days with me." Hopestill, either because she was harassed by the business which the wedding involved, or because she could think of no way to refuse the invitation graciously, did not answer, a breach of manners that had already had serious consequences. The elder Mrs. McAllister had told the story everywhere, and making use of her daughter's unwittingly accurate phrase, repeated often, "The wedding is too hasty for me. Marian and I both wish they'd wait until June."

Sitting at the aisle in the middle of the church, casually dressed in tweeds, Mr. Harry Morgan slouched against the side of the pew, his chin in his hand, his eyes closed. He had not been invited, as I well enough knew because I had checked over the list of guests. But I was not in the least surprised to see him although I could not be certain of his motive, whether he had come to tease Hopestill or if he was in love with her and wished to torment himself, or if it was that, desiring to escape suspicion, he had thought it the better policy not to hide himself away. He had, if this last was his intention, made a serious mistake in his costume, and continued, throughout the ceremony, to make an even graver error in his indolent attitude and his drowsy grin, for he was most conspicuous in that church full of people whose dress was all so similar it was virtually a uniform, and thus he was set down by everyone who saw him—and he escaped the notice of very few—as vain and impudent, for in gainsaying the decrees of custom he was usurping custom's power. His presence relieved me on one point and troubled me on another. Evidently Hopestill had not been seeing him, as I had suspected from time to time, for if she had she would have told him not to come. What disturbed me was that since he apparently thought there was nothing odd in his coming this morning and coming with so blatant an air of indifference, there was no reason to suppose that Hopestill and Philip and their friends would be deprived of his company in the future. Perhaps he had come today for the simple reason that he wanted to see Hopestill, to refresh his memory of her beauty and to determine, from the expression on her face and the way she walked, whether his further siege of her would be rewarding.

In the hush that forewarned the wedding march, a hush that fell upon the flesh as well as on the ears so that the guests froze briefly in their postures of kneeling or leaning toward their neighbors, tears of excitement boiled over my eyelids and half-screened the four bridesmaids in their green tulle dresses, preceding the maid of honor whose medieval velvet gown, a deeper shade than theirs, was like the outer leaf and theirs the paler inside ones.

The dazzled guests watched the proud flower for whose protection and enhancement the leaves had been created: a chaste and perfect column draped in satin as pure as the wax of the tapers on the altar and outdoing their flame with the hair that blazed through a calotte of pearls. Her face, white as her finery and her lilies, wore an expression of solemnity befitting the occasion, although, as I heard someone whisper, there should have been something of a smile in her countenance, if not upon her lips then at least within her eyes, for joy should be in proportion equal to the other feelings of the partaker of this particular sacrament. Her look, to me, was one instinct with death, yet death less chill than that which now like a layer beneath her skin gave off a waxen luminosity and imparted to her movement a brittleness as though the soft integuments of skin and cloth concealed a metal mechanism. Her thin fingers were tightly curled on the Admiral's arm. Harry Morgan had turned, with all the others, and while I could not see her face, I knew by his, when she had passed by, that a sign had passed between them, for his mouth curved into a serene smile as if he had half-won his battle.

It seemed to me, as they joined before the minister, that Hopestill shuddered. If this was seen by anyone else—indeed, if it occurred at all—it was attributed to her nervousness, the understandable and appropriate reluctance of a girl about to relinquish her virginity by so public a ritual. With a tidal rustling, the audience sat down, arranged their hands in their laps, and adjusted their spectacles like people anticipating a well-known and beloved piece of music. It was, to be sure, an artistic performance, for the minister, wreathed in benign smiles, posed his literary questions and offered up his prayers with the intonations of a Shakespearean actor, which grace of pitch and diction was afterward to evoke from Reverend McAllister the remark that the service had been "nothing but rhetoric." I was astonished at the brevity of the cross-examination, and before I had accustomed myself to the idea that something of great importance was going on, the whole thing was over and the man and wife were coming back down the aisle, arm in arm, smiling to their well-wishers, their faces illuminated by the sunlight into which they were walking. Hopestill did not fail to include her husband in her dispensation of impartial smiles, but her hand that clutched the bouquet of flowers was clenched like stone.

The drawing room, the library, the dining room overflowed with cawing guests and the stairs were packed with two lanes, one ascending to view the wedding presents, the other coming down. As soon as I had offered my congratulations, I pushed my way through the throngs to Miss Pride, who had got rid of her hat and looked refreshed.

"There are two or three things I want you to attend to," she said to me. "Come along with me and I'll show you."

I followed her docilely down the hall to the door of the pantry, where she instructed me to post myself in order to see that the dirty dishes were immediately sent down on the dumbwaiter to be washed and sent up again so that everyone might be served. The waiters, who were perfectly capable of managing by themselves, regarded me with such wounded displeasure that for the half hour I stood on guard I did not utter a word, but leaned against the window where the sunlight was warm, drinking the remains of champagne in the glasses that came out from the other rooms. Once I closed my eyes to feel the sun on my lids and when I opened them again saw Harry Morgan lounging up against the door giving me what I could only call a once-over. Fearing that if Miss Pride chanced to come into the pantry and saw us there together she might surmise that I was responsible for this intrusion, and being, moreover, greatly perturbed by his prowling eyes, I exclaimed, "My God!" and he, straightening up, extended his hand as he said, "May I share your quiet inglenook, dear, just we two?" One of the accommodators, a portly middle-aged man with a bald head and a frowning face turned on him a look of avuncular disapproval as he pushed past with a tray of glasses and I said, "It's very crowded in here."

"Well, then, let's find a place that isn't crowded. I can't go back into that crush."

"Nobody asked you to," I said, so nervous that I was obliged to put down the glass I was holding for fear of dropping it. "Nobody asked you to come in the first place."

"What kind of talk is that? I am guest Number One. I came at the urgent invitation of the doctor himself. No one asked me, indeed!"

He laughed openly at my perplexity. "Well, in that case," I said, "You ought to join the party."

I myself, feeling that my services in the pantry were dispensable, went out, taking up a place between the long buffet table and the doors to the drawing room which had been slid back all the way, there to examine the implications of the conversation I had just had. I was prevented from a long study by the Admiral who, with old Mrs. McAllister, appeared slowly making his way toward the refreshment table. "Ah," he cried, spotting me, "here we have an ally. Sonie, what could you do in the way of a hot bird and a cold bottle for two old fellows? I'm hungry as a bear. I tell you, giving away a young lady is hard work. It's a strain on the heart! Particularly if you wanted her for your granddaughter-in-law." He winked at his companion. "Well, all's well that ends well, as they say. And while I'm about consoling myself, ma'am, let me congratulate you on getting a pippin for the boy."

"Much obliged," said Mrs. McAllister coldly. "I think Hope looks ill."

"Ill? Why, ma'am, though you're a woman, you don't know women. What female creature ever looked well on her wedding day? I always say the expression shouldn't be 'white as a ghost' but 'white as a bride.' And the whiter they are, the prettier, what?"

Mrs. McAllister received a plate of sole and salad and a glass of champagne from me. Refusing from that moment forward to discuss the wedding, the wedding breakfast, or the bride and groom, she commenced on an analysis of Amy Brooks's water colors, in which she displayed more affection than intelligence, Amy being the bride she had coveted for her grandson. "The sweet thing, knowing that I don't get about, brought a whole portfolio full of them to me yesterday and I was perfectly charmed. She has real talent." She went on to describe in particular a little scene Amy had done of the hemlocks in the Arboretum. While I nodded with interest and even volunteered a few comments ("How much I should like to see the picture. No, I have never been to the Arboretum, but I hope to go on Lilac Sunday," et cetera), Reverend McAllister edged his way up to us. "How much champaign would you say Lucy Pride ordered for this collation?" he asked me. I told him exactly: twelve cases. He raised his eyebrows, appalled. "If all the money spent on drink were handed over to the missionaries, we would have a Christian world."

Mrs. McAllister, who had wanted her son to go into the Navy, had often been heard to speak like a pagan. She snapped at him, "I hope that time never comes, Son, for I feel that there are times when one *needs* alcohol. Now, for example. At weddings and at funerals." Her voice had risen to an impassioned shriek and her son put his finger to his solemn lips. "Hush, Mother, they say it takes very little to go to one's head when one is advanced in years."

The Admiral snorted, "Your mother can take care of herself, old man. She hasn't had enough to drink, that's her trouble. Hand me your glass, ma'am, and let me refill it."

"Good afternoon," said Miss Pride crisply from behind us. "Ah, Sonie, I see you're taking over out here. I don't know what I would do without you. Well, and have you seen our poor lambs, Sarah? They're complaining that their arms ache from shaking hands and their faces hurt from smiling. They groaned when I told them they must stay another hour at least."

"At least," rejoined the old lady staring hard at Miss Pride. "Why, I daresay that less than half of Boston has had a chance to congratulate them. My dear Lucy, you have outdone yourself!"

By this time, however, the crowd was beginning to thin. Hopestill beckoned to me. "Go up with me, will you, Sonie?" she whispered. I glanced toward her maid-of-honor and she said impatiently, "I've arranged that, don't worry." Philip's face was fixed in a smile that revealed his teeth which were so regular and white they looked almost false. The adjective "sanitary" flashed across my mind as I took in his clear intellectual eyes, his fair hair, his meticulously cared-for person, and in that moment, I preferred his bride upon whose cheek there was a light streak of dirt and who was frankly exhausted and was making no attempts to conceal the fact. I told her that I would meet her in her room and she left when she had said something to Philip who, looking at me as if he had never seen me before, formally shook my hand, not altering his grin in the least. I laughed uneasily and said, "I've already congratulated you once, don't you remember?" and he replied, "How stingy you are! Can't you congratulate a man twice on the happiest day of his life?" But there was in his voice a note of such staggering unhappiness, so taut an irony that I could make only a feeble rejoinder, told him I must hurry up to Hopestill, that I wished him all the happiness, that I . . .

Hopestill had flung her bouquet down the stair well, but one flower, limp and ragged at the edges, was caught in the pointed cuff of her wedding dress. She was waiting in her sitting room for me and she could have been waiting ten years, she had changed so much. The structure of her face was loose, as though the sagging muscles had weakened the mortised bones. There was a starched pallor on her thin lips, a narrow canniness in her eyes, and the skin, in the brief time since I had seen her in the church, had lost that shimmer which had seemed to be touched by the moon rather than the sun, and was ashen now, darkening to a bruised blue beneath her eyes. She had had a drink and, when I came in, put down her glass. There was a newly opened bottle of whisky on the table near where she stood.

"By God, he can wait for me!" she cried. "I'll go down when I'm God damned good and ready." And she sank into one of the winged chairs and poured herself another drink.

"It was a very nice wedding," I said.

"Lock the door, Sonie. I won't have any of them coming in here! I won't! I wish I were dead!"

I locked the door as she ordered me and reluctantly returned. She directed me to sit down opposite her and she said, "I really mean it: I wish I were dead. All I've accomplished today, all I've accomplished in my whole life, is that I've transferred myself from one martinet to another."

"You didn't have to marry him."

She got to her feet and glared at me. "I'm sure I don't know why I've taken you into my confidence, and you can jolly well forget this. Now I'm going to dress."

The crowd had thinned considerably when I went down. In the vestibule, I heard a woman remark, "I wouldn't mind if my income were cut to fifteen thousand. I'd just go out to my farm for the whole year." And another voice replied, "Of course it wouldn't go hard with you, Augusta. Why, you have a fortune in your roses if you'd only do something about it." Augusta, whom I immediately knew to be Philip's aunt, laughed heartily, "That's what my nephew tells me, but he's a pipe dreamer. I'm so glad that at least one of his pipe dreams has come true. Hope is the sweetest girl in Boston, I've always felt."

Hopestill was coming down the stairs and in her carefully composed face there was no sign of the fright and anger that had made her burst out to me in her room. She joined Philip at the door and they went out, sped on by the uproar of the guests who had lingered.

"At any rate," Miss Pride was saying at my elbow, "I haven't lost this one," and she slipped her arm through mine. She linked her other in the Admiral's, and three abreast, we went down the hall toward the library. "We'll quickly get rid of Ichabod," whispered Miss Pride nodding in the direction of Reverend McAllister, "and then we three can have a nice talk."

"Right-o," said the Admiral. "Ain't it a pity my wife had to miss this! I'm gay as a lark. Aren't you, Sonie?"

"Oh, yes, sir!" I cried. Miss Pride released us both and after she had gently closed the door behind us, switched off the ceiling light.

The sun had gone behind a cloud and the library was shadowy and cold. "There now," she said. "It's cozy. It's just right to have this sort of *Dämmerung* follow a wedding. It is the anticlimax to these affairs that I like most."

CHRISTOPHER LA FARGE

1947

The Three Aspects

To Mrs. Arthur Everard the whole incident appeared anachronistic and obscure, although it was obviously picturesque. That an apparently ordinary country woman like Laura Pellett could have had the strength and determination to horsewhip her strong husband and then lock him up in a shed was astonishing. That such a thing could occur in 1947 was both primitive and funny, while quite beyond any rational explanation that she could see. The somewhat sordid turnabout ending to the story merely made the whole matter more confusing.

"I guess that neither of us," Mrs. Everard said to her friend Mrs. Walters, "has sufficient knowledge of Rhode Island—or, for that matter, of New England—to have a key to these people anyway."

"No," said Mrs. Walters. "It's different from Virginia. Is Mrs. Pellett the one you get your milk from, that angular female?"

"Yes," said Mrs. Everard. "She's delivered the milk since we moved here in 1943, when Arthur first went to Quonset. Milk and eggs. Sometimes vegetables too. But she's always seemed very ordinary—a plain sort of woman, tall, but flat-chested, not a bit attractive, and kept herself very much to herself. The only odd thing about her was that she usually had her husband, Leroy, in the truck with her. It must have cut a whole lot of his working day. But anyway, there he sat. He never got out or I never saw him do it. She herself made the deliveries. For a while I'd figured he was crippled or something."

"Was he?" asked Mrs. Walters.

"No, not a bit," Mrs. Everard said. "I've seen him since, a little closer; he's tall, looks well made, with dark hair. Not unattractive, a rather weak but humorous face. They have no children, I believe."

"How did you run into all this, then?"

"I drove over to the Pelletts' to see if they had any sweet corn. I'd forgotten to ask her in the morning when she was here. There wasn't anyone at the house—it was all locked up—and I heard a funny sort of noise from the barns and walked over toward them. There was a shed, it was padlocked shut and it had no window, and I could hear a man singing inside. He was singing, 'What shall we do with the drunken sailor?' "

"Gosh!" said Mrs. Walters. "Go on!"

"Well, I knocked on the door and I asked him if Mrs. Pellett was home and he said no, she wasn't, and would I look and see if the padlock on the door was really locked? I looked and it was. He said, 'Well, then there's nothing to do. My wife'll be home soon. She's got the key. You got any cigarettes?' I said I had and he said he'd certainly be obliged if I'd pass some under the door to him. I shoved my pack of cigarettes under and I asked him if he had matches and he said, 'Yes, I got some and I'm obliged to you. You just go back along now. Any message you'd like me to give her?' I told him of the corn and he said they had some and he'd see his wife brought some over in the morning. It was the damnedest conversation. He didn't sound a bit angry or embarrassed, and he laughed—he actually laughed—and he said, 'Well, this is different than talking on the telephone, ain't it?' I had to laugh too. Then I left. As I was driving out, a woman who had been leaning on the fence—I guess she'd been watching the whole thing—waved at me and I stopped the car. Her name is Mrs. Cloud."

"Is that the fat woman that lives next door to the Pelletts?" Mrs. Walters asked. "The one they call Ma?"

"Yes. She's really monstrous, isn't she? She frightens me. When I'd stopped she said, 'You been looking for Laura Pellett?' I said I had. 'He still locked in that shed?' she asked me. I said there was a man there, I supposed it was Mr. Pellett. 'That's right,' she said. 'It's Leroy,' and she laughed, and went on. 'My guy!' she said—I love that expression—'My guy! you should have seen her take the whip to him!' 'Whip?' I said. 'Yes indeed,' she said. 'She come home about noon and she seen him in the orchard talking to that young Sybilla Greene lives acrost the road, and she had this whip with her and she took the whip right to him. He never said a word, he just laughed, and that Sybilla, she ran off yelling like a house afire, and then Laura Pellett, she locked him up in the shed. Just marched him in there and locked him up. He got no dinner and she left in the truck. No accounting for folks' behavior, is there? I guess there'll be quite a reconciliation to this. Pity you couldn't have let him loose.' I wish I could imitate her exact words and accent for you. Well, then she grinned at me and turned around and walked off without another word. It made me feel very uncomfortable and sorry I'd stopped, in a way. I just came home then. But it really is frightfully funny, isn't it? So completely screwball."

"Darnedest thing I ever heard of," said Mrs. Walters. "How old are the Pelletts?"

"It's hard to say. Around thirty-five, I guess. But it's just a guess."

"What happened when Mrs. Pellett got home?"

"Well," said Mrs. Everard, "all I know is what I've picked up since. It may be pure gossip, but everyone knows it. Anyway, it's all the nineteenth century, not the twentieth. They say she let him out that evening, and then that night, after she'd gone to sleep, he got up and took every stitch of clothes, man's or woman's, out of the house with him. He went to his mother's house, and in the morning Mrs. Pellett had to go to Mrs. Cloud and ask for the loan of some clothes. They say she didn't have on even a nightgown, that she was wrapped up in a blanket. Just think of having to do that! Yet she made the deliveries right on time that morning, just the same, dressed in something that hung around her like a tent, and she looked—well, it's hard to describe—she looked quite calm, almost content. She didn't even seem to be embarrassed. When I saw her, all she said was, 'Here you are, Mrs. Everard. I brought you the corn. I look a sight, don't I?' and she smiled at me. Honestly, she looked *happy*. It's true, you couldn't miss it, although I know it doesn't make any sense."

"No, it really doesn't," said Mrs. Walters.

"Particularly," said Mrs. Everard, "with her husband off on a drunk."

"Golly, did he go on a drunk?"

"Well, I didn't actually see them," Mrs. Everard said, "but apparently everyone else did. Leroy and his mother. The mother must be nearly seventy, they tell me, and they go on drunks about twice a year. I gather that this time they took his mother's horse and buggy and got very drunk together and drove all over the town singing songs and laughing like crazy. That took two days—they say it's always two days—and then Leroy went home."

"Gosh!" said Mrs. Walters. "I do wish I'd seen that. Have you seen them since then?"

"Every day," said Mrs. Everard. "She comes in the truck with him. She's got her own clothes back now. She makes the deliveries, and he sits in the cab and never moves out of it. I've longed to get a look at him, but I've never had the excuse. But she looks, she *still* looks, contented in that sort of dumb way. I'm damned if I see what the content comes from."

"They must all of them be crazy," Mrs. Walters said.

"That's what it seems like," said Mrs. Everard. "But goodness! There's some key to it, only *I* haven't got it. Maybe they really are all crazy. Who knows? But in 1947!"

When Ma Cloud saw Sybilla come into the Pelletts' orchard, she watched from the kitchen window of her house. She saw Leroy leave the barns and go out and join the girl there, and she thought it was funny Laura had left him at home. Must be one of the cows sick or something, nothing else would explain it. That Laura was certainly a jealous woman.

When she saw Laura come back in the truck, about fifteen minutes later, and earlier than usual, Ma Cloud got right out and went to the fence where she could see better. A body wouldn't want to miss this. No, sir.

She watched Laura light into Leroy with the horsewhip and she could hear Sybilla scream as she ran away. Well, she thought, that little slut come for no good, she'd ought to be the one was whipped. Ma found it unbelievably exciting to watch the whipping, it made her tingle all over, it made her think of her own youth and her own passions and the men she'd had. The only thing that surprised her was when Laura locked up Leroy in the shed. She'd expected they'd go into the house together and make it up, plenty. That's what she'd a done, when she was young.

But Laura went into the house and nothing further happened, so Ma went back to her kitchen and made herself dinner, but she kept an eye out the window from then on. She saw Laura go to the barn and to the vegetable garden, and she watched her drive off in the truck again. Well, folks acted funny. You couldn't tell what they'd do.

She heard that Everard woman's car, and she got right out of the house to the fence again. I ain't going to miss this, she said to herself. Mrs. Everard was pretty and she might let Leroy out, he might just be closed in, not locked in. It was as good as a play to watch that young woman standing by the shed and talking through it to Leroy. Ma couldn't hear what they said, but she could imagine it. My guy! she thought, that Laura's a fool! Mrs. Everard, she's twice as pretty as that Sybilla, and these summer people from out of town, like her, they had no morals, not to speak of. Or so it seemed.

It was a great disappointment when Mrs. Everard left the shed and started back down the lane in her car. The shed must have been padlocked. But anyway, it gave you someone to talk to about it. She waved to the young woman and when she stopped, Ma told her all about it—well, not all about it, but about the whipping. Telling it, it all took place again in her own mind and she could feel the same acute pleasure once more. And it was fun to watch the woman's expression, it was half eager, half shocked. It was as though she knew she shouldn't be setting there, she so high and mighty, and be gossiping like this and yet she couldn't help herself. It'll learn her, said Ma to herself. I bet now she wishes she'd let him out of that shed.

About six o'clock Ma saw Laura come home and let Leroy out of the shed, and she watched him go to the house. It was funny, again, that Laura didn't follow him in. It was against nature. But she stayed at her window till she saw Laura come back from the garden with a big basket full of ears of corn and go indoors. That was too hard to take for long. She lifted her huge bulk out of her chair and she went to the porch and she waited there until it was getting dark. Then she walked over to the Pelletts' house. If they caught her, she'd say she'd come to borrow a little shortening. If they didn't, maybe she could get a peek in a window.

She got near the house without being seen, and she looked in, and all she could see was Laura sitting in one chair and sewing and Leroy smoking in another and both of them as silent as the grave. She stood there a long time, till her old legs ached, and finally Laura got up without a word and went into the bedroom and closed the door, and a little while later Leroy lighted a new cigar and he went in after her. But when she moved around to that side of the house, the shades were drawn, close, and she could do nothing but go home and go to bed herself. Still, a body could imagine what went on. Or could you? They didn't act like they'd made up, not any, and there was Leroy smoking cigars in the bedroom, and the Lord knew Laura had made plenty fuss about that lately. Well, thing to do was to see how they behaved in the morning.

Ma Just about died of excitement when Laura turned up at seven in the morning with nothing on but a blanket.

"Can I borrow a dress, Ma?" she said.

"What you want a dress for?" Ma said. "You been burnt out?"

"No," Laura said. "Leroy has gone to his ma, and he took all my clothes."

Looking at the expression on Laura's face, Ma felt herself getting excited again. "Where's your nightgown, child?"

She saw the color run up into Laura's pale face. "It went with the rest of the clothes," Laura said.

"Well," said Ma, "I'll see what I got that won't fall off of you. I got some of my daughter's things, though she's a lot bigger'n you be." She turned away to rummage in a cupboard, and the sense of excitement was tingling all through her. My guy, she thought, I wish I could-a seen in that room last night. How'd he git the nightgown?

"So Leroy's gone to his ma," she said, "I guess that'll mean he's off again for a few days."

"Seems so," said Laura.

"She's certainly a gay old lady," said Ma. She handed a slip and a cotton housedress and some sneakers to Laura. "Try these, and if they don't fit, we'll try something else. Need a nightgown?"

"No, thank you," Laura said and she blushed hotly again. "Thank you, Ma, these'll do," and she fair ran out of the house.

Small wonder, thought Ma. Now Leroy and his old ma would get as drunk as lords and go cavorting around the countryside. Always had been a queer family. Old man Pellett just like Leroy. Must be God knows how many little Pellett bastards in South County, number of women he chased after. And now Leroy following in his tracks. Well, just showed what a fool Laura was to try to lock him up, to try to stop him by taking him along in the truck when he could be doing a day's work at home. You couldn't stop that sort of thing, not with human nature the way it was. Only funny thing was, why did Laura seem so calm about it? Had she jest give up? Well, she'd better. She'd better get accustomed to the Pelletts after living with one of them for fifteen years. Or get herself an extra man. But, my good guy, thought Ma Cloud, she ain't got the looks to git a man now, let alone hold one. It was going to be real interesting to have them for neighbors. Exciting, too.

When Laura came home that noon, she saw Leroy and Sybilla in the orchard and a great many things went through her mind at once, quite clearly, though not in words. She felt her love—her passion—for her husband rise in her like a hot wave, and with it a sick feeling of sadness at their childlessness and guilt at her recent behavior toward Leroy. She understood that Leroy was doing this completely on purpose or he wouldn't be seeing Sybilla in the orchard but somewhere else, out of sight of the house and her. She understood that Sybilla must be far gone toward Leroy, or she would never have consented to meet him there—and it made Leroy unbearably attractive and desirable.

Less clearly but still forcefully, she saw that she had been foolish to deny herself to him because of their fight over the smoking in bed and that only her foolishness had caused all this to happen, and that the best thing to do would be to retreat from the impossible, stubborn position she had taken, pretend not to have seen them, and tell Leroy later that he could smoke in bed again—and that his smoking would—would stop *nothing* ever again.

But however much she saw and knew and understood in that intense moment, it was impossible for her to make herself act otherwise than she had to act—as she knew, indeed, that Leroy was goading her to act. Sybilla was young; she was not. Sybilla was pretty, she had a lovely young figure; and Laura knew she herself was plain and that she had spread and that her figure was gone forever, even without childbearing. The pattern she had set up so long ago, the being always together, the refusal ever to let Leroy go out of her sight, was too strong now. It had worked, they had been happy, the— the whole of life, nights and days, had been good and fulfilled, whatever anyone thought or said of them. It was only the recent quarrel, this difference of her making, that had brought on the present crisis. And the crisis had become too acute, too dangerous, to let her be calm or sensible. Her rage rose in proportion to its uselessness and she seized the old whip on the porch and ran out to the orchard.

You just had to bring things to a head, somehow, and even if this meant that sooner or later Leroy would go on another of his drunks, when he came back it would be all over, they could begin again. She was driven by a force greater than reason. Perhaps Laura might have calmed down if Sybilla hadn't screamed so loudly or if Leroy hadn't laughed. The combination was too much, and even though she saw old Ma Cloud leaning on the fence and watching, she began to lay into Leroy with the whip. He just protected his face with his arms and stood there laughing, and Sybilla screamed again and ran off yelling at the top of her lungs.

Laura continued to whip Leroy until Sybilla was out of sight. Then she stopped.

"Now!" she said. "Now! You git to the sheepshed, you Leroy, or you'll git some more of this."

"Mad, ain't you?" Leroy said and he grinned.

She cut at his legs again with the whip.

"Jesus, woman!" he said. "You got no sense. Why should I mind the shed? House ain't no use to me, is it? She's pretty, ain't she?"

"You git to that shed," Laura cried.

He walked past her and Laura followed him, close enough to lash him again with the whip if she had to, but Leroy went straight to the shed and into it and sat down on a box there. Without hesitation, Laura closed the doors on him and padlocked them shut.

"You're a hawg for work, Laura," he called out to her. "Here I set, thinkin' choice thoughts, *choice* thoughts, and you got to do all the work. My!"

"You set there till you're ready to see what a skunk you are," she said.

"Fetch me my cigarettes," he said. "Or even better, my cigars. I left 'em in the house. I'm going to make me up a bed here—to smoke in."

"You'll git no cigarettes or cigars now nor later," she yelled at him. "I'll hide you again when I do let you out." She heard him laugh and it made her so angry that she almost undid the padlock again to give him another taste of the whip, but she changed her mind and she went to the house instead. She'd have liked to take a cut at old Ma Cloud, too.

She cooked dinner, but she didn't take any out to Leroy. She worked in the garden till three and then she took the truck to North Ferry for shopping. When she got back it was about six and she went to the shed. She could hear nothing there.

"You still there?" she said.

"I'm right here," he said. "I got a message for you."

"Who?" she asked.

"Well, it ain't from Ma Cloud, and it ain't from Sybilla Greene," he said. "It's from Mrs. Everard. She wants some sweet corn for tomorrow." His voice took on almost the exact intonation of Mrs. Everard's. "You all had better scurry right out and pick it now before dark, honey," he said.

Laura stood there in a mood composed half of anger and half of reluctant amusement.

"You want to come out?" she said.

"Why, sure," he said. "Any time suits you."

Not knowing what else to do, she unlocked the door and Leroy came out. Without a word to her, he walked to the house. When he got there he called back to her, "Don't forgit the corn," and he went inside.

She picked the corn and she came in and got supper ready. Leroy was smoking and looking at the ceiling. They never said a word to each other all evening. At nine o'clock Laura went to bed. Just as she started to turn out the light, Leroy came in.

"No," he said. "Leave the light on. I been in enough darkness for a while." He was smoking a cigar.

He undressed and he stood before her naked.

"Nice welts," he said pointing to the scars of her whip on his legs and body. "You use a whip real handy, don't you?"

Laura felt her whole soul turn over in pain at the sight of those welts and at the lightness, the detached tone of his voice. She watched him get into his pajamas, but when he got into bed and lay there puffing at the cigar, the whole structure she had erected collapsed on her and she turned away from him and burst into tears.

He must have put out his cigar at once and turned off the light, because it was only seconds later that she was in his arms and everything was as it had always been since they got married. She didn't have to tell him that he could smoke all he wanted to, in bed or out, that she'd never refuse him this love again—he'd know all that without her telling, because that was what love meant.

When she woke in the morning she was still naked and there wasn't a stitch of clothes in the whole house. He'd even taken her nightgown that she'd flung to the floor. She'd have got angry again if it hadn't been for the note, left on the kitchen table.

"Gone to get drunk with my ma," it said. "See how you like having to set in one place alone. Don't catch cold. Be back Thursday, feel too good to set quiet now. Don't worry any. Leroy."

It made her so happy that she didn't care at all about having to wrap herself up in a blanket and go over, even to Ma Cloud's to borrow some clothes. Why should she care *who* knew that Leroy loved her?

SHIRLEY JACKSON

1950

The Summer People

The Allisons' country cottage, seven miles from the nearest town, was set prettily on a hill; from three sides it looked down on soft trees and grass that seldom, even at midsummer, lay still and dry. On the fourth side was the lake, which touched against the wooden pier the Allisons had to keep repairing, and which looked equally well from the Allisons' front porch, their side porch or any spot on the wooden staircase leading from the porch down to the water. Although the Allisons loved their summer cottage, looked forward to arriving in early summer and hated to leave in the fall, they had not troubled themselves to put in any improvements, regarding the cottage itself and the lake as improvement enough for the life left to them. The cottage had no heat, no running water except the precarious supply from the backyard pump, and no electricity. For seventeen summers, Janet Allison had cooked on a kerosene stove, heating all their water; Robert Allison had brought buckets full of water daily from the pump and read his paper by kerosene light in the evenings; and they had both, sanitary city people, become stolid and matter-of-fact about their backhouse. In the first two years they had gone through all the standard vaudeville and magazine jokes about backhouses and by now, when they no longer had frequent guests to impress, they had subsided to a comfortable security which made the backhouse, as well as the pump and the kerosene, an indefinable asset to their summer life.

In themselves, the Allisons were ordinary people. Mrs. Allison was fifty-eight years old and Mr. Allison sixty; they had seen their children outgrow the summer cottage and go on to families of their own and seashore resorts; their friends were either dead or settled in comfortable year-round houses, their nieces and nephews vague. In the winter they told one another they could stand their New York apartment while waiting for the summer; in the summer they told one another that the winter was well worth while, waiting to get to the country.

Since they were old enough not to be ashamed of regular habits, the Allisons invariably left their summer cottage the Tuesday after Labor Day, and were as invariably sorry when the months of September and early October turned out to be pleasant and almost insufferably barren in the city; each year they recognized that there was nothing to bring them back to New York, but it was not until this year that they overcame their traditional inertia enough to decide to stay in the cottage after Labor Day.

"There isn't really anything to take us back to the city," Mrs. Allison told her husband seriously, as though it were a new idea, and he told her, as though neither of them had ever considered it, "We might as well enjoy the country as long as possible."

Consequently, with much pleasure and a slight feeling of adventure, Mrs. Allison went into their village the day after Labor Day and told those natives with whom she had dealings, with a pretty air of breaking away from tradition, that she and her husband had decided to stay at least a month longer at their cottage.

"It isn't as though we had anything to take us back to the city," she said to Mr. Babcock, her grocer. "We might as well enjoy the country while we can."

"Nobody ever stayed at the lake past Labor Day before," Mr. Babcock said. He was putting Mrs. Allison's groceries into a large cardboard carton, and he stopped for a minute to look reflectively into a bag of cookies. "Nobody," he added.

"But the city!" Mrs. Allison always spoke of the city to Mr. Babcock as though it were Mr. Babcock's dream to go there. "It's so hot—you've really no idea. We're always sorry when we leave."

"Hate to leave," Mr. Babcock said. One of the most irritating native tricks Mrs. Allison had noticed was that of taking a trivial statement and rephrasing it downward, into an even more trite statement. "I'd hate to leave myself," Mr. Babcock said, after deliberation, and both he and Mrs. Allison smiled. "But I never heard of anyone ever staying out at the lake after Labor Day before."

"Well, we're going to give it a try," Mrs. Allison said, and Mr. Babcock replied gravely, "Never know till you try."

Physically, Mrs. Allison decided, as she always did when leaving the grocery after one of her inconclusive conversations with Mr. Babcock, physically, Mr. Babcock could model for a statue of Daniel Webster, but mentally . . . it was horrible to think into what old New England Yankee stock had

degenerated. She said as much to Mr. Allison when she got into the car, and
he said, "It's generations of inbreeding. That and the bad land."

Since this was their big trip into town, which they made only once
every two weeks to buy things they could not have delivered, they spent all
day at it, stopping to have a sandwich in the newspaper and soda shop, and
leaving packages heaped in the back of the car. Although Mrs. Allison was
able to order groceries delivered regularly, she was never able to form any
accurate idea of Mr. Babcock's current stock by telephone, and her lists of
odds and ends that might be procured was always supplemented, almost beyond their need, by the new and fresh local vegetables Mr. Babcock was selling temporarily, or the packaged candy which had just come in. This trip
Mrs. Allison was tempted, too, by the set of glass baking dishes that had
found themselves completely by chance in the hardware and clothing and
general store, and which had seemingly been waiting there for no one but
Mrs. Allison, since the country people, with their instinctive distrust of anything that did not look as permanent as trees and rocks and sky, had only
recently begun to experiment in aluminum baking dishes instead of iron-
ware, and had, apparently within the memory of local inhabitants, discarded
stoneware in favor of iron.

Mrs. Allison had the glass baking dishes carefully wrapped, to endure
the uncomfortable ride home over the rocky road that led up to the Allisons'
cottage, and while Mr. Charley Walpole, who, with his younger brother Al-
bert, ran the hardware-clothing-general store (the store itself was called
Johnson's, because it stood on the site of the old Johnson cabin, burned fifty
years before Charley Walpole was born), laboriously unfolded newspapers to
wrap around the dishes, Mrs. Allison said, informally, "Course, I *could* have
waited and gotten those dishes in New York, but we're not going back so
soon this year."

"Heard you was staying on," Mr. Charley Walpole said. His old fingers
fumbled maddeningly with the thin sheets of newspaper, carefully trying to
isolate only one sheet at a time, and he did not look up at Mrs. Allison as he
went on, "Don't know about staying on up there to the lake. Not after Labor
Day."

"Well, you know," Mrs. Allison said, quite as though he deserved an explanation, "it just seemed to us that we've been hurrying back to New York
every year, and there just wasn't any need for it. You know what the city's
like in the fall." And she smiled confidingly up at Mr. Charley Walpole.

Rhythmically he wound string around the package. He's giving me a
piece long enough to save, Mrs. Allison thought, and she looked away quickly to avoid giving any sign of impatience. "I feel sort of like we belong here,
more," she said. "Staying on after everyone else has left." To prove this, she
smiled brightly across the store at a woman with a familiar face, who might
have been the woman who sold berries to the Allisons one year, or the

woman who occasionally helped in the grocery and was probably Mr. Babcock's aunt.

"Well," Mr. Charley Walpole said. He shoved the package a little across the counter, to show that it was finished and that for a sale well made, a package well wrapped, he was willing to accept pay. "Well," he said again. "Never been summer people before, at the lake after Labor Day."

Mrs. Allison gave him a five-dollar bill, and he made change methodically, giving great weight even to the pennies. "Never after Labor Day," he said, and nodded at Mrs. Allison, and went soberly along the store to deal with two women who were looking at cotton house dresses.

As Mrs. Allison passed on her way out she heard one of the women say acutely, "Why is one of them dresses one dollar and thirty-nine cents and this one here is only ninety-eight?"

"They're great people," Mrs. Allison told her husband as they went together down the sidewalk after meeting at the door of the hardware store. "They're so solid, and so reasonable, and so *honest*."

"Makes you feel good, knowing there are still towns like this," Mr. Allison said.

"You know, in New York," Mrs. Allison said, "I might have paid a few cents less for these dishes, but there wouldn't have been anything sort of personal in the transaction."

"Staying on to the lake?" Mrs. Martin, in the newspaper and sandwich shop, asked the Allisons. "Heard you was staying on."

"Thought we'd take advantage of the lovely weather this year," Mr. Allison said.

Mrs. Martin was a comparative newcomer to the town; she had married into the newspaper and sandwich shop from a neighboring farm, and had stayed on after her husband's death. She served bottled soft drinks, and fried egg and onion sandwiches on thick bread, which she made on her own stove at the back of the store. Occasionally when Mrs. Martin served a sandwich it would carry with it the rich fragrance of the stew or the pork chops cooking alongside for Mrs. Martin's dinner.

"I don't guess anyone's ever stayed out there so long before," Mrs. Martin said. "Not after Labor Day, anyway."

"I guess Labor Day is when they usually leave," Mr. Hall, the Allisons' nearest neighbor, told them later, in front of Mr. Babcock's store, where the Allisons were getting into their car to go home. "Surprised you're staying on."

"It seemed a shame to go so soon," Mrs. Allison said. Mr. Hall lived three miles away; he supplied the Allisons with butter and eggs, and occasionally, from the top of their hill, the Allisons could see the lights in his house in the early evening before the Halls went to bed.

"They usually leave Labor Day," Mr. Hall said.

The ride home was long and rough; it was beginning to get dark, and Mr. Allison had to drive very carefully over the dirt road by the lake. Mrs. Allison lay back against the seat, pleasantly relaxed after a day of what seemed whirlwind shopping compared with their day-to-day existence; the new glass baking dishes lurked agreeably in her mind, and the half bushel of red eating apples, and the package of colored thumbtacks with which she was going to put up new shelf edging in the kitchen. "Good to get home," she said softly as they came in sight of their cottage, silhouetted above them against the sky.

"Glad we decided to stay on," Mr. Allison agreed.

Mrs. Allison spent the next morning lovingly washing her baking dishes, although in his innocence Charley Walpole had neglected to notice the chip in the edge of one; she decided, wastefully, to use some of the red eating apples in a pie for dinner, and, while the pie was in the oven and Mr. Allison was down getting the mail, she sat out on the little lawn the Allisons had made at the top of the hill, and watched the changing lights on the lake, alternating gray and blue as clouds moved quickly across the sun.

Mr. Allison came back a little out of sorts; it always irritated him to walk the mile to the mailbox on the state road and come back with nothing, even though he assumed that the walk was good for his health. This morning there was nothing but a circular from a New York department store, and their New York paper, which arrived erratically by mail from one to four days later than it should, so that some days the Allisons might have three papers and frequently none. Mrs. Allison, although she shared with her husband the annoyance of not having mail when they so anticipated it, pored affectionately over the department store circular, and made a mental note to drop in at the store when she finally went back to New York, and check on the sale of wool blankets; it was hard to find good ones in pretty colors nowadays. She debated saving the circular to remind herself, but after thinking about getting up and getting into the cottage to put it away safely somewhere, she dropped it into the grass beside her chair and lay back, her eyes half closed.

"Looks like we might have some rain," Mr. Allison said, squinting at the sky.

"Good for the crops," Mrs. Allison said laconically, and they both laughed.

The kerosene man came the next morning while Mr. Allison was down getting the mail; they were getting low on kerosene and Mrs. Allison greeted the man warmly; he sold kerosene and ice, and, during the summer, hauled garbage away for the summer people. A garbage man was only necessary for improvident city folk; country people had no garbage.

"I'm glad to see you," Mrs. Allison told him. "We were getting pretty low."

The kerosene man, whose name Mrs. Allison had never learned, used a hose attachment to fill the twenty-gallon tank which supplied light and heat and cooking facilities for the Allisons; but today, instead of swinging down from his truck and unhooking the hose from where it coiled affectionately around the cab of the truck, the man stared uncomfortably at Mrs. Allison, his truck motor still going.

"Thought you folks'd be leaving," he said.

"We're staying on another month," Mrs. Allison said brightly. "The weather was so nice, and it seemed like—"

"That's what they told me," the man said. "Can't give you no oil, though."

"What do you mean?" Mrs. Allison raised her eyebrows. "We're just going to keep on with our regular—"

"After Labor Day," the man said. "I don't get much oil myself after Labor Day."

Mrs. Allison reminded herself, as she had frequently to do when the disagreement with her neighbors, that city manners were no good with country people; you could not expect to over-rule a country employee as you could a city worker, and Mrs. Allison smiled engagingly as she said, "But can't you get extra oil, at least while we stay?"

"You see," the man said. He tapped his finger exasperatingly against the car wheel as he spoke. "You see," he said slowly, "I order this oil. I order it down from maybe fifty, fifty-five miles away. I order back in June, how much I'll need for the summer. Then I order again . . . oh, about November. Round about now it's starting to get pretty short." As though the subject were closed, he stopped tapping his finger and tightened his hands on the wheel in preparation for departure.

"But can't you give us *some?*" Mrs. Allison said. "Isn't there anyone else?"

"Don't know as you could get oil anywheres else right now," the man said consideringly. "*I* can't give you none." Before Mrs. Allison could speak, the truck began to move; then it stopped for a minute and he looked at her through the back window of the cab. "Ice?" he called. "I could let you have some ice."

Mrs. Allison shook her head; they were not terribly low on ice, and she was angry. She ran a few steps to catch up with the truck, calling, "Will you try to get us some? Next week?"

"Don't see's I can," the man said. "After Labor Day, it's harder." The truck drove away, and Mrs. Allison, only comforted by the thought that she could probably get kerosene from Mr. Babcock, or, at worst, the Halls, watched it go with anger. "Next summer," she told herself. "Just let *him* try coming around next summer!"

There was no mail again, only the paper, which seemed to be coming doggedly on time, and Mr. Allison was openly cross when he returned. When Mrs. Allison told him about the kerosene man he was not particularly impressed.

"Probably keeping it all for a high price during the winter," he commented. "What's happened to Anne and Jerry, do you think?"

Anne and Jerry were their son and daughter, both married, one living in Chicago, one in Far West; their dutiful weekly letters were late; so late, in fact, that Mr. Allison's annoyance at the lack of mail was able to settle on a legitimate grievance. "Ought to realize how we wait for their letters," he said. "Thoughtless, selfish children. Ought to know better."

"Well, dear," Mrs. Allison said placatingly. Anger at Anne and Jerry would not relieve her emotions toward the kerosene man. After a few minutes she said, "Wishing won't bring the mail, dear. I'm going to go call Mr. Babcock and tell him to send up some kerosene with my order."

"At least a postcard," Mr. Allison said as she left.

As with most of the cottage's inconveniences, the Allisons no longer noticed the phone particularly, but yielded to its eccentricities without conscious complaint. It was a wall phone, of a type still seen in only few communities; in order to get the operator, Mrs. Allison had first to turn the sidecrank and ring once. Usually it took two or three tries to force the operator to answer, and Mrs. Allison, making any kind of telephone call, approached the phone with resignation and a sort of desperate patience. She had to crank the phone three times this morning before the operator answered, and then it was still longer before Mr. Babcock picked up the receiver at his phone in the corner of the grocery behind the meat table. He said "Store?" with the rising inflection that seemed to indicate suspicion of anyone who tried to communicate with him by means of this unreliable instrument.

"This is Mrs. Allison, Mr. Babcock. I thought I'd give you my order a day early because I wanted to be sure and get some—"

"What say, Mrs. Allison?"

Mrs. Allison raised her voice a little; she saw Mr. Allison, out on the lawn, turn in his chair and regard her sympathetically. "I said, Mr. Babcock, I thought I'd call in my order early so you could send me—"

"Mrs. Allison?" Mr. Babcock said. "You'll come and pick it up?"

"Pick it up?" In her surprise Mrs. Allison let her voice drop back to its normal tone and Mr. Babcock said loudly, "What's that, Mrs. Allison?"

"I thought I'd have you send it out as usual," Mrs. Allison said.

"Well, Mrs. Allison," Mr. Babcock said, and there was a pause while Mrs. Allison waited, staring past the phone over her husband's head out into the sky. "Mrs. Allison," Mr. Babcock went on finally, "I'll tell you, my boy's been working for me went back to school yesterday and now I got no one to deliver. I only got a boy delivering summers, you see."

"I thought you *always* delivered," Mrs. Allison said.

"Not after Labor Day, Mrs. Allison," Mr. Babcock said firmly. "You never been here after Labor Day before, so's you wouldn't know, of course."

"Well," Mrs. Allison said helplessly. Far inside her mind she was saying, over and over, can't use city manners on country folk, no use getting mad.

"Are you *sure?*" she asked finally. "Couldn't you just send out an order today, Mr. Babcock?"

"Matter of fact," Mr. Babcock said, "I guess I couldn't, Mrs. Allison. It wouldn't hardly pay, delivering with no one else out at the lake."

"What about Mr. Hall?" Mrs. Allison asked suddenly, "the people who live about three miles away from us out here? Mr. Hall could bring it out when he comes."

"Hall?" Mr. Babcock said. "John Hall? They've gone to visit her folks upstate, Mrs. Allison."

"But they bring all our butter and eggs," Mrs. Allison said, appalled.

"Left yesterday," Mr. Babcock said. "Probably didn't think you folks would stay on up there."

"But I told Mr. Hall . . ." Mrs. Allison started to say, and then stopped. "I'll send Mr. Allison in after some groceries tomorrow," she said.

"You got all you need till then," Mr. Babcock said, satisfied; it was not a question, but a confirmation.

After she hung up, Mrs. Allison went slowly out to sit again in her chair next to her husband. "He won't deliver," she said. "You'll have to go in tomorrow. We've got just enough kerosene to last till you get back."

"He should have told us sooner," Mr. Allison said.

It was not possible to remain troubled long in the face of the day; the country had never seemed more inviting, and the lake moved quietly below them, among the trees, with the almost incredible softness of a summer picture. Mrs. Allison sighed deeply in the pleasure of possessing for themselves that sight of the lake, with the distant green hills beyond, the gentleness of the small wind through the trees.

The weather continued fair; the next morning Mr. Allison, duly armed with a list of groceries, with "kerosene" in large letters at the top, went down the path to the garage, and Mrs. Allison began another pie in her new baking dishes. She had mixed the crust and was starting to pare the apples when Mr. Allison came rapidly up the path and flung open the screen door into the kitchen.

"Damn car won't start," he announced, with the end-of-the-tether voice of a man who depends on a car as he depends on his right arm.

"What's wrong with it?" Mrs. Allison demanded, stopping with the paring knife in one hand and an apple in the other. "It was all right on Tuesday."

"Well," Mr. Allison said between his teeth, "it's not all right on Friday."

"Can you fix it?" Mrs. Allison asked.

"No," Mr. Allison said, "I can not. Got to call someone, I guess."

"Who?" Mrs. Allison asked.

"Man runs the filling station, I guess." Mr. Allison moved purposefully toward the phone. "He fixed it last summer one time."

A little apprehensive, Mrs. Allison went on paring apples absentmindedly, while she listened to Mr. Allison with the phone, ringing, waiting, finally giving the number to the operator, then waiting again and giving the number again, giving the number a third time, and then slamming down the receiver.

"No one there," he announced as he came into the kitchen.

"He's probably gone out for a minute," Mrs. Allison said nervously; she was not quite sure what made her so nervous, unless it was the probability of her husband's losing his temper completely. "He's there alone, I imagine, so if he goes out there's no one to answer the phone."

"That must be it," Mr. Allison said with heavy irony. He slumped into one of the kitchen chairs and watched Mrs. Allison paring apples. After a minute, Mrs. Allison said soothingly, "Why don't you go down and get the mail and then call him again?"

Mr. Allison debated and then said, "Guess I might as well." He rose heavily and when he got to the kitchen door he turned and said, "But if there's no mail—" and leaving an awful silence behind him, he went off down the path.

Mrs. Allison hurried with her pie. Twice she went to the window to glance at the sky to see if there were clouds coming up. The room seemed unexpectedly dark, and she herself felt in the state of tension that preceded a thunderstorm, but both times when she looked the sky was clear and serene, smiling indifferently down on the Allisons' summer cottage as well as on the rest of the world. When Mrs. Allison, her pie ready for the oven, went a third time to look outside, she saw her husband coming up the path; he seemed more cheerful, and when he saw her, he waved eagerly and held a letter in the air.

"From Jerry," he called as soon as he was close enough for her to hear him, "at last—a letter!" Mrs. Allison noticed with concern that he was no longer able to get up the gentle slope of the path without breathing heavily; but then he was in the doorway, holding out the letter. "I saved it till I got here," he said.

Mrs. Allison looked with an eagerness that surprised her on the familiar handwriting of her son; she could not imagine why the letter excited her so, except that it was the first they had received in so long; it would be a pleasant, dutiful letter, full of the doings of Alice and the children, reporting progress with his job, commenting on the recent weather in Chicago, closing with love from all; both Mr. and Mrs. Allison could, if they wished, recite a pattern letter from either of their children.

Mr. Allison slit the letter open with great deliberation, and then he spread it out on the kitchen table and they leaned down and read it together.

"*Dear Mother and Dad,*" it began, in Jerry's familiar, rather childish, handwriting, "*Am glad this goes to the lake as usual, we always thought you came back too soon and ought to stay up there as long as you could. Alice says that now that you're not as young as you used to be and have no demands on your time, fewer friends, etc., in the city, you ought to get what fun you can while you can. Since you two are both happy up there, it's a good idea for you to stay.*"

Uneasily Mrs. Allison glanced sideways at her husband; he was reading intently, and she reached out and picked up the empty envelope, not knowing exactly what she wanted from it. It was addressed quite as usual, in Jerry's handwriting, and was postmarked "Chicago." Of course it's postmarked Chicago, she thought quickly, why would they want to postmark it anywhere else? When she looked back down at the letter, her husband had turned the page, and she read on with him: "*–and of course if they get measles, etc., now, they will be better off later. Alice is well, of course; me too. Been playing a lot of bridge lately with some people you don't know, named Carruthers. Nice young couple, about our age. Well, will close now as I guess it bores you to hear about things so far away. Tell Dad old Dickson, in our Chicago office, died. He used to ask about Dad a lot. Have a good time up at the lake, and don't bother about hurrying back. Love from all of us, Jerry.*"

"Funny," Mr. Allison commented.

"It doesn't sound like Jerry," Mrs. Allison said in a small voice. "He never wrote anything like . . . " She stopped.

"Like what?" Mr. Allison demanded. "Never wrote anything like what?"

Mrs. Allison turned the letter over, frowning. It was impossible to find any sentence, any word, even, that did not sound like Jerry's regular letters. Perhaps it was only that the letter was so late, or the unusual number of dirty fingerprints on the envelope.

"I don't *know*," she said impatiently.

"Going to try that phone call again," Mr. Allison said.

Mrs. Allison read the letter twice more, trying to find a phrase that sounded wrong. Then Mr. Allison came back and said, very quietly, "Phone's dead."

"What?" Mrs. Allison said, dropping the letter.

"Phone's dead," Mr. Allison said.

The rest of the day went quickly; after a lunch of crackers and milk, the Allisons went to sit outside on the lawn, but their afternoon was cut short by the gradually increasing storm clouds that came up over the lake to the cottage, so that it was as dark as evening by four o'clock. The storm delayed, however, as though in loving anticipation of the moment it would break over the summer cottage, and there was an occasional flash of lightning, but no rain. In the evening Mr. and Mrs. Allison, sitting close together inside their cottage, turned on the battery radio they had brought with them from New York. There were no lamps lighted in the cottage, and the only light came from the lightning outside and the small square glow from the dial of the radio.

The slight framework of the cottage was not strong enough to withstand the city noises, the music and the voices, from the radio, and the Allisons could hear them far off echoing across the lake, the saxophones in the New York dance band wailing over the water, the flat voice of the girl vocalist going inexorably out into the clean country air. Even the announcer, speaking glowingly of the virtues of razor blades, was no more than an inhuman voice sounding out from the Allisons' cottage and echoing back, as though the lake and the hills and the trees were returning it unwanted.

During one pause between commercials, Mrs. Allison turned and smiled weakly at her husband. "I wonder if we're supposed to . . . *do* anything," she said.

"No," Mr. Allison said consideringly. "I don't think so. Just wait."

Mrs. Allison caught her breath quickly, and Mr. Allison said, under the trivial melody of the dance band beginning again, "The car had been tampered with, you know. Even I could see that."

Mrs. Allison hesitated a minute and then said very softly, "I suppose the phone wires were cut."

"I imagine so," Mr. Allison said.

After a while, the dance music stopped and they listened attentively to a news broadcast, the announcer's rich voice telling them breathlessly of a marriage in Hollywood, the latest baseball scores, the estimated rise in food prices during the coming week. He spoke to them, in the summer cottage, quite as though they still deserved to hear news of a world that no longer reached them except through the fallible batteries on the radio, which were already beginning to fade, almost as though they still belonged, however tenuously, to the rest of the world.

Mrs. Allison glanced out the window at the smooth surface of the lake, the black masses of the trees, and the waiting storm, and said conversationally, "I feel better about that letter of Jerry's."

"I knew when I saw the light down at the Hall place last night," Mr. Allison said.

The wind, coming up suddenly over the lake, swept around the summer cottage and slapped hard at the windows. Mr. and Mrs. Allison involuntarily moved closer together, and with the first sudden crash of thunder, Mr. Allison reached out and took his wife's hand. And then, while the lightning flashed outside, and the radio faded and sputtered, the two old people huddled together in their summer cottage and waited.

The Ledge

On Christmas morning before sunup the fisherman embraced his warm wife and left his close bed. She did not want him to go. It was Christmas morning. He was a big, raw man, with too much strength, whose delight in winter was to hunt the sea ducks that flew in to feed by the outer ledges, bare at low tide.

As his bare feet touched the cold floor and the frosty air struck his nude flesh, he might have changed his mind in the dark of this special day. It was a home day, which made it seem natural to think of the outer ledges merely as some place he had shot ducks in the past. But he had promised his son, thirteen, and his nephew, fifteen, who came from inland. That was why he had given them his present of an automatic shotgun each the night before, on Christmas Eve. Rough man though he was known to be, and no spoiler of boys, he kept his promises when he understood what they meant. And to the boys, as to him, home meant where you came for rest after you had had your Christmas fill of action and excitement.

He legs astride, his arms raised, the fisherman stretched as high as he could in the dim privacy of his bedroom. Above the snug murmur of his wife's protest he heard the wind in the pines and knew it was easterly as the boys had hoped and he had surmised the night before. Conditions would be ideal, and when they were, anybody ought to take advantage of them. The birds would be flying. The boys would get a man's sport their first time outside on the ledges.

His son at thirteen, small but steady and experienced, was fierce to grow up in hunting, to graduate from sheltered waters and the blinds along the shores of the inner bay. His nephew at fifteen, an overgrown farm boy, had a farm boy's love of the sea, though he could not swim a stroke and was often sick in choppy weather. That was the reason his father, the fisherman's brother, was a farmer and chose to sleep in on the holiday morning at his brother's house. Many of the ones the farmer had grown up with were regularly seasick and could not swim, but they were unafraid of the water. They could not have dreamed of being anything but fishermen. The fisherman himself could swim like a seal and was never sick, and he would sooner die than be anything else.

He dressed in the cold and dark, and woke the boys gruffly. They tumbled out of bed, their instincts instantly awake while their thoughts still fumbled slumbrously. The fisherman's wife in the adjacent bedroom heard them apparently trying to find their clothes, mumbling sleepily and happily to each other, while her husband went down to the hot kitchen to fry eggs— sunny-side up, she knew, because that was how they all liked them.

Always in winter she hated to have them go outside, the weather was so treacherous and there were so few others out in case of trouble. To the fisherman these were no more than woman's fears, to be taken for granted and laughed off. When they were first married, they fought miserably every fall because she was after him constantly to put his boat up until spring. The fishing was all outside in winter, and though prices were high the storms made the rate of attrition high on gear. Nevertheless he did well. So she could do nothing with him.

People thought him a hard man, and gave him the reputation of being all out for himself because he was inclined to brag and be disdainful. If it was true, and his own brother was one of those who strongly felt it was, they lived better than others, and his brother had small right to criticize. There had been times when in her loneliness she had yearned to leave him for another man. But it would have been dangerous. So over the years she had learned to shut her mind to his hard-driving, and take what comfort she might from his unsympathetic competence. Only once or twice, perhaps, had she gone so far as to dwell guiltily on what it would be like to be a widow.

The thought that her boy, possibly because he was small, would not be insensitive like his father, and the rattle of dishes and smell of frying bacon downstairs in the kitchen shut off from the rest of the chilly house, restored the cozy feeling she had had before she was alone in bed. She heard them after a while go out and shut the back door.

Under her window she heard the snow grind drily beneath their boots, and her husband's sharp, exasperated commands to the boys. She shivered slightly in the envelope of her own warmth. She listened to the noise of her son and nephew talking elatedly. Twice she caught the glimmer of their lights on the white ceiling above the window as they went down the path to the shore. There would be frost on the skiff and freezing suds at the water's edge. She herself used to go gunning when she was younger; now, it seemed to her, anyone going out like that on Christmas morning had to be incurably male. They would none of them think about her until they returned and piled the birds they had shot on top of the sink for her to dress.

Ripping into the quiet pre-dawn cold she heard the hot snarl of the outboard taking them out to the boat. It died as abruptly as it had burst into life. Two or three or four or five minutes later the big engine broke into a warm reassuring roar. He had the best of equipment, and he kept it in the best of condition. She closed her eyes. It would not be too long before the others would be up for Christmas. The summer drone of the exhaust deepened. Then gradually it faded in the wind until it was lost at sea, or she slept.

The engine had started immediately in spite of the temperature. This put the fisherman in a good mood. He was proud of his boat. Together he and the two boys heaved the skiff and outboard onto the stern and secured it athwartships. His son went forward along the deck, iridescent in the ray of the light the nephew shone through the windshield, and cast the mooring pennant loose into darkness. The fisherman swung to starboard, glanced at his compass, and headed seaward down the obscure bay.

There would be just enough visibility by the time they reached the headland to navigate the crooked channel between the islands. It was the only nasty stretch of water. The fisherman had done it often in fog or at night—he always swore he could go anywhere in the bay blindfolded—but there was no sense in taking chances if you didn't have to. From the mouth of the channel he could lay a straight course for Brown Cow Island, anchor the boat out of sight behind it, and from the skiff set their tollers off Devil's Hump three hundred yards to seaward. By then the tide would be clearing the ledge and they could land and be ready to shoot around half-tide.

It was early, it was Christmas, and it was farther out than most hunters cared to go in this season of the closing year, so that he felt sure no one would be taking possession ahead of them. He had shot thousands of ducks there in his day. The Hump was by far the best hunting. Only thing was you had to plan for the right conditions because you didn't have too much time. About four hours was all, and you had to get it before three in the afternoon when the birds left and went out to sea ahead of nightfall.

They had it figured exactly right for today. The ledge would not be going under until after the gunning was over, and they would be home for supper in good season. With a little luck the boys would have a skiff-load of birds to show for their first time outside. Well beyond the legal limit, which was no matter. You took what you could get in this life, or the next man made out and you didn't.

The fisherman had never failed to make out gunning from Devil's Hump. And this trip, he had a hunch, would be above the ordinary. The westerly wind would come up just stiff enough, the tide was right, and it was going to storm by tomorrow morning so the birds would be moving. Things were perfect.

The old fierceness was in his bones. Keeping a weather eye to the murk out front and a hand on the wheel, he reached over and cuffed the boys playfully as they stood together close to the heat of the exhaust pipe running up through the center of the house. They poked back at him and shouted above the drumming engine, making bets as they always did on who would shoot the most birds. This trip they had the thrill of new guns, the best money could buy, and a man's hunting ground. The black retriever wagged at them and barked. He was too old and arthritic to be allowed in December water, but he was jaunty anyway at being brought along.

Groping in his pocket for his pipe, the fisherman suddenly had his high spirits rocked by the discovery that he had left his tobacco at home. He swore. Anticipation of a day out with nothing to smoke made him incredulous. He searched his clothes, and then he searched them again, unable to believe the tobacco was not somewhere. When the boys inquired what was wrong he spoke angrily to them, blaming them for being in some devious way at fault. They were instantly crestfallen and willing to put back after the tobacco, though they could appreciate what it meant only through his irritation. But he bitterly refused. That would throw everything out of phase. He was a man who did things the way he set out to do.

He clamped his pipe between his teeth, and twice more during the next few minutes he ransacked his clothes in disbelief. He was no stoic. For one relaxed moment he considered putting about the gunning somewhere nearer home. Instead he held his course and sucked the empty pipe, consoling himself with the reflection that at least he had whiskey enough if it got too uncomfortable on the ledge. Peremptorily he made the boys check to make certain the bottle was really in the knapsack with the lunches where he thought he had taken care to put it. When they reassured him, he despised his fate a little less.

The fisherman's judgment was as usual accurate. By the time they were abreast of the headland there was sufficient light so that he could wind his way among the reefs without slackening speed. At last he turned his bow toward open ocean, and as the winter dawn filtered upward through long layers of smoky cloud on the eastern rim his spirits rose again with it.

He opened the throttle, steadied on his course, and settled down to the two-hour run. The wind was stronger but seemed less cold coming from the sea. The boys had withdrawn from the fisherman and were talking together while they watched the sky through the windows. The boat churned solidly through a light chop, flinging spray off her flaring bow. Astern the headland thinned rapidly till it lay like a blackened sill on the grey water. No other boats were abroad.

The boys fondled their new guns, sighted along the barrels, worked the mechanisms, compared notes, boasted, and gave each other contradictory advice. The fisherman got their attention once and pointed at the horizon. They peered through the windows and saw what looked like a black scum floating on top of gently agitated water. It wheeled and tilted, rippled, curled, then rose, strung itself out and became a huge raft of ducks escaping over the sea. A good sign.

The boys rushed out and leaned over the washboards in the wind and spray to see the flock curl below the horizon. Then they went and hovered around the hot engine, bewailing their lot. If only they had been already out and waiting. Maybe these ducks would be crazy enough to return later and be slaughtered. Ducks were known to be foolish.

In due course and right on schedule they anchored at mid-morning in the lee of Brown Cow Island. They put the skiff overboard and loaded it with guns, knapsacks, and tollers. The boys showed their eagerness by being clumsy. The fisherman showed his in bad temper and abuse which they silently accepted in the absorbed tolerance of being boys. No doubt they laid it to lack of tobacco.

By outboard they rounded the island and pointed due east in the direction of a ridge of foam which could be seen whitening the surface three hundred yards away. They set the decoys in a broad, straddling vee opening wide into the ocean. The fisherman warned them not to get their hands wet, and when they did he made them carry on with red and painful fingers, in order to teach them. Once they got their numbed fingers inside their oilskins and hugged their warm crotches. In the meantime the fisherman had turned the skiff toward the patch of foam where as if by magic, like a black glossy rib of earth, the ledge had broken through the belly of the sea.

Carefully they inhabited their slippery nub of the North American continent, while the unresting Atlantic swelled and swirled as it had for eons round the indomitable edges. They hauled the skiff after them, established themselves as comfortably as they could in a shallow sump on top, lay on their sides a foot or so above the water, and waited, guns in hand.

In time the fisherman took a thermos bottle from the knapsack and they drank steaming coffee, and waited for the nodding decoys to lure in the first flight to the rock. Eventually the boys got hungry and restless. The fisherman let them open the picnic lunch and eat one sandwich apiece, which they both shared with the dog. Having no tobacco the fisherman himself would not eat.

Actually the day was relatively mild, and they were warm enough at present in their woolen clothes and socks underneath oilskins and hip boots. After a while, however, the boys began to feel cramped. Their nerves were agonized by inactivity. The nephew complained and was severely told by the fisherman—who pointed to the dog, crouched unmoving except for his white rimmed eyes—that part of doing a man's hunting was learning how to wait.

But he was beginning to have misgivings of his own. This could be one of those days where all the right conditions masked an incalculable flaw.

If the fisherman had been alone, as he often was, stopping off when the necessary coincidence of tide and time occurred on his way home from hauling trawls, and had plenty of tobacco, he would not have fidgeted. The boys' being nervous made him nervous. He growled at them again. When it came it was likely to come all at once, and then in a few moments to be over. He warned them not to slack off, never to slack off, to be always ready. Under his rebuke they kept their tortured peace, though they could not help shifting and twisting until he lost what patience he had left and bullied them into lying still. A duck could see an eyelid twitch. If the dog could go without moving, so could they.

"Here it comes!" the fisherman said tersely at last.

The boys quivered with quick relief. The flock came in downwind, quartering slightly, myriad, black, and swift.

"Beautiful—" breathed the fisherman's son.

"All right," said the fisherman, intense and precise. "Aim at singles in the thickest part of the flock. Wait for me to fire and then don't stop shooting till your gun's empty." He rolled up onto his elbow and spread his legs to brace himself. The flock bore down, arrowy and vibrant, then a hundred yards beyond the decoys it veered off.

"They're going away!" the boys cried, sighting in.

"Not yet!" snapped the fisherman. "They're coming round."

The flock changed shape, folded over itself, and drove into the wind in a tight arc. "Thousands—" the boys hissed through their teeth. All at once a whistling storm of black and white broke over the decoys.

"Now!" the fisherman shouted. "Perfect!" And he opened fire at the flock just as it hung suspended in momentary chaos above the tollers. The three pulled their triggers and the birds splashed into the water, until the last report went off unheard, the last smoking shell flew unheeded over their shoulders, and the last of the routed flock scattered diminishing, diminishing, diminishing in every direction.

Exultantly the boys dropped their guns, jumped up and scrambled for the skiff.

"I'll handle that skiff!" the fisherman shouted at them. They stopped. Gripping the painter and balancing himself he eased the skiff into the water stern first and held the bow hard against the side of the rock shelf the skiff had rested on. "You stay here," he said to his nephew. "No sense in all three of us going in the boat."

The boy on the reef gazed at the grey water rising and falling hypnotically along the glistening edge. It had dropped about a foot since their arrival. "I want to go with you," he said in a sullen tone, his eyes on the streaming eddies.

"You want to do what I tell you if you want to gun with me," answered the fisherman harshly. The boy couldn't swim, and he wasn't going to have him climbing in and out of the skiff any more than necessary. Besides, he was too big.

The fisherman took his son in the skiff and cruised round and round among the decoys picking up dead birds. Meanwhile the other boy stared unmoving after them from the highest part of the ledge. Before they had quite finished gathering the dead birds, the fisherman cut the outboard and dropped to his knees in the skiff. "Down!" he yelled. "Get down!" About a dozen birds came tolling in. "Shoot—shoot!" his son hollered from the bottom of the boat to the boy on the ledge.

The dog, who had been running back and forth whining, sank to his belly, his muzzle on his forepaws. But the boy on the ledge never stirred. The ducks took late alarm at the skiff, swerved aside and into the air, passing with a whirr no more than fifty feet over the head of the boy, who remained on the ledge like a statue, without his gun, watching the two crouching in the boat.

The fisherman's son climbed on the ledge and held the painter. The bottom of the skiff was covered with feathery black and white bodies with feet upturned and necks lolling. He was jubilant. "We got twenty-seven!" he told his cousin. "How's that? Nine apiece. Boy—" he added, "what a cool Christmas!"

The fisherman pulled the skiff onto its shelf and all three went and lay down again in anticipation of the next flight. The son, reloading, patted his gun affectionately. "I'm going to get me ten next time," he said. Then he asked his cousin, "Whatsamatter—didn't you see the strays?"

"Yeah," the boy said.

"How come you didn't shoot at 'em?"

"Didn't feel like it," replied the boy, still with a trace of sullenness.

"You stupid or something?" The fisherman's son was astounded. "What a highlander!" But the fisherman, though he said nothing, knew that the older boy had had an attack of ledge fever.

"Cripes!" his son kept at it. "I'd at least of tried."

"Shut up," the fisherman finally told him, "and leave him be."

At slack water three more flocks came in, one right after the other, and when it was over, the skiff was half full of clean, dead birds. During the subsequent lull they broke out the lunch and ate it all and finished the hot coffee. For a while the fisherman sucked away on his cold pipe. Then he had himself a swig of whiskey.

The boys passed the time contentedly jabbering about who shot the most—there were ninety-two all told—which of their friends they would show the biggest ones to, how many each could eat at a meal provided they didn't have to eat any vegetables. Now and then they heard sporadic distant gunfire on the mainland, at its nearest point about two miles to the north. Once far off they saw a fishing boat making in the direction of home.

At length the fisherman got a hand inside his oilskins and produced his watch.

"Do we have to go now?" asked his son.

"Not just yet," he replied. "Pretty soon." Everything had been perfect. As good as he ever had it. Because he was getting tired of the boys' chatter he got up, heavily in his hip boots, and stretched. The tide had turned and was coming in, the sky was more ashen, and the wind had freshened enough so that whitecaps were beginning to blossom. It would be a good hour before they had to leave the ledge and pick up the tollers. However, he guessed they would leave a little early. On account of the rising wind he doubted there would be much more shooting. He stepped carefully along the back of the ledge, to work his kinks out. It was also getting a little colder.

The whiskey had begun to warm him, but he was unprepared for the sudden blaze that flashed upward inside him from belly to head. He was standing looking at the shelf where the skiff was. Only the foolish skiff was not there!

For the second time that day the fisherman felt the deep vacuity of disbelief. He gaped, seeing nothing, but the flat shelf of rock. He whirled, started toward the boys, slipped, recovered himself, fetched a complete circle, and stared at the unimaginably empty shelf. Its emptiness made him feel as if everything he had done that day so far, his life so far, he had dreamed. What could have happened? The tide was still nearly a foot below. There had been no sea to speak of. The skiff could hardly have slid off by itself. For the life of him, consciously careful as he inveterately was, he could not now remember hauling it up the last time. Perhaps in the heat of hunting, he had left it to the boy. Perhaps he could not remember which was the last time.

"Christ—" he exclaimed loudly, without realizing it because he was so entranced by the invisible event.

"What's wrong, Dad?" asked his son, getting to his feet.

The fisherman went blind with uncontainable rage. "Get back down there where you belong!" he screamed. He scarcely noticed the boy sink back in amazement. In a frenzy he ran along the ledge thinking the skiff might have been drawn up at another place, though he knew better. There was no other place.

He stumbled, half falling, back to the boys who were gawking at him in consternation, as though he had gone insane. "God damn it!" he yelled savagely, grabbing both of them and yanking them to their knees. "Get on your feet!"

"What's wrong?" his son repeated in a stifled voice.

"Never mind what's wrong," he snarled. "Look for the skiff—it's adrift!" When they peered around he gripped their shoulders, brutally facing them about. "Downwind–" He slammed his fist against his thigh. "Jesus!" he cried, struck to madness by their stupidity.

At last he sighted the skiff himself, magically bobbing along the grim sea like a toller, a quarter of a mile to leeward on a direct course for home. The impulse to strip himself naked was succeeded instantly by a queer calm. He simply sat down on the ledge and forgot everything except the marvelous mystery.

As his awareness partially returned he glanced toward the boys. They were still observing the skiff speechlessly. Then he was gazing into the clear young eyes of his son.

"Dad," asked the boy steadily, "what do we do now?"

That brought the fisherman upright. "The first thing we have to do," he heard himself saying with infinite tenderness as if he were making love, "is think."

"Could you swim it?" asked his son.

He shook his head and smiled at them. They smiled quickly back, too quickly. "A hundred yards maybe, in this water. I wish I could," he added. It was the most intimate and pitiful thing he had ever said. He walked in circles round them, trying to break the stall his mind was left in.

He gauged the level of the water. To the eye it was quite stationary, six inches from the shelf at this second. The fisherman did not have to mark it on the side of the rock against the passing of time to prove to his reason that it was rising, always rising. Already it was over the brink of reason, beyond the margins of thought–a senseless measurement. No sense to it.

All his life the fisherman had tried to lick the element of time, by getting up earlier and going to bed later, owning a faster boat, planning more than the day would hold, and tackling just one other job before the deadline fell. If, as on rare occasions he had the grand illusion, he ever really had beaten the game, he would need to call on all his reserves of practice and cunning now.

He sized up the scant but unforgivable three hundred yards to Brown Cow Island. Another hundred yards behind it his boat rode at anchor, where, had he been aboard, he could have cut in a fathometer to plumb the profound and occult seas, or a ship-to-shore radio on which in an interminably short time he would have heard his wife's voice talking to him over the air about homecoming.

"Couldn't we wave something so somebody would see us?" his nephew suggested.

The fisherman spun round. "Load your guns!" he ordered. They loaded as if the air had suddenly gone frantic with birds. "I'll fire once and count to five. Then you fire. Count to five. That way they won't just think it's only somebody gunning ducks. We'll keep doing that."

"We've only got just two-and-a-half boxes left," said his son.

The fisherman nodded, understanding that from beginning to end their situation was purely mathematical, like the ticking of the alarm clock in his silent bedroom. Then he fired. The dog, who had been keeping watch over the decoys, leaped forward and yelped in confusion. They all counted off, fired the first five rounds by threes, and reloaded. The fisherman scanned first the horizon, then the contracting borders of the ledge, which was the sole place the water appeared to be climbing. Soon it would be over the shelf.

They counted off and fired the second five rounds. "We'll hold off a while on the last one," the fisherman told the boys. He sat down and pondered what a trivial thing was a skiff. This one he and the boy had knocked together in a day. Was a gun, manufactured for killing.

His son tallied up the remaining shells, grouping them symmetrically in threes on the rock when the wet box fell apart. "Two short," he announced. They reloaded and laid the guns on their knees.

Behind thickening clouds they could not see the sun going down. The water, coming up, was growing blacker. The fisherman thought he might have told his wife they would be home before dark since it was Christmas day. He realized he had forgotten about its being any particular day. The tide would not be high until two hours after sunset. When they did not get in by nightfall, and could not be raised by radio, she might send somebody to hunt for them right away. He rejected this arithmetic immediately, with a sickening shock, recollecting it was a two-and-a-half hour run at best. Then it occurred to him that she might send somebody on the mainland who was nearer. She would think he had engine trouble.

He rose and searched the shoreline, barely visible. Then his glance dropped to the toy shoreline at the edges of the reef. The shrinking ledge, so sinister from a boat, grew dearer minute by minute as though the whole wide world he gazed on from horizon to horizon balanced on its contracting rim. He checked the water level and found the shelf awash.

Some of what went through his mind the fisherman told to the boys. They accepted it without comment. If he caught their eyes they looked away to spare him or because they were not yet old enough to face what they saw. Mostly they watched the rising water. The fisherman was unable to initiate a word of encouragement. He wanted one of them to ask him whether somebody would reach them ahead of the tide. He would have found it possible to say yes. But they did not inquire.

The fisherman was not sure how much, at their age, they were able to imagine. Both of them had seen from the docks drowned bodies put ashore out of boats. Sometimes they grasped things, and sometimes not. He supposed they might be longing for the comfort of their mothers, and was astonished, as much as he was capable of any astonishment except the supreme one, to discover himself wishing he had not left his wife's dark, close, naked bed that morning.

"Is it time to shoot now?" asked his nephew.

"Pretty soon," he said, as if he were putting off making good on a promise. "Not yet."

His own boy cried softly for a brief moment, like a man, his face averted in an effort neither to give nor show pain.

"Before school starts," the fisherman said, wonderfully detached, "we'll go to town and I'll buy you boys anything you want."

With great difficulty, in a dull tone as though he did not in the least desire it, his son said after a pause, "I'd like one of those new thirty-horse outboards."

"All right," said the fisherman. And to his nephew, "How about you?"

The nephew shook his head desolately. "I don't want anything," he said.

After another pause the fisherman's son said, "Yes he does, Dad. He wants one too."

"All right—" the fisherman said again, and said no more.

The dog whined in uncertainty and licked the boys' faces where they sat together. Each threw an arm over his back and hugged him. Three strays flew in and sat companionably down among the stiff-necked decoys. The dog crouched, obedient to his training. The boys observed them listlessly. Presently, sensing something untoward, the ducks took off, splashing the wave tops with feet and wingtips, into the dusky waste.

The sea began to make up in the mountain wind, and the wind bore a new and deathly chill. The fisherman, scouring the somber, dwindling shadow of the mainland for a sign, hoped it would not snow. But it did. First a few flakes, then a flurry, then storming past horizontally. The fisherman took one long, bewildered look at Brown Cow Island three hundred yards dead to leeward, and got to his feet.

Then it shut in, as if what was happening on the ledge was too private even for the last wan of light of the expiring day.

"Last round," the fisherman said austerely.

The boys rose and shouldered their tacit guns. The fisherman fired into the flying snow. He counted methodically to five. His son fired and counted. His nephew. All three fired and counted. Four rounds.

"You've got one left, Dad," his son said.

The fisherman hesitated another second, then he fired the final shell. Its pathetic report, like the spat of a popgun, whipped away on the wind and was instantly blanketed in falling snow.

Night fell all in a moment to meet the ascending sea. They were not barely able to make one another out through driving snowflakes, dim as ghosts in their yellow oilskins. The fisherman heard a sea break and glanced down where his feet were. They seemed to be wound in a snowy sheet. Gently he took the boys by the shoulders and pushed them in front of him, feeling with his feet along the shallow sump to the place where it triangulated into a sharp crevice at the highest point of the ledge. "Face ahead," he told them. "Put the guns down."

"I'd like to hold mine, Dad," begged his son.

"Put it down," said the fisherman. "The tide won't hurt it. Now brace your feet against both sides and stay there."

They felt the dog, who was pitch black, running up and down in perplexity between their straddled legs. "Dad," said his son, "what about the pooch?"

If he had called the dog by name it would have been too personal. The fisherman would have wept. As it was he had all he could do to keep from laughing. He bent his knees, and when he touched the dog hoisted him under one arm. The dog's belly was soaking wet.

So they waited, marooned in their consciousness, surrounded by a monstrous tidal space which was slowly, slowly closing them out. In this space the periwinkle beneath the fisherman's boots was king. While hovering airborne in his mind he had an inward glimpse of his house as curiously separate, like a June mirage.

Snow, rocks, seas, wind the fisherman had lived by all his life. Now he thought he had never comprehended what they were, and he hated them. Though they had not changed. He was deadly chilled. He set out to ask the boys if they were cold. There was no sense. He thought of the whiskey, and sidled backward, still holding the awkward dog, till he located the bottle under water with his toe. He picked it up squeamishly as though afraid of getting his sleeve wet, worked his way forward and bent over his son. "Drink it," he said, holding the bottle against the boy's ribs. The boy tipped his head back, drank, coughed hotly, then vomited.

"I can't," he told his father wretchedly.

"Try—try—" the fisherman pleaded, as if it meant the difference between life and death.

The boy obediently drank, and again he vomited hotly. He shook his head against his father's chest and passed the bottle forward to his cousin, who drank and vomited also. Passing the bottle back, the boys dropped it in the frigid water between them.

When the waves reached his knees the fisherman set the warm dog loose and said to his son, "Turn around and get upon my shoulders." The boy obeyed. The fisherman opened his oilskin jacket and twisted his hands behind him through his suspenders, clamping the boy's booted ankles with his elbows.

"What about the dog?" the boy asked.

"He'll make his own way all right," the fisherman said. "He can take the cold water." His knees were trembling. Every instinct shrieked for gymnastics. He ground his teeth and braced like a colossus against the sides of the submerged crevice.

The dog, having lived faithfully as though one of them for eleven years, swam a few minutes in and out around the fisherman's legs, not knowing what was happening, and left them without a whimper. He would swim and swim at random by himself, round and round in the blinding night, and when he had swum routinely through the paralyzing water all he could, he would simply, in one incomprehensible moment, drown. Almost the fisherman, waiting out infinity, envied him his pattern.

Freezing seas swept by, flooding inexorably up and up as the earth sank away imperceptibly beneath them. The boy called out once to his cousin. There was no answer. The fisherman, marveling on a terror without voice, was dumbly glad when the boy did not call again. His own boots were long full of water. With no sensation left in his straddling legs he dared not move them. So long as the seas came sidewise against his hips, and then sidewise against his shoulders, he might balance—no telling how long. The upper half of him was what felt frozen. His legs, disengaged from his nerves and his will, he came to regard quite scientifically. They were the absurd, precarious axis around which reeled the surged universal tumult. The waves would come on; he could not visualize how many tossing reinforcements lurked in the night beyond—inexhaustible numbers, and he wept in supernatural fury at each because it was higher, till he transcended hate and took them, swaying like a convert, one by one as they lunged against him and away aimlessly into their own undisputed, wild realm.

From his hips upward the fisherman stretched to his utmost as a man does whose spirit reaches out of dead sleep. The boy's head, none too high, must be at least seven feet above the ledge. Though growing larger every minute, it was a small light life. The fisherman meant to hold it there, if need be, through a thousand tides.

By and by the boy, slumped on the head of his father, asked, "Is it over your boots, Dad?"

"Not yet," the fisherman said. Then through his teeth he added, "If I fall—kick your boots off—swim for it—downwind—to the island. . . ."

"You . . . ?" the boy finally asked.

The fisherman nodded against the boy's belly. "—Won't see each other," he said.

The boy did for the fisherman the greatest thing that can be done. He may have been too young for perfect terror, but he was old enough to know there were things beyond the power of any man. All he could do he did, trusting his father to do all he could, and asking nothing more.

The fisherman, rocked to his soul by a sea, held his eyes shut upon the interminable night.

"Is it time now?" the boy said.

The fisherman could hardly speak. "Not yet," he said. "Not just yet. . . ."

As the land mass pivoted toward sunlight the day after Christmas, a tiny fleet of small craft converged off shore like iron filings to a magnet. At daybreak they found the skiff floating unscathed off the headland, half full of ducks and snow. The shooting *had* been good, as someone hearing on the mainland the previous afternoon had supposed. Two hours afterward they found the unharmed boat adrift five miles at sea. At high noon they found the fisherman at ebb tide, his right foot jammed cruelly into a glacial crevice of the ledge beside three shotguns, his hands tangled behind him in his suspenders, and under his right elbow a rubber boot with a sock and a live starfish in it. After dragging unlit depths all day for the boys, they towed the fisherman home in his own boat at sundown, and in the frost of evening, mute with discovering purgatory, laid him on his wharf for his wife to see.

She, somehow, standing on the dock as in her frequent dream, gazing at the fisherman pure as crystal on the icy boards, a small rubber boot still frozen under one clenched arm, saw him exaggerated beyond remorse or grief, absolved of his mortality.

KURT VONNEGUT, JR.

1961

Who Am I This Time?

The North Crawford Mask and Wig Club, an amateur theatrical society I belong to, voted to do Tennessee Williams' *A Streetcar Named Desire* for the spring play. Doris Sawyer, who always directs, said she couldn't direct this time because her mother was so sick. And she said the club ought to develop some other directors anyway, because she couldn't live forever, even though she'd made it safely to seventy-four.

So I got stuck with the directing job, even though the only thing I'd ever directed before was the installation of combination aluminum storm windows and screens I'd sold. That's what I am, a salesman of storm windows and doors, and here and there a bathtub enclosure. As far as acting goes, the highest rank I ever held on stage was either butler or policeman, whichever's higher.

I made a lot of conditions before I took the directing job, and the biggest one was that Harry Nash, the only real actor the club has, had to take the Marlon Brando part in the play. To give you an idea of how versatile Harry is, inside of one year he was Captain Queeg in *The Caine Mutiny Court Martial*, then Abe Lincoln in *Abe Lincoln in Illinois* and then the young architect in *The Moon is Blue*. The year after that, Harry Nash was Henry the Eighth in *Anne of the Thousand Days* and Doc in *Come Back Little Sheba*, and I was after him for Marlon Brando in *A Streetcar Named Desire*. Harry wasn't at the meeting to say whether he'd take the part or not. He never came to meetings.

He was too shy. He didn't stay away from meetings because he had some-thing else to do. He wasn't married, didn't go out with women – didn't have any close men friends either. He stayed away from all kinds of gatherings because he never could think of anything to say or do without a script.

So I had to go down to Miller's Hardware Store, where Harry was a clerk, the next day and ask him if he'd take the part. I stopped off at the tele-phone company to complain about a bill I'd gotten for a call to Honolulu, I'd never called Honolulu in my life.

And there was this beautiful girl I'd never seen before behind the counter at the phone company, and she explained that the company had put in an automatic billing machine and that the machine didn't have all the bugs out of it yet. It made mistakes. "Not only did I not call Honolulu," I told her, "I don't think anybody in North Crawford ever has or will."

So she took the charge off the bill, and I asked her if she was from around North Crawford. She said no. She said she just came with the new billing machine to teach local girls how to take care of it. After that, she said, she would go with some other machine to someplace else. "Well," I said, "as long as people have to come along with the machines, I guess we're all right."

"What?" she said.

"When machines start delivering themselves," I said, "I guess that's when the people better start really worrying."

"Oh," she said. She didn't seem very interested in that subject, and I wondered if she was interested in anything. She seemed kind of numb, almost a machine herself, an automatic phone-company politeness machine.

"How long will you be in town here?" I asked her.

"I stay in each town eight weeks, sir," she said. She had pretty blue eyes, but there sure wasn't much hope or curiosity in them. She told me she had been going from town to town like that for two years, always a stranger.

And I got it in my head that she might make a good Stella for the play. Stella was the wife of the Marlon Brando character, the wife of the character I wanted Harry Nash to play. So I told her where and when we were going to hold tryouts, and said the club would be very happy if she'd come.

She looked surprised, and she warmed up a little. "You know," she said, "that's the first time anybody ever asked me to participate in any community thing."

"Well," I said, "there isn't any other way to get to know a lot of nice people faster than to be in a play with 'em."

She said her name was Helene Shaw. She said she might just surprise me – and herself. She said she just might come.

You would think that North Crawford would be fed up with Harry Nash in plays after all the plays he'd been in. But the fact was that North Crawford probably could have gone on enjoying Harry forever, because he was never Harry on stage. When the maroon curtain went up on the stage in the gymnasium of the Consolidated Junior-Senior High School, Harry, body and soul, was exactly what the script and the director told him to be.

Somebody said one time that Harry ought to go to a psychiatrist so he could be something important and colorful in real life, too—so he could get married anyway, and maybe get a better job than just clerking in Miller's Hardware Store for fifty dollars a week. But I don't know what a psychiatrist could have turned up about him that the town didn't already know. The trouble with Harry was he'd been left on the doorstep of the Unitarian Church when he was a baby, and he never did find out who his parents were.

When I told him there in Miller's that I'd been appointed director, that I wanted him in my play, he said what he always said to anybody who asked him to be in a play—and it was kind of sad, if you think about it.

"Who am I this time?" he said.

So I held the tryouts where they're always held—in the meeting room on the second floor of the North Crawford Public Library. Doris Sawyer, the woman who usually directs, came to give me the benefit of all her experience. The two of us sat in state upstairs, while the people who wanted parts waited below. We called them upstairs one by one.

Harry Nash came to the tryouts, even though it was a waste of time. I guess he wanted to get that little bit more acting in.

For Harry's pleasure, and our pleasure, too, we had him read from the scene where he beats up his wife. It was a play in itself, the way Harry did it, and Tennessee Williams hadn't written it all either. Tennessee Williams didn't write the part, for instance, where Harry, who weight about one hundred forty-five, who's about five feet eight inches tall, added fifty pounds to his weight and four inches to his height by just picking up a playbook. He had a short little double-breasted bellows-back grade-school graduation suit coat on and a dinky little red tie with a horsehead on it. He took off the coat and tie, opened his collar, then turned his back to Doris and me, getting up steam for the part. There was a great big rip in the back of his shirt, and it looked like a fairly new shirt too. He'd ripped it on purpose, so he could be that much more like Marlon Brando, right from the first.

When he faced us again, he was huge and handsome and conceited and cruel. Doris read the part of Stella, the wife, and Harry bullied that old, old lady into believing that she was a sweet, pregnant girl married to a sexy gorilla who was going to beat her brains out. She had me believing it too. And I read the lines of Blanche, her sister in the play, and darned if Harry didn't scare me into feeling like a drunk and faded Southern belle.

And then, while Doris and I were getting over our emotional experiences, like people coming out from under ether, Harry put down the playbook, put on his coat and tie, and turned into the pale hardware-store clerk again.

"Was–was that all right?" he said, and he seemed pretty sure he wouldn't get the part.

"Well," I said, "for a first reading, that wasn't too bad."

"Is there a chance I'll get the part?" he said. I don't know why he always had to pretend there was some doubt about his getting a part, but he did.

"I think we can safely say we're leaning powerfully in your direction," I told him.

He was very pleased. "Thanks! Thanks a lot!" he said, and he shook my hand.

"Is there a pretty new girl downstairs?" I said, meaning Helene Shaw.

"I didn't notice," said Harry.

It turned out that Helen Shaw *had* come for the tryouts, and Doris and I had our hearts broken. We thought the North Crawford Mask and Wig Club was finally going to put a really good-looking, really young girl on stage, instead of one of the beat-up forty-year-old women we generally have to palm off as girls.

But Helene Shaw couldn't act for sour apples. No matter what we gave her to read, she was the same girl with the same smile for anybody who had a complaint about his phone bill.

Doris tried to coach her some, to make her understand that Stella in the play was a very passionate girl who loved a gorilla because she needed a gorilla. But Helen just read the lines the same way again. I don't think a volcano could have stirred her up enough to say, "Oo."

"Dear," said Doris, "I'm going to ask you a personal question.

"All right," said Helene.

"Have you ever been in love?" said Doris. "The reason I ask," she said, "remembering some old love might help you put more warmth in your acting."

Helene frowned and thought hard. "Well," she said, "I travel a lot, you know. And practically all the men in the different companies I visit are married and I never stay anyplace long enough to know many people who aren't."

"What about school?" said Doris. "What about puppy love and all the other kinds of love in school?"

So Helene thought hard about that, and then she said, "Even in school I was always moving around a lot. My father was a construction worker, following jobs around, so I was always saying hello or good-by to someplace, without anything in between."

"Um," said Doris.

"Would movie stars count?" said Helene. "I don't mean in real life. I never knew any. I just mean up on the screen."

Doris looked at me and rolled her eyes. "I guess that's a love of a kind," she said.

And then Helene got a little enthusiastic. "I used to sit through movies over and over again," she said, "and pretend I was married to whoever the man movie star was. They were the only people who came with us. No matter where we moved, movie stars were there."

"Uh huh," said Doris.

"Well, thank you, Miss Shaw," I said. "You go downstairs and wait with the rest. We'll let you know."

So we tried to find another Stella. And there just wasn't one, not one woman in the club with the dew still on her. "All we've got are Blanches," I said, meaning all we had were faded women who could play the part of Blanche, Stella's faded sister. "That's life, I guess–twenty Blanches to one Stella."

"And when you find a Stella," said Doris, "it turns out she doesn't know what love is."

Doris and I decided there was one last thing we could try. We could get Harry Nash to play a scene along with Helene. "He just might make her bubble the least little bit," I said.

"That girl hasn't got a bubble in her," said Doris.

So we called down the stairs for Helene to come back on up, and we told somebody to go find Harry. Harry never sat with the rest of the people at tryouts–or at rehearsals either. The minute he didn't have a part to play, he'd disappear into some hiding place where he could hear people call him, but where he couldn't be seen. At tryouts in the library he generally hid in the reference room, passing the time looking at flags of different countries in the front of the dictionary.

Helene came back upstairs, and we were very sorry and surprised to see that she'd been crying.

"Oh, dear," said Doris. "Oh, my–now what on earth's the trouble, dear?"

"I was terrible, wasn't I?" said Helene, hanging her head.

Doris said the only thing anybody can say in an amateur theatrical society when somebody cries. She said, "Why, no dear–you were marvelous."

"No, I wasn't," said Helene. "I'm a walking icebox, and I know it."

"Nobody could look at you and say that," said Doris.

"When they get to know me, they can say it," said Helene. "When people get to know me, that's what they *do* say," Her tears got worse. "I don't want to be the way I am," she said. "I just can't help it, living the way I've lived all my life. The only experiences I've had have been in crazy dreams of movie stars. When I meet somebody nice in real life, I feel as though I were in some kind of big bottle, as though I couldn't touch that person, no matter how hard I tried." And Helene pushed on air as though it were a big bottle all around her.

"You ask me if I've ever been in love," she said to Doris. "No—but I want to be. I know what this play's about. I know what Stella's supposed to feel and why she feels it. I—I—I—" she said, and her tears wouldn't let her go on.

"You what, dear?" said Doris gently.

"I—" said Helene, and she pushed on the imaginary bottle again. "I just don't know how to begin," she said.

There was heavy clumping on the library stairs. It sounded like a deep-sea diver coming upstairs in his lead shoes. It was Harry Nash, turning himself into Marlon Brando. In he came, practically dragging his knuckles on the floor. And he was so much in character that the sight of a weeping woman made him sneer.

"Harry," I said, "I'd like you to meet Helene Shaw. Helene—this is Harry Nash. If you get the part of Stella, he'll be your husband in the play." Harry didn't offer to shake hands. He put his hands in his pockets, and he hunched over, and he looked her up and down, gave her looks that left her naked. Her tears stopped right then and there.

"I wonder if you two would play the fight scene," I said, "and then the reunion scene right after it."

"Sure," said Harry, his eyes still on her. Those eyes burned up clothes faster than she could put them on. "Sure," he said, "if Stell's game."

"What?" said Helene. She'd turned the color of cranberry juice.

"Stell—Stella," said Harry. "That's you. Stell's my wife."

I handed the two of them playbooks. Harry snatched his from me without a word of thanks. Helene's hands weren't working very well, and I had to kind of mold them around the book.

"I'll want something I can throw," said Harry.

"What?" I said.

"There's one place where I throw a radio out a window," said Harry. "What can I throw?"

So I said an iron paperweight was the radio, and I opened the window wide. Helene Shaw looked scared to death.

"Where you want us to start?" said Harry, and he rolled his shoulders like a prizefighter warming up.

"Start a few lines back from where you throw the radio out the window," I said.

"O.K., O.K.," said Harry, warming up, warming up. He scanned the stage directions. "Let's see," he said, "after I throw the radio, she runs off stage, and I chase her, and I sock her one."

"Right," I said.

"O.K., baby," Harry said to Helene, his eyelids drooping. What was about to happen was wilder than the chariot race in *Ben Hur.* "On your mark," said Harry. "Get ready, baby. Go!"

When the scene was over, Helene Shaw was as hot as a hod carrier, as limp as an eel. She sat down with her mouth open and her head hanging to one side. She wasn't in any bottle any more. There wasn't any bottle to hold her up and keep her safe and clean. The bottle was gone.

"Do I get the part or don't I?" Harry snarled at me.

"You'll do," I said.

"You said a mouthful!" he said. "I'll be going now. . . . See you around, Stella," he said to Helene, and he left. He slammed the door behind him.

"Helene?" I said. "Miss Shaw?"

"Mf?" she said.

"The part of Stella is yours," I said. "You were great!"

"I was?" she said.

"I had no idea you had that much fire in you, dear," Doris said to her.

"Fire?" said Helene. She didn't know if she was afoot or on horseback.

"Skyrockets! Pinwheels! Roman candles!" said Doris.

"Mf," said Helene. And that was all she said. She looked as though she were going to sit in the chair with her mouth open forever.

"Stella," I said.

"Huh?" she said.

"You have my permission to go."

So we started having rehearsals four nights a week on the stage of the Consolidated School. And Harry and Helene set such a pace that everybody in the production was half crazy with excitement and exhaustion before we'd rehearsed four times. Usually a director has to beg people to learn their lines, but I had no such trouble. Harry and Helene were working so well together that everybody else in the cast regarded it as a duty and an honor and a pleasure to support them.

I was certainly lucky—or thought I was. Things were going so well, so hot and heavy, so early in the game that I had to say to Harry and Helene after one love scene, "Hold a little something back for the actual performance, would you please? You'll burn yourselves out."

I said that at the fourth or fifth rehearsal, and Lydia Miller, who was playing Blanche, the faded sister, was sitting next to me in the audience. In real life, she's the wife of Verne Miller. Verne owns Miller's Hardware Store. Verne was Harry's boss.

"Lydia," I said to her, "have we got a play or have we got a play?"

"Yes," she said, "you've got a play, all right." She made it sound as though I'd committed some kind of crime, done something just terrible. "You should be very proud of yourself."

"What do you mean by that?" I said.

Before Lydia could answer, Harry yelled at me from the stage, asked if I was through with him, asked if he could go home. I told him he could and, still Marlon Brando, he left, kicking furniture out of his way and slamming doors. Helene was left all alone on the stage, sitting on a couch with the same gaga look she'd had after the tryouts. The girl was that drained.

I turned to Lydia again and I said, "Well—until now, I thought I had every reason to be happy and proud. Is there something going on I don't know about?"

"Do you know that girl's in love with Harry?" said Lydia.

"In the play?" I said.

"What play?" said Lydia. "There isn't any play going on now, and look at her up there." She gave a sad cackle. "You aren't directing this play."

"Who is?" I said.

"Mother Nature at her worst," said Lydia. "And think what it's going to do to that girl when she discovers what Harry really is." She corrected herself. "What Harry really isn't," she said.

I didn't do anything about it, because I didn't figure it was any of my business. I heard Lydia try to do something about it, but she didn't get very far.

"You know," Lydia said to Helene one night, "I once played Ann Rutledge, and Harry was Abraham Lincoln."

Helene clapped her hands. "That must have been heaven!" she said.

"It was, in a way," said Lydia. "Sometimes I'd get so worked up, I'd love Harry the way I'd love Abraham Lincoln. I'd have to come back to earth and remind myself that he wasn't ever going to free the slaves, that he was just a clerk in my husband's hardware store."

"He's the most marvelous man I ever met," said Helene.

"Of course, one thing you have to get set for, when you're in a play with Harry," said Lydia, "is what happens after the last performance."

"What are you talking about?" said Helene.

"Once the show's over," said Lydia, "whatever you thought Harry was just evaporates into thin air."

"I don't believe it," said Helene.

"I admit it's hard to believe," said Lydia.

Then Helene got a little sore. "Anyway, why tell me about it?" she said. "Even if it is true, what do I care?"

"I—I don't know," said Lydia, backing away. "I—I just thought you might find it interesting."

"Well, I don't," said Helene.

And Lydia slunk away, feeling about as frowzy and unloved as she was supposed to feel in the play. After that nobody said anything more to Helene to warn her about Harry, not even when word got around that she'd told the telephone company that she didn't want to be moved around anymore, that she wanted to stay in North Crawford.

So the time finally came to put on the play. We ran it for three nights—Thursday, Friday, and Saturday—and we murdered those audiences. They believed every word that was said on stage, and when the maroon curtain came down they were ready to go to the nut house along with Blanche, the faded sister.

On Thursday night the other girls at the telephone company sent Helene a dozen red roses. When Helene and Harry were taking a curtain call together, I passed the roses over the footlights to her. She came forward for them, took one rose from the bouquet to give to Harry. But when she turned to give Harry the rose in front of everybody, Harry was gone. The curtain came down on that extra little scene—that girl offering a rose to nothing and nobody.

I went backstage, and I found her still holding that one rose. She'd put the rest of the bouquet aside. There were tears in her eyes. "What did I do wrong?" she said to me. "Did I insult him some way?"

"No," I said. "He always does that after a performance. The minute it's over, he clears out as fast as he can."

"And tomorrow he'll disappear again?"

"Without even taking off his makeup."

"And Saturday?" she said. "He'll stay for the cast party on Saturday, won't he?"

"Harry never goes to parties," I said. "When the curtain comes down on Saturday, that's the last anybody will see of him till he goes to work on Monday.

"How sad," she said.

Helene's performance on Friday night wasn't nearly so good as Thursday's. She seemed to be thinking about other things. She watched Harry take off after curtain call. She didn't say a word.

On Saturday she put on the best performance yet. Ordinarily it was Harry who set the pace. But on Saturday Harry had to work to keep up with Helene.

When the curtain came down on the final curtain call, Harry wanted to get away, but he couldn't. Helene wouldn't let go his hand. The rest of the cast and the stage crew and a lot of well-wishers from the audience were all standing around Harry and Helene, and Harry was trying to get his hand back.

"Well," he said, "I've got to go."

"Where?" she said.

"Oh," he said, "home."

"Won't you please take me to the cast party?" she said.

He got very red. "I'm afraid I'm not much on parties," he said. All the Marlon Brando in him was gone. He was tongue-tied, he was scared, he was shy—he was everything Harry was famous for being between plays.

"All right," she said. "I'll let you go – if you promise me one thing."

"What's that?" he said, and I thought he would jump out a window if she let go of him then.

"I want you to promise to stay here until I get you your present," she said.

"Present?" he said, getting even more panicky.

"Promise?" she said.

He promised. It was the only way he could get his hand back. And he stood there miserably while Helene went down to the ladies' dressing room for the present. While he waited, a lot of people congratulated him on being such a fine actor. But congratulations never made him happy. He just wanted to get away.

Helene came back with the present. It turned out to be a little blue book with a big red ribbon for a place marker. It was a copy of *Romeo and Juliet*. Harry was very embarrassed. It was all he could do to say "Thank you."

"The marker marks my favorite scene," said Helene.

"Um," said Harry.

"Don't you want to see what my favorite scene is?" she said.

So Harry had to open the book to the red ribbon.

Helene got close to him, and read a line of Juliet's. " 'How cam'st thou hither, tell me, and wherefore?' " she read. " 'The orchard walls are high and hard to climb, and the place death, considering who thou art, if any of my kinsmen find thee here.' " She pointed to the next line. "Now, look at what Romeo says," she said.

"Um," said Harry.

"Read what Romeo says," said Helene.

Harry cleared his throat. He didn't want to read the line, but he had to. " 'With love's light wings did I o'erperch these walls,' " he read out loud in his everyday voice. But then a change came over him. " 'For stony limits cannot hold love out,' " he read, and he straightened up, and eight years dropped away from him, and he was brave and gay. " 'And what love can do, that dares love attempt,' " he read, " 'therefore thy kinsmen are no let to me.' "

" 'If they do see thee they will murther thee,' " said Helene, and she started him walking toward the wings.

" 'Alack!' " said Harry, " 'there lies more peril in thine eye than twenty of their swords.' " Helene led him toward the backstage exit. " 'Look thou but sweet,' " said Harry, " 'and I am proof against their enmity.' "

" 'I would not for the world they saw thee here,' " said Helene, and that was the last we heard. The two of them were out the door and gone.

They never did show up at the cast party. One week later they were married.

They seem very happy, although they're kind of strange from time to time, depending on which play they're reading to each other at the time.

I dropped into the phone company office the other day, on account of the billing machine was making dumb mistakes again. I asked her what plays she and Harry'd been reading lately.

"In the past week," she said, "I've been married to Othello, been loved by Faust and been kidnaped by Paris. Wouldn't you say I was the luckiest girl in town?"

I said I thought so, and I told her most of the women in town thought so too.

"They had their chance," she said.

"Most of 'em couldn't stand the excitement," I said. And I told her I'd been asked to direct another play. I asked if she and Harry would be available for the cast. She gave me a big smile and said, "Who are we this time?"

CURTIS K. STADTFELD

1972

The Line Fence

They had shared a line fence for over forty years. One hundred and sixty rods long, half a mile, it stretched back from the road to the woods where it just sort of petered out, as they used to say, down in a swamp where the cows didn't go anyway. The fence wasn't maintained there even in the years when they both ran a lot of cattle. Paul farmed eighty acres on the east side of the fence. His farm was in a conventional shape, a quarter mile wide by half a mile long, eighty rods by a hundred and sixty. George was on the west side, and he had a hundred and twenty acres, in an L shape, so he shared line fences with three other farmers. But the line he shared with Paul was the longest, and the most important. The men who owned the other farms lived in houses separated by roads or woods from George's farm, so Paul was his closest neighbor, all those years.

They worked in each other's sight most of the time. The land lay on a great slope, with Paul's farm above George's. Paul could look down on the other farm while he worked, keep an eye on things, almost as though he were in an airplane. Once in a while he would get in his car, drive around on the road, come to tell George that cows were out or someone's cattle were in his corn, something like that. If they had not been friendly, George might have thought of him as a snoop, a spy, the way he could look at things. But no unfriendliness could outlast forty years of sharing a line fence. In any case, they had been boys together, had been friends in the cautious way that farm neighbors are friends. Their work had kept them together, and they had never fought over the fence.

There was bound to be a little friction, with a fence that long shared for

223

so many years, bound to be a little irritation once in a while when livestock broke through. But that had happened no more than half a dozen times in nearly half a century, and it was nothing at all compared to the many times they had shared help, worked on the fence together, talked over it about the crops or cattle, given each other a hand with one chore or another.

The fence had pretty well fallen down in recent years. Neither of them had kept a head of cattle on his land for more than a decade. There was no need any more to keep up the fence. Most of the posts were rotted just about off at ground level. Several of them had fallen, broken off by an animal or a child or the wind or just simply with the gravity of time. Where the other posts were still good, the broken ones would lean over, still held off the ground but swaying in the wind, pulling at the wires. There were four barbed strands—"bob wire" they called it, in their slightly flat accents—and they were rusting, breaking, settling into the grass, growing into the trees that stood here and there in the fence row, substituting for posts. And of course the grass, untended by horse or cow, had grown up, season after season, had matured and fallen down, tangled with the weeds, built up the fertility for the little wild cherry brush that was making a comeback now that no one pruned it.

The first thirty years of the neighborness, the fences had been important. Paul kept Holsteins, rough rangy animals, always with a little extra touch of wildness in them because Paul had little compassion for his cattle. He was one of the few farmers around who numbered his cows rather than naming them. He never groomed them, never spoke to them, let the bull run loose with them in the late summer for breeding. In the early years, he had kept horses, too, three or four, wild and unattended as the cows.

George kept Durhams for a long time, big red and roan cows, shaggy and shy. But he switched to Guernseys, dairy cows, smaller, higher bred, more delicate by nature than the Holsteins, more domesticated because they were cared for by George's swarm of children, who named them and petted them and brushed and combed them and showed them at local fairs—who made friends of them.

So the herds had to be kept apart by the line fence because George's children did not want the big rough Holsteins upsetting the Guernseys, and George did not want to take a chance of having one of his cows bred by the Holstein bull.

Also, there was usually a piece of corn along the line, or potatoes, and the fence kept the cows out of that.

By tradition—both men believed it to be common law, though neither had ever checked—a man was responsible for the half of the line fence that was on his right as he faced his neighbor's land. So if the cows got out, it was easy to tell whose fence had been broken through. If much crop was destroyed, there might have been damages to pay besides fixing the fence. So it was a good idea to keep your half of the line in good repair.

It was Paul's end that drifted down into the woods; George's was straight except for a place where a sink hole pocked the line and all year, except in the late summer, the fence there was under water, at least for the bottom wire or so.

The custom had become a tradition with them. Sometime in the spring, George would walk out of his house, up to where his section of the fence came to an end near the road, and begin to walk along, carrying a scythe or corn knife, a hammer in the loop on his overalls and a pair of fence pliers in his pocket, lugging a little bag of staples. He would trim back the weeds and grass, kick at the posts to see if any was shaky, replace staples if they were coming loose. If more than one or two posts needed replacement, it would be a job marked for a morning when the fields were too wet to work, or for a Saturday, when the boys were home from school to help.

Paul's wife, who was not a busybody but for other reasons had plenty of time to watch out the window, would tell her husband that George was checking the fence. Paul would gather up his own tools and staples, and start walking the line from his end.

Through the years, neither of them had ever made any attempt to mark the center post that divided George's half of the line fence from Paul's. Some years, they might meet two-thirds of the way to one end, another year, toward the other end, depending on which section weathered the winter best. But they never divided it up sharply; it was their line fence, and they kept it together, and they never quarreled over it.

George would point out to his sons that the fence was an example of how things evened out in the world, if a man just did what he was supposed to do without worrying too much about whether he was doing too much. Paul's big cows, and especially the bull, were harder on the fence than the Guernseys, George would explain, so you might think that Paul should take a bigger share of the responsibility for keeping up the fence. But on the other lines, no one ever ran cattle at all, and the other owners had to keep up their half of the fence for George's cattle. That's the way the world was, he would explain—just follow the rules and things will even out sooner or later.

There were some good stories about the line fence to be told in the winter. There was the day that George and his sons were dumping trash into the pothole, and Paul's big bull was tearing at the fence, pawing the ground, scaring hell out of everyone. George had recently come by a rat terrier, a tiny tense little whirlwind of a dog, and the dog was eyeing the bull with considerable interest. When it seemed that the fence was about to yield, George pointed to the bull and told the dog to "sic'em."

The terrier, too fast to know fear, darted down and nipped the bull on the nose. The bull was startled and turned to dispatch the little nuisance. The terrier pulled one of his favorite tricks, a little thing he used to do to cows to show them he meant business. He would jump, grab the tail up high near the top, and slide down it, keeping his teeth gripped and letting his weight pull him along the tail. Once was usually enough to convince a cow that the dog was to be obeyed. It got the bull's attention, too, and he spun to find his tormentor. The terrier was very quick; he could run down a squirrel in a wood lot, and a Holstein bull is much slower than a squirrel. The dog bit the bull on the ear, then ran around, took a nip or two at the scrotum. The bull capitulated, ran bellowing toward the barn, the dog nipping along happily and biting at every tender part he could reach.

That night, after the chores were done, Paul drove down in his Hudson. "What did you do to my bull? He won't even come out of the barnyard. Every once in a while, he goes up and peeks over the hill and bellers and runs back to hide under the overchute." He and George had a good laugh about such a little dog putting such a big bull in his place.

And there was the time the Canadian thistles began to spread in a big circular patch with its center at the line fence. George waited all summer until the moon was in the right sign and the thistles' round purple flowers were full, and then took a scythe and gave another to his son, who was in high school at the time, studying agriculture, and who did not believe in the sign of the moon as it related to crops. But to humor his father, he went out with him and they cut the thistles, right up to the line fence. For years, Paul's thicket of thistles flourished, but the patch ended abruptly at the fence and it never reestablished itself on George's farm. There was no logical reason for this, but there it was, and it made for much story-telling and head-shaking.

Those times were long past, and the fence had fallen in. George's family had grown and gone, no one staying with him on the land, working instead in factories and offices in distant cities. He had sold the cattle when the last of his boys left, and Paul had sold his when arthritis cramped his hands so he could not milk or handle a hay fork in comfort. Paul and his wife had no children. She was a mental invalid, sometimes sitting at the window for weeks staring out without comment, sometimes playing her piano, now and then feeling well enough to go for a ride with Paul in the Hudson. She spent some years in an institution; her last few at home. She died in the winter, one cold afternoon, after she had awakened from a nap and seemed bright and whole again. They had about an hour, and then she died.

George's wife, weary from the hard years and the work of raising eight children in the harshness of a farm home, had died the winter before. Both men took money from the government now.

Yet the habits had taken deep roots over the years. And one spring day, George walked out, up the road to where the line fence began, and started along it. As he reached the top of the first hill, he stopped and looked up at Paul's farm, and saw his neighbor walking stiffly down the lane toward his own half of the line fence.

George found that he could not walk the line as he once did. The matted grass and weeds had grown too thick, the puzzle of fallen posts and wire too tangled. He wanted, though, to cut out the cherry brush that was invading. He had brought along his jackknife, sharpened the night before. He came to the first wild cherry shrub, and stopped. It was no shrub. The little sapling trunk that George had planned to slash with his jackknife was nearly four inches in diameter, the tree some twenty feet high — big enough to shade four or five cows.

He stood before the tree for a little while, and finally folded the knife and dropped it back in his pocket. He turned and looked down toward the barn, where the brush was growing up around the fences since the cattle had stopped bothering it. Some of it was as big as this tree, George saw. He hadn't realized how big it was, it had grown up so slowly. Gradually, year by year, slipping in when a man's back was turned, taking over again. And no one there to help him, no cows to pen in the barnyard overnight once in a while so they would chew back the brush, no one to get out an ax and take down the trees.

He had a good ax, although it might need sharpening. He had hung it up in the garage last fall, there by the door. Or was it the fall before. It seemed that he had spent much more time in recent years hanging things up for the last time. In earlier years, when he and the farm were young, he had hung things up with a flourish when he knew he was through with them.

He had hung up the corn planter one day, because he had a tractor and he could afford an automatic two-row planter. He had hung up the hand grain-broadcaster when he bought the old Superior nine-hole drill. He had hung up the milk stool when the milker was working, and he had hung up the crosscut saw when he got his first chain saw.

He walked along the line fence again, toward Paul, who was making a little better time. Maybe he didn't notice the cherries, George thought. Or maybe he just didn't care.

Every posthole, George had dug, or he had supervised the digging. With shovels, later a posthole digger, hard work even where the soil was soft, brutal in dry clay or if you hit a big stone two feet down and had to start the hole over somewhere else.

My God, how many postholes had he dug! Four hundred eighty rods of line fence alone, a post every rod. Two rows of fence along the lane, full length of the eighty and across to the back forty. Cross fences at least seven or eight of them, eighty rods long each. Average life of a cedar post, five or six years. He gave up trying to figure it out, but he could count them all in the muscles of his back and shoulders, all those postholes; all the posts, too—he had cut many of them from his own cedar swamp, cut and peeled and cured them and then planted them and put the wire on them and braced them in the corners. His shoulders remembered them all.

They met near a place where a fence had once crossed George's land. His oldest son had taken the fence row out fifteen years ago to make room for strips, longer, more efficient. God, it was good to see those fences go. But then his son had gone too, and George had neither fence nor son. "How's it look?" he asked Paul.

The other man snorted. "Like hell. Take two younger men a week to get it in shape. Goddam thing couldn't hold a sick sheep."

Now, of course, if they wanted to replace the fence, they would put an auger on the back of the tractor, dig the postholes by power, twenty or thirty an hour, or simply put in steel posts. Nothing to it, except strength and money. And a reason for doing it.

"George, I've wanted to come down and talk with you since Velda died." Good God, what a name for a farm wife! But she had been so beautiful and strong when they were married, and she could sing like an angel. She and Paul used to walk down the road to the church on Sunday and sing together in the choir and the priest would speak the mass softly so everyone could listen. She had not looked frail at all.

"I went to the funeral."

"I know, George, I know. Did I ever tell you that when we had that little time, those few minutes before she died, that she asked for you and Mary? How you were? I don't think she remembered that you'd had children. She asked how you were, the two of you."

"I'm proud that she asked. We always thought a lot of her, you know."

"I told her you were fine, both of you. I didn't tell her that Mary had died. We just talked about people and places and things for a while, the first time in thirty years she had more than just a minute or two. Most of the people she wanted to talk about are dead, and I've forgotten where some of the places are." He looked up toward the big unpainted house, almost hidden among the untrimmed trees in the overgrown yard.

After a minute, he turned back, brushing his eyes with a glove. "But I wanted you to know something else. I've thought about it a lot, how lonely you must be since Mary died and the kids all gone. I see they come up sometimes on a weekend, but it's not the same, I know."

Not the same. These two men had gone to school together, hunted watermelons in the dark of fall evenings from Model T Fords. They had filled each other's silos thirty falls, helped in each other's fields in emergencies. There had been eight children for George, only one had died. From the time the first was born until the last left home was over thirty years. There were two dozen grandchildren, some of them he hardly knew, and his wife was dead a year and a half. The big house, so noisy for so long, was quiet now. No, it wasn't the same.

"Well," Paul said, "I want you to know it's the same for me. You'd think that after all these years, caring for her and worrying and wondering and all, that it would have been a relief, finally. I almost thought it would be. There were times, George, years ago, when I looked forward to it, God help me. But now she's gone and, by God, George, I miss her as much as you miss your Mary. I just wanted you to know."

Their eyes did not meet again. But they stood for a few minutes, looking past each other at the empty fields. Then Paul lurched away, and hobbled up the lane.

That was in the spring–and now it was a week before Christmas and George decided to mention something to Paul–something he'd had on his mind since Mary had died, and especially since they had buried Velda. If Paul's house had a light at the side that faced George's house, George could check it at night before he went to bed. He could come out on his back porch and look up the long slope and see if things were all right with Paul, see if the light was on. It would be nice if Paul would put a light back there. After all, George thought, Paul has been up there all these years with my lights to check. It probably hasn't occurred to him that I'd like his house to have a light that I can see, too.

George decided that he'd drive up later and mention it to Paul. The light might help a little, make it less lonely while they watched.

ALICE ADAMS

1973

Alternatives

It is the summer of 1935, and there are two people sitting at the end of a porch. The house is in Maine, at the edge of a high bluff that overlooks a large and for the moment peaceful lake. Tom Todd and Barbara Rutherford. They have recently met (she and her husband are house-guests of the Todds). They laugh a lot, they are excited about each other, and they have no idea what to do with what they feel. She is a very blond, bright-eyed girl in her twenties, wearing very short white shorts, swinging long thin legs below the high hammock on which she is perched, looking down at Tom. He is a fair, slender man with sad lines beside his mouth, but (not now!) now he is laughing with Babs. Some ten years older than she, he is a professor, writing a book on Shelley (Oh wild West Wind!) but the Depression has had unhappy effects on his university (Hilton, in the Middle South): 10 percent salary cuts, cancellation of sabbaticals. He is unable to finish his book (no promotion); they rely more and more on his wife's small income from her bookstore. And he himself has been depressed—but not now. What a girl, this Babs!

The house itself is old, with weathered shingles that once were green, and its shape is peculiar; it used to be the central lodge for a camp for under-privileged girls that Jessica Todd owned and ran before her marriage to Tom. The large, high living room is still full of souvenirs from that era: group pic-tures of girls in bloomers and middies, who danced or rather posed in dis-creet Greek tunics, and wore headbands; and over the fireplace, just below a moldering deer's head, there is a mouse-nibbled triangular felt banner, once dark green, that announced the name of the camp: Wabuwana. Why does

Jessica keep all those things around, as though those were her happiest days? No one ever asked. Since there were no bedrooms Tom and Jessica sleep in a curtained-off alcove, with not much privacy; two very small rooms that once were storage closets are bedrooms for their children, Avery and Devlin. Babs and her husband, Wilfred Rutherford, have been put in a tent down the path, on one of a row of gray plank tent floors where all the camper girls used to sleep. Babs said, "How absolutely divine – I've never slept in a tent." "You haven't?" Jessica asked. "I think I sleep best in tents."

A narrow screened-in porch runs the length of the house, and there is a long table out there – too long for just the four Todds, better (less lonely) with even two guests. The porch widens at its end, making a sort of round room, where Tom and Babs now are, not looking at the view.

Around the house there are clumps of hemlocks, tall Norway pines, white pines, and birches that bend out from the high bank. Across the smooth bright lake are the White Mountains, the Presidential Range – sharp blue Mount Adams and farther back, in the exceptionally clear days of early fall, such as this day is, you can see Mount Washington silhouetted. Lesser, gentler slopes take up the foreground: Mount Pleasant, Douglas Hill.

Beside Babs in the hammock lies a ukelele – hers, which Tom wants her to play.

"Oh, but I'm no good at *all*, she protests. "Wilfred can't stand it when I play!"

"I'll be able to stand it, I can promise you that, my dear."

Her accent is very Bostonian, his Southern; both tendencies seem to intensify as they talk together.

She picks up the instrument, plucks the four strings as she sings, "My dog has fleas."

"So does Louise," he sings mockingly, an echo. Tom is fond of simple ridiculous jokes but he feels it necessary always to deliver them as though someone else were talking. In fact, he says almost everything indirectly.

They both laugh, looking at each other.

They are still laughing when Jessica comes out from the living room where she has been reading (every summer she rereads Jane Austen) and walks down the length of the porch to where they are, and says "Oh, a ukelele, how nice, Barbara. Some of our girls used to play."

Chivalrous Tom gets up to offer his chair – "Here you are, old dear." She did not want to sit so close to the hammock but does anyway, a small shapeless woman on the edge of her chair.

Jessica is only a few years older than Tom but she looks considerably more so, with graying hair and sad brown eyes, a tightly compressed mouth. She has strong and definite Anglo-Saxon notions about good behavior (they all do, this helpless group of American Protestants, Tom and Jessica, Barbara and Wilfred) which they try and almost succeed in passing on to their children. Jessica wears no makeup and is dressed in what she calls "camp clothes," meaning things that are old and shabby (what she thinks she deserves). "Won't you play something for us?" she asks Babs.

"Perhaps you will succeed in persuasion where I have failed," says Tom. As he sees it, his chief duty toward his wife is to be unfailingly polite, and he always is, although sometimes it comes across a little heavily.

Of course Jessica feels the currents between Babs and Tom but she accepts what she senses with melancholy resignation. There is a woman at home whom Tom likes too, small, blond Irene McGinnis, and Irene is crazy about Tom—that's clear—but nothing happens. Sometimes they kiss; Jessica has noticed that Verlie, the maid, always hides Tom's handkerchiefs. Verlie also likes Tom. Nothing more will happen with Babs. (But she is wrong.) It is only mildly depressing for Jessica, a further reminder that she is an aging, not physically attractive woman, and that her excellent mind is not compelling to Tom. But she is used to all that. She sighs, and says, "I think there's going to be a very beautiful sunset," and she looks across the lake to the mountains. "There's Mount Washington," she says.

Then the porch door bangs open and Wilfred walks toward them, a heavy, dark young man with sleeves rolled up over big hairy arms; he has been washing and polishing his new Ford. He is a distant cousin of Jessica's. "Babs, you're not going to play that thing, are you?"

"No, darling, I absolutely promise."

"Well," Tom says, "surely it's time for a drink?"

"It surely is," says Babs, giggling, mocking him.

He gestures as though to slap at the calf of her long leg, but of course he does not; his hand stops some inches away.

Down a wide pine-needled path, some distance from the lodge, there is a decaying birchbark canoe, inside which white Indian pipes grow. They were planted years back by the camper girls. Around the canoe stands a grove of pines with knotted roots, risen up from the ground, in which chipmunks live. Feeding the chipmunks is what Jessica and Tom's children do when they aren't swimming or playing on the beach. Skinny, dark Avery and smaller, fairer Devlin—in their skimpy shorts they sit cross-legged on the pine needles, making clucking noises to bring out the chipmunks.

A small chipmunk comes out, bright-eyed, switching his tail back and forth, looking at the children, but then he scurries off.

Devlin asks, "Do you like Babs?" He underlines the name, meaning that he thinks it's silly.

"She's OK." Avery's voice is tight; she is confused by Babs. She doesn't know whether to think, as her mother probably does, that Bab's white shorts are too short, that she is too dressed up in her pink silk shirt for camp, or to be pleased at the novel sort of attention she gets from Babs, who said last night at dinner, "You know, Avery, when you're a little older you should have an evening dress this color," and pointed to the flame-gold gladioli on the table, in a gray stone crock.

"Her shorts are too short," says Devlin.

"What do you know about clothes? They're supposed to be short—*shorts*." Saying this, for a moment Avery feels that she *is* Babs, who wears lipstick and anything she wants to, whom everyone looks at.

"Mother doesn't wear shorts, ever."

"So what? You think she's well dressed?"

Devlin is appalled; he has no idea what to make of what she has said. "I'll tell!" He is desperate. "I'll tell her what you said."

"Just try, you silly little sissy. Come on, I'll race you to the lodge."

Both children scramble up, Avery first, of course, and run across the slippery pines, their skinny brown legs flashing between the trees, and arrive at the house together and slam open the screen door and tear down the length of the porch to the cluster of grown-ups.

"Mother, do you know what Avery said?"

"No, darling, but please don't tell me unless it was something very amusing." This is out of character for Jessica, and Devlin stares at his mother, who strokes his light hair, and says, "Now, let's all be quiet. Barbara is going to play a song."

Babs picks up her ukelele and looks down at it as she begins her song, which turns out to be a long ballad about a lonely cowboy and a pretty city girl. She has an attractive, controlled alto voice. She becomes more and more sure of herself as she goes along, and sometimes looks up and smiles around at the group—at Tom—as she sings.

Tom has an exceptional ear, as well as a memory for words; somewhere, sometime, he has heard that ballad before, so that by the time she reaches the end he is singing with her, and they reach the last line together, looking into each other's eyes with a great stagy show of exaggeration; they sing together, "And they loved forever more."

But they are not, that night, lying hotly together on the cold beach, furiously kissing, wildly touching everywhere. That happens only in Tom's mind, as he lies next to Jessica and hears her soft sad snores. In her cot, in the tent, Babs sleeps very soundly, as she always does, and she dreams of the first boy she ever kissed, whose name was not Tom.

In the late forties, almost the same group gathers for dinner around a large white restaurant table, the Buon Gusto, in San Francisco. There are Tom and Jessica, and Babs, but she is without Wilfred, whom she has just divorced in Reno. Devlin is there, Devlin grown plump and sleek, smug with his new job of supervising window display at the City of Paris. Avery is there, with her second husband, fat, intellectual Stanley. (Her first marriage, to Paul Blue, the black trumpet player, was annulled; Paul was already married, and his first wife had lied about the divorce.)

Tom and Barbara have spent the afternoon in bed together, in her hotel room—that old love finally consummated. They are both violently aware of the afternoon behind them; they are partly still there, together in the tangled sea-smelling sheets. Barbara presses her legs close. Tom wonders if there is any smell of her on him that anyone could notice.

No one notices anything; they all have problems of their own.

In the more than ten years since they were all in Maine Jessica has sunk further into her own painful and very private despair. She is not fatter, but her body has lost all definition, and her clothes are deliberately middle-aged, as though she were eager to be done with being a sexual woman. Her melancholy eyes are large, darkly shadowed; below them her cheeks sag, and the corners of her mouth have a small sad downward turn. Tom is always carrying on—the phrase she uses to herself—with someone or other; she has little energy left with which to care. But sometimes, still, a lively rebellious voice within her cries out that it is all cruelly unfair; she has done everything that she was taught a wife is expected to do; she has kept house and cared for children and listened to Tom, laughed at his jokes and never said no when he felt like making love—done all those things, been a faithful and quiet wife when often she didn't want to at all, and there he is, unable to keep his eyes off Babs, laughing at all *her* jokes.

Tom has promised Barbara that he will leave Jessica; this winter they will get a divorce, and he will apply for a teaching job at Stanford or U.C., and he and Babs will live in San Francisco; they are both in love with the city.

Avery has recently begun psychoanalysis with a very orthodox Freudian; he says nothing, and she becomes more and more hysterical—she is lost! And now this untimely visit from her parents; agonized, she questions them about events of her early childhood, as though to get her bearings. "Was I nine or ten when I had whooping cough?"

"What?" says Jessica, who had daringly been embarked on an alternative version of her own life, in which she did not marry Tom but instead went on to graduate school herself, and took a doctorate in Classics. (But who would have hired a woman professor in the twenties?) "Tom, I'd love another drink," she says. "Barbara? you too?" Late in her life Jessica has discovered the numbing effects of drink—you can sleep.

"Oh, yes, divine."

Sipping what is still his first vermouth, Devlin repeats to himself that most women are disgusting. He excepts his mother. He is sitting next to Babs, and he cannot stand her perfume, which is Joy.

Looking at Jessica, whom, curiously, she has always liked, Barbara feels a chill in her heart. Are they doing the right thing, she and Tom? He says they are; he says Jessica has her bookstore and her student poet friends ("Fairies, most of them, from the look of them," Tom says), and that living with him does not make her happy at all; he has never made her happy. Is he only talking to himself, rationalizing? Barbara doesn't know.

All these people, so many of them Southern, make Avery's husband, Stanley, feel quite lost; in fact, he finds it hard to understand anything they say. Tom is especially opaque: the heavy Southern accent and heavier irony combine to create confusion, which is perhaps what Tom intends. Stanley thinks Tom is a little crazy, and feels great sympathy for Jessica, whom he admires. And he thinks: poor Avery, growing up in all that—no wonder Devlin's queer and Avery has to go to a shrink. Stanley feels an awful guilt toward Avery, for not supplying all that Tom and Jessica failed to give her, and for his persistent "premature ejaculations"—and putting the phrase in quotes is not much help.

"I remember your whooping cough very well indeed," says Tom, pulling in his chin so that the back of his head jerks up; it is a characteristic gesture, an odd combination of self-mockery and self-congratulation. "It was the same summer you pushed Harry McGinnis into the swimming pool." He turns to Stanley, who is as incomprehensible to him as he is to Stanley, but he tries. "Odd gesture, that. Her mother and I thought she had a sort of 'crush' on young Harry, and then she went and pushed him into the pool." He chuckles. "Don't try to tell me that ladies aren't creatures of whim, even twelve-year-old girls."

"I was nine," says Avery, and does not add: you had a crush on Harry's mother, you were crazy about Irene that summer.

Jessica thinks the same thing, and she and Avery are both looking at Tom, so that he feels the thought.

"I remember teasing Irene about the bathing suit she wore that day," he says recklessly, staring about with his clear blue eyes at the unfamiliar room.

"What was it like?" asks Barbara, very interested.

"Oh, some sort of ruffled thing. You know how those Southern gals are," he says, clearly not meaning either his wife or his daughter.

"I must have thought the whooping cough was a sort of punishment," Avery says. "For having a crush on Harry, as you put it."

"Yes, probably," Jessica agrees, being herself familiar with many varieties of guilt. "You were awful sick—it was terrible. There was nothing we could do."

"When was the first summer you came to Maine?" Devlin asks Babs, coldly curious, nearly rude. It is clear that he wishes she never had.

"1935. In September. In fact September ninth," she says, and then blushes for the accuracy of her recall, and looks at Tom.

"Verlie took care of me," says Avery, still involved with her whooping cough.

Jessica sighs deeply. "Yes, I suppose she did."

Almost ten years later, in the middle fifties, Tom and Barbara are married. In the chapel of the little church, the Swedenborgian, in San Francisco, both their faces stream with tears as the minister says those words.

In her forties, Barbara is a striking woman still, with her small disdainful nose, her sleekly knotted pale hair, and her beautiful way of walking, holding herself forward like a present. She has aged softly, as very fine-skinned very blond women sometimes do. And Tom is handsome still; they make a handsome couple (they always have).

Avery is there; she reflects that she is now older than Barbara was in 1935, that summer in Maine. She is almost thirty, divorced from Stanley, and disturbingly in love with two men at once. Has Barbara never loved anyone but Tom? (Has she?) Avery sees their tears as highly romantic.

She herself is a nervy, attractive girl with emphatic dark eyebrows, large dark eyes, and a friendly soft mouth, heavy breasts on an otherwise slender body. She wishes she had not worn her black silk suit, despite its chic; two friends have assured her that no one thought about wearing black to weddings anymore, but now it seems a thing not to have done. "I wore black to my father's wedding"—thank God she is not still seeing Dr. Gunderscheim, and will use that sentence only as a joke. Mainly, Avery is wondering which of the two men to marry, Charles or Christopher. (The slight similarity of the names seems ominous—what does it mean?) This wondering is a heavy obsessive worry to her; it drags at her mind, pulling it down. Now for the first time, in the small dim chapel, candlelit, it wildly occurs to her that perhaps she should marry neither of them, perhaps she should not marry at all, and she stares about the chapel, terrified.

"I pronounce you man and wife," says the minister, who is kindly, thin, white-haired. He is very old; in fact he quietly dies the following year.

And then, almost as though nothing had happened, they have all left the chapel: Tom and Barbara, Avery and Devlin, who was Tom's best man. ("I have my father away," is another of Avery's new post-wedding jokes.) But something has happened: Tom and Barbara are married. They don't believe it either. He gives her a deep and prolonged kiss (why does it look so awkward?) which embarrasses Devlin, so that he stares up and down the pretty, tree-lined street. He is thinking of Jessica, who is dead.

And he passionately wishes that she had not died, savagely blames Tom and Barbara for that death. Trivial, entirely selfish people—so he sees them; he compares the frivolity of their connection with Jessica's heavy suffering. Since Jessica's death Devlin has been in a sort of voluntary retreat. He left his window-display job and most of his friends; he stays at home on the wrong side of Telegraph Hill, without a view. He reads a lot and listens to music and does an occasional watercolor. He rarely sees Avery, and disapproves of what he understands to be her life. ("You don't think it's dykey, the way you sleep around?" was the terrible sentence he spoke to her, on the eve of Jessica's funeral, and it has never been retracted.) Sometimes in his fantasies it is ten years back, and Tom and Jessica get a divorce and she comes out to live in San Francisco. He finds her a pretty apartment on Telegraph Hill and her hair grows beautifully white and she wears nice tweeds and entertains at tea. And Tom and Barbara move to hell—Los Angeles or Mexico or somewhere. Most people who know him assume Devlin to be homosexual; asexual is actually the more accurate description.

They stand there, that quite striking group, all blinking in a brilliant October sun that instantly dries all tears; for several moments they are all transfixed there, unable to walk, all together, to their separate cars, to continue to the friend's house where there is to be the wedding reception. (Why this hesitation? do none of them believe in the wedding? what is a marriage?)

Five years later, in the early sixties, Avery drives up to Maine from Hilton, for various reasons which do not include a strong desire to see Tom and Barbara. She has been married to Christopher for four years, and she came out from San Francisco to Hilton to see how it was away from him. Away from him she fell wildly in love with a man in Hilton named Jason Valentine, and now (for various reasons) she has decided that she needs some time away from Jason.

She drives smoothly, quietly, along the pine-needled road in her Corvair to find no one there. No car.

But the screen door is unlatched, and she goes in, stepping up from the old stone step onto the long narrow porch, from which the long table has been removed, replaced with a new one that is small and round. (But where did they put the old one?) And there are some bright yellow canvas chairs, new and somehow shocking against the weathered shingled wall.

Inside the house are more violent changes, more bright new fabrics: curtains, bandanna-red, and a bandanna bedspread on the conspicuous wide bed. Beside the fireplace is a white wicker sofa (new) with chintz cushions—more red. So much red and so much newness make Avery dizzy; almost angrily she wonders where the old things are, the decaying banners and sepia photographs of girls in Greek costumes. She goes into the kitchen and it is all painted yellow, into what was the large closet where she used to sleep—but a wall has been knocked out between her room and Devlin's; it is all one room now, a new room, entirely strange, with a new iron bed, a crocheted bedspread, which is white. Is that where they will expect her to sleep? She wishes there were a phone. Tomorrow she will have to drive into town to call Jason at his studio.

Needing a drink, Avery goes back into the kitchen, and finds a bottle of an unfamiliar brand of bourbon. She gets ice from the refrigerator (terrifyingly new–so white!), water from the tap–thank God, the same old sink. With her clutched drink she walks quickly through the living room to the porch, down to the end. She looks out across the lake with sentimentally teared eyes, noting that it is clear but not quite clear enough to see Mount Washington.

Being in love with Jason, who is a nonpracticing architect (he would rather paint), who worries about his work (his nonwork), who loves her but is elusive (she has no idea when they will see each other again), has tightened all Avery's nerves: she is taut, cries easily, and is all concentrated on being in love with Jason.

A car drives up, a Mustang–Barbara is faithful to Fords. And there they are saying, "Avery, but we didn't ex*pect* you, we went into *Port*land, for *lob*sters. Oh, dear, how awful, we only bought *two*!" Embracing, laughing. Tears (why?) in everyone's eyes.

They settle down, after packages are put away, Avery's bags in the new guest room, and they watch the sunset: a disappointing pale pastel. And they drink a lot.

Barbara is nervous, both because of this shift in schedule and because of Avery, whom she regards as an intellectual, like Tom. She is always afraid of what Avery will say–a not-unfounded fear. Also, she is upset about the prospect of two lobsters for three people.

What he considers her untimely arrival permits Tom's usual ambivalence about Avery to yield to a single emotion: extreme irritation. How inconsiderate she is–always has been! Besides, he was looking forward to his lobster.

Avery chooses this unpropitious moment to announce that she is leaving Christopher. "We've been making each other miserable," she says. "We have been, for a long time." She trails off.

Tom brightens, "Well, old dear, I always think incompatibility is a good reason not to live together." He has no notion of his own prurience in regard to his daughter.

She does. She says, "Oh, Christ."

Barbara goes into the kitchen to divide up the lobster; a skilled hostess, she does quite well, and she makes a good mayonnaise, as she listens to the jagged sounds of the quarrel on the porch. Avery and Tom. She sighs.

Now darkness surrounds the house, and silence, except for a faint soft lapping of small waves on the shore and tiny noises from the woods: small animals shifting weight on the leaves, a bird moving on a branch.

"Although I have what I suppose is an old-fashioned prejudice against divorce," Tom unfortunately says.

"Christ, is that why you stayed married to mother and made her as miserable as you could? Christ, I have a prejudice against misery!" Avery feels her voice (and herself) getting out of control.

Barbara announces dinner, and they go to the pretty new table, where places are set, candles lit. Barbara distributes the lobster, giving Tom the major share, but he scowls down at his plate.

As Avery does at hers—in Hilton, with Jason, she was generally too overstimulated, too "in love" to eat; now she is exhausted and very hungry. She turns to Barbara, as though for help. "Don't you ever wish you'd got married before you did? What a waste those years were. That time in San Francisco, why not then?"

Startled, Barbara has no idea what to answer. She has never allowed herself to think in these terms, imaginatively to revise her life. "I feel lucky we've had these years we have had," she says—which, for her, is the truth. She loves Tom; she feels that she is lucky to be his wife.

"But those last years were horrible for mother," Avery says. "You might have spared her that time."

"I think I might be in a better position than you to be the judge of that." Enraged, Tom takes a characteristic stance: his chin thrust out, he is everyone's superior—he is especially superior to women and children, particularly his own.

"Oh, yeah?" In her childhood, this was considered the rudest remark one could make; then Avery would never have said it to Tom. "You think she just plain died of a heart attack, don't you? Well, her room was full of empty sherry bottles. All over. Everywhere those drab brown empty bottles, smelling sweet. Julia told me, when she cleaned it out."

This information (which is new) is so shocking (and so absolutely credible) to Tom that he must dismiss it at once. His desperate and hopeless guilts toward Jessica have forced him to take a sanctimonious tone in speaking of her. He must dismiss this charge at once. "As a matter of fact, Julia is quite unreliable, as Verlie was," he says.

Avery explodes. "Julia is unreliable! Verlie was! Christ—why? because they're black? because they're women?"

Barbara has begun to cry. "You've got to stop this," she says. "Why quarrel about the past? It's over—"

Tom and Avery stare at each other, in terrible pain; they would like to weep, to embrace, but they are unable to do either.

Tom draws himself up stiffly—stiffly he turns to Barbara. "You're quite right, old dear," he says.

Several things attack Avery's mind at once: one, that she would like to say, goddam you both, or something obscene, and take off down the turnpike, back to Boston; two, she is too drunk for the turnpike; and three, she has just noticed that Tom speaks to Barbara exactly as though she were Jessica, as though neither of them were people but something generic named Wife.

And so the moment goes, the awful emotions subside, and they all retreat to trivia. Although Avery's hands still shake, she comments on the mayonnaise (she is not excruciatingly Southern Jessica's daughter for nothing), which Barbara gratefully takes up.

"I'm never sure it will come out right," she says. "I've had the most embarrassing failures, but of course tonight, just for family—" She is unable to finish the sentence, or to remember what she meant.

Later, during the next few years before Tom's death, Avery looks back and thinks that yes, she should have left then, drunk or not. She could have found a motel. That would have been a strong gesture, a refusal to put up with any more of what she saw as Tom's male imperialism, his vast selfishness. (But poor Avery was constantly plagued with alternatives; she constantly rewrote her life into new versions in which she did not marry Stanley. Or Christopher. Sometimes she thought she should have stayed with Paul Blue; in that version, of course, he was not married.) After Tom died she thought that perhaps it was just as well she hadn't left, but she was never quite sure.

Against everyone's advice, early in the summer after Tom died, Barbara drove alone to Maine. Even Devlin had called to dissuade her (in fact ever since Tom's funeral, to which Avery did not even come—Tom had died while she was in Mount Zion Hospital being treated for depression—a new and warm connection had been established between Barbara and Devlin; they wrote back and forth; she phoned him for various pieces of advice—she had begun to rely on him as she was used to relying on Tom).

Devlin said, "Darling Barbara, do you see it as an exercise in masochism? I wouldn't have thought it of you."

"Angel, you don't understand. I love that house. I've been extremely happy there."

"Barbara, let me be blunt: don't you think you'll be fantastically lonely?"

"No, I don't."

And so, after visits with friends and relatives in Boston, Barbara drives on to Maine in her newest Ford, and arrives in a twilight of early July. She parks near the house, gets out, pausing only briefly to observe the weather, which is clear, and to smile at the warm familiar smell of pines. Then she walks briskly over to the porch and opens the padlock on the screen door.

Her first reaction, stepping up onto the porch, could be considered odd: she decides that those yellow chairs are wrong for the porch. This pleases her: changing them for something else will give her something to do. She enters the living room, sniffs at the musty, airless space, and goes into the kitchen, where last summer she hid a bottle of bourbon in the flour bin. (Sometimes stray hunters or fishermen break into the house and take things.) No one has taken it, and she makes herself a good stiff drink, and goes to the rounded end of the porch, to sit and rest.

And much more clearly than she can remember anything that happened last month, last winter or fall, she sees that scene of over thirty years ago, sees Tom (how young he was, how handsome), as he urged her to play her ukelele (play what? did he name a song?), and she sees Jessica come out to where they are (making some reference to the girls who used to come to camp–poor Jessica), and Wilfred, as always angrily serious, puffing although not yet fat, and then wild, skinny Avery (why did she and Jason Valentine not marry?) and frightened Devlin, holding his mother's arm. She sees all those people, and herself among them, and for an instant she has a sense that she *is* all of them–that she is Jessica as well as Barbara, is Wilfred, Avery, Devlin, and Tom.

But this is an unfamiliar mood, or sense, for her, and she shakes it off, literally shaking her head and lifting her chin. She remembers then that she put the old chairs and the table in the shed next to the kitchen.

Three days later Barbara has restored the lodge to what (to herself) she calls its "old look." The old chairs and old long table are back. She has even put up some of Jessica's old pictures in the living room.

She has no idea why she made such an effort, except that she firmly believes (always has) in the efficacy of physical work; she was driven by a strong, controlling instinct, and she also believes in her instincts. She even laughs to herself at what could seem a whim, and in writing a note to Devlin she says, "You'd have thought I was restoring Williamsburg, and you should see my blisters!"

And so at the end of her day she is seated there at the end of the porch, and everything but herself looks just as it did when she first saw it. She drinks the two stiff highballs that she allows herself before dinner, and she remembers all the best times with Tom, San Francisco hotels and Paris honeymoon, the big parties in Hilton, and she sheds a few tears, but she does not try to change anything that happened. She does not imagine an altered, better life that she might have had.

MARK HELPRIN

1980

A Vermont Tale

Many years ago, when I was so young that each snowfall threatened to bar the door and mountain lions came down from the north to howl below my window, my sister and I were sent for an entire frozen January to the house of our grandparents in Vermont. Our mother and father had been instructed by the court in the matter of their difficult and unbecoming love, and that, somehow, was the root of our journey.

After several hours of winding along the great bays of the ice-cluttered Hudson, we arrived in Manhattan only to discover that we had hardly begun. Our father took us to the Oyster Bar, where we tried to eat oysters and could not. Then he found a way to the high glass galleries in Grand Central, where we watched in astonishment as people far below moved in complete silence, smoothly crossing the strong, sad light which descended in wide columns to the floor. We were told that Vermont would be colder than Putnam County, where we lived, the snow deeper, the sky clearer. We were told that we had been there before in the winter but did not remember, that our summer image of the house had been snowed in, and that our grandfather had, of all things, snowshoes.

We were placed in the care of a tremendously fat conductor on a green steam-driven train called Star of the North, which long after darkness had the temerity to charge out into the black cold, and speed through snow-covered fields and over bridges at the base of which murderous ice groped and cut. We knew that outside the windows a man without his coat would either find fire or die. We sensed as well that the warmth in the train and its bright lights were not natural but, rather, like the balancing of a sword at the tip of a magician's finger – an achieved state, from which an overconfident calculation, a graceless move, an accident of steel might hurl us into the numbing water of one of the many rivers over which the conductor had passed so often that he gave it no thought. We feared many things – especially that our parents would not come back together and that we would never go home again. And there was the nagging suspicion that our grandfather had turned into an illogical ogre, who, for unimaginable reasons, chose to wear shoes made of snow.

At midnight, the conductor brought us a pewter tureen of black-bean soup. He explained that the kitchen had just shut down, and that this was the last food until breakfast. We had had our filet of sole in the dining car, and were not hungry at all. But the way he bustled about the soup, and his excitement at having spirited it to us, created an unforeseen appetite. In company of the steam whistle and the glittering ice formed against our window, we finished it and dispatched a box of crackers besides. My sister was young enough so that the conductor could take her on his endless lap and show her how to blow across her spoon to cool the soup. She loved it. And I remember my own fascination with the gold watch chain which, across his girth, signified the route between Portugal and Hawaii.

All through the night, the Star of the North rushed on, its whistle gleaming across frost-lined valleys. We were both in the upper bunk. My sister asked if morning would come. I replied that I was sure it would.

"What will it be like?" she asked.

"I don't know," I answered, but she was already asleep.

The cold outside was magical, colder than anything we had known.

White River Junction had frozen into place, caught as it crept up the hill. The morning was so bright that it seemed like a dream flooded by spotlights. It was a shock to breathe the cold air, and our grandparents saw at once that we were not warm enough in our camel-colored loden coats.

"Don't you children have Christmas hats?" asked my grandfather.

Not knowing exactly what these were, I kept silent for fear of giving the wrong answer.

"Well," he said quietly, "we're going to have to get you kids Christmas hats and goose vests."

Christmas hats were knit caps of the softest, whitest wool. In a band around the center were ribbons of color representing the spectrum, from a shimmering deep violet to dark orange. Goose vests were quilted down-filled silk. They came to us in wire baskets shooting along a maze of overhead track in a store so vast and full of stuff that it seemed like the world's central repository for things. A distant clerk pulled hard on a hanging lever and there was an explosive report after which the basket careered across the room like a startled pheasant. In the store were high thin windows, through which we saw a perfectly blue sky, parts of the town, an ice-choked river, and brown trees and evergreens on the opposite bank, standing on the hill like a dumbfounded herd. We bought so much in that store that we completely filled the pickup truck with sacks, boxes, packages, bags, and bushel baskets. We bought, among other things, apples, lamb, potatoes, oranges, mint, coffee, wine, sugar, pepper, chocolate, thread, nails, balsa wood, color film, shoe wax, flour, cinnamon, maple sugar, salt fish, matches, toys, and a dozen children's books–good long thick ones with beautiful pictures and heavy fragrant paper.

Then we drove off in the truck. I sat in the middle and my sister was on my grandmother's lap, her little head pointed straight at the faraway white mountains visible through the windshield. I saw my grandmother looking at the way my sister's eyes were focused on the distance; in my grandmother's restrained smile, lit by bright light coming shadowless from the north, was more love than I have ever seen since. They both had blue eyes; and I felt only pain, because I knew that the moment would pass–as it did.

With tire chains singing and the heater blowing, we drove all the way up into Addison County, to the empty quarter, where there are few towns. It seemed odd, after coming all that way, when my grandfather told me that we were close to New York. "The boy doesn't understand," said my grandmother. "We'll have to get a map." Then she looked at me: "You don't understand." Of course, I knew that, especially since I had just heard it declared a minute before. "New York goes all the way up to Canada, and so does Vermont. Massachusetts and Connecticut are in between, but alongside New York. You and Julia came through Connecticut and Massachusetts. But New York was always on your left, to the west."

"Oh," I said.

On a bluff high above a rushing river, we pulled into a shed at the end of a long snow-covered road. The river forked above my grandparents' land, and came together again south of it. In winter, one could not cross the boiling rapids except by a cable car, which went from the shed to a pine grove behind their barn. The cable car was cream-colored and blue, and had come, we were told, from Switzerland. The two hundred acres were a perfect island.

This island was equally divided into woods, pasture, and lakes. The woods were evergreen, and my grandfather picked up fallen branches whenever he came upon them (for kindling), so that the floor was open and clear, covered only with pine needles and an occasional grouping of ferns. The pines were tall and widely spaced. Horses could gallop through the columned shadows. The chamber formed by these trees extended for acres, in some places growing very dark, and to walk through it was fearsome and delightful. Always, the wind whistled through the trees. If you looked around and saw only this forest, it seemed as if you were underground. But a glance upward showed sky through green.

The pastures were fenced with split rail and barbed wire, covered with deep snow, spread about in patches of five or ten acres in the woods and on the sides of hills. They rolled all over the island and were host to wind and drifts; they were the places to ski or go race the horses on trails that had been packed down by daily use. Half in woods, half in pasture, was the house – white frame with black shutters, many fireplaces, and warm plank floors which gave off resinous squeaks. Between the house and the river was the barn, in which were two horses, a loft of clean hay, a workshop, and a pair of retrievers – one gold and one black – whose tails were forever waving back and forth in approval and contentment.

At the island's center were two lakes. One, of about five acres, lay open to the north wind and was isolated from the winter sun by a pine-clad rise to its south. This lake froze so that its surface was as slick as a mirror. When it was not covered with snow, it was the perfect place to skate. The second lake was no more than three acres, and it lay in the lee of the rise, open to the sun. A salt spring dropped water to it over falls of ten or fifteen feet. It was bordered by pines and forest-green rocks on the north, and opened to a pasture below. This lake was nearly hidden, and it was never completely frozen.

After a few trips in the cable car, we got the provisions and supplies into the house and spent a long time unpacking and putting away what we had bought. My grandfather and I took turkeys, hams, chickens, roasts, and wheels of cheese into a cold smokehouse. When he lit the fire there, I was poised to run from a great conflagration, and was surprised that it crept slowly, with hardly any flame. That night, we smelled not only sweet fires in the house but a dark, antique scent from chips smoldering under hanging meat and fowl.

Our room was in the attic. It had a big window through which we could see mountain ranges and clouds beyond the meadows. At night a vast portion of sky was visible from our bed. When I opened my eyes after being asleep, the stars were so ferociously bright that I had to squint. They were not passive and mute as they sometimes are, but they shone out and burned like white fire. I have never fallen asleep without thinking of them. They made me imagine white lions, perhaps because the phosphorescent burning was like a roar of light. A fireplace was in the room; a picture of Melville (the handsomest man I have ever seen, surely not so much for what he looked like but for what he was); wooden pegs on which to hang our goose vests and Christmas hats; shelves and shelves of illustrated books. Most remarkably, the ceiling was painted a deep luminous blue.

As the days became calibrated into wide periods of light and dark, we lost track even of the weeks, much less the hours. Later, when I was wounded in war, they shot me full of morphine. The slow bodiless breathing was just like the way time passed in that crystalline January.

We were possessed by the flawless isolation and the numbing cold. Perhaps we lost ourselves so easily because of the exquisite tiredness after so many hours outdoors, or perhaps because Julia and I had been waiting tensely and were suddenly freed. In the days, we rode the horses, and the dogs followed. At first, the four of us went out, with the children sitting forward on the saddles. Soon, though, I did my own riding. My grandmother and Julia would go back into the house and I would mount their horse. Then my grandfather and I galloped all over the island, dashing through the pines, crossing meadows, riding hard to prospects overlooking the thunderous white forks of the river. Much work was needed just to take care of the horses, to curry, to shovel, to fork down their hay from the loft. We split wood and carried it into the house, stocking all the fireplaces every night for at least one good burn. We baked pies according to a special system, in which my grandmother made pie for the grownups and we followed her, step by step, with a children's pie, which, no matter what we did, always looked like a shanty. My sister kept the house completely free of dust. It was a game for her, and she polished everything in sight.

"It's sad," said my grandfather.

"Why?" asked his blue-eyed wife, still strikingly beautiful.

"The child is so upset that she's become obsessed. Today, she was dusting for two hours, telling herself stories and singing. She's afraid to sit still."

"She's as happy as she can be in the circumstances."

"I don't know," he said. "How do you reach a child caught up like that? You can't just talk to her."

"All we have to do is love her, and that's easy."

In late afternoon as it grew dark we would come into the house and read, or be read to, until dinner. After we had cleaned up, we had a fire in the living room and read some more. An old radio brought in a classical station which sounded so far away that it seemed to be Swiss. Sometimes we took walks in the moonlight, and sometimes we stayed out for as long as we could and looked through a telescope at the moon and planets. By about eight, we were always so tired that we hardly moved, and just sat staring at the fire. Then my grandfather would throw on some logs and say, "Enough of this nonsense! Are we sloths? Certainly not! There are things to do. Let's do them."

In a sudden burst of energy, my grandmother would go to the piano, he would return to his book, Julia would pull down the watercolors, the fire would blaze, and I would become hypnotized by Hottentots and Midwestern drainage canals within the dentist-yellow *National Geographic*s. Then we would go to bed, as exhausted as if we had just spent time in a great city at Christmas. Sleep came easily when the nights were clear and the sky pulsed.

But the nights were not always clear. In the middle of January, we had a great blizzard. We could neither ride, nor ski, nor walk for very long with the snowshoes. High drifts made it extremely difficult just to get the wood in. The sky was gray; my grandfather's bad leg made him limp about; and we all began to grow pale. Instead of putting more logs on the fire and waking up, we let the flame go into coals, and we moved slowly upstairs to sleep. The blizzard lasted for days. We felt as if we were in the Arctic, and we learned to wince slightly at the word "Canada." I wondered if indeed all things came to sad and colorless ends.

Then something happened. One night, when the wind was so fierce that we heard trees crash down in the forest, we were just about to get into bed, and my grandfather had turned out all the lights and was coming up the stairs. From high above in the swirl of raging wind and snow came a frightening, wonderful, mysterious sound.

Neither of the nightingale nor of the wolf but somewhere in between, as meaningful and mournful as a life spent in the most solitary places, strong and yet sad, as clear as cold water and ever so beautiful, it was the cry of the loon. It sounded for all the world like one of Blake's angels, and as it hovered above our house, circling our bed, we thought it was God come to take us. My grandfather rushed to the landing.

"They're back!" he cried.

"It can't be," said my grandmother, looking up. "Not after ten years. They must be others."

"No," he said. "I know them too well."

The sound kept circling and we listened for many minutes with our heads thrown back and our eyes traversing to and fro against the pitch of the roof. Then there was quiet.

"What was it?" I asked, noticing for the first time that my sister had grasped my waist and still held tightly.

"Arctic Loons," he said. "Two Arctic Loons. Isn't it a beautiful sound? I'll tell you about them."

"When?"

"Now," he said, and went to light the fire.

My grandmother dragged in a chair, and she and my grandfather sat facing us. We were propped up in bed, covered by a giant satin goose blanket. It was very late for my sister, and she looked drugged. But she was terrified, and she stared ahead without a blink. She wore a white flannel gown with tiny blue stars all over it. My grandmother rocked back and forth, hardly ever taking her eyes from us. My grandfather leaned forward as if he were about to enter communion with the blazing fire.

Then he turned with startling concentration. My grandfather was six and one-half feet tall and as thin as a switch. He was rocking back and forth, and he mesmerized us as if we were a jury and he a great lawyer of the nineteenth century. The fire roared upward at the stone, diverging into ragged orange tongues. "What is a loon? What is a loon? What is a loon?" he said, so that our mouths dropped open in astonishment.

"You heard it, did you not? Can you tell me that the creature has no soul? Doesn't it sound, in its sad call, like a man? Did they not sound like singers? Remember, first of all, that we have our idea of angels from the birds. For they are gentle and perfect in a way we will never be. For more than a hundred million years they have been soaring. They found the union of peace and ecstasy so long ago that we cannot even imagine the time. But that does not answer your simple question.

"A loon is a bird. Tomorrow, you will see it. It is extremely fine to look at, so sleek and clean of line that it puts an arrow to shame. It is circumpolar, which means that it lives in both the Eastern and the Western hemispheres. It can swim on the water and under it, and it is a strong flier. Tonight we heard two Arctic Loons. When winter comes in the polar regions, they go south. But rarely do they appear on the Atlantic Coast, and when they do they winter on the sea, where the water, though cold, is not frozen, and where there are plenty of fish.

"When I came back from the First War, your grandmother and I bought this place and began to spend the summers here. The house was up, but most of the pasture was not cleared, the barn had yet to be built, and the only way over the river was by a cable ferry on which everything got a thorough wetting. For years, we were here only in the summer, but one winter I came to stay alone.

"It was almost impossible to cross the river on the ferry. Had it capsized into the freezing waters, I would have drowned. The sheriff of the county advised me not to cross, but I did, and soon I was snowed in and everything was completely quiet. In those days, I was trying to write my dissertation. Before you become a professor, you have to write a book which is boring enough so that even you cannot bear to read it over. Once you have done this, you are free to write as you please, but can't. After I had been in the war, it was hard to write such a book because, well, I was so happy just to be alive—so happy that for years afterward I often did crazy things."

My grandmother glanced leftward into the darkness above the roof beams, conveying both skepticism and amusement. But, when she returned her gaze to my grandfather's face, she seemed almost bitter.

"For example," my grandfather continued. "In Cambridge, Harvard students were supposed to be afraid of the town toughs, who always gathered in large groups at street corners. Though I knew my way around (after having been there for ten years), I would sometimes approach such a group and say, 'Which one of you duds knows enough words to direct me to Kirkland Street?' That, believe me, took courage. And then, once, I stood up in a crowded lecture and asked the professor: 'What is the difference between a mailbox and the backside of a hippopotamus?" He immediately said, 'I don't know,' to which I answered that I would be glad to mail his letters for him. I believe it was the shock of war. I hope it was the shock of war. It took me a while to straighten out.

"After a few days in the house, struggling to write my chapters, I grew restless and began to walk around in the woods. We did not have horses then. I went to the big lake and found that it had a snowless surface. I skated there for a week before I went to the little lake, to see if perhaps I could skate there, too. When I saw that it was clear of ice, I remembered that it was salty and sheltered. As I was sitting, skates hung over my shoulder, my face to the sun, a fleet of birds sailed gracefully from under a rock ledge to the center of the lake. There were at least a dozen loons—paired up, healthy, unaware of my presence. I moved back so that they would not see me, and when I left I resolved to watch them in secret.

"This I did, and soon learned their habits. Early in the morning, the first flight—as I called it—would take off from the lake with great effort. It was so hard for them to get airborne that it seemed as if they would crash against the opposite shore, but they rose just before the land and flew southward. This they did two at a time until about noon, when the first pair returned. The last flight returned just at darkness. Then they would go up on the bank and sleep in nests they had made of fern, pine needles, and reeds.

"Though their transition to flight was awkward, they flew magnificently—as I learned later, up to sixty miles per hour. Because of their great speed, I was at first unable to follow them. But one day I was in town and had just stepped out of the post office, when I saw two of them flying by in the same direction as the road. You can imagine the surprise of the sheriff when I jumped into his idling car and ordered him to follow the loons. He did, and we discovered that they fed in a wide section of the river, where there were many fish but where the loons could not have lived because the water ran too fast. I watched them over time and found that they lived in mated pairs, that they kept faith, and that they showed great concern and tenderness for one another. In fact, their loyalty and intimacy were as beautiful to observe as their graceful bodies of brown, white, and gray.

"I soon discovered an attached pair which seemed to be special. Though the female was not as majestic as some, and though she modestly moved about her business and did not lord it over the group as others did, she was extraordinarily beautiful—despite her imperfections, or perhaps because of them. She had a gentleness, a quietness, a tentativeness, which showed how finely she was aware of the sad beauty in the life they lived. You could see the seasons on her face, and that she felt and suffered deeply. Nonetheless, she was a strong and robust flier. This combination intrigued me, this union of gentleness and strength.

"Her mate was full of energy and wounds. Part of his foot was missing. A great gash was cut into his wing. You see, he and others like him had flown into the hunters' guns. Fishermen think that loons steal their catch. This is incorrect, and yet the loons are hunted down time and again, and their number steadily decreases. This may explain why they had chosen a small lake in lieu of an abundant sea.

"Anyway, he was alternately gregarious and reclusive. Sometimes he led or harried the others, and sometimes he would not go near them. For her, this was most difficult. Loons are good fliers and graceful swimmers. They can stay under water for several minutes, and they have been observed to dive as far as two hundred and fifty feet below the surface. But on land they can hardly move, because they are, I think, the only bird whose leg is mainly within the body, so much are they like swimmers. When moving on land, they waddle and they fall. Many, many times, he went up onshore and pushed for the woods. I saw her looking after him. It pained her to see him moving so awkwardly into the thicket, where perhaps a fox might get him. It made her feel as if she were not loved. For if she were, she thought, why would he take such risks? But he was driven in all directions and frequently made her feel alone and apart. And yet she loved him, and she loved him very strongly, despite what appeared to be her reticence.

"They would lie up against one another, have long conversations in their many voices, circle the lake, and sometimes put their faces together so that their eyes touched. The days passed one after another until it became irredeemably dark. Then, from the north, another group of loons came winging in and threw the lake into chaos. They were unattached, and their arrival electrified the others.

"She felt immediately threatened because of his curiosity and the way he had always wandered away. This frightened her, and she kept to herself, closing off to him. All *he* knew was that she became colder and colder. He did not realize that she loved so much that her fear ran ahead of her, and he began to take up with the group from the north. He paid much attention to one in particular—a brilliant female, with whom one day he flew off to the feeding place, where the river was fast and full of fish.

"She was so hurt that she could not even think. And when he returned, enthused and energized, she was hurt all the more. But it would have passed had he not done it again and again, until she was forced to go alone south to the feeding place, and fish alone in front of all while he was occupied with the new one. And she flew back alone, her heart beating against the rhythm of her wings, her eyes nearly blind, for she loved him so much, and he had betrayed her.

"As time passed, the pain was too much for her to bear, and she left. Her departure worked through him like a harrow, and all was changed. As in the classical Greek and Latin romances, he realized what he had done, and, more to the point, how valuable she was and how he loved her, and he was thrashed with remorse. He set out to find her. Despite his skill and experience as a flier and a fighter, it was extremely difficult. She had gone to a lake deep, deep in the wilderness and very far away."

"Baltimore," said my grandmother, startling herself, and then realizing that it was late and that the story would have to continue on the next night. "Besides," she said to my grandfather, "if the blizzard keeps up you won't be able to take the children to the small lake. They can see the loons the day after tomorrow."

When they had kissed us good night and opened the window enough so that the room began to cool rapidly and hard, dry crystals of snow were blown in only to disappear in the darkness beyond the bed, we were left alone in the light of the fire. Breathing hard, my little sister stared at the flames, her eyes all welled up. It was like a fever night, when there is no relief. In those reddened nights, little children first conjured up the idea of Hell. I tried, as I always did, to be very grownup. But I really couldn't.

It snowed so hard the next day that the air was like tightly loomed cloth. Drifts covered the porch and reclined against the windows. The house was extremely quiet. We had stayed up late and were tired from days of being trapped inside. My grandfather and grandmother said hardly a word, not even to one another.

When it darkened—and it darkened early—we began to anticipate resumption of the tale as if we were awaiting Christmas morning: the four of us in a small room with a sky-blue ceiling, an enginelike fire steadily cascading like a forge, snow against the window, the goose blanket spread out silky and white like a winter meadow, and the story unraveling in dancing shadows. Before we knew it, the yellow disc in the clock plunged downward and was replaced by a sparkling white moon and stars on a background of blue. The moon had a strange smile, and I thought that he must have been born on that island a long time before, and spent his life in the perfect quiet—season after season, silent snow after silent snow.

My grandfather put two more split logs on the fire in our room, and started once again to tell us about the loons. I looked at the ceiling and imagined them as they had been the night before, poised above us, treading with brown wings on the agitated air.

"He hardly knew what he was in for," said the old man closing his eyes briefly and then opening them as he began the tale. "He was so good-spirited that he envisioned a fast flight to a lake found out by skill, swooping to re-union, and then beginning where they had left off. But he didn't count on two things. The first was her feeling that she had been horribly betrayed, and the second, and more immediate, was the problem of how to find her.

"He set off, rising into the air with a rush from his wings. He flew for many miles, and after a day he did not see her on any of the lakes beneath. He stayed one night on a large lake where it was cold and there were no living things, but only a whistling mysterious wind. He traversed the dark northern lakes as if they were chambers in a great cavern, always alone, fly-ing through the relentless cold, day after day and week after week, with his eyes sharp and his great strength serving him well, until he had flown enough for several migrations and was nearly beaten. The ice cut him; he was pursued by hungry forest animals; and in all those regions of empty whiteness he never came upon another of his kind."

"How do you know?" I asked. He looked at me imperiously, greatly offended. I began to be frightened of him.

"Because I know," he said, and from then on I did not dare to question him, although I did wonder how he could know such a thing.

"For months, he read the terrain and searched for the proper signs. Then, as he was about to land on one of a chain of lakes, he saw a flight of many loons far off in the distance, disappearing over a hill of bare trees.

"He sprinted toward them. Since he had flown all day, he was lithe and hot, and caught them so quickly that they thought an eagle had flown into their midst. She was there! He spotted her at the edge, in company of several others. He dived at them and drove them off, and then flew level with her, on the same course as the rest but at a distance.

"She would not look at him, and she acted as if he were dead to her. After they landed, she, to his great sadness, went off with another. But he could easily see that she did not love the other. Nor was the other a cham-pion, a strong flier, or wounded by the hunters' guns.

"All his persuasion, his sorrow, meant nothing to her. She seemed deter-mined to spend her life, without feeling, in the presence of strangers. So he left without her. It was painful for him to see her recede into the distance as he flew away.

"Alone on the little lake, he did not know what to do. He had got to know her so well, and come to love her so deeply, that he did not feel that he could ever love another. He began to think of the hunters' guns. It gave him great pleasure to imagine flying against them, even though he would be killed. But he was kept from this by the chance that she would return. He waited. Days passed, months. As the seasons turned and it was winter once again, he realized that he had lost his chance. If at the end of another winter she did not return, he would then set off to seek out the hunters.

"When storms came down from the north in the second winter, he realized that she would not return. For she would by then have been driven south. Nor did the others arrive, and he found himself in sole possession of the lake. He made no more forays into the trees and brush. He stopped singing on clear nights. Until that time, he had sung loudly and beautifully in hope that she would use the sound to guide herself back. On those nights in the fall when the air is refined and clear and the moon beats down by black shadows in a straight white line, he had sung the last out of himself. As winter took hold, he moved in a trance, determined to find the hunters in the spring. Her image so frequently filled the darkness before him that he did not trust his sanity.

"Sensible loons (if there can be such a term) were supposed to get on with work. But he cared little for making himself fat with fish and could not see years ahead of simply eating. The winter closed him in. He would sit in the disheveled nest and stare without feeling as the sun refracted through ice and water. The blue sky seemed to run through his eyes like a brook.

"But one day in early March, when the sun was hot enough to usher out some light green and the blue lakes seemed soft and new, he glanced up at a row of whitened Alpine clouds and saw a speck sailing among them as if in a wide circle. It was a bird, far away, alone in the sky, orienting. And then the bird slid down the sides of the clouds and beat her way around them and fell lower and lower in a great massive glide, swooping up sometimes, turning a little, and finally pointing like an arrow to the lake.

"He trembled from expectation and fear. But he knew her flight. He knew the courage she had always had, despite her frailty, in coursing the clouds. And on that last run, as she came closer and closer, she became an emblem of herself. He sped to the middle of the lake with all the energy he had unwittingly saved. The blood was rushing through him as if he had been flying for a day, and she swooped over his head, turned in the air like an eagle, and landed by him in a crest of white water."

When my grandfather said that, his hands were before him and he sat bolt upright in his chair. My sister closed her eyes and let out a sigh. This, my grandmother liked very much. For the little girl had been tensed and contorted awaiting the outcome. Suddenly, the circling of the loons above the house made perfect sense. It was as if winter were somehow over, though that was far from true.

As my sister slept profoundly, it was my turn to spend a fever night. Though it was deathly cold, there was enough light to think upon, and I troubled until morning.

Very early, when I could sleep only in fits and starts, I arose and jumped quietly to the floor. Everyone was asleep. It was light, but it still snowed. I put on my clothes and boots and went down the stairs. There was ice on the inside of the windows. Not knowing about condensation, or much else, I thought the ice had come through the glass. Outside, I put on snowshoes and heatedly made my way around the house. I could hear the snow falling. It sounded like a slow and endless fire. I caught whiffs from the smoke shed, and was aware of a vague sweet smell from the house chimneys.

I followed the tops of the fence posts and the straight ribbon between the trees which showed the road. The snowshoes were too big and I tumbled several times into the snow, discovering in both delight and horror that it came up to my chin. But, puffing along the top of the drifts, I finally came to the lake. It was partially covered by ice, on which lay a slope of snow.

Under the rock ledge, a wide space of open water smelled fresh even from a distance. The snow came down in steady lines, but I squinted and made out two gliding forms, hardly visible, moving as if in the severest of all mysteries. I dared not approach them, though I could have. They seemed like lions on the plain, or spirits, or frightening angels.

Then I turned at the sound of snowshoes and saw my grandmother coming up the rise to where I stood. When she reached me, she put her hand on my shoulder and looked hard at the loons. She, too, looked sleepless.

"I heard you," she said, "when you left the house. Do you see them?"

For reasons I could not discern, I began to cry. She dropped to her knees, kneeling on her snowshoes, and took me in her arms. She didn't have to say anything. For I saw that her eyes . . . her eyes, though beautiful and blue, were as cold as ice.

JOYCE CAROL OATES

1980

Presque Isle

At about the time the gulls' crazy shrieking woke Jean-Marie, her mother Eunice was halfway to Skye Harbor in the little red Fiat. But then the Fiat caught fire: Eunice happened to glance in the rearview mirror and saw clouds of angry white-gray smoke. Oh my God, she said, not again . . . Her first instinct was to brake to a stop, right on the road. But the road was narrow. And the shoulder sloped away to a deep sandy ditch. So she drove, at five miles an hour, to Jake's Service on the outskirts of Skye Harbor.

Where the owner, Jake, who knew Eunice's former husband, James, and knew all about the wealthy Scudders, hid his contempt, and said he would do what he could on the car—but that make, he said, was a pile of junk. Eunice blinked tears angrily out of her eyes. She had to fight the impulse to weep in front of strangers; there was never any temptation to weep at home. Yes, all right, I know, Eunice said, this is the second time it has happened, can you fix it?–that's all I want to know. Jake was charmingly unkempt, and his bib-overalls were stiff with grease. That make of car, he said, was a pile of junk. He didn't know what he could do with it. He couldn't be responsible.

Eunice decided to forget about the groceries, no doubt someone else would be driving in, wasn't Kim planning on a luncheon for a dozen or more people?–and went to the liquor store instead, where she spent $67 in ten minutes. She used the telephone there to call the lodge but no one answered. She hung up, and dialed again, because her hands were shaking slightly and she might have misdialed . . . that happened sometimes. But no one answered.

It was almost 11:00. Too early for her guests to be out on the beach (and the air was uncomfortably chilly–the sky was one of those hammered-tin skies), but late for them to be sleeping. Though maybe not Eunice thought, staring at her watch, because everyone had been up late the night before. How late, she didn't know. She had fallen onto her bed, half-dressed, around 2:30. She really couldn't remember.

Something odd had happened the night before, something unpleasant and unexpected, but she couldn't remember. She supposed she would remember, in time. That usually happened.

The taxi driver helped her with the liquor–the bottles had been placed, for convenience, in a cardboard carton–and drove her the seven miles out to the tip of Presque Isle, to the Scudder camp. It was easiest simply to call it that, since everyone on Presque Isle knew where it was, the Scudder camp, though Eunice detested the name Scudder, and was contemplating a name change–maybe the resumption of her maiden name (Pemberton–a nice enough name, though somewhat prim), or a new name entirely (Maas, Hugo, Woolf, Lorraine–and there was still the possibility of Kleiboldt, if she and Reed did get married after all). The Scudder camp was really a compound. Fifty acres, a ten-foot chain-link fence (which needed repairs, Eunice knew, but *she* wasn't going to bother), no-trespassing signs every forty feet. The Scudders had owned it for generations, though in recent years, with everyone dying off, and James's trips to Brazil, it was rarely used and would probably have to be sold. But then it was an investment–it was real estate– palpable, as James's accountant would say. Eunice didn't know. She tried not to care. In this phase of her life a sense of fatality overcame her, or was it perhaps a sense of destiny ("destiny" had a nobler ring), and she found it halfway pleasant. I have been active, I have been *scrambling*, she thought, for too many years.

The taxi driver commented, as everyone did, on the beautiful view of the ocean–the handsome "cottages"–the stand of tall, perfectly straight Scots pine. It was impressive, yes. Eunice remembered how impressed she had been, twenty-five years ago, and intimidated, which had been part of James's design, certainly. Or his mother's. She wondered if Reed had been impressed, last week. He had said nothing except, What's all the way across there– Spain, Portugal?–Morocco? Eunice said she didn't know exactly, she thought it might be France.

Oh yes, Reed had said something more–were the people around the camp, Presque Isle people, in James's hire? (By "people" Reed meant "servants" though he couldn't bring himself to use the word, and by "hire" he meant were they spies for Eunice's former husband.)

But they were safe, Eunice explained. They were safe now. James had turned 180 degrees (if that was the correct expression) and was now going to be very liberal and tolerant, even sympathetic; there would be no more detectives; no more grubby nonsense. You're grown up now, Eunice, he said, chuckling sadly, you're a big girl now, and though he had disappointed her in the past by lying he had never lied in quite *that* style. So they had the camp for the entire month of August and it was only August 8.

As Eunice paid the driver, her sharp eye darted everywhere–to the little cottage by the sea-cliff path called Windy Dells, to Sunny Haven, the Pines, and the main lodge–but no one seemed to be around.

She walked in the kitchen door, struggling with the carton of bottles, and had the surprise of her life–there was Jean-Marie–leaning against the kitchen sink, smoking a cigarette, obviously waiting for her. She saw me carrying this box, Eunice thought, and didn't even–

What are you doing here! she heard herself cry out.

What? said Jean-Marie.

I mean–did you say–what about music camp?–Eunice stammered.

I *told* you last night about music camp, Jean-Marie said.

You did? You told me? Last night–?

Mother, I explained it all last night, don't you remember? Jean-Marie said with that hateful quizzical little smile of hers. I got here last night, don't you remember? . . . These guys were driving to Quebec, I ran into them at Polly's new place, in the Village, I told you about it last night, you seemed to be listening.

Well, you shouldn't scare me like that, Eunice said.

She began putting bottles away, noisily.–You know what my nerves are like, she said.

She could feel her face growing warm. And red. Oh yes–it would be blotched with red! Though why *she* should be embarrassed she didn't know. After all, Reed and Jean-Marie had already met. In June, in the city. Lunch at a pub on Third Avenue, a visit to the Metropolitan, where, in the Egyptian wing, Reed had made them giggle by warning a group of black boys, junior-high-aged, that there was an ancient mummy's curse on anyone who fooled around in the presence of the dead. (The boys had slipped away from their teacher and were acting a bit rowdy.) Jean-Marie had been *very* amused.

It was erroneous to think, as Eunice sometimes did when she wasn't thinking clearly, that Reed was young enough to be her son. He wasn't: he was twenty-seven. And Jean-Marie was only sixteen. Her sixteenth birthday had been back in May.–Did James bring you here? Is he in town? Eunice heard herself asking.

For God's sake, Mother, Jean-Marie said, exhaling smoke from her nostrils in a harsh dramatic gesture (picked up, Eunice supposed, from one of James's "model" friends), I *told* you about last night.

Are you in contact with James.

Well–not exactly–but he knows about the music school–he knows it wasn't working out.

And what about the tuition? Eunice asked. She opened the refrigerator and looked inside but couldn't remember what she wanted.

Jean-Marie shrugged her shoulders.

Your father isn't going to like it, Eunice said nervously.

He already *knows*, Jean-Marie said.

I'm just so shaky, the car broke down and I should call the garage, but the man there is so rude. Eunice said, shutting the refrigerator door with a thud, and everything is so . . . You aren't supposed to hitchhike, Jean-Marie. You know that.

I didn't hitchhike. It was a *ride*.

And they drove you all the way to Skye Harbor—?

They let me out at the exit. By Plainsboro.

And then you hitchhiked!

Mother, it's only fifteen miles.

But then how did you get out here?

What do you mean—out here?

Out here. To the camp.

I said—I got a ride.

To Skye Harbor, and then—?

To Skye Harbor, yes, and then he was nice enough to drive me out here, Jean-Marie said patiently.

But this was another person, wasn't it! Eunice said.

Oh Mother, for God's sake, it's only fifteen miles from the Plainsboro exit, Jean-Marie said, flicking ashes into the sink. Anyway I told you last night. I told Reed last night, she said with a queer little smile.

Reed? When did you see Reed?

Down on the beach!—you were all down on the beach when I got here, Jean-Marie said.

Eunice remembered, now. And her face grew hotter.

Well—you shouldn't sneak up on me and scare me, she said, yanking open a drawer, you know what my nerves are like—you didn't give me any warning—just walked away from that camp—and you said, you promised, you'd stay there!—you said how beautiful it was in Virginia and you never wanted to leave and the city air is foul, you were never coming home again—

She crouched down to open a cupboard door. Her knees bent fatly.

Mother, Jean-Marie said, with that faint air of incredulity, of polite astonishment, that so exasperated both her parents—she had come back from St. Ann's with it, at the age of fourteen—Mother, what the hell are you looking for?

The telephone book! I am looking for the telephone book! Eunice shouted.

It wasn't in the kitchen, so mother and daughter searched in the other room—a long high-ceilinged room with a dozen windows, screened, and a large fieldstone fireplace, and wicker furniture with yellow-and-green striped cushions, now rather faded. Jean-Marie found the telephone book in one of the window seats. He should have given you a card or something, at the garage, she said. She flicked through the telephone book. Some of the pages are missing, she said.

Well he didn't *give* me any card, Eunice said angrily.

Here's my old guitar, Jean-Marie said, I didn't know I left it out here. She laughed and wiped at her nose with her fingers. —So this is where it is.

She began plucking away at the strings energetically. Eunice looked through the telephone book, in the yellow pages, trying to remember the name of the garage—it was a man's name, a very simple name.

The exhaust was on fire, Eunice said. And that disgusting little man said the care was a pile of junk . . .

Jean-Marie strummed away, faster and faster. In a high thin voice she sang, O Shenandoah, I love your daughter . . . O Shenandoah, I'm bound to leave you . . .

In the kitchen, Eunice poured herself a tall glass of tomato juice and added a touch of vodka. And lemon. Her hands were shaking badly because too much was going on: the car breaking down, Jean-Marie showing up unannounced, everyone sleeping late. (Though she heard—she *thought* she heard—heavy footsteps overhead. Someone going barefoot down the hall, to the bathroom. Did the footsteps come from her room, hers and Reed's? Or Kim's? Or maybe it was that girl from Ireland, what was her name . . .)

Jean-Marie slouched in the doorway, picking at the guitar, at single strings. Her fingers were quick and impatient, as if she halfway wanted to break the strings. There's something called Jake's Garage, she said.

Jake's—! Yes, that's it, Eunice said, closing the telephone book; but in the next moment she snatched it up again, to look for the number. Oh God, I just can't send your father another bill, she said. You know I had that awful root canal work last winter . . .

Jean-Marie strummed and sang, John Henry he had a little woman, woman dressed in green, she used to come to the . . . used to come to the mountain every day, just to hear John Henry's hammer ring, Oh God, just to hear John Henry's hammer ring . . . She said, in a flat, low voice: Reed didn't seem very friendly last night. In fact he seemed a little unfriendly.

Well—

I don't think he remembered me, actually.

Of course he remembered you! Eunice said, turning the pages nervously. It's just that . . . he . . . he's sometimes . . . he's sometimes moody . . . And you came unannounced . . . And there's some tension between him and that boy Kim . . . you know . . . did you meet Kim . . . the photographer . . .

Oh yes: Kim! Jean-Marie said, laughing.

Eunice swallowed a large mouthful of her drink. Someone was running upstairs, along the corridor.

It sounds as if your guests are up, at least, Jean-Marie said.

Well—it's our vacation, Eunice said weakly.

Did Reed go to Arizona, after all?

Arizona? Why Arizona?

Wasn't there some film or something?—Tucson?—he was saying, in June, he might get a grant from the film institute or whatever it's called—

I don't think that came through, Eunice said.

He had the script mostly written, didn't he?

Jean-Marie, I don't know, why don't you ask him yourself . . .

Eunice had found the number and was about to dial. Her fingers *were* shaking. —Niall Sullivan, that was her name. That charming pug-nosed girl from Ireland.

Reed was distinctly unfriendly last night, Jean-Marie said, running her fingernails sharply across the strings. And Kim too. Oh yes, Kim! And what's-her-name—Sandra.

Honey, you took us by surprise, Eunice said. You know how Reed feels about James.

What's that got to do with me? Jean-Marie asked, opening her eyes wide, as if such a thought had never occurred to her.

I've got to telephone that awful man . . . You wouldn't like to do it for me, Jean-Marie, would you?

Look—you invited me here, Jean-Marie said. *You invited me.*

Of course I invited you, honey, you're always welcome, but we had agreed—you seemed so enthusiastic—the music camp, the mountains—

You're just worried about the fucking tuition, aren't you, Jean-Marie said.

Jean-Marie, Eunice said sharply, I don't *want* you to use that kind of language, I've told you a dozen times . . .

There was a pounding on the stairs, and Kim ran into the kitchen in his bathing trunks, barefoot—short tanned bustling Kim, said to be half Greek and half Spanish, a handsome smiling boy in his early thirties. His dark hair was graying, there were sharp laugh lines around his mouth, but he looked extremely young. He was a quite successful photographer in New York. Eunice was always meeting people who knew him, since she had become acquainted with him—but wasn't that always the way—everyone knew everyone else. Ah, Eunice, he said, blinking, hello Eunice, good morning Eunice!—and Jean-Marie—it *is* Jean-Marie?—yes? Good morning, but is it a *good* morning, the sky looks disappointing again, and I have these people due in an hour and a half for lunch, and I haven't even *begun* thinking—! He shivered, hugging himself. Eunice noted, sipping at her drink, that there were goose pimples on his arms and shoulders, and that his fingernails were turning mauve. She liked Kim very much. He was so high-spirited, so good-natured. And talented as well. She was not in the slightest jealous of Kim. —

What's that you have, Eunice, he asked sniffing, may I join you?–may I help myself? It's so wretched, waking up, he laughed, baring his splendid white teeth at Eunice and Jean-Marie, it becomes more of an effort every *morning*.

He splashed vodka into a tall blue glass and added a few inches of tomato juice, humming loudly. Eunice saw, but discounted, the odd white strained look on her daughter's face.

Fourteen people are driving out from the city, Kim said, taking a swallow, half-closing his eyes, and I can't begin to *think* about them . . . I intended to make a perfectly delicious curry dish, chicken with diced celery and cucumbers and apples, and slivered almonds, and pineapple, of course, fresh pineapple . . . and as a first course a soup of my own invention . . . and fruit with rum for dessert, maybe a little yogurt . . . plain sugarless astringent yogurt . . . But I couldn't force myself out of bed, and the morning is practically gone, and I'm just going to ask them to turn right around again and I'll take them to lunch at . . . what is that place . . . the lighthouse . . . Reed hates it but I think it's perfectly adequate . . . the lighthouse, he said, snapping his fingers, what is it . . . !

Just The Lighthouse, Jean-Marie said. That's its name.

I should make that call, Eunice said apathetically. She lifted up the receiver and listened to the dial tone. So that I *know* what is going on . . .

One of my guests, Kim said, drawing in his breath luxuriously, is an epileptic.

An epileptic? Eunice said, But–

Oh, he's perfectly safe, Kim said, I doubt that he'll have a fit in front of us, they control these things with pills now, you know. One can lead a normal life, an *almost* normal life, he said, winking at Jean-Marie who was staring stonily at him, the way things are today . . . medical technology . . . that sort of thing. He had colored slightly, perhaps at Jean-Marie's rude stare. His thick eyelashes fluttered. –Oh there was this boy, this pathetic boy, in my high school geometry class, and he choked and fell out of his seat in the aisle and had a fit, right there in the class, a terrible convulsive fit, just like that, his nose was bleeding and blood splashed on the floor and the desks and the girls' skirts . . . and I almost fainted, myself . . . I'm such a coward . . . And you know it just goes on and on: he flopped around like a huge fish.

Did he choke? Jean-Marie asked.

Well–the teacher fortunately had her wits about her, and put something under his tongue, Kim said, giggling, I think it was, actually, an emery board–you know, for filing your fingers. So he didn't die, and he said afterward he didn't remember a thing! But they just go on and on, you know. Those fits.

That must have been terrible, Eunice said.

She was staring at the tile floor and seeing star-splashes of red against the simulated slate.

They go on and on, it seems for hours−! Kim said, shivering.

What happened to him then? Jean-Marie asked.

What do you mean? They came in to get him, he was carried out, taken to a hospital, Kim said.

Jean-Marie strummed the guitar. The chords were harsh and flat.

I mean, the rest of his life, she said, what happened to him the rest of his life . . .

Kim started at her, sipping at his tall drink, as if he had never heard of such a peculiar question. Well, he said finally, with a small laugh and a glance at Eunice, I really don't *know* about the rest of his life.

Eunice looked from Jean-Marie to Kim, and from Kim to Jean-Marie again. Her hands were shaking and it terrified her that her head might begin to shake too. (James's mother, in her dotage, the skinny neck trembling, the soft hairless dewlaps quivering. As if with feeling. Anger. Intensity of some sort. But not at all, not at all−she wasn't the slightest bit of trouble, the nurses bragged, she could just sit by herself for hours and hours and never complained if the television went on the blink!−she was one of their pets at the Home.) So she put the receiver down carefully.

It was rude, Jean-Marie's cold pinched stare. The girl had a long pale horsey face, and her forehead had broken out again, which was why she had combed bangs down practically to her eyebrows. She *might* have been pretty, anyway attractive, with her urgent gray stare that was like James's, and her cute snubbed nose like Eunice's, if only her skin would clear up. (She refused to go back to the dermatologist. And probably failed to take her antibiotic pills every morning.) She might have been very pretty, Eunice used to say, if only she wouldn't *think* so hard that the skin between her eyebrows puckered.

Many years ago, Jean-Marie had slipped away in one of those child-sized sailboats, no more than five feet long, and by the time they missed her she was carried out to sea . . . no, into the Bay . . . they were at the Martzes' place in North Carolina . . . and the Coast Guard rescued her. There was a regular Coast Guard boat, and a helicopter too. Eunice had been terrified, but of course her little girl was perfectly all right, just a bit sunburned, and her photograph was in the paper (the Martzes sent them several copies, for fun) above the caption ADVENTUROUS LITTLE MISS RESCUED BY COAST GUARD. Jean-Marie had been nine at the time.

Out here, at Presque Isle, a helicopter sometimes appeared, making a terrific din. Another Coast Guard helicopter, patrolling the beach. James had made such a fuss, one August, that the officers in Skye Harbor told their men to avoid the Scudder compound; James had threatened to get an injunction against them, or sue them for disturbing the peace. He was a friend of the lieutenant governor's at the time−he had designed a controversial but very striking house for him, in the hills near the state capitol. The house had received a great deal of publicity, not all of it favorable, but Skye Harbor did not want any trouble with James Scudder in any case. His family had once owned half of Presque Isle.

The telephone rang. Eunice knew it was James—she had jinxed herself, thinking of him.

Mother, aren't you going to answer it, Jean-Marie giggled, it's right under your *hand*.

There were footsteps overhead, and on the stairs, and Eunice caught sight of Reed on his way out—swimming trunks, coral sweatshirt, thick coarse wiry dark hair. Behind him, Niall Sullivan, carrying towels and manila folders. (They were working on a project together—authentic folk songs from the West Coast of Ireland—Niall was a Dublin girl, actually—though she had recently received a Ph.D. degree in Anglo-Irish studies at Yale.) Evidently they were not hungry for breakfast.

Eunice picked up the phone and of course it was James.

Kim hurried after Reed and Niall, and Jean-Marie chose that very moment to let her guitar fall, and go rummage through the refrigerator. Suddenly she was hungry. She hadn't eaten for eighteen hours or more.

Of course it was James, and Eunice had no choice but to talk with him. He sounded distant and formal, inquiring about tax records—boxes of tax records—going back to 1974—in their apartment in the city. At first Eunice thought he was blaming her because something was lost, then she thought, gripping the receiver and staring down at her open-toed Italian shoes, at her gay brave pink-bronze painted toenails (now beginning to chip—Reed had painted them himself, for fun, one sunny afternoon on the beach when they had all been in excellent spirits), he's lost a box of receipts and he will be furious with me because I had the cleaning woman throw them out, and she had even begun to apologize when it became clear that the material wasn't lost at all and James was not blaming her: he was only asking permission to enter the apartment.

Eunice was distracted by her daughter's behavior. Jean-Marie was squatting before the refrigerator, picking and sampling, poking her finger in the liver paté (which should have been wrapped up, it was dismayingly expensive and would last another five days), scooping up a quavering pinkish paste Eunice couldn't identify at first—oh yes, it was caviar: but it had not been especially good—making faces, sniffing, wriggling her eyebrows. The eyebrows were too thick to be attractive: like James's: growing hard and blunt and dark over the staring gray eyes. What on earth *was* the girl doing . . . She had opened a can of Tab and was drinking it thirstily, her head flung back, the tendons in her neck working. A hungry creature, ravenously hungry, like something that had crept in from outdoors driven by a ferocious hunger it could not control . . . Outside someone was yelling, it sounded like Reed.

James was asking: could she call home, tell the doorman to let him in, have the key ready for him, he'd like to bring the records to Lou (Lou was James's tax lawyer) this afternoon . . . Eunice, distracted, had to ask James to repeat himself. Which always annoyed him.

What was Reed yelling about? One of the girls—Sandra Reinert—yelled an answer. The keys to her car? (She drove a Renault station wagon, a charming little vehicle.) Towels? Eunice wanted to cup her hand over the receiver and call out that there were plenty of towels in the downstairs closet, the girl had done a load of laundry yesterday afternoon. But she didn't want to confuse James.

Jean-Marie was gnawing at a hunk of cheese, still squatting in front of the refrigerator. Close the door, you're wasting energy, Eunice whispered, but she didn't hear. She was eating Stilton cheese, Eunice winced to see her, wasn't it awfully strong like that . . . ? Eunice reached over to poke Jean-Marie on the shoulder. Make yourself a real breakfast, she said. Jean-Marie wiped her fingers on her soiled white bell-bottoms and pulled open one of the bottom drawers, and discovered the heel of a loaf of French bread, which she began to nibble at immediately, though it must have been stale—it was days old.

Odd, how Jean-Marie didn't glance at her mother, or make signals, asking her to say hello to James, or not to let him know she was here: at one time she had been an impish little monkey if anyone was on the phone. Tell Daddy hello, tell Daddy come back here right away, tell Daddy to land by parachute . . . I did hear you, James, Eunice said, sipping carefully at her drink (for if he heard the ice cubes clink he would know at once—he always did), you needn't speak as if I'm deaf.

Jean-Marie opened another can of Tab, and shut the refrigerator door with her foot, rather hard. She bounced up, her breasts wobbling inside that shapeless, unbecoming mustard-yellow jersey; Eunice could not help but think that the girl's body was as sullen and antagonistic as her face.

Jean-Marie? What about Jean-Marie? Eunice said cautiously.

Mother and daughter now exchanged a glance—razor-quick, alarmed.

Well, Eunice said faintly, as far as I know . . . I don't know . . . instruction in the flute, I remember that . . . and something like music theory . . . harmonics . . . it's written down somewhere but . . . Yes it's said to be a lovely place. Mountains, and . . .

A call came in on James's other phone, and he asked Eunice to wait. She poured herself another inch or two of vodka. Jean-Marie finished the second can of Tab, drinking like a truck driver, as if she were violently thirsty. Her hard little nipples showed through the jersey blouse and Eunice could not help but stare at them, blinking.

You know it makes me nervous, someone eavesdropping, she said to Jean-Marie.

I'm not eavesdropping, for Christ's sake! Jean-Marie laughed. As if I gave a shit what you two talk about.

Jean-Marie! Eunice hissed.

Oh fuck Jean-Marie, Jean-Marie laughed.

Eunice swiped at her with the flat of her hand, and caught her on the side of the head; but not hard; Jean-Marie only giggled.

You don't love me, you don't love any of us, Eunice whispered, her hand pressed over the receiver, I just don't *know* why you came here . . .

Polly threw me out, 's why, Jean-Marie said.

James? Eunice said shakily. James? Are you there?

He was still on the other line, making her wait. That was exactly like him, that rudeness: but she hadn't the strength to hang up.

Outside, Reed and Kim and Niall were headed for the beach. Reed and Kim wore sunglasses though the sky was still gunmetal-gray. Eunice watched them through the screen. What was Kim carrying? A guitar?

Hello James? Eunice said anxiously. I'm afraid I will have to hang up here—I've got to make an emergency call. James?

The line crackled emptily.

Eunice stared at her slow wriggling toes and thought, How vulnerable, how exposed, do they belong to me, and suddenly she was seeing again the Fine Arts building of her undergraduate days, she was on the third floor landing peering up to the fourth floor where the Architecture Department was housed, and where brilliant ambitious young men like James Scudder were working for graduate degrees . . . Eunice was studying interior design, she liked to say, in recent years, that she had had a career "in interior design," but of course that wasn't true: her grades were all C's, she had managed only a single B- and that was a gift from a sympathetic woman teacher who liked to encourage women students: Eunice hadn't any talent at all, and not much enthusiasm for a career. She had been vastly relieved as well as happy when James Scudder asked her to marry him . . . Relieved too when she was finally pregnant, after three years of trying. Now I have done it, she thought, gloating. *Now.*

Jean-Marie, her daughter, now sixteen years old, pirouetting about the kitchen as if she both wanted, and did not want, Eunice to tell James about her. Let me talk to Daddy! Put me on the phone! Daddy, Daddy! When are you coming back! Did you get me a present! . . . An enormous doll from Rio de Janeiro, three feet tall, with a prettily blank porcelain face and rosebud lips: but it was too *big*, it stared too bluntly at Jean-Marie who burst into tears at the sight of it. I hate it! Take it away Mommy! I *hate* it!

Eunice stared at her daughter and remembered suddenly that Jean-Marie was the one who had helped her to bed he night before. Jean-Marie, sniffing and wiping her nose. But why? Crying. Puffy-eyed. But why?

On the beach, the icy-cold surf stinging her toes. Reed and Niall singing at the top of their lungs: With a down, derry-derry-derry down, down! Reed gripped her tight. His steel-hard arms closed about her, tight, tight. Laughing, protesting, she as whirled around and around and around . . . Hey nonny, nonny-nonny! Hey nonny nonny-no! The others clapped their hands. The transistor radio was turned up as high as it would go, but the station was distant, the rock music marred by static. Someone appeared at the top of the sea-cliff path, a girl in white bell-bottoms, and no one knew who she was, until she came slipping and scrambling down the path . . .

Later, much later, Jean-Marie had helped Eunice up to the lodge, and up to the room. Where Reed's things were tossed about: jeans, sports shirts, underwear, a handsome linen sports coat with a cuff button missing. Eunice had collapsed onto the bed and Jean-Marie, sobbing, had pulled off her sandals, and loosened her clothing, and wiped the vomit from her mouth . . . The white cashmere sweater from Scotland, someone's Christmas gift from years ago, had been folded with desperate neatness and laid on the ladder-back chair by the window.

Jean-Marie pirouetted again, and did an awkward split. (She had once studied "modern dance" for several months, at St. Ann's.) She said, giggling, You know, Mother, I saw something strange last night. *I saw something strange.* Can you guess what it was?

Eunice shook her head impatiently, indicating the telephone. But James was still on the other line.

Jean-Marie said, First I was going to sleep in Windy Dells, but I changed my mind, I thought maybe I should be closer to you, if you needed me, so I slept down the hall in my old room. There wasn't any linen on the bed but I didn't mind, I slept on top of the bedspread. The rest of them stayed down on the beach for a long time, I fell asleep listening to them, then I woke up and it was quiet and very dark and I didn't know where I was at first, until I heard the surf . . . Mother? Are you listening?

I'm trying to talk to your father! Eunice hissed.

I got up to go to the bathroom, Jean-Marie said in her quick flat voice, and when I opened the door there was Reed and what's-his-name with the curly graying hair . . . Reed had only a shirt on, nothing but a shirt on, and the other one, Curlylocks, Kim, baby-faced Kim, was kneeling on the floor in front of him, and they were really going at it . . . I mean Reed had hold of Kim's head with both hands and he wasn't about to let go, no sir . . . I ran back to my room and pulled the bedspread up over my head, I said *I didn't see right, I didn't see anything,* and all the while, Mother you were snoring your head off—poor Mother!

James returned to the line with an abrupt click. He began speaking rapidly and earnestly about a client from White Plains, a meeting scheduled for later that afternoon, so could Eunice please telephone the doorman and leave instructions *immediately* . . .

I don't want you in that apartment any more! Eunice cried. I don't want you pawing through my things!

James protested—he *certainly* didn't want to paw through her things.

We've been through this, Eunice said wildly, I've begged you to stop harassing me—interfering with my private life—

James shouted something. Eunice began to sob. She held the receiver out to Jean-Marie. I can't tolerate this, Eunice said, twenty-five years—it's your turn—you will have to help me—

Jean-Marie, frightened, began to back away.

You and your filthy mouth, miss, Eunice whispered, shaking the receiver at her. Filthy, lying . . . Malicious . . .

I saw what I saw! Jean-Marie said.

Filthy, lying . . . If your father ever knew . . .

I saw you—all of you! I won't forget! Jean-Marie shouted.

She ran out of the kitchen. Eunice shouted something incoherent after her. She was so upset her entire body shook, her teeth were chattering, a terrible weight pressed against her chest. You liar! Filthy-mouthed liar! she shouted. But the doorway was empty.

Two fat angry tears rolled down her cheeks, immense as rocks on a hillside. Something whined like a mosquito, a tiny voice, and Eunice realized that James was still talking to her, the fool didn't know a thing that was going on, wasn't that just like him—! Eunice said hotly and harshly: Your daughter is sick! She has an imagination filthy and sick as a schizophrenic's! And *ugly*—you don't know how ugly!

James tried to speak but Eunice interrupted. You don't know! You're only the father! *What do you know!*

She slammed the receiver down, trembling.

She strode into the other room.

Jean-Marie? Where are you?

She retrieved her drink, and took a large swallow. It was tepid, it had no taste. She pressed the glass against her warm forehead but it did little good.

The room smelled faintly of ashes though no fire had been lit in the fireplace for many months. Jean-Marie was nowhere around. The lid of the window-seat was raised. What had they been looking for? The telephone book? Oh Jesus, Eunice thought, the pressure increasing in her chest, I have to telephone the *garage* . . .

She stood at the foot of the stairs, gripping the railing for support. Jean-Marie! she called. Come back down here at once!

She wondered why she had insisted upon giving her baby daughter such a pretentious name—she wondered why James had not dissuaded her.

Jean-Marie! she shouted.

But Jean-Marie did not reply, of course, and Eunice hadn't the strength for the stairs, not at the moment. She studied her watch. Five minutes to twelve. Unless the watch had stopped. A Saturday in early August, and the sky was beginning to clear, and they had several weeks at Presque Isle . . . Reed would regain his good spirits once the sun came out: simple things pleased him. And James had not been angry, he had not accused her of anything.

Eunice stood at the foot of the stairs for some time, until her breathing returned to normal. Finally, Jean-Marie appeared above, looking disheveled and puffy-eyed. Mother and daughter stared at each other in silence. Well—! Eunice said, after a long moment. Jean-Marie stared at her. Her face was long and pale, her skin looked coarse. The downward cast of her mouth was sullen, but contrite as well. Still, she was silent: stubborn and silent: not a word of apology.

You can call that awful man at the garage, Eunice said.

Jean-Marie did not acquiesce. But she did not refuse either.

WARD JUST

1983

About Boston

Beth was talking and I was listening. She said, "This was years ago. I was having a little tryst. On a Thursday, in New York, in the afternoon. He telephoned: 'Is it this Thursday or next?' I told him it was never, if he couldn't remember the *week*. Well." She laughed. "It makes your point about letters. Never would've happened if we'd written letters because you write something and you remember it. Don't you?"

"Usually," I said.

"There isn't a record of anything anymore, it's just telephone calls and bad memory."

"I've got a filing cabinet full of letters," I said, "and most of them are from ten years ago and more. People wrote a lot in the sixties, maybe they wanted a record of what they thought. There was a lot to think about, and it seemed a natural thing to do, write a letter to a friend, what with everything that was going on."

"I wonder if they're afraid," she said.

"No written record? No," I said. "They don't have the time. They won't make the time and there aren't so many surprises now, thanks to the sixties. We're surprised-out. They don't write and they don't read either."

"That one read," she said, referring to the man in the tryst. "he read all the time—history, biography. Sports books, linebackers' memoirs, the strategy of the full-court press." She lowered her voice. "And politics."

'Well," I said. I knew who it was now.

"But he didn't know the week." She lit a cigarette, staring at the match a moment before depositing it, just so, in the ashtray. "You always wrote letters."

269

I smiled. "A few close friends."

She smiled back. "Where do you think we should begin?"

"Not at the beginning."

"No, you know that as well as I do."

I said, "Probably better."

"Not better," she said.

"I don't know if I'm the man—"

"No," she said firmly. She stared at me across the room, then turned to look out the window. It was dusk, and the dying sun caught the middle windows of the Hancock tower, turning them a brilliant, wavy orange. In profile, with her sharp features and her short black hair, she looked like a schoolgirl. She said, "You're the man, all right. I want you to do it. I'd feel a lot more comfortable, we've known each other so long. Even now, after all this time, we don't have to finish sentences. It'd be hard for me, talking about it to a stranger."

"Sometimes that's easiest," I said.

"Not for me it isn't."

"All right," I said at last. "But if at any time it gets awkward for you—" I was half hoping she'd reconsider. But she waved her hand in a gesture of dismissal, subject closed. She was sitting on the couch in the corner of my office, and now she rose to stand at the window and watch the last of the sun reflected on the windows of the Hancock. A Mondrian among Turners, she had called it, its blue mirrors a new physics in the Back Bay. And who cared if in the beginning its windows popped out like so many ill-fitting contact lenses. The Hancock governed everything around it, Boston's past reflected in Boston's future. And it was miraculous that in the cascade of falling glass the casualties were so few.

I watched her: at that angle and in the last of the light her features softened and she was no longer a schoolgirl. I checked my watch, then rang my assistant and said she could lock up; we were through for the day. I fetched a yellow legal pad and a pen and sat in the leather chair, facing Beth. She was at the window, fussing with the cord of the venetian blind. She turned suddenly, with a movement so abrupt that I dropped my pad; the blind dropped with a crash. There had always been something violent and unpredictable in her behavior. But now she only smiled winningly, nodded at the sideboard, and asked for a drink before we got down to business.

I have practiced law in the Back Bay for almost twenty-five years. After Yale I came to Boston with the naïve idea of entering politics. The city had a rowdy quality I liked; it reminded me of Chicago, a city of neighborhoods, which wasn't ready for reform. But since I am a lapsed Catholic, neither Irish nor Italian, neither Yankee nor Democrat nor rich, I quickly understood that for me there were no politics in Boston. Chicago is astronomically remote from New England, and it was of no interest to anyone that I had been around politicians most of my life and knew the code. My grandfather had been, briefly, a congressman from the suburbs of Cook County, and I knew how to pull strings. But in Boston my antecedents precluded everything but good-government committees and the United Way.

Beth and I were engaged then, and Boston seemed less daunting than New York, perhaps because she knew it so intimately; it was her town as Chicago was mine. I rented an apartment in the North End and for the first few months we were happy enough, I with my new job and she with her volunteer work at the Mass. General. We broke off the engagement after six months—the usual reasons—and I looked up to find myself behind the lines in enemy territory. I had misjudged Boston's formality and its network of tribal loyalties and had joined Hamlin & White, one of the old State Street firms. I assumed that H,W—as it had been known for a hundred years—was politically connected. An easy error to make, for the firm was counsel to Boston's largest bank and handled the wills and trusts of a number of prominent Brahmin Republicans, and old Hamlin had once been lieutenant governor of Massachusetts. In Chicago that would have spelled political, but in Boston it only spelled probate. There were thirty men in the firm, large for Boston in those days. The six senior men were Hamlin and Hamlin Junior and White III, and Chelm, Warner, and Diuguid. Among the associates were three or four recognizable Mayflower names. The six senior men were all physically large, well over six feet tall and in conspicuous good health, by which I mean ruddy complexions and propensity to roughhouse. They all had full heads of hair, even old Hamlin, who was then eighty. Their talk was full of the jargon of sailing and golf, and in their company I felt the worst sort of provincial rube.

Of course I was an experiment—a balding, unathletic Yale man from Chicago, of middling height, of no particular provenance, and book-smart. I was no one's cousin and no one's ex-roommate. But I was engaged to a Boston girl and I had been first in my class at Yale and the interview with Hamlin Junior had gone well. All of them in the firm spoke in that hard, open-mouthed bray peculiar to Massachusetts males of the upper classes. The exception was Hamlin Junior, who mumbled. When it was clear, after two years, that their experiment had failed—or had not, at any event, succeeded brilliantly—it was Hamlin Junior who informed me. He called me into his dark-brown office late one afternoon, poured me a sherry, and rambled for half an hour before he got to the point, which was that I was an excellent lawyer mumble mumble damned able litigator mumble mumble but the firm has its own personality, New England salt sort of thing ha-ha mumble sometimes strange to an outsider but it's the way we've always done things mumble question of style and suitability, sometimes tedious but can't be helped wish you the best you're a damned able trial man, and of course you've a place here so long's you want though in fairness I wanted mumble make it known that you wouldn't be in the first foursome as it were mumble mumble. Just one question, I've always wondered: 'S really true that you wanted to go into politics here?

It was my first professional failure, and in my anger and frustration I put it down to simple snobbery. I did not fit into their clubs, and I hated the North Shore and was not adept at games. I was never seen "around" during the winter or on the Cape or the Islands or in Maine in the summer. I spent my vacations in Europe, and most weekends I went to New York, exactly as I did when I was at law school in New Haven. New York remains the center of my social life. Also, I was a bachelor. Since the breakup of my engagement, I had become an aggressive bachelor. Beth was bitter and I suspected her of spreading unflattering stories. Of course this was not true, but in my humiliation I believed that it was and that as a consequence the six senior men had me down as homosexual. In addition, I was a hard drinker in a firm of hard drinkers though unlike them I never had whiskey on my breath in the morning and I never called in sick with Monday grippe. I could never join in the hilarious retelling of locker-room misadventures. They drank and joked. I drank and didn't joke.

When I left H,W, I opened an office with another disgruntled provincial —he was from Buffalo, even farther down the scale of things than Chicago— half expecting to fail but determined not to and wondering what on earth I would do and where I would go, now that I'd been drummed out of my chosen city: blackballed. Young litigators are not as a rule peripatetic: you begin in a certain city and remain there; you are a member of the bar, you know the system, you build friendships and a clientele and a reputation. Looking back on it, Deshais and I took a terrible risk. But we worked hard and prospered, and now there are twenty lawyers in our firm, which we have perversely designed to resemble a squad of infantry in a World War II propaganda movie: Irish, Italians, Jews, three blacks in the past ten years, one Brahmin, Deshais, and me. Of course we are always quarreling; ours is not a friendly, clubby firm. In 1974, we bought a private house, a handsome brownstone, in the Back Bay, only two blocks from my apartment on Commonwealth Avenue. This is so convenient, such an agreeable way to live—it is my standard explanation to my New York friends who ask why I remain here—that we decided not to expand the firm because it would require a larger building and all of us love the brownstone, even the younger associates who must commute from Wayland or Milton. Sometimes I think it is the brownstone and the brownstone alone that holds the firm together.

I suppose it is obvious that I have no affection for this spoiled city and its noisy inhabitants. It is an indolent city. It is racist to the bone and in obvious political decline and like any declining city is by turns peevish and arrogant. It is a city without civility or civic spirit, or Jews. The Jews, with their prodigious energies, have tucked themselves away in Brookline, as the old aristocrats, with their memories and trust funds, are on the lam on the North Shore. Remaining are the resentful Irish and the furious blacks. Meanwhile, the tenured theory class issues its pronouncements from the safety of Cambridge, confident that no authority will take serious notice. So the city of Boston closes in on itself, conceited, petulant, idle, and broke.

I observe this from a particular vantage point. To my surprise, I have become a divorce lawyer. The first cases I tried after joining forces with Deshais were complicated divorce actions. They were women referred to me by Hamlin Junior, cases considered – I think he used the word "fraught" – too mumble "fraught" for H,W. In Chicago we used the word "messy," though all this was a long time ago; now they are tidy and without fault. However, then as now there was pulling and hauling over the money. Hamlin Junior admired my trial work and believed me discreet and respectable enough to represent in the first instance his cousin and in the second a dear friend of his wife's. He said that he hoped the matter of the cousin would be handled quietly, meaning without a lengthy trial and without publicity, but that if the case went to trial he wanted her represented by a lawyer ahem who was long off the tee. You know what it is you must do? he asked. I nodded. At that time divorces were purchased; you bought a judge for the afternoon. Happily, the cousin was disposed of in conference, quietly and very expensively for her husband. The success of that case caused Hamlin Junior to send me the second woman, whose disposition was not quite so quiet. Fraught it certainly was, and even more expensive.

I was suddenly inside the bedroom, hearing stories the obverse of those I had heard after hours at H,W. The view from the bedroom was different from the view from the locker room. It was as if a light-bulb joke had been turned around and told from the point of view of the bulb. Hundred-watt Mazda shocks WASP couple! I discovered that I had a way with women in trouble. That is precisely because I do not pretend to understand them, as a number of my colleagues insist that they "understand women." But I do listen. I listen very carefully, and then I ask questions and listen again. Then they ask me questions and I am still listening hard, and when I offer my answers they are brief and as precise as I can make them. And I never, never overpromise. No woman has ever rebuked me with "But you *said*, and now you've broken your word."

The cousin and the wife's friend were satisfied and told Hamlin Junior, who said nothing to his colleagues. He seemed to regard me as the new chic restaurant in town, undiscovered and therefore underpriced; it would become popular soon enough, but meanwhile the food would continue excellent and the service attentive and the bill modest. For years he referred clients and friends to me, and I always accepted them even when they were routine cases and I had to trim my fees. And when Hamlin Junior died, I went to his funeral, and was not at all startled to see so many familiar female faces crowding the pews.

My divorce business was the beginning, and there was a collateral benefit—no, bonanza. I learned how money flows in Boston, and where; which were the rivers and which were the tributaries and which were the underground streams. Over the years, I have examined hundreds of trusts and discovered a multiformity of hidden assets, liquid and solid, floating and stationary, lettered and numbered, aboveground and below. The trusts are of breathtaking ingenuity, the product of the flintiest minds in Massachusetts, and of course facilitated over the years by a willing legislature. And what has fascinated me from the beginning is this: The trust that was originally devised to avoid taxes or to punish a recalcitrant child or to siphon income or to "protect" an unworldly widow or to reach beyond the grave to control the direction of a business or a fortune or a marriage can fall apart when faced with the circumstances of the present, an aggrieved client, and a determined attorney.

This is not the sort of legal practice I planned, but it is what I have. Much of what I have discovered in divorce proceedings I have replicated in my trust work, adding a twist here and there to avoid unraveling by someone like me, sometime in the future. Wills and trusts are now a substantial part of my business, since I have access to the flintiest minds in Massachusetts. Turn, and turn about. However, it is a risible anomaly of the upper classes of Boston that the estates have grown smaller and the trusts absurdly complex—Alcatraz to hold juvenile delinquents.

So one way and another I am in the business of guaranteeing the future. A trust, like a marriage, is a way of getting a purchase on the future. That is what I tell my clients, especially the women; women have a faith in the future that men, as a rule, do not. I am careful to tell my clients that although that is the objective, it almost never works; or it does not work in the way they intend it to work. It is all too difficult reading the past, without trying to read the future as well. It is my view that men, at least, understand this, having, as a rule, a sense of irony and proportion. At any event, this is my seat at the Boston opera. It is lucrative and fascinating work. There was no compelling reason, therefore, not to listen to the complaint of Beth Earle Doran Greer, my former fiancée.

She said quietly, "It's finished."

I said nothing.

She described their last year together, the two vacations and the month at Edgartown, happy for the most part. They had one child, a boy, now at boarding school. It had been a durable marriage, fifteen years; the first one had lasted less than a year, and she had assumed that despite various troubles this one would endure. Then last Wednesday he said he was leaving her and his lawyer would be in touch.

"Has he?"

"No," she said.

"Who is he?"

She named a State Street lawyer whom I knew by reputation. He was an excellent lawyer. I was silent again, waiting for her to continue.

"Frank didn't say anything more than that."

"Do you know where he is?"

"I think he's at the farm." I waited again, letting the expression on my face do the work. There were two questions. Is he alone? Do you want him back? She said again, "It's finished." Then, the answer to the other question: "There is no one else." I looked at her, my face in neutral. She said, "Hard as that may be to understand."

Not believe, *understand;* a pointed distinction. I nodded, taking her at her word. It was hard, her husband was a great bon vivant.

"That's what he says, and I believe him. His sister called me to say that there isn't anybody else, but I didn't need her to tell me. Believe me, I know the signs. There isn't a sign I don't know and can't see a mile away, and he doesn't show any of them. Five years ago—that was something else. But she's married and not around anymore, and that's over and done with. And besides, if there was someone else he'd tell me. It'd be like him."

I nodded again and made a show of writing on my pad.

"And there isn't anyone else with me either."

"Well," I said, and smiled.

"Is it a first?"

I laughed quietly. "Not a first," I said. "Maybe a second."

She laughed, and lit a cigarette. "You were afraid it would be another cliché, she would be twenty and just out of Radcliffe. Meanwhile, I would've taken up with the garage mechanic or the gamekeeper. Or Frank's best friend; they tell me that's chic now." She looked at me sideways and clucked. "You know me better than that. Clichés aren't my style."

I said, "I never knew you at all."

"Yes, you did," she said quickly. I said nothing. "You always listened, in those days you were a very good listener. And you're a good listener now."

"The secret of my success," I said. But I knew my smile was getting thinner.

"The mouthpiece who listens," she said. "That's what Nora told me, when she was singing your praises. Really, she did go on. Do they fall in love with you, like you're supposed to do with a psychiatrist?"

Nora was a client I'd represented in an action several years before, a referral from Hamlin Junior. She was a great friend of Beth's but a difficult woman and an impossible client. I said, "No."

"It was a pretty good marriage," she said after a moment's pause. "You'd think, fifteen years . . . " I leaned forward, listening. Presently, in order to focus the conversation, I would ask the first important question: What is it that you want me to do now? For the moment, though, I wanted to hear more. I have never regarded myself as a marriage counselor, but it is always wise to know the emotional state of your client. So far, Beth seemed admirably rational and composed, almost cold-blooded. I wondered if she had ever consulted a psychiatrist, then decided she probably hadn't. There was something impersonal about her locution "like you're supposed to." She said abruptly, "How did you get into this work? It's so unlike you. Remember the stories you told me about your grandfather and his friend? The relationship they had, and how that was the kind of lawyer you wanted to be?"

I remembered all right, but I was surprised that she did. My grandfather and I were very close, and when I was a youngster we lunched together every Saturday. My father drove me to the old man's office, in an unincorporated area of Cook County, near Blue Island. I'd take the elevator to the fourth floor, the building dark and silent on Saturday morning. My grandfather was always courteous and formal, treating me as he would treat an important adult. On Saturday mornings my grandfather met with Tom. Tom was his lawyer. I was too young to know exactly what they were talking about, though as I look back on it, their conversation was in a private language. There was a "matter" that needed "handling," or "a man"–perhaps "sound," perhaps "a screwball"–who had to be "turned." Often there was a sum of money involved–three, four, fi' thousand dollars. These questions would be discussed sparely, long pauses between sentences. Then, as a signal that the conversation was near its end, my grandfather would say, "Now this is what I want to do," and his voice would fall. Tom would lean close to the old man, listening hard; I never saw him make a note. Then, "Now you figure out how I can do it." And Tom would nod, thinking, his face disappearing into the collar of his enormous camel's-hair coat. He never removed the coat, and he sat with his gray fedora in both hands, between his knees, turning it like the steering wheel of a car. When he finished thinking, he would rise and approach me and gravely shake hands. Then he would offer me a piece of licorice from the strand he kept in his coat, the candy furry with camel's hair. He pressed it on me until I accepted. I can remember him saying goodbye to my grandfather and, halting at the door, smiling slightly and winking. Tom would exit whistling, and more often than not my grandfather would make a telephone call, perhaps two, speaking inaudibly into the receiver. Finally, rumbling in his basso profundo, he would make the ritual call to the Chicago Athletic Club to reserve his usual table for two, "myself and my young associate."

In those days children were not allowed in the men's bar, so we ate in the main dining room, a huge chamber with high ceilings and a spectacular view of the lakefront. We sat at a table by the window, and on a clear day we could see Gary and Michigan City to the southeast. Long-hulled ore boats were smudges on the horizon. Once, during the war, we saw a pocket aircraft carrier, a training vessel for Navy pilots stationed at Great Lakes. The old man would wave his hand in the direction of the lake and speak of the Midwest as an ancient must have spoken of the Fertile Crescent: the center of the world, a homogeneous, God-fearing, hardworking *region*, its interior position protecting it from its numerous enemies. With a sweep of his hand he signified the noble lake and the curtain of smoke that hung over Gary's furnaces, thundering even on Saturdays. Industry, he'd say, *heavy* industry working at one hundred percent of capacity. Chicagoland, foundry to the world. His business was politics, he said; and his politics was business. "We can't let them take it away from us, all this . . . "

When the old man died, Tom was his principal pallbearer. It was a large funeral; the governor was present with his suite, along with a score or more of lesser politicians. Tom was dry-eyed, but I knew he was grieving. At the end of it he came over to me and shook my hand, solemnly as always, and said, "Your grandfather was one of the finest men who ever lived, a great friend, a great Republican, a great American, and a great client." I thought that an extraordinary inventory and was about to say so when he gripped my arm and exclaimed, "You ever need help of any kind, you come to me. That man and I . . . " He pointed at my grandfather's casket, still aboveground under its green canopy, then tucked his chin into the camel's hair. "We've been through the mill, fought every day of our lives. I don't know what will happen without him." He waved dispiritedly at the gravestones around us, stones as far as the eye could see, and lowered his voice so that I had to bend close to hear. "The world won't be the same without him," Tom said. "The Midwest's going to hell."

Tom died a few years later, without my having had a chance to take him up on his offer. But from my earliest days in that fourth-floor office I knew I would be a lawyer. I wanted to be Tom to someone great, and prevent the world from going to hell. Tom was a man who listened carefully to a complex problem, sifting and weighing possibilities. Then, settled and secure in his own mind, he figured a way to get from here to there. It was only an idiosyncrasy of our legal system that the route was never a straight line.

"I mean," she said brightly, leaning forward on the couch, "listening to a bunch of hysterical women with their busted marriages, that wasn't what I expected at all."

"They are not always hysterical," I said, "and some of them are men."

"And you never married," she said.

That was not true, but I let it pass.

"No," she said, rapping her knuckles on the coffee table. "You *were* married. I heard that, a long time ago. I heard that you were married, a whirlwind romance in Europe, but then it broke up right away."

"That's right," I said.

"She was French."

"English," I said.

"And there were no children."

"No," I said. We were silent while I walked to the sideboard, made a drink for myself, and refilled hers.

"Do you remember how we used to talk, that place on Hanover Street we used to go to, all that pasta and grappa? I practiced my Italian on them. Always the last ones out the door, running down Hanover Street to that awful place you had on—where was it?"

"North Street," I said.

"North Street. We'd get to dinner and then we'd go to your place and you'd take me back to Newton in your red Chevrolet. Three, four o'clock in the morning. I don't know how you got any work done, the hours we kept."

I nodded, remembering.

"And of course when I heard you'd been sacked at H,W, I didn't know what to think, except that it was for the best." She paused. "Which I could've told you if you'd asked." I handed her the highball and sat down, resuming my lawyerly posture, legs crossed, the pad in my lap. "Do you ever think about your grandfather? Or what would've happened if you'd gone back to Chicago instead of following me here? Whether you'd've gone into politics, like him?"

"I don't follow you," I said. "We came together. It was where we intended to live, together."

"Whatever." She took a long swallow of her drink. "Chicago's such a different place from Boston, all that prairie. Boston's close and settled and old, so charming." I listened, tapping the pencil on my legal pad. It was dark now. At night the city seemed less close and settled. The cars in the street outside were bumper to bumper, honking. There was a snarl at the intersection, one car double-parked and another stalled. A car door slammed and there were angry shouts. She looked at me, smiling. "I don't want anything particular from him."

I made a note on my pad.

"I have plenty of money; so does he. Isn't that the modern way? No punitive damages?" She hesitated. "So there won't be any great opportunity to delve into the assets. And Frank's trust. Or mine."

I ignored that. "Of course there's little Frank."

She looked at me with the hint of a malicious grin. "How did you know his name?"

"Because I follow your every movement," I said, with as much sarcasm as I could muster. "For Christ's sake, Beth. I don't know how I know his name. People like Frank Greer always name their children after themselves."

"Don't get belligerent," she said. "A more devoted father—" she began and then broke off.

"Yes," I said.

"—he's devoted to little Frank." She hesitated, staring out the window for a long moment. She was holding her glass with both hands, in her lap. She said, "What was the name of that man, your grandfather's lawyer?"

"Tom," I said.

"God, yes," she said, laughing lightly. "Tom, one of those sturdy midwestern names."

"I think," I said evenly, "I think Tom is a fairly common name. I think it is common even in Boston."

She laughed again, hugely amused. "God, yes, it's common."

I glared at her, not at all surprised that she remembered which buttons worked and which didn't. Beth had an elephant's memory for any man's soft spots. Why Tom was one of mine was not so easily explained; Beth would have one explanation, I another. But of course she remembered. My background was always a source of tension between us, no doubt because my own attitude was ambiguous. She found my grandfather and Tom . . . quaint. They were colorful provincials, far from her Boston milieu, and she condescended to them exactly as certain English condescend to Australians.

"It's a riot," she said.

"So," I said quietly, glancing at my watch. "What is it that you want me to do now?"

"A quick, clean divorce," she said. "Joint custody for little Frank, though it's understood he lives with me. Nothing changes hands, we leave with what we brought, *status quo ante*. I take my pictures, he takes his shotguns. Except, naturally, the house in Beverly. It's mine anyway, though for convenience it's in both our names. He understands that."

"What about the farm?"

"We split that, fifty-fifty."

"Uh-huh," I said.

"Is it always this easy?"

"We don't know how easy it'll be," I said carefully. "Until I talk to his lawyer. Maybe it won't be easy at all. It depends on what he thinks his grievances are."

"He hasn't got any."

"Well," I said.

"So it'll be easy," she said, beginning to cry.

We had agreed to go to dinner after meeting in my office. I proposed the Ritz; she countered with a French restaurant I had never heard of. She in-

sisted, Boylston Street nouvelle cuisine, and I acceded, not without complaint. I told her about a client, a newspaperman who came to me every six
years for his divorce. The newspaperman said that the nouvelle cuisine
reminded him of the nouveau journalisme – a colorful plate, agreeably subtle,
wonderfully presented with inspired combinations, and underdone. The por-
tions were small, every dish had a separate sauce, and you were hungry
when you finished. A triumph of style over substance.

She listened patiently, distracted.

I was trying to make her laugh. "But I can get a New York strip here,
which they'll call an entrecôte, and there isn't a lot you can do to ruin a
steak. Though they will try."

"You haven't changed," she said bleakly.

"Yes, I have," I said. "In the old days I would've been as excited about
this place as you are. I'd know the names of the specialties of the house and
of the chef. In the old days I was al dente as the veggies. But not anymore."
I glanced sourly around the room. The colors were pastel, various tints of
yellow, even to a limp jonquil in the center of each table, all of it illuminated
by candles thin as pencils and a dozen wee chandeliers overhead. It was very
feminine and not crowded; expensive restaurants rarely were in Boston now;
the money was running out.

"I'm sorry about the tears," she said.

I said, "Don't be."

"I knew I was going to bawl when I made that remark about Tom and
you reacted."

"Yes," I said. I'd known it too.

"It made me sad. It reminded me of when we were breaking up and all
the arguments we had."

I smiled gamely. "I was al dente then, and I broke easily." I knew what
she was leading up to, and I didn't want it. When the waiter arrived I ordered whiskey for us both, waiting for the little superior sneer and feeling
vaguely disappointed when he smiled pleasantly and flounced off. I started
to tell her a story but she cut me off, as I knew she would.

"It reminded me of that ghastly dinner and how awful everything was
afterward."

I muttered something noncommittal, but the expression on her face told
me she wanted more, so I said it was over and forgotten, part of the buried
past, etcetera. Like hell. We had argued about the restaurant that night, as
we had tonight, except I won and we went to the Union Oyster House. My
parents were in town, my father ostensibly on business; in fact they were in
Boston to meet Beth. The dinner did not go well from the beginning; the
restaurant was crowded and the service indifferent. My parents didn't seem
to care, but Beth was irritated – "The Union Oyster Tourist Trap" – and that
in turn put me on edge, or perhaps it was the other way around. Halfway

through dinner, I suspect in an effort to salvage things, my father shyly handed Beth a wrapped package. It was a bracelet he had selected himself; even my mother didn't know about it. It was so unlike him, and such a sweet gesture, tears jumped to my eyes. Even before she opened it, I knew it would not be right. Beth had a particular taste in jewelry and as a consequence rarely wore any. I hoped she could disguise her feelings, but as it happened she giggled. And did not put the bracelet on, but hurried it into her purse, after leaning over the table and kissing my father. He did not fail to notice the bracelet rushed out of sight. Probably he didn't miss the giggle, either. In the manner of families, after a suitable silent interval my father and I commenced to quarrel. On the surface it was a quarrel about businessmen and professional men, but actually it had to do with the merits of the East and the merits of the Midwest and my father's knowledge that I had rejected the values of his region. The Midwest asserted its claims early, and if you had a restless nature you left. It forced you to leave; there were no halfway measures in the heartland, at that time a province as surely as Franche-Comté or Castile, an interior region pressed by the culture of the coasts, defensive, suspicious, and claustrophobic. When I left I tried to explain to him that a New Yorker's restlessness or ambition could take him to Washington as a Bostonian's could take him to New York, the one city representing power and the other money. No midwesterner, making the momentous decision to leave home, would go from Chicago to Cleveland or from Minneapolis to Kansas City. These places are around the corner from one another. The Midwest is the same wherever you go, the towns larger or smaller but the culture identical. Leaving the Midwest, one perforce rejects the Midwest and its values, its sense of inferiority–so I felt then–prevented any return. In some way it had failed. What sound reason could there be for leaving God's country, the very soul of the nation, to live and work on the cluttered margins? It had failed you and you had failed it, whoring after glitter. My father's chivalry did not allow him to blame "that girl" publicly, but I knew that privately he did. Too much–too much Boston, too much money, too determined, too self-possessed. He hated to think that his son–flesh of my flesh, blood of my blood!–could be led out of Chicagoland by a woman. The image I imagine it brought to his mind was of an ox dumbly plodding down a road, supervised by a young woman lightly flicking its withers with a stick. That ghastly dinner!

"The thing is." She smiled wanly, back in the present now: that is, her own life, and what she had made of it. "It's so–*tiresome*. I know the marriage is over, it's probably been finished for years. But starting over again. I don't want to start over again. I haven't the energy." She sighed. "He's said for years that he's got to find himself. He's forty-eight years old and he's lost and now he wants to be found. And I'm sure he will be."

"Usually it's the other way around," I said. "These days, it's the women who want to find themselves. Or get lost, one or the other."

"Frank has a feminine side." I nodded, thinking of Frank Greer as a pastel. Frank in lime-green and white, cool and pretty as a gin and tonic. "But the point isn't Frank," Beth said. "It's me. I don't want to start over again. I started over again once and that didn't work and then I started over again and it was fun for a while and then it was a routine, like everything else. I like the routine. And I was younger then."

I did not quite follow that, so I said, "I know."

"Liar," she said. "How could you? You've never been married."

"Beth," I said.

She looked at me irritably. "That doesn't count. You've got to be married for at least five years before it's a marriage. And there have to be children, or at least a child. Otherwise it's just shacking up and you can get out of it as easily and painlessly as you got into it, which from the sound of yours was pretty easy and painless."

I looked away while the waiter set down our drinks and, with a flourish, the menus.

"How long ago was it?"

"Almost twenty years ago," I said.

"Where is she now?"

I shrugged. I had no idea. When she left me she went back to London. I heard she had a job there; then, a few years ago, I heard she was living in France, married, with children. Then I heard she was no longer in France, but somewhere else on the Continent, unmarried now.

"That's what I mean," she said. "You don't even know where she *is*."

"Well," I said. "She knows where I am."

"What was her name?"

"Rachel," I said.

Beth thought a moment. "Was she Jewish?"

"Yes," I said.

Beth made a little sound, but did not comment. The amused look on her face said that my father must have found Rachel even more unsuitable than Beth. As it happened, she was right, but it had nothing to do with Rachel's Jewishness. She was a foreigner with pronounced political opinions. "And you like living alone," Beth said.

"At first I hated it," I said. "But I like it now and I can't imagine living any other way. It's what I do, live alone. You get married, I don't. Everyone I know gets married and almost everyone I know gets divorced."

"Well, you see it from the outside."

"It's close enough," I said.

"Yes, but it's not *real*." She glanced left into Boylston Street. It was snowing, and only a few pedestrians were about, bending into the wind. She shivered when she looked at the stiff-legged pedestrians, their movements so spiritless and numb against the concrete of the sidewalk, the sight bleaker still by contrast with the pale monochrome and the fragrance of the restaurant. Outside was a dark, malicious, European winter, Prague perhaps, or Moscow. "We might've made it," she said tentatively, still looking out the window.

I said nothing. She was dead wrong about that.

She sat with her chin in her hand, staring into the blowing snow. "But we were so different, and you were so bad."

The waiter was hovering and I turned to ask him the specialties of the day. They were a tiny bird en croûte, a fish soufflé, and a vegetable ensemble. Beth was silent, inspecting the menu; she had slipped on a pair of half-glasses for this chore. I ordered a dozen oysters and an entrecôte, medium well. I knew that if I ordered it medium well I had a fair chance of getting it medium rare. Then I ordered a baked potato and a Caesar salad and another drink. The waiter caught something in my tone and courteously suggested that medium well was excessive. I said all right, if he would promise a true medium rare. Beth ordered a fish I never heard of and called for the wine list. The waiter seemed much happier dealing with Beth than with me. They conferred over the wine list for a few moments, and then he left.

She said, "You're always so defensive."

"I don't like these places, I told you that." I heard the Boston whine in my voice and retreated a step. "The waiter's okay."

"You never did like them," she said. "But at least *before* . . . " She shook her head, exasperated.

"Before, what?" I asked.

"At least you were a provincial, there was an excuse."

I pulled at my drink, irritated. But when I saw her smiling slyly I had to laugh. Nothing had changed, though we had not seen each other in fifteen years and had not spoken in twenty. The occasion fifteen years ago was a wedding reception. I saw her standing in a corner talking to Frank Greer. She was recently divorced from Doran. I was about to approach to say hello; then I saw the expression on her face and withdrew. She and Greer were in another world, oblivious of the uproar around them, and I recognized the expression: it was the one I thought was reserved for me. Now, looking at her across the restaurant table, it was as if we had never been apart, as if our attitudes were frozen in aspic. We were still like a divided legislature, forever arguing over the economy, social policy, the defense budget, and the cuisine in the Senate dining room. The same arguments, conducted in the same terms; the same old struggle for control of our future. Her prejudice, my pride.

"You have to tell me one thing." She turned to inspect the bottle the waiter presented, raising her head so she could see through the half-glasses. She touched the label of the wine with her fingernails and said yes, it was fine, excellent really, and then, turning, her head still raised, she assured me that I would find it drinkable, since it came from a splendid little chateau vineyard near the Wisconsin Dells. The waiter looked at her dubiously and asked whether he should open it now and put it on ice, and she said yes, of course, she wanted it so cold she'd need her mittens to pour it. I was laughing and thinking how attractive she was, a woman whose humor improved with age, if she would just let up a little on the other. Also, I was waiting for the "one thing" I would have to tell her.

I said, "You're a damn funny woman."

"I have good material," she said.

"Not always," I replied.

"The one thing," she said, "that I can't figure out. Never could figure out. Why did you stay here? This isn't your kind of town at all, never was. It's so circumspect, and sure of itself. I'm surprised you didn't go back to Chicago after you were canned by H,W."

"I like collapsing civilizations," I said. "I'm a connoisseur of collapse and systems breakdown and bankruptcy—moral, ethical, and financial. So Boston is perfect." I thought of the town where I grew up, so secure and prosperous then, so down-at-heel now, the foundry old, exhausted, incidental, and off the subject. We lived in Chicago's muscular shadow and were thankful for it, before the world went to hell. "And I wasn't about to be run out of town by people like that," I added truculently.

"So it was spite," she said.

"Not spite," I said equably. "Inertia."

"And you're still spending weekends in New York?"

I nodded. Not as often now as in the past, though.

"Weird life you lead," she said.

I said, "What's so weird about it?"

"Weekdays here, weekends in New York. And you still have your flat near the brownstone, the same one?"

I looked at her with feigned surprise. "How did you know about my flat?"

"For God's sake," she said. "Nora's a friend of mine."

It was never easy to score a point on Beth Earle. I said, "I've had it for almost twenty years. And I'll have it for twenty more. It's my Panama Canal. I bought it, I paid for it, it's mine, and I intend to keep it."

She shook her head, smiling ruefully. She said that she had lived in half a dozen houses over the years and remembered each one down to the smallest detail: the color of the tile in the bathroom and the shape of the clothes closet in the bedroom. She and Doran had lived in Provincetown for a year, and then had moved to Gloucester. That was when Doran was trying to paint. Then, after Doran, she lived alone in Marblehead. When she was married to Frank Greer they went to New York, then returned to Boston; he owned an apartment on Beacon Hill. They lived alone there for two years, and then moved to Beverly–her idea; she was tired of the city. She counted these places on her fingers. "Six," she said. "And all this time, you've been in the same place in the Back Bay." She was leaning across the table, and now she looked up. The waiter placed a small salad in front of her and the oysters in front of me. The oysters were Cotuits. She signaled for the wine and said that "Monsieur" would taste. She told the waiter I was a distinguished gourmet, much sought after as a taster, and that my wine cellar in Michigan City was the envy of the region. She gave the impression that the restaurant was lucky to have me as a patron. The waiter shot me a sharp look and poured the wine into my glass. I pronounced it fine. Actually, I said it was "swell," and then, gargling heartily, "dandy." I gave Beth one of the oysters and insisted that she eat it the way it was meant to be eaten, naked out of the shell, without catsup or horseradish. She sucked it up, and then leaned across the table once again. "Don't you miss them, the arguments? The struggle, always rubbing off someone else? The fights, the friction–?"

I laughed loudly. "Miss them to death," I said.

We finished the bottle of white, and ordered a bottle of red; she said she preferred red with fish. I suspected that that was a concession to my entrecôte, which at any event was rare and bloody. She continued to press, gently at first, then with vehemence. She was trying to work out her life and thought that somehow I was a clue to it. At last she demanded that I describe my days in Boston. She wanted to know how I lived, the details, "the quotidian." I was reluctant to do this, having lived privately for so many years. Also, there was very little to describe. I had fallen into the bachelor habit of total predictability. Except to travel to the airport and the courts, I seldom left the Back Bay. My terrain was bordered by the Public Garden and the Ritz, Storrow Drive, Newbury Street, the brownstone where I worked and Commonwealth Avenue where I lived. I walked to work, lunched at the Ritz, took a stroll in the Garden, returned to the brownstone, and at seven or so went home. People I knew tended to live in the Back Bay or on the Hill, so if I went out in the evening I walked. Each year it became easier not to leave the apartment; I needed an exceptional reason to do so. I liked my work and worked hard at it.

She listened avidly, but did not comment. The waiter came to clear the table and offer dessert. We declined, ordering coffee and cognac.

"What kind of car do you have?" she asked suddenly.

I said I didn't own one.

"What kind of car does she own?"

I looked at her: Who?

"Your secretary," she said. "I hear you have a relationship with your secretary."

"She's been my assistant for a very long time," I said.

"Her car," Beth said.

I said, "A Mercedes."

"Well," she said.

"Well, what?"

"Well, nothing," she said. "Except so do I."

"Two cheers for the Krauts," I said.

"Is she a nice woman?"

I laughed. "Yes," I said. "Very. And very able."

"She approves of the arrangement."

"Beth," I said.

Beth said, "I wonder what she gets out of it?"

"She won't ever have to get divorced," I said. "That's one thing she gets out of it."

"Was she the woman in the outer office?"

"Probably," I said.

Beth was silent a moment, toying with her coffee cup. There was only one other couple left in the restaurant, and they were preparing to leave. "You were always secretive," she said.

"You were not exactly an open book."

She ignored that. "It's not an attractive trait, being secretive. It leaves you wide open."

For what? I wondered. I looked at her closely, uncertain whether it was she talking or the wine. We were both tight, but her voice had an edge that had not been there before. I poured more coffee, wondering whether I should ask the question that had been in my mind for the past hour. I knew I would not like the answer, whatever it was, but I was curious. Being with her again, I began to remember things I had not thought of in years; it was as if the two decades were no greater distance than the width of the table, and I had only to lean across the space and take her hand to be twenty-five again. The evening had already been very unsettling and strange; no reason, I thought, not to make it stranger still.

I said quietly, "How was I so bad?"

"You never let go," she said. "You just hung on for dear life."

"Right," I said. I had no idea what she was talking about.

"Our plans," she began.

"Depended on me letting go?"

She shrugged. "You tried to fit in and you never did."

"In Boston," I said.

She moved her head, yes and no; apparently the point was a subtle one. "I didn't want to come back here and you insisted. I was depending on you to take me away, or at least make an independent life. You never understood that I had always been on the outs with my family."

I stifled an urge to object. I had never wanted to come to Boston. It was where she lived. It was her town, not mine. Glorious Boston, cradle of the Revolution. I had no intrinsic interest in Boston, I only wanted to leave the Midwest. Boston was as good a city as any, and she lived there –

"You were such a damn good *listener.*" She bit the word off, as if it were an obscenity. "Better than you are now, and you're pretty good now. Not so good at talking, though. You listened so well a woman forgot that you never talked yourself, never let on what it was *that was on your mind.* Not one of your strong points, talking."

"Beth," I said evenly. She waited, but I said nothing more; there was nothing more to say anyhow, and I knew the silence would irritate her.

"And it was obvious it would never work; we never got grounded here. And it was obvious you never would, you could never let go of your damned prairie *complexe d'infériorité.* And as a result you were" – she sought the correct word – "*louche.*"

"I am not André Malraux," I said. "What the hell does that mean?"

"It means secretive," she said. "And something more. Furtive."

"Thanks," I said.

"It's a mystery to me why I'm still here. Not so great a mystery as you, but mystery enough. You had to lead the way, though, and you didn't. And I knew H,W was a mistake."

"It was your uncle who suggested it," I said.

"After you asked him," she said.

"At your urging," I said.

"When it looked like you wouldn't land anything and I was tired of the griping."

"You were the one who was nervous," I said.

"I didn't care where we lived," she said. "That was the point you never got." Her voice rose, and I saw the waiter turn and say something to the maître d'. The other couple had left and we were alone in the restaurant. Outside, a police car sped by, its lights blazing, but without sirens. The officer in the passenger seat was white-haired and fat, and he was smoking a cigar. It had stopped snowing but the wind was fierce, blowing debris and rattling windows. The police car had disappeared. I motioned to the waiter for the check. But Beth was far from finished.

"So I married Doran."

"And I didn't marry anybody."

"You married Rachel."

"According to you, Rachel doesn't count."

"Neither did Doran."

The waiter brought the check and I automatically reached for my wallet. She said loudly, "No," and I looked at her, momentarily confused. I had forgotten it was her treat. I had become so absorbed in the past; always when we had been together, I had paid, and it seemed cheap of me to let her pay now. But that was what she wanted and I had agreed to it. She had the check in her hand and was inspecting it for errors. Then, satisfied, she pushed it aside along with a credit card. She exhaled softly and turned to look out the window.

She said quietly, talking to the window, "Do you think it will be easy?"

"I don't know," I said.

"Please," she said. She said it hesitantly, as if the word were unfamiliar. "Just tell me what you think. I won't hold you to it, if you're wrong."

"His lawyer," I began.

"Please," she said again, more forcefully.

"You're asking me for assurances that I can't give. I don't know."

"Just a guess," she said. "In your line of work you must make guesses all the time. Make one now, between us. Between friends."

"Well, then," I said. "No."

"The first one was easy."

"Maybe this will be too," I said.

"But you don't think so."

"No," I said. I knew Frank Greer.

She said, "You're a peach." She put on her glasses.

I did not reply to that.

"I mean it," she said.

Apparently she did, for she looked at me and smiled warmly.

"I have disrupted your life."

I shook my head, No.

"Yes I have. That's what I do sometimes, disrupt the lives of men."

There was so much to say to that, and so little to be gained. I lit a cigarette, listening.

With a quick movement she pushed the half-glasses over her forehead and into her hair, all business. "Get in touch with him tomorrow. Can you do that?"

"Sure," I said.

"And let me know what he says, right away."

"Yes," I said.

"I don't think it's going to be so tough."

"I hope you're right," I said.

"But I've always been an optimist where men are concerned."

I smiled and touched her hand. I looked at her closely, remembering her as a young woman; I knew her now and I knew her then, but there was nothing in between. That was undiscovered territory. I saw the difficulties ahead. They were big as mountains. Annapurna-sized difficulties, a long slog at high altitudes, defending Beth. I took my hand away and said, "You can bail out any time you want, if this gets difficult or awkward. I know it isn't easy. I can put you in touch with any one of a dozen—" She stared at me for a long moment. In the candlelight her face seemed to flush. Suddenly I knew she was murderously angry.

"I think you're right," she said.

"Look," I began.

"Reluctant lawyers are worse than useless." She took off her glasses and put them in her purse. When she snapped the purse shut it sounded like a pistol shot.

"I'll call you tomorrow," I said. I knew that I had handled it badly, but there was no retreat now.

She stood up and the waiter swung into position, helping her with her chair and bowing prettily from the waist.

Outside on Boylston Street the wind was still blowing, and the street was empty except for two cabs at the curb. We stood a moment on the sidewalk, not speaking. She stood with her head turned away, and I thought for a moment she was crying. But when she turned her head I saw the set of her jaw. She was too angry to cry. She began to walk up the street, and I followed. The wind off the Atlantic was vicious. I thought of it as originating in Scotland or Scandinavia, but of course that was wrong. Didn't the wind blow from west to east? This one probably originated in the upper Midwest or Canada. It had a prairie feel to it. We both walked unsteadily with our heads tucked into our coat collars. I thought of Tom and his camel's-hair coat. At Arlington Street she stopped and fumbled for her keys, and then resumed the march. A beggar was at our heels, asking for money. I turned, apprehensive, but he was a sweet-faced drunk. I gave him a dollar and he ambled off. Her car was parked across the street from the Ritz, a green Mercedes convertible with her initials in gold on the door. The car gleamed in the harsh white light of the streetlamps. She stooped to unlock the door, and when she opened it the smell of leather, warm and inviting, spilled into the frigid street. I held the door for her, but she did not get in. She stood looking at me, her face expressionless. She started to say something, but changed her mind. She threw her purse into the back seat and the next thing I knew I was reeling backward, then slipping on an icy patch and falling. Her fist had come out of nowhere and caught me under the right eye. Sprawled on the sidewalk, speechless, I watched her get into the car and drive away. The smell of leather remained in my vicinity.

The doorman at the Ritz had seen all of it, and now he hurried across Arlington Street. He helped me up, muttering and fussing, but despite his best intentions he could not help smiling. He kept his face half turned away so I would not see. Of course he knew me; I was a regular in the bar and the café.

Damn woman, I said. She could go ten with Marvin Hagler.

He thought it all right then to laugh.

Not like the old days, I said.

Packed quite a punch, did she, sir? Ha-ha.

I leaned against the iron fence and collected my wits.

Anything broken? he asked.

I didn't think so. I moved my legs and arms, touched my eye. It was tender but there was no blood. I knew I would have a shiner and wondered how I would explain that at the office.

Let's get you into the bar, he said. A brandy—

No. I shook my head painfully and reached for my wallet. The doorman waited, his face slightly averted as before. I found a five, then thought better of it and gave him a twenty. He didn't have to be told that twenty dollars bought silence. He tucked the money away in his vest and tipped his hat, frowning solicitously.

You wait here one minute, he said. I'll fetch a cab.

No need, I replied. Prefer to walk. I live nearby.

I know, he said, looking at me doubtfully. Then, noticing he had customers under the hotel canopy, he hurried back across the street. I watched him go, assuring the people with a casual wave of his hand that the disturbance was a private matter, minor and entirely under control.

I moved away too, conscious of being watched and realizing that I was very tight. I was breathing hard and could smell my cognac breath. I felt my eye beginning to puff and I knew that I would have bruises on my backside. I decided to take a long way home and walked through the iron gate into the Garden. There was no one about, but the place was filthy, papers blowing everywhere and ash cans stuffed to overflowing. The flurries had left a residue of gray snow. I passed a potato-faced George Washington on horseback on my way along the path to the statue facing Marlborough Street. This was my favorite. Atop the column a physician cradled an unconscious patient, "to commemorate the discovery that the inhaling of ether causes insensibility to pain. First proved to the world at the Mass. General Hospital." It was a pretty little Victorian sculpture. On the plinth someone had scrawled *Up the I.R.A.* in red paint.

I exited at the Beacon Street side. A cab paused, but I waved him on. I labored painfully down Beacon to Clarendon and over to Commonwealth, my shoes scuffing little shards of blue glass, hard and bright as diamonds; this was window glass from the automobiles vandalized nightly. While I waited at the light a large American sedan pulled up next to me, its fender grazing my leg, two men and a woman staring menacingly out the side windows. I took a step backward, and the sedan sped through the red light, trailing rock music and laughter. Tires squealed as the car accelerated, wheeling right on Newbury.

My flat was only a few blocks away. I walked down the deserted mall, my eyes up and watchful. Leafless trees leaned over the walkway, their twisted branches grotesque against the night sky. I walked carefully, for there was ice and dog shit everywhere. The old-fashioned streetlights, truly handsome in daytime, were useless now. It was all so familiar; I had walked down this mall every day for twenty years. Twenty years ago, when there was no danger after dark, Rachel and I took long strolls on summer evenings trying to reach an understanding, and failing. I remembered her musical voice and her accent; when she was distressed she spoke rapidly, but always with perfect diction. I looked up, searching for my living-room window. I was light-headed now and stumbling, but I knew I was close. The Hancock was to my left, as big as a mountain and as sheer, looming like some futuristic religious icon over the low, crabbed sprawl of the Back Bay. I leaned against a tree, out of breath. There was only a little way now; I could see the light in the window. My right eye was almost closed, and my vision blurred. The wind bit into my face, sending huge tears running down my cheeks. I hunched my shoulders against the wind and struggled on, through the empty streets of the city I hated so.

RUSSELL BANKS

1984

Sarah Cole:
A Type of
Love Story

To begin, then, here is a scene in which I am the man and my friend Sarah Cole is the woman. I don't mind describing it now, because I'm a decade older and don't look the same now as I did then, and Sarah is dead. That is to say, on hearing this story you might think me vain if I looked the same now as I did then, because I must tell you that I was extremely handsome then. And if Sarah were not dead, you'd think I were cruel, for I must tell you that Sarah was very homely. In fact, she was the homeliest woman I have ever known. Personally, I mean. I've *seen* a few women who were more unattractive than Sarah, but they were clearly freaks of nature or had been badly injured or had been victimized by some grotesque, disfiguring disease. Sarah, however, was quite normal, and I knew her well, because for three and a half months we were lovers.

Here is the scene. You can put it in the present, even though it took place ten years ago, because nothing that matters to the story depends on when it took place, and you can put it in Concord, New Hampshire, even though that is indeed where it took place, because it doesn't matter where it took place, so it might as well be Concord, New Hampshire, a place I happen to know well and can therefore describe with sufficient detail to make the story believable. Around six o'clock on a Wednesday evening in late May a man enters a bar. The place, a cocktail lounge at street level with a restaurant upstairs, is decorated with hanging plants and unfinished wood paneling, butcherblock tables and captain's chairs, with a half dozen darkened, thickly upholstered booths along one wall. Three or four men between the ages of twenty-five and thirty-five are drinking at the bar, and they, like the man who has just entered, wear three piece suits and loosened neckties. They are probably lawyers, young, unmarried lawyers gossiping with their brethren over martinis so as to postpone arriving home alone at their whitewashed townhouse apartments, where they will fix their evening meals in radar ranges and, afterwards, while their tv's chuckle quietly in front of them, sit on their couches and do a little extra work for tomorrow. They are, for the most part, honorable, educated, hard-working, shallow, and moderately unhappy young men. Our man, call him Ronald, Ron, in most ways is like these men, except that he is unusually good-looking, and that makes him a little less unhappy than they. Ron is effortlessly attractive, a genetic wonder, tall, slender, symmetrical, and clean. His flaws, a small mole on the left corner of his square but not-too-prominent chin, a slight excess of blond hair on the tops of his tanned hands, and somewhat underdeveloped buttocks, insofar as they keep him from resembling too closely a men's store mannequin, only contribute to his beauty, for he is beautiful, the way we usually think of a woman as being beautiful. And he is nice, too, the consequence, perhaps, of his seeming not to know how beautiful he is, to men as well as women, to young people, even children, as well as old, to attractive people, who realize immediately that he is so much more attractive than they as not to be competitive with them, as well as unattractive people, who see him and gain thereby a comforting perspective on those they have heretofore envied for their good looks.

Ron takes a seat at the bar, unfolds the evening paper in front of him, and before he can start reading, the bartender asks to help him, calling him "Sir," even though Ron has come into this bar numerous times at this time of day, especially since his divorce last fall. Ron got divorced because, after three years of marriage, his wife had chosen to pursue the career that his had interrupted, that of a fashion designer, which meant that she had to live in New York City while he had to continue to live in New Hampshire, where his career had got its start. They agreed to live apart until he could continue his career near New York City, but after a few months, between conjugal visits, he started sleeping with other women, and she started sleeping with other men, and that was that. "No big deal," he explained to friends, who liked both Ron and his wife, even though he was slightly more beautiful than she. "We really were too young when we got married, college sweethearts. But we're still best friends," he assured them. They understood. Most of Ron's friends were divorced by then too.

Ron orders a scotch and soda, with a twist, and goes back to reading his paper. When his drink comes, before he takes a sip of it, he first carefully finishes reading an article about the recent reappearance of coyotes in northern New Hampshire and Vermont. He lights a cigarette. He goes on reading. He takes a second sip of his drink. Everyone in the room, the three or four men scattered along the bar, the tall, thin bartender, and several people in the booths at the back, watches him do these ordinary things.

He has got to the classified section, is perhaps searching for someone willing to come in once a week and clean his apartment, when the woman who will turn out to be Sarah Cole leaves a booth in the back and approaches him. She comes up from the side and sits next to him. She's wearing heavy, tan cowboy boots and a dark brown, suede cowboy hat, lumpy jeans and a yellow tee shirt that clings to her arms, breasts, and round belly like the skin of a sausage. Though he will later learn that she is thirty-eight years old, she looks older by about ten years, which makes her look about twenty years older than he actually is. (It's difficult to guess accurately how old Ron is, he looks anywhere from a mature twenty-five to a youthful forty, so his actual age doesn't seem to matter.)

"It's not bad here at the bar," she says, looking around. "More light, anyhow. Whatcha readin'?" she asks brightly, planting both elbows on the bar.

Ron looks up from his paper with a slight smile on his lips, sees the face of a woman homelier than any he has ever seen or imagined before, and goes on smiling lightly. He feels himself falling into her tiny, slightly crossed, dark brown eyes, pulls himself back, and studies for a few seconds her mottled, pocked complexion, bulbous nose, loose mouth, twisted and gapped teeth, and heavy but receding chin. He casts a glance over her thatch of dun-colored hair and along her neck and throat, where acne burns against gray skin, and returns to her eyes, and again feels himself falling into her.

"What did you say?" he asks.

She knocks a mentholated cigarette from her pack, and Ron swiftly lights it. Blowing smoke from her large, wing-shaped nostrils, she speaks again. Her voice is thick and nasal, a chocolate-colored voice. "I asked you whatcha readin', but I can see now." She belts out a single, loud laugh. "The paper!"

Ron laughs, too. "The paper! *The Concord Monitor!*" He is not hallucinating, he clearly sees what is before him and admits—no, he asserts—to himself that he is speaking to the most unattractive woman he has ever seen, a fact which fascinates him, as if instead he were speaking to the most beautiful woman he has ever seen or perhaps ever will see, so he treasures the moment, attempts to hold it as if it were a golden ball, a disproportionately heavy object which—if he doesn't hold it lightly and with precision and firmness—will slip from his hand and roll across the lawn to the lip of the well and down, down to the bottom of the well, lost to him forever. It will be merely a memory, something to speak of wistfully and with wonder as over the years the image fades and comes in the end to exist only in the telling. His mind and body waken from their sleepy self-absorption, and all his attention focuses on the woman, Sarah Cole, her ugly face, like a wart hog's, her thick, rapid voice, her dumpy, off-center wreck of a body, and to keep this moment here before him, he begins to ask questions of her, he buys her a drink, he smiles, until soon it seems, even to him, that he is taking her and her life, its vicissitudes and woe, quite seriously.

He learns her name, of course, and she volunteers the information that she spoke to him on a dare from one of the two women still sitting in the booth behind her. She turns on her stool and smiles brazenly, triumphantly, at her friends, two women, also homely (though nowhere as homely as she) and dressed, like her, in cowboy boots, hats and jeans. One of the women, a blond with an underslung jaw and wearing heavy eye makeup, flips a little wave at her, and as if embarrassed, she and the other woman at the booth turn back to their drinks and sip fiercely at straws.

Sarah returns to Ron and goes on telling him what he wants to know, about her job at the Rumford Press, about her divorced husband who was a bastard and stupid and "sick," she says, as if filling suddenly with sympathy for the man. She tells Ron about her three children, the youngest, a girl, in junior high school and boy-crazy, the other two, boys, in high school and almost never at home anymore. She speaks of her children with genuine tenderness and concern, and Ron is touched. He can see with what pleasure and pain she speaks of her children; he watches her tiny eyes light up and water over when he asks their names.

"You're a nice woman," he informs her.

She smiles, looks at her empty glass. "No. No, I'm not. But you're a nice man, to tell me that."

Ron, with a gesture, asks the bartender to refill Sarah's glass. She is drinking white Russians. Perhaps she has been drinking them for an hour or two, for she seems very relaxed, more relaxed than women usually do when they come up and without introduction or invitation speak to him.

She asks him about himself, his job, his divorce, how long he has lived in Concord, but he finds that he is not at all interested in telling her about himself. He wants to know about her, even though what she has to tell him about herself is predictable and ordinary and the way she tells it unadorned and clichéd. He wonders about her husband. What kind of man would fall in love with Sarah Cole?

2

That scene, at Osgood's Lounge in Concord, ended with Ron's departure, alone, after having bought Sarah's second drink, and Sarah's return to her friends in the booth. I don't know what she told them, but it's not hard to imagine. The three women were not close friends, merely fellow workers at Rumford Press, where they stood at the end of a long conveyor belt day after day packing *TV Guides* into cartons. They all hated their jobs, and frequently after work, when they worked the day shift, they would put on their cowboy hats and boots, which they kept all day in their lockers, and stop for a drink or two on their way home. This had been their first visit to Osgood's, a place that, prior to this, they had avoided out of a sneering belief that no one went there but lawyers and insurance men. It had been Sarah who had asked the others why that should keep them away, and when they had no answer for her, the three had decided to stop at Osgood's. Ron was right, they had been there over an hour when he came in, and Sarah was a little drunk. "We'll hafta come in here again," she said to her friends, her voice rising slightly.

Which they did, that Friday, and once again Ron appeared with his evening newspaper. He put his briefcase down next to his stool and ordered a drink and proceeded to read the front page, slowly, deliberately, clearly a weary, unhurried, solitary man. He did not notice the three women in cowboy hats and boots in the booth in back, but they saw him, and after a few minutes Sarah was once again at his side.

"Hi."

He turned, saw her, and instantly regained the moment he had lost when, the previous night, once outside the bar, he had forgotten about the ugliest woman he had ever seen. She seemed even more grotesque to him now than before, which made the moment all the more precious to him, and so once again he held the moment as if in his hands and began to speak with her, to ask questions, to offer his opinions and solicit hers.

I said earlier that I am the man in this story and my friend Sarah Cole, now dead, is the woman. I think back to that night, the second time I had seen Sarah, and I tremble, not with fear but in shame. My concern then, when I was first becoming involved with Sarah, was merely with the moment, holding onto it, grasping it wholly as if its beginning did not grow out of some other prior moment in her life and my life separately and at the same time did not lead into future moments in our separate lives. She talked more easily than she had the night before, and I listened as eagerly and carefully as I had before, again, with the same motives, to keep her in front of me, to draw her forward from the context of her life and place her, as if she were an object, into the context of mine. I did not know how cruel this was. When you have never done a thing before and that thing is not simply and clearly right or wrong, you frequently do not know if it is a cruel thing, you just go ahead and do it, and maybe later you'll be able to determine whether you acted cruelly. That way you'll know if it was right or wrong of you to have done it in the first place.

While we drank, Sarah told me that she hated her ex-husband because of the way he treated the children. "It's not so much the money," she said, nervously wagging her booted feet from her perch on the high barstool. "I mean, I get by, barely, but I get them fed and clothed on my own okay. It's because he won't even write them a letter or anything. He won't call them on the phone, all he calls for is to bitch at me because I'm trying to get the state to take him to court so I can get some of the money he's s'posed to be paying for child support. And he won't even think to talk to the kids when he calls. Won't even ask about them."

"He sounds like a bastard," I said.

"He is, he is," she said. "I don't know why I married him. Or stayed married. Fourteen years, for Christ's sake. He put a spell over me or something. I don't know," she said with a note of wistfulness in her voice. "He wasn't what you'd call good-looking."

After her second drink, she decided she had to leave. Her children were at home, it was Friday night and she liked to make sure she ate supper with them and knew where they were going and who they were with when they went out on their dates. "No dates on schoolnights," she said to me. "I mean, you gotta have rules, you know."

I agreed, and we left together, everyone in the place following us with his or her gaze. I was aware of that, I knew what they were thinking, and I didn't care, because I was simply walking her to her car.

It was a cool evening, dusk settling onto the lot like a gray blanket. Her car, a huge, dark green Buick sedan at least ten years old, was battered, scratched, and almost beyond use. She reached for the door handle on the driver's side and yanked. Nothing. The door wouldn't open. She tried again. Then I tried. Still nothing.

Then I saw it, a V-shaped dent in the left front fender creasing the fender where the door joined it, binding the metal of the door against the metal of the fender in a large crimp that held the door fast. "Someone must've backed into you while you were inside," I said to her.

She came forward and studied the crimp for a few seconds, and when she looked back at me, she was weeping. "Jesus, Jesus, Jesus!" she wailed, her large, frog-like mouth wide open and wet with spit, her red tongue flopping loosely over gapped teeth. "I can't pay for this! I *can't!*" Her face was red, and even in the dusky light I could see it puff out with weeping, her tiny eyes seeming almost to disappear behind wet cheeks. Her shoulders slumped, and her hands fell limply to her sides.

Placing my briefcase on the ground, I reached out to her and put my arms around her body and held her close to me, while she cried wetly into my shoulder. After a few seconds, she started pulling herself back together and her weeping got reduced to sniffling. Her cowboy hat had been pushed back and now clung to her head at a precarious, absurdly jaunty angle. She took a step away from me and said, "I'll get in the other side."

"Okay," I said almost in a whisper. "That's fine."

Slowly, she walked around the front of the huge, ugly vehicle and opened the door on the passenger's side and slid awkwardly across the seat until she had positioned herself behind the steering wheel. Then she started the motor, which came to life with a roar. The muffler was shot. Without saying another word to me, or even waving, she dropped the car into reverse gear and backed it loudly out of the parking space and headed out the lot to the street.

I turned and started for my car, when I happened to glance toward the door of the bar, and there, staring after me, were the bartender, the two women who had come in with Sarah, and two of the men who had been sitting at the bar. They were lawyers, and I knew them slightly. They were grinning at me. I grinned back and got into my car, and then, without looking at them again, I left the place and drove straight to my apartment.

3

One night several weeks later, Ron meets Sarah at Osgood's, and after buying her three white Russians and drinking three scotches himself, he takes her back to his apartment in his car—a Datsun fastback coupe that she says she admires—for the sole purpose of making love to her.

I'm still the man in this story, and Sarah is still the woman, but I'm telling it this way because what I have to tell you now confuses me, embarrasses me, and makes me sad, and consequently, I'm likely to tell it falsely. I'm likely to cover the truth by making Sarah a better woman than she actually was, while making myself appear worse than I actually was or am; or else I'll do the opposite, make Sarah worse than she was and me better. The truth is, I was pretty, extremely so, and she was not, extremely so, and I knew it and she knew it. She walked out the door of Osgood's determined to make love to a man much prettier than any she had seen up close before, and I walked out determined to make love to a woman much homelier than any I had made love to before. We were, in a sense, equals.

No, that's not exactly true. (You see? This is why I have to tell the story the way I'm telling it.) I'm not at all sure she feels as Ron does. That is to say, perhaps she genuinely likes the man, in spite of his being the most physically attractive man she has ever known. Perhaps she is more aware of her homeliness than of his beauty, just as he is more aware of her homeliness than of his beauty, for Ron, despite what I may have implied, does not think of himself as especially beautiful. He merely knows that other people think of him that way. As I said before, he is a nice man.

Ron unlocks the door to his apartment, walks in ahead of her, and flicks on the lamp beside the couch. It's a small, single bedroom, modern apartment, one of thirty identical apartments in a large brick building on the heights just east of downtown Concord. Sarah stands nervously at the door, peering in.

"Come in, come in," he says.

She steps timidly in and closes the door behind her. She removes her cowboy hat, then quickly puts it back on, crosses the livingroom, and plops down in a blond easychair, seeming to shrink in its hug out of sight to safety. Ron, behind her, at the entry to the kitchen, places one hand on her shoulder, and she stiffens. He removes his hand.

"Would you like a drink?"

"No . . . I guess not," she says, staring straight ahead at the wall opposite where a large framed photograph of a bicyclist advertises in French the Tour de France. Around a corner, in an alcove off the living room, a silver-gray ten-speed bicycle leans casually against the wall, glistening and poised, slender as a thoroughbred race-horse.

"I don't know," she says. Ron is in the kitchen now, making himself a drink. "I don't know . . . I don't know."

"What? Change your mind? I can make a white Russian for you. Vodka, cream kahlua, and ice, right?"

Sarah tries to cross her legs, but she is sitting too low in the chair and her legs are too thick at the thigh, so she ends, after a struggle, with one leg in the air and the other twisted on its side. She looks as if she has fallen from a great height.

Ron steps out from the kitchen, peers over the back of the chair, and watches her untangle herself, then ducks back into the kitchen. After a few seconds, he returns. "Seriously. Want me to fix you a white Russian?"

"No."

Ron, again from behind, places one hand onto Sarah's shoulder, and this time she does not stiffen, though she does not exactly relax, either. She sits there, a block of wood, staring straight ahead.

"Are you scared?" he asks gently. Then he adds, "*I* am."

"Well, no, I'm not scared." She remains silent for a moment. "You're scared? Of what?" She turns to face him but avoids his eyes.

"Well . . . I don't do this all the time, you know. Bring home a woman I . . . ," he trails off.

"Picked up in a bar"

"No. I mean, I like you, Sarah, I really do. And I didn't just pick you up in a bar, you know that. We've gotten to be friends, you and me."

"You want to sleep with me?" she asks, still not meeting his steady gaze.

"Yes." He seems to mean it. He does not take a gulp or even a sip from his drink. He just says, "Yes," straight out, and cleanly, not too quickly, either, and not after a hesitant delay. A simple statement of a simple fact. The man wants to make love to the woman. She asked him, and he told her. What could be simpler?

"Do you want to sleep with *me?*" he asks.

She turns around in the chair, faces the wall again, and says in a low voice, "Sure I do, but . . . it's hard to explain."

"What? But what?" Placing his glass down on the table between the chair and the sofa, he puts both hands on her shoulders and lightly kneads them. He knows he can be discouraged from pursuing this, but he is not sure how easily. Having got this far without bumping against obstacles (except the ones he has placed in his way himself), he is not sure what it will take to turn him back. He does not know, therefore, how assertive or how seductive he should be with her. He suspects that he can be stopped very easily, so he is reluctant to give her a chance to try. He goes on kneading her doughy shoulders.

"You and me . . . we're real different." She glances at the bicycle in the corner.

"A man . . . and a woman," he says.

"No, not that. I mean, different. That's all. Real different. More than you . . . you're nice, but you don't know what I mean, and that's one of the things that makes you so nice. But we're different. Listen," she says, "I gotta go. I gotta leave now."

The man removes his hands and retrieves his glass, takes a sip, and watches her over the rim of the glass, as, not without difficulty, she rises from the chair and moves swiftly toward the door. She stops at the door, squares her hat on her head, and glances back at him.

"We can be friends. Okay?"

"Okay. Friends."

"I'll see you again down at Osgood's, right?"

"Oh, yeah, sure."

"Good. See you," she says, opening the door.

The door closes. The man walks around the sofa, snaps on the television set, and sits down in front of it. He picks up a *TV Guide* from the coffee table and flips through it, stops, runs a finger down the listings, stops, puts down the magazine and changes the channel. He does not once connect the magazine in his hand to the woman who has just left his apartment, even though he knows she spends her days packing *TV Guide*s into cartons that get shipped to warehouses in distant parts of New England. He'll think of the connection some other night, but by then the connection will be merely sentimental. It'll be too late for him to understand what she meant by "different."

4

But that's not the point of my story. Certainly it's an aspect of the story, the political aspect, if you want, but it's not the reason I'm trying to tell the story in the first place. I'm trying to tell the story so that I can understand what happened between me and Sarah Cole that summer and early autumn ten years ago. To say we were lovers says very little about what happened; to say we were friends says even less. No, if I'm to understand the whole thing, I have to say the whole thing, for, in the end, what I need to know is whether what happened between me and Sarah Cole was right or wrong. Character is fate, which suggests that if a man can know and then to some degree control his character, he can know and to that same degree control his fate.

But let me go on with my story. The next time Sarah and I were together we were at her apartment in the south end of Concord, a second floor flat in a tenement building on Perley Street. I had stayed away from Osgood's for several weeks, deliberately trying to avoid running into Sarah there, though I never quite put it that way to myself. I found excuses and generated interests in and reasons for going elsewhere after work. Yet I was obsessed with Sarah by then, obsessed with the idea of making love to her, which, because it was not an actual *desire* to make love to her, was an unusually complex obsession. Passion without desire, if it gets expressed, may in fact be a kind of rape, and perhaps I sensed the danger that lay behind my obsession and for that reason went out of my way to avoid meeting Sarah again.

Yet I did meet her, inadvertently, of course. After picking up shirts at the cleaner's on South Main and Perley Streets, I'd gone down Perley on my way to South State and the post office. It was a Saturday morning, and this trip on my bicycle was part of my regular Saturday routine. I did not remember that Sarah lived on Perley Street, although she had told me several times in a complaining way – it's a rough neighborhood, packed dirt yards, shabby apartment buildings, the carcasses of old, half-stripped cars on cinderblocks in the driveways, broken red and yellow plastic tricycles on the cracked sidewalks – but as soon as I saw her, I remembered. It was too late to avoid meeting her. I was riding my bike, wearing shorts and tee shirt, the package containing my folded and starched shirts hooked to the carrier behind me, and she was walking toward me along the sidewalk, lugging two large bags of groceries. She saw me, and I stopped. We talked, and I offered to carry her groceries for her. I took the bags while she led the bike, handling it carefully, as if she were afraid she might break it.

At the stoop we came to a halt. The wooden steps were cluttered with half-opened garbage bags spilling egg shells, coffee grounds, and old food wrappers to the walkway. "I can't get the people downstairs to take care of their garbage," she explained. She leaned the bike against the bannister and reached for her groceries.

"I'll carry them up for you," I said. I directed her to loop the chain lock from the bike to the bannister rail and snap it shut and told her to bring my shirts up with her.

"Maybe you'd like a beer?" she said as she opened the door to the darkened hallway. Narrow stairs disappeared in front of me into heavy, damp
darkness, and the air smelled like old newspapers.

"Sure," I said and followed her up.

"Sorry there's no light. I can't get them to fix it."

"No matter. I can see you and follow along," I said, and even in the dim
light of the hall I could see the large, dark blue veins that cascaded thickly
down the backs of her legs. She wore tight, white-duck bermuda shorts,
rubber shower sandals, and a pink sleeveless sweater. I pictured her in the
cashier's line at the supermarket. I would have been behind her, a stranger,
and on seeing her, I would have turned away and studied the covers of the
magazines, *TV Guide, People, The National Enquirer,* for there was nothing of
interest in her appearance that in the hard light of day would not have
slightly embarrassed me. Yet here I was inviting myself into her home,
eagerly staring at the backs of her ravaged legs, her sad, tasteless clothing,
her poverty. I was not detached, however, was not staring at her with scien-
tific curiosity, and because of my passion, did not feel or believe that what I
was doing was perverse. I felt warmed by her presence and was flirtatious
and bold, a little pushy, even.

Picture this. The man, tanned, limber, wearing red jogging shorts,
Italian leather sandals, a clinging net tee shirt of Scandinavian design and
manufacture, enters the apartment behind the woman, whose dough colored
skin, thick, short body, and homely, uncomfortable face all try, but fail to
hide themselves. She waves him toward the table in the kitchen, where he
sets down the bags and looks good-naturedly around the room. "What about
the beer you bribed me with?" he asks. The apartment is dark and cluttered
with old, oversized furniture, yard sale and second-hand stuff bought originally for a large house in the country or a spacious apartment on a boulevard
forty or fifty years ago, passed down from antique dealer to used furniture
store to yard sale to thrift shop, where it finally gets purchased by Sarah
Cole and gets lugged over to Perley Street and shoved up the narrow stairs,
she and her children grunting and sweating in the darkness of the hallway
—overstuffed armchairs and couch, huge, ungainly dressers, upholstered
rocking chairs, and in the kitchen, an old maple desk for a table, a half dozen
heavy oak diningroom chairs, a high, glass-fronted cabinet, all peeling,
stained, chipped and squatting heavily on a dark green linoleum floor.

The place is neat and arranged in a more or less orderly way, however,
and the man seems comfortable there. He strolls from the kitchen to the
livingroom and peeks into the three small bedrooms that branch off a hallway behind the livingroom. "Nice place!" he calls to the woman. He is studying the framed pictures of her three children arranged like an altar atop the
buffet. "Nice looking kids!" he calls out. They are. Blond, round-faced, clean,
and utterly ordinary-looking, their pleasant faces glance, as instructed,

slightly off camera and down to the right, as if they are trying to remember the name of the capital of Montana.

When he returns to the kitchen, the woman is putting away her groceries, her back to him. "Where's that beer you bribed me with?" he asks again. He takes a position against the doorframe, his weight on one hip, like a dancer resting. "You sure are quiet today, Sarah," he says in a low voice. "Everything okay?"

Silently, she turns away from the grocery bags, crosses the room to the man, reaches up to him, and holding him by the head, kisses his mouth, rolls her torso against his, drops her hands to his hips and yanks him tightly to her, and goes on kissing him, eyes closed, working her face furiously against his. The man places his hands on her shoulders and pulls away, and they face each other, wide-eyed, as if amazed and frightened. The man drops his hands, and the woman lets go of his hips. Then, after a few seconds, the man silently turns, goes to the door, and leaves. The last thing he sees as he closes the door behind him is the woman standing in the kitchen doorframe, her face looking down and slightly to one side, wearing the same pleasant expression on her face as her children in their photographs, trying to remember the capital of Montana.

5

Sarah appeared at my apartment door the following morning, a Sunday, cool and rainy. She had brought me the package of freshly laundered shirts I'd left in her kitchen, and when I opened the door to her, she simply held the package out to me as if it were a penitent's gift. She wore a yellow rain slicker and cap and looked more like a disconsolate schoolgirl facing an angry teacher than a grown woman dropping a package off at a friend's apartment. After all, she had nothing to be ashamed of.

I invited her inside and she accepted my invitation. I had been reading the Sunday *New York Times* on the couch and drinking coffee, lounging through the gray morning in bathrobe and pajamas. I told her to take off her wet raincoat and hat and hang them in the closet by the door and started for the kitchen to get her a cup of coffee, when I stopped, turned, and looked at her. She closed the closet door on her yellow raincoat and hat, turned around, and faced me.

What else can I do? I must describe it. I remember that moment of ten years ago as if it occurred ten minutes ago, the package of shirts on the table behind her, the newspapers scattered over the couch and floor, the sound of windblown rain washing the sides of the building outside, and the silence of the room, as we stood across from one another and watched, while we each simultaneously removed our own clothing, my robe, her blouse and skirt, my pajama top, her slip and bra, my pajama bottom, her underpants, until we

were both standing naked in the harsh, gray light, two naked members of
the same species, a male and a female, the male somewhat younger and less
scarred than the female, the female somewhat less delicately constructed
than the male, both individuals pale-skinned with dark thatches of hair in
the area of their genitals, both individuals standing slackly, as if a great,
protracted tension between them had at last been released.

We made love that morning in my bed for long hours that drifted easily
into afternoon. And we talked, as people usually do when they spend half a
day or half a night in bed together. I told her of my past, named and described the people I had loved and had loved me, my ex-wife in New York, my
brother in the Air Force, my father and mother in their condominium in
Florida, and I told her of my ambitions and dreams and even confessed some
of my fears. She listened patiently and intelligently throughout and talked
much less than I. She had already told me many of these things about herself, and perhaps whatever she had to say to me now lay on the next inner
circle of intimacy or else could not be spoken of at all.

During the next few weeks we met and made love often and always at
my apartment. On arriving home from work, I would phone her, or if not,
she would phone me, and after a few feints and dodges, one would suggest to
the other that we get together tonight, and a half hour later she'd be at my
door. Our love-making was passionate, skillful, kindly, and deeply satisfying.
We didn't often speak of it to one another or brag about it, the way some
couples do when they are surprised by the ease with which they have
become contented lovers. We did occasionally joke and tease each other,
however, playfully acknowledging that the only thing we did together was
make love but that we did it so frequently there was no time for anything
else.

Then one hot night, a Saturday in August, we were lying in bed atop the
tangled sheets, smoking cigarettes and chatting idly, and Sarah suggested
that we go out for a drink.

"Now?"

"Sure. It's early. What time is it?"

I scanned the digital clock next to the bed. "Nine-forty-nine."

"There. See?"

"That's not so early. You usually go home by eleven, you know. It's
almost ten."

"No, it's only a little after nine. Depends on how you look at things.
Besides, Ron, it's Saturday night. Don't you want to go out and dance or
something? Or is this the only thing you know how to do?" she teased and
poked me in the ribs. "You know how to dance? You like to dance?"

"Yah, sure . . . sure, but not tonight. It's too hot. And I'm tired."

But she persisted, happily pointing out that an air-conditioned bar would be cooler than my apartment, and we didn't have to go to a dance bar, we could go to Osgood's. "As a compromise," she said.

I suggested a place called the El Rancho, a restaurant with a large, dark cocktail lounge and dance bar located several miles from town on the old Portsmouth highway. Around nine the restaurant closed and the bar became something of a roadhouse, with a small country-western houseband and a clientel drawn from the four or five villages that adjoined Concord on the north and east. I had eaten at the restaurant once but had never gone to the bar, and I didn't know anyone who had.

Sarah was silent for a moment. Then she lit a cigarette and drew the sheet over her naked body. "You don't want anybody to know about us, do you? Do you?"

"That's not it . . . I just don't like gossip, and I work with a lot of people who show up sometimes at Osgood's. On a Saturday night especially."

"No," she said firmly. "You're ashamed of being seen with me. You'll sleep with me, but you won't go out in public with me."

"That's not true, Sarah."

She was silent again. Relieved, I reached across her to the bedtable and got my cigarettes and lighter.

"You owe me, Ron," she said suddenly, as I passed over her. "You owe me."

"What?" I lay back, lit a cigarette, and covered my body with the sheet.

"I said, 'You owe me.' "

"I don't know what you're talking about, Sarah. I just don't like a lot of gossip going around, that's all. I like keeping my private life private, that's all. I don't *owe* you anything."

"Friendship you owe me. And respect. Friendship and respect. A person can't do what you've done with me without owing them friendship and respect."

"Sarah, I really don't know what you're talking about," I said. "I am your friend, you know that. And I respect you. I really do."

"You really think so, don't you?"

"Yes."

She said nothing for several long moments. Then she sighed and in a low, almost inaudible voice said, "Then you'll have to go out in public with me. I don't care about Osgood's or the people you work with, we don't have to go there or see any of them," she said. "But you're gonna have to go to places like the El Rancho with me, and a few other places I know, too, where there's people *I* work with, people *I* know, and maybe we'll even go to a couple of parties, because *I* get invited to parties sometimes, you know. I have friends, and I have some family, too, and you're gonna have to meet my family. My kids think I'm just going around bar-hopping when I'm over here with you, and I don't like that, so you're gonna have to meet them so I can tell them where I am when I'm not at home nights. And sometimes you're gonna come over and spend the evening at my place!" Her voice had risen as she heard her demands and felt their rightness until now she was almost shouting at me. "You *owe* that to me. Or else you're a bad man. It's that simple."

It was.

6

The handsome man is over-dressed. He is wearing a navy blue blazer, taupe shirt open at the throat, white slacks, white loafers. Everyone else, including the homely woman with the handsome man, is dressed appropriately, dressed, that is, like everyone else—jeans and cowboy boots, blouses or cowboy shirts or tee shirts with catchy sayings printed across the front, and many of the women are wearing cowboy hats pushed back and tied under their chins. The man doesn't know anyone at the bar or, if they're at a party, in the room, but the woman knows most of the people there, and she gladly introduces him. The men grin and shake his hand, slap him on his jacketed shoulder, ask him where he works, what's his line, after which they lapse into silence. The women flirt briefly with their faces, but they lapse into silence even before the men do. The woman with the man in the blazer does most of the talking for everyone. She talks for the man in the blazer, for the men standing around the refrigerator, or if they're at a bar, for the other men at the table, and for the other women, too. She chats and rambles aimlessly through loud monologues, laughs uproariously at trivial jokes, and drinks too much, until soon she is drunk, thick-tongued, clumsy, and the man has to say her goodbyes and ease her out the door to his car and drive her home to her apartment on Perley Street.

This happens twice in one week, and then three times the next—at the El Rancho, at the Ox Bow in Northwood, at Rita's and Jimmy's apartment on Thorndike Street, out in Warner at Betsy Beeler's new house, and, the last time, at a cottage on Lake Sunapee rented by some kids in shipping at Rumford Press. Ron no longer calls Sarah when he gets home from work; he waits for her call, and sometimes, when he knows it's she, he doesn't answer the phone. Usually, he lets it ring five or six times, and then he reaches down and picks up the receiver. He has taken his jacket and vest off and loosened his tie and is about to put supper, frozen manicotti, into the radar range.

"Hello?"

"*Hi.*"

"How're you doing?"

"*Okay, I guess. A little tired.*"

"Still hung-over?"

"*No. Not really. Just tired. I hate Mondays.*"

"You have fun last night?"

"*Well, yeah, sorta. It's nice out there, at the lake. Listen,*" she says, brightening. "*Whyn't you come over here tonight? The kids're all going out later, but if you come over before eight, you can meet them. They really want to meet you.*"

"You told them about me?"

"*Sure. Long time ago. I'm not supposed to tell my own kids?*"

Ron is silent.

"*You don't want to come over here tonight. You don't want to meet my kids. No, you don't want my kids to meet you, that's it.*"

"No, no, it's just . . . I've got a lot of work to do . . . "

"*We should talk,*" she announces in a flat voice.

"Yes," he says, "we should talk."

They agree that she will meet him at his apartment, and they'll talk, and they say goodbye and hang up.

While Ron is heating his supper and then eating alone at his kitchen table and Sarah is feeding her children, perhaps I should admit, since we are nearing the end of my story, that I don't actually know that Sarah Cole is dead. A few years ago I happened to run into one of her friends from the press, a blond woman with an underslung jaw. Her name, she reminded me, was Glenda, she had seen me at Osgood's a couple of times and we had met at the El Rancho once when I had gone there with Sarah. I was amazed that she could remember me and a little embarrassed that I did not recognize her at all, and she laughed at that and said, "You haven't changed much, mister!" I pretended to recognize her, but I think she knew she was a stranger to me. We were standing outside the Sears store on South Main Street, where I had gone to buy paint. I had recently remarried, and my wife and I were redecorating my apartment.

"Whatever happened to Sarah?" I asked Glenda. "Is she still down at the press?"

"Jeez, no! She left a long time ago. Way back. I heard she went back with her ex-husband. I can't remember his name. Something Cole."

I asked her if she was sure of that, and she said no, she had only heard it around the bars and down at the press, but she had assumed it was true. People said Sarah had moved back with her ex-husband and was living in a trailer in a park near Hooksett, and the whole family had moved down to Florida that winter because he was out of work. He was a carpenter, she said.

"I thought he was mean to her. I thought he beat her up and everything. I thought she hated him," I said.

"Oh, well, yeah, he was a bastard, all right. I met him a couple of times, and I didn't like him. Short, ugly, and mean when he got drunk. But you know what they say."

"What do they say?"

"Oh, you know, about water seeking its own level."

"Sarah wasn't mean when she was drunk."

The woman laughed. "Naw, but she sure was short and ugly!"

I said nothing.

"Hey, don't get me wrong, I liked Sarah. But you and her . . . well, you sure made a funny-looking couple. She probably didn't feel so self-conscious and all with her husband," the woman said seriously. "I mean, with you . . . all tall and blond, and poor old Sarah . . . I mean, the way them kids in the press room used to kid her about her looks, it was embarrassing just to hear it."

"Well . . . I loved her," I said.

The woman raised her plucked eyebrows in disbelief. She smiled. "Sure, you did, honey," she said, and she patted me on the arm. "Sure, you did." Then she let the smile drift off her face, turned and walked away.

When someone you have loved dies, you accept the fact of his or her death, but then the person goes on living in your memory, dreams and reveries. You have imaginary conversations with him or her, you see something striking and remind yourself to tell your loved one about it and then get brought up short by the knowledge of the fact of his or her death, and at night, in your sleep, the dead person visits you. With Sarah, none of that happened. When she was gone from my life, she was gone absolutely, as if she had never existed in the first place. It was only later, when I could think of her as dead and could come out and say it, my friend Sarah Cole is dead, that I was able to tell this story, for that is when she began to enter my memories, my dreams, and my reveries. In that way I learned that I truly did love her, and now I have begun to grieve over her death, to wish her alive again, so that I can say to her the things I could not know or say when she was alive, when I did not know that I loved her.

7

The woman arrives at Ron's apartment around eight. He hears her car, because of the broken muffler, blat and rumble into the parking lot below, and he crosses quickly from the kitchen and peers out the livingroom window and, as if through a telescope, watches her shove herself across the seat to the passenger's side to get out of the car, then walk slowly in the dusky light toward the apartment building. It's a warm evening, and she's wearing her white bermuda shorts, pink sleeveless sweater, and shower sandals. Ron hates those clothes. He hates the way the shorts cut into her flesh at the crotch and thigh, hates the large, dark caves below her arms that get exposed by the sweater, hates the flapping noise made by the sandals.

Shortly, there is a soft knock at his door. He opens it, turns away and crosses to the kitchen, where he turns back, lights a cigarette, and watches her. She closes the door. He offers her a drink, which she declines, and somewhat formally, he invites her to sit down. She sits carefully on the sofa, in the middle, with her feet close together on the floor, as if she were being interviewed for a job. Then he comes around and sits in the easy chair, relaxed, one leg slung over the other at the knee, as if he were interviewing her for the job.

"Well," he says, "you wanted to talk."

"Yes. But now you're mad at me. I can see that. I didn't do anything, Ron."

"I'm not mad at you."

They are silent for a moment. Ron goes on smoking his cigarette. Finally, she sighs and says, "You don't want to see me anymore, do you?"

He waits a few seconds and answers, "Yes. That's right." Getting up from the chair, he walks to the silver-gray bicycle and stands before it, running a fingertip along the slender cross-bar from the saddle to the chrome plated handlebars.

"You're a son of a bitch," she says in a low voice. "You're worse than my ex-husband." Then she smiles meanly, almost sneers, and soon he realizes that she is telling him that she won't leave. He's stuck with her, she informs him with cold precision. "You think I'm just so much meat, and all you got to do is call up the butcher shop and cancel your order. Well, now you're going to find out different. You *can't* cancel your order. I'm not meat, I'm not one of your pretty little girlfriends who come running when you want them and go away when you get tired of them. I'm *different*. I got nothing to lose, Ron. Nothing. You're stuck with me, Ron."

He continues stroking his bicycle. "No, I'm not."

She sits back in the couch and crosses her legs at the ankles. "I think I *will* have that drink you offered."

"Look, Sarah, it would be better if you go now."

"No," she says flatly. "You offered me a drink when I came in. Nothing's changed since I've been here. Not for me, and not for you. I'd like that drink you offered," she says haughtily.

Ron turns away from the bicycle and takes a step toward her. His face has stiffened into a mask. "Enough is enough," he says through clenched teeth. "I've given you enough."

"Fix me a drink, will you, honey?" she says with a phony smile.

Ron orders her to leave.

She refuses.

He grabs her by the arm and yanks her to her feet.

She starts crying lightly. She stands there and looks up into his face and weeps, but she does not move toward the door, so he pushes her. She regains her balance and goes on weeping.

He stands back and places his fists on his hips and looks at her. "Go on and leave, you ugly bitch," he says to her, and as he says the words, as one by one they leave his mouth, she's transformed into the most beautiful woman he has ever seen. He says the words again, almost tenderly. "Leave, you ugly bitch." Her hair is golden, her brown eyes deep and sad, her mouth full and affectionate, her tears the tears of love and loss, and her pleading, out-stretched arms, her entire body, the arms and body of a devoted woman's cruelly rejected love. A third time he says the words. "Leave me, you disgust-ing, ugly bitch." She is wrapped in an envelope of golden light, a warm, dense haze that she seems to have stepped into, as into a carriage. And then she is gone, and he is alone again.

He looks around the room, as if searching for her. Sitting down in the easy chair, he places his face in his hands. It's not as if she has died; it's as if he has killed her.

ABOUT THE AUTHORS

ALICE ADAMS · 1926–   Alice Adams was born August 14, 1926, in Fredericksburg, Virginia, and educated at Radcliffe College (B.A., 1946). A writer of short stories and novels, she has worked at office jobs and taught at various colleges. "Alternatives" (first appeared in the *Atlantic Monthly*, April, 1973, and was chosen for *Prize Stories, 1974: The O. Henry Awards*, where it was designated the third best American short story published in 1973. In 1982 she received the O. Henry Special Award for Continuing Achievement. Her short-story collections include *Beautiful Girl* (1979), *To See You Again* (1982), *Molly's Dog* (1983) and *Return Trips* (1983). Of interest to New Englanders is her novel *Superior Women* (1984), which tracks four women's experiences at Radcliffe and thereafter.

THOMAS BAILEY ALDRICH · 1836–1907   Thomas Bailey Aldrich was born November 11, 1836, in Portsmouth, New Hampshire and died March 19, 1907, in Boston, Massachusetts. He was a poet, editor (of *Atlantic Monthly*, among other magazines), and short-story writer. The death of his father forced him to forgo an education at Harvard. "Marjorie Daw," which first appeared in the *Atlantic Monthly*, April, 1873, is his most famous work, and Martha Foley included it in her *200 Years of Great American Stories* (1975). Of interest to younger New Englanders is his novel about growing up in Portsmouth, New Hampshire, *The Story of a Bad Boy* (1869).

RUSSELL BANKS · 1940–   Russell Banks was born March 28, 1940, in Newton, Massachusetts, and educated at the University of North Carolina (A.B., 1967). A novelist and short-story writer, he has taught writing at several colleges, including the University of New Hampshire, New England College, and Emerson College. "Sarah Cole: A Type of Love Story" first appeared in *The Missouri Review* in 1984, and was chosen for *The Best American Short Stories, 1985*. His short-story collection *Trailerpark* (1981) and novel *Hamilton Stark* (1978) are both set in New Hampshire. Two other novels, *The Book of Jamaica* (1980) and *Continental Drift* (1985), feature New Hampshire protagonists in the exotic settings of Jamaica and Florida.

STEPHEN VINCENT BENÉT · 1898–1943   Stephen Vincent Benét was born July 22, 1898, in Bethlehem, Pennsylvania, and died March 13, 1943, in New York City. A poet and short-story writer, he was educated at Yale (B.A., 1919 and M.A., 1920) and the Sorbonne in Paris, and later lived in Rhode Island for several years. His *John Brown's Body* (1928) and *Western Star* (1943) both won the Pulitzer Prize for Poetry. His best-known story is "The Devil and Daniel Webster," which first appeared in the *Saturday Evening Post*, October 24, 1936, and was chosen for the *O. Henry Memorial Award Prize Stories of 1937*, where it was designated the best American short story published in 1936. It was later successfully filmed as *All That Money Can Buy* (1941).

JAMES GOULD COZZENS · 1903–1978   James Gould Cozzens was born August 19, 1903 in Chicago, Illinois, the parents of New England stock, lived for several years in Williamstown, Massachusetts, and died August 9, 1978, in Stuart, Florida. A novelist and short-story writer, he was educated at Kent School in Connecticut and at Harvard University. He worked as a tutor, librarian, advertising executive, editor, and Air Force officer before becoming a full-time writer. Though he won the Pulitzer Prize in 1949 for *Guard of Honor, By Love Possessed* (1957), which was filmed in 1961, was his most successful novel. "Total Stranger" first appeared in the *Saturday Evening Post*, February 15, 1936, and was chosen for the *O. Henry Memorial Award Prize Stories of 1936*, where it was designated the best American short story published in 1936.

DOROTHY (DOROTHEA) CANFIELD FISHER · 1879-1958 Dorothea Canfield (Fisher) was born February 17, 1879, in Lawrence, Kansas, and died November 9, 1958, in Arlington, Vermont. A novelist, nonfiction, and short-story writer, she was educated at Ohio State University (Ph.B., 1899), the Sorbonne in Paris, and Columbia University (Ph.D., 1905), and spent much time from 1923 on living on a farm near Arlington, Vermont. Her short-story collections include *Hillsboro People* (1915) and *A Harvest of Stories, From a Half Century of Writing* (1956). "The Bedquilt," which is considered one of her best stories, first appeared in *Harper's Magazine*, November, 1906. Of interest to young New Englanders is her novel *Understood Betsy* (1916), which recounts a young girl's happy move from the Midwest to New England.

MARY WILKINS FREEMAN · 1852-1930 Mary Wilkins (Freeman) was born October 31, 1852, in Randolph, Massachusetts, and died March 13, 1930, in Metuchen, New Jersey. After her education at Mount Holyoke Seminary (now College) was cut short because of bad health, she lived with her family in West Brattleboro, Vermont. She returned to Randolph in 1883 until she married in 1902 and moved to Metuchen, New Jersey. Her shorter works have greater acclaim than her novels and "The Revolt of Mother," which first appeared in *Harper's Magazine*, September, 1890, is one of her finest stories. Indeed, Martha Foley included it in her anthology *200 Years of Great American Stories* (1975). Collections of interest to New Englanders include *A New England Nun and Other Stories* (1891) and the *Best Stories of Mary Wilkins Freeman* (1927).

LAWRENCE SARGENT HALL · 1915-   Lawrence Sargent Hall was born April 23, 1915, in Haverhill, Massachusetts. A college teacher (Bowdoin and Columbia), scholar, short-story writer, and novelist, he was educated at Bowdoin College (A.B., 1936) and Yale University (Ph.D., 1941). "The Ledge" was first published in *The Hudson Review*, Winter, 1958–1959, and was chosen for *Prize Stories, 1960: The O. Henry Awards*, where it was designated the best American short story published in 1959. Of interest to New Englanders are his critical study *Hawthorne: Critic of Society* (1943) and his novel *Stowaway* (1961).

NATHANIEL HAWTHORNE · 1804-1864 Nathaniel Hathorne (he added the "w") was born July 4, 1804, in Salem, Massachusetts, and died May 19, 1864, near Plymouth, New Hampshire. One of America's four most important nineteenth-century writers, he was educated at Bowdoin College (baccalaureate, 1825) and lived most of his life in New England. "Young Goodman Brown," considered to be one of his most important stories, first appeared in the *New-England Magazine*, April, 1835, and was included in his first book, *Twice Told Tales* (1837). Other collections, such as *Moses From an Old Manse* (1846), followed, but he achieved popular acclaim only after the publication of his two classic novels about New England and the New England character: *The Scarlet Letter* (1850) and *The House of Seven Gables* (1851).

MARK HELPRIN · 1947-   Mark Helprin is this anthology's enigma wrapped in a riddle. The only personal information we have about him is his birthdate: 1947. An acclaimed short-story writer and novelist, his works include *Dove of the East and Other Stories* (1975), *Refiner's Fire: The Life and Adventures of Marshall Pearl, A Foundling* (1977), *Ellis Island and Other Stories* (1981), and *Winter's Tale* (1984). "A Vermont Tale" first appeared in the *New Yorker*, March 3, 1980.

SHIRLEY JACKSON · 1919-1965 Shirley Jackson was born December 14, 1919, in San Francisco, California, and died August 8,1965, in North Bennington, Vermont. A novelist and short-story writer, she was educated at the University of Rochester and Syracuse University (B.A., 1940). For many years she lived in Bennington, where her husband taught at

Goddard College. "The Summer People," like many of her stories, sports a vague New England presence. It first appeared in *Charm*, September, 1950, and was chosen for *Best American Short Stories, 1951*. Of interest to New Englanders is her novel *The Haunting of Hill House* (1959), which was successfully filmed as *The Haunting* (1963).

HENRY JAMES · 1843-1916 Henry James was born April 15, 1843, in New York City, and died February 28, 1916, in London. A novelist and short-story writer, he moved permanently to England in 1876. Several of his short stories, however, feature New England protagonists or settings, probably because he spent time at Newport, Rhode Island, and was educated at Harvard. Indeed, "Osborne's Revenge," which first appeared in *Galaxy*, July, 1868, is set in Newport during the years when Edith Wharton, who became a close friend, summered there. Another work of interest to New Englanders is the novella *Daisy Miller* (1878).

WARD JUST · 1935- Ward Just was born September 5, 1935, in Michigan City, Indiana, and educated at Trinity College in Hartford, Connecticut. A journalist, novelist, and short-story writer, he lived for a while in Warren, Vermont, but now resides in Paris. His works include the *Congressman Who Loved Flaubert and Other Washington Stories* (1973) and his most popular novel, *The American Ambassador* (1987). "About Boston" first appeared in the *Atlantic Monthly*, December, 1983, and was chosen for *Prize Stories, 1985: The O. Henry Awards*.

CHRISTOPHER LA FARGE · 1897-1956 Christopher La Farge was born December 10, 1897, in New York City, and died January 5, 1956, in Providence, Rhode Island. Educated at Groton, Harvard (A.B., 1920), and the Pennsylvania School of Architecture (B.Arch., 1923), he was an architect, poet, short-story writer, novelist, and painter who lived much of his life in Rhode Island. "The Three Aspects" first appeared in *'47 – The Magazine of the Year*, and was chosen for the *O. Henry Memorial Award Prize Stories of 1948*. Also of interest to New Englanders is *The Sudden Guest* (1946), his most popular novel, which is set in Rhode Island during a hurricane.

SINCLAIR LEWIS · 1885-1951 (Harry) Sinclair Lewis was born February 7, 1885, in Sauk Centre, Minnesota, and died January 10, 1951, in Rome. A journalist, novelist, and short-story writer, he was educated at Yale University (A.B., 1908) and spent considerable time on farms in Barnard, Vermont, and South Williamstown, Massachusetts. The first American to receive the Nobel Prize for Literature, his novels include *Main Street* (1920), *Babbitt* (1922), *Arrowsmith* (1926), for which he won the Pulitzer Prize, and *Elmer Gantry* (1927). "Land," which is considered one of his finest short stories, first appeared in the *Saturday Evening Post*, September 12, 1931.

H. P. LOVECRAFT · 1890-1937 H(oward) P(hilips) Lovecraft was born August 20, 1890, in Providence, Rhode Island, and died March 15, 1937, in the same city. Though poor health prevented him from attending college and personal inclination limited travel, he carried on voluminous correspondences through magazines and with individuals. Ironically, though he boosted the careers of many writers such as Robert Bloch and August Derleth, he himself experienced relatively little financial or critical success during his lifetime. "The Haunter of the Dark," which first appeared in *Weird Tales*, December, 1936, is the most reprinted story ever set in Rhode Island. Part of the influential Cthulhu Mythos, "The Haunter of the Dark," is one of his best stories, and its protagonist is but a thinly disguised Robert Bloch, who had previously killed off Lovecraft in another literary work.

JOYCE CAROL OATES · 1938- Joyce Carol Oates was born June 16, 1938, in Lockport, New York, and educated at Syracuse University (B.A., 1960) and the University of Wisconsin (M.A., 1961). She is a short-story writer, novelist, poet, playwright, and college teacher (primarily at Princeton). Exceptionally talented and prolific, she has received the O. Henry Award for Continuing Achievement in 1970 and 1986 and the National Book Award in 1970 for *Them*. "Presque Isle," which first appeared in *Agni Review*, in 1980, was reprinted in *The Best American Short Stories, 1981*, and later transformed into a play (1984).

CURTIS K. STADTFELD · 1935–   Curtis K. Stadtfeld was born April 9, 1935, in Remus, Michigan, and raised on a farm. He was educated at Michigan State University (B.A., 1957) and Eastern Michigan University (M.A., 1969). A short-story writer and novelist, he has worked primarily as a journalist and college professor. "The Line Fence," which may be his most famous story, was first published in *Yankee*, December, 1972. Other works include the novel *From the Land and Back* (1972).

JEAN STAFFORD · 1915–1979   Jean Stafford was born July 1, 1915, in Covina, California, and died March 26, 1979, in White Plains New York. She was educated at the University of Colorado (B.A., 1936, and M.A., 1936) and Heidelberg University. A novelist, short-story writer, and college teacher, she lived for a number of years in Connecticut, Maine, and Massachusetts. Her story "The Wedding: Beacon Hill," which first appeared in *Harper's Bazaar*, August, 1944, was chosen for the *Best American Short Stories of 1945*. It is a self-contained, prepublished, and substantially shorter chapter from her most famous novel, *Boston Adventure* (1944). Her short stories, which were assembled as *The Collected Stories of Jean Stafford*, received the Pulitzer Prize in 1970.

JAMES THURBER · 1894–1961   James Thurber was born December 8, 1894, in Columbus, Ohio, and died November 2, 1961, in New York City. Educated at Ohio State University, he was a journalist, editor (the first editor of the *New Yorker*), humorist, cartoonist, and short-story writer. His story "The Secret Life of Walter Mitty," which appeared in the *New Yorker*, March 18, 1939, is one of his most famous works. It was successfully filmed in 1949, but the setting was changed to Perth Amboy, New Jersey and New York City. Other works of interest include *My Life and Hard Times* (1933), *My World – and Welcome to It* (1942), and *The Thurber Carnival* (1945).

KURT VONNEGUT, JR. · 1922–   Kurt Vonnegut, Jr., was born November 11, 1922, in Indianapolis, Indiana, and educated at Cornell University, Carnegie Institute of Technology, and University of Chicago (M.A., 1971). A novelist and short-story writer, he has worked in public relations and as a journalist and college instructor (including Harvard University). His works include *Cat's Cradle* (1963), *Welcome to the Monkey House: A Collection of Short Works* (1968), and *Slaughterhouse Five* (1969), and in 1985 he received an Emmy Award for the teleplay of his story "D. P." "Who Am I This Time?" first appeared in the *Saturday Evening Post*, December 16, 1961, under the title "My Name is Everyone" and has subsequently been dramatized for the Arts and Entertainment Network.

EDITH WHARTON · 1862–1937   Edith Newbold Jones (Wharton) was born January 24, 1862, in New York City, and died August 11, 1937, near Saint-Brice-Sous-Foret, France. Educated by tutors, she summered in Newport, Rhode Island, while growing up. Later she lived in Newport and Lenox, Massachusetts, before moving to France, where she spent much of her later life. She was awarded the Pulitzer Prize twice: for literature in 1921 for *The Age of Innocence* (1920) (a novel about Newport society) and for drama in 1935 for *The Old Maid*. Her most satirical story, "Xingu," first appeared in *Scribner's Magazine*, March, 1911. Another work of interest to New Englanders is the powerful novella *Ethan Frome* (1911).

ABOUT THE EDITORS

ROBERT TAYLOR is a Boston-based book and art critic. In metropolitan journalism his positions have ranged from reporter to daily columnist to book editor of *The Boston Globe* to critic-at-large; he is a professor of English at Wheaton College, Norton, Massachusetts, and has published a novel and three works of nonfiction, most recently a biography, *Fred Allen: His Life and Wit*.

MARTIN H. GREENBERG and CHARLES G. WAUGH are the country's most prolific anthologists. The former teaches political science at the University of Wisconsin at Green Bay. The latter teaches speech and psychology at the University of Maine at Augusta.